THE END OF WINTER

The End Of Winter

T. D. Griggs

First published 2004 by S. Fischer Verlag GmbH, Frankfurt am Main, Germany

This edition printed by CreateSpace, An Amazon.com Company

ISBN 13: 978-1491041963
ISBN 10: 149104196X

T.D Griggs was born in London and has lived and worked on four continents. He holds British and Australian nationality and has worked variously as a truck driver, journalist, film extra, MD of a successful communications consultancy, and – for about seven sweaty hours – as a volunteer fire fighter. Despite that, much of the Australian bush survives.

He has written many short stories and three other novels, including the father-son drama *The Warning Bell* (written as Tom Macaulay) and - under his own name - the Victorian epic *Distant Thunder* and the international bestseller *Redemption Blues*.

T. D. Griggs is also a professional business writer with an international client base. He has degrees in English and archaeology, and now lives with his wife Jenny in Oxford, UK.

To find out more, visit www.tdgriggs.co.uk or follow him on Twitter @TDGRIGGS1.

For Jenny:

**For how should I forget the wisdom that you brought,
The comfort that you made?**

W. B. Yeats
'Under Saturn'

ACKNOWLEDGMENTS

Like the humans who create them, novels are born naked and rely on the nurture and protection of those around them. Most of these nurturers will go unacknowledged, or are simply and cruelly forgotten, as the story gains in strength and starts to outgrow them.

Some few are remembered here, with apologies to all the other protectors who have cast a kindly eye over this tale, nodding with quiet satisfaction as it has developed.

In London, my thanks as ever to Peta Nightingale and Mark Lucas at my UK agency, LAW, for their friendship, good humour and unending passion for the book. And a word of gratitude, too, for the team at Médecins sans Frontières, who took time away from their far more important work to advise me on the details and ethos of their splendid and noble organization. I just hope nobody died while they were reading my book.

In Oxford, my gratitude goes once again to my long-suffering wife Jenny, who has always stood behind this novel as she has stood behind everything else I've ever written, done, or even thought about. Thanks, too, to my neighbours in Warwick Street and beyond, who put up with my incessant ramblings at dinner parties as the story took shape, and always contrived to sound interested. Some of them even bought it.

And special thanks to my two medical advisers, Campbell 'Two Hammers' Hand in Oxford, and in Sydney Dr John Baffsky and his team, including Professor Buchbrenner, Father O'Malley, Sister Nipples and Phil Slyme. Dr Baffsky's taste for fiction is, apparently, even stranger than my own....

T. D. GRIGGS
Oxford 2013

PROLOGUE

M y father's last farewell was on a winter night twenty-five years ago.

This is how I remember it.

My homework was spread out before me on the Formica tabletop in the kitchen. The three of them, home from the restaurant for two hours now, were growing raucous in the sitting room. They brayed with laughter and their embarrassing music was turned up too loud and they shouted at one another over it. I hated it when they got this way. I didn't feel like laughing. My father was leaving for Africa in ten hours. He would be away for months in some wild and remote place where men hunted with spears and the harsh sun burned down on brittle scrub. And he wasn't going to take me with him. I was thirteen. I thought it entirely probable I would never laugh again.

The music sank away and Anthony rose to his feet. His plump penguin figure filled my wedge of vision through the door. He couldn't have been past forty, but even then he dressed in antique fashion, rumpled pinstripe with a breast pocket handkerchief.

He lifted his glass. 'To Duncan.'

His voice was resonant, the way it got after a few brandies. I could almost hear my father imitating him; he was a wicked mimic and spared no-one, least of all his oldest friend.

I closed my book with a slap, in the hope that they would hear and that it would disturb their stupid party. My mother glanced at me from under Anthony's raised arm. There was something hostile in that look. She would lose my father in a few hours too, and she was not about to give up those hours to me. She turned away, and the toast was repeated to the clinking of glasses and more laughter, and suddenly the party was over. A moment later they came clattering into the kitchen on their way to the back door, loud and rosy and dazzled by the harsher light.

Anthony was beaming behind his spectacles but not quite making eye contact with anyone. He shrugged himself clumsily into his coat, his gestures all a little large. I knew he was upset at the parting, despite the hilarity. There were times when I thought Anthony ridiculous, but he did his best to be a friend to me when my father was away, and I felt a surge of fellow feeling for him now.

'We'll keep them safe, won't we, Michael, old chap?' Anthony touched my shoulder tentatively: he was a bachelor, unused to children. 'Your mother and the little ones? We'll keep an eye on them for the intrepid traveller, won't we?'

I didn't answer. I felt suddenly tearful, and I knew Anthony could tell.

'Action, my lad,' he boomed, putting on that bluff manner of his. '*Action téméraire!* We'll go out somewhere special, the two of us. That's what's needed to keep our minds occupied. Bold action!'

Anthony often said this, but his idea of bold action was a trip to the opera or an expedition to some antiques market. Neither prospect did much for me. He stood there looking less like a man capable of bold action than anyone I had ever seen. But then in a second my mother was kissing him on the cheek and pulling his coat around him in a protective fashion and steering him towards the back door and telling him the cab wouldn't wait. She was fond of Anthony but I knew that she wanted to get rid of him.

A swirl of cold air as the door opened and I heard Anthony's hurrying footsteps on the path and a taxi drew away. My mother put her back against the door to shut it against the winter wind, and rubbed her bare arms. Her smile drained away. Her eyes were fixed on my father's. He leaned against the wall opposite, smoking a cigar, inspecting the knuckles of his right hand. He was a lean, good looking man with an easy confidence about him, but now he seemed ill at ease. I knew that this was the time they had dreaded, when the last distraction was removed, and they had a clear view of one another.

'Go on up, Pat,' my father said gently, but still without looking at her. 'I won't be a minute.'

She walked straight past him out of the kitchen. She did not say anything. Her back was unnaturally stiff as she disappeared through the living room and rhythm of her steps on the stairs had an awkward urgency.

My father looked at me through his cigar smoke, and as he did so he recovered his poise. The cigar made him look louche. He pulled down the corners of his mouth and raised his eyebrows at me. I knew this one: man-to-man solidarity in the face of female dramatics. I hated him for such obvious tactics. He wanted to go away with a fiercer longing than I wanted him to stay, that was the truth, and I hated that most of all.

He looked at the cigar. 'Filthy things. It's that Anthony Gilchrist makes me do it.' He looked around for an ashtray, failed to find one in the kitchen and went back into the sitting room. Presumably he found one there, for when he came back, puckering his mouth in comic distaste, he no longer had the cigar. He pulled out the chair opposite me and sat down.

'Give me a break, son,' he said quite suddenly, in a tone he had never before used to me. 'This is my job.'

'You could get another bloody job.' My voice was strangled.

'I'm a project engineer, Mike. I have to go where the projects are. It doesn't mean I like leaving you all.'

'Deb and Paul don't care if you go away. They're only young. They forget in two days.' I was astonished to hear myself talking like this. My face was hot and my voice seemed to come from somewhere beyond me. 'And Mum gets to come out and see you every trip.'

'It's not a holiday, Mike. You'd be bored.'

Bored? I stared at him in disbelief that he could say anything so absurd.

'You'll be back at school soon,' he said, to reassure himself. He reached over and slid my homework towards him and riffled through the pages as if he had never seen a schoolbook before. 'It'll be better then.'

There was no point in me saying anything. The gulf was too huge. I thought of that rain-swept boarding school in the Midlands and pictured in contrast the world he moved in – hot dust, four-wheel drives, emerald forests and rivers the colour of coffee. How could he possibly imagine that I would prefer to have *my* life than to share in his? There was no point trying to talk to anyone who misunderstood me so thoroughly, or – worse – who pretended to.

'They ever teach you about Ulysses, Mike?' he asked abruptly, setting the book aside.

'The novel or the Greek?'

He gave me a wry look. 'It wasn't meant to be multiple choice. Ulysses spent ten years sailing home to Ithaca from the Trojan Wars. But he got there in the end, back to his wife and kids. When he was ready. When the Gods were ready to let him.'

I said nothing.

'Ithaca's a real place,' he said, as I had somehow known he would. 'It's a Greek island, in the Ionian Sea. Did you know that? I always thought it would be something special to go there. Maybe we should go there together one day, all of us.'

'When?' I demanded quickly.

He opened his mouth to answer, but at that moment there was a sound from upstairs, muffled and indistinct. A dropped ornament, perhaps. We both heard it, as we were intended to. My father and I looked up at the ceiling and then at one another, and I knew in that moment that we would never go to Ithaca together, nor to anywhere else.

He reached across and squeezed my wrist. 'I need you to take care of them all while I'm gone, Mike. Just for a few months.'

Anger burned like a coal inside me. But my father didn't see it. He released my wrist, got to his feet and smiled at me as if we'd just resolved everything. Then he walked quietly away through the sitting room and I heard the stair treads creak under his weight. When the noises had died away upstairs – running water, softly closing doors – I went into the sitting room. A couple of empty bottles stood on the table and glasses marked with red wine were perched on the arms of chairs. The place stank of cigar smoke. There was an atlas open on the floor in front of the gas fire, showing a brightly coloured map of Africa. I turned off the fire and the humming stereo, went back into the kitchen and turned out the lights. I stood for a long time in the dark, listening to the pinging of the fire as it cooled and the buffeting of the wind against the window.

Then I opened the back door and stepped out into the winter darkness. A wild night, a highwayman's night, with black trees lashing the suburban gardens and sleet driving horizontally between the smug houses. I shuddered, the wind cutting through my thin clothes. It was bitterly cold but at least out here I was free, I was a spirit, a free spirit in the night and the storm, part of it, perhaps the heart of it. I was filled with wild defiance. Take care of them? Let them take care of themselves. I turned the key in the lock behind me and ran blindly away down the empty black street.

CHAPTER ONE

It was eerily quiet, quieter even than it should have been: no voices, no clink of digging, no rumble of bulldozers or earthmovers. The quake had levelled the buildings on either side into low mountains of rubble. Yellow dust hung in the air, tasting of cement and – more strongly now – of decay. We stood in a group close to the jeep, gazing around us. Sweat gathered on my back in the climbing heat.

Stella's boots crunched on the grit as she shifted behind me, a tiny signal to remind me that she was there, part reassurance and part impatience. I shaded my eyes without looking at her. Far below us, on the broken road from Caracas, the truck carrying Patrick and Julio and their equipment was still motionless between fields of cane so brilliant in the sun that they hurt the eye. Even from here I could make out their ant figures scurrying around the crippled vehicle. Patrick, the logistics specialist, would be cursing and kicking the wheels.

I turned to the driver. 'This is the place?'

He muttered doubtfully to himself in Spanish and fumbled for his map. The sound of the crinkling paper was very loud in the waiting silence. I knew it was the place, but I wanted time to think. I didn't like to be stuck up here in the midst of this desolation with the rest of the team stranded and out of reach. I didn't like Stella's eyes on my back. I didn't like the thought of what might be asked of us, of what we would not be able to do.

I heard the tramp of boots and a Venezuelan army major came striding around the shoulder of the rubble mountain towards us. He seemed to me to have sprung out of nowhere. He was a very big man, an inch or two taller than I was, and he would have been an intimidating presence. But as he drew close I could see that his eyes were dull with weariness and his skin and hair were caked with dust and sweat. He wore a khaki neckerchief over his mouth, and this and the holstered pistol on his hip made him look like a cartoon bandit. I stepped forward to meet him, but at the last moment someone out of sight shouted and a dog yipped excitedly and the major raised his hand like a policeman on point duty and I stopped in my tracks. The invisible dog started barking again, more insistently this time.

The major tugged down the neckerchief and called over his shoulder, but without taking his eyes off me. '*Que pasa?*'

The answer came back, garbled but jubilant, and there were more voices now, frantic voices, though I could not understand the words. The major kept his eyes on me as he listened.

'I'm Michael Severin.' I said, and touched the Médecins Sans Frontières insignia on my tunic. 'Someone should be expecting us.'

The major looked from me to Stella. 'You have come to help us?' He seemed incredulous, or perhaps amused, and for a moment I saw the hopeless irony in this situation as clearly as he did: one man and one woman, against an earthquake.

'There are two more of us,' I said, and realised how doubly absurd that sounded, 'but the truck's stuck down in the valley.'

He lifted his chin in acknowledgment. He showed no surprise at our problems. They must have counted for little against what he had seen in the last two days. His name – P.Rivera – stood out in white letters on a black plastic tag above his shirt pocket. He looked again at my Médecins Sans Frontières badge. He stared dully at me.

I said, 'Should we move?'

'Perhaps, yes.'

The major took a step away and then remembered something. He looked from me to Stella and drew himself up to his full height. 'I am to… I wish to thank you. For coming to us. In case it is forgotten later. In case the words are not spoken.' To my embarrassment he saluted crisply and held the salute for a full fifteen seconds. I heard Stella shift uncomfortably behind me. I was about to say something flippant but when I looked up I saw that Major Rivera's eyes were full of tears.

The dog scrambled from the hole first, a brown-and-white spaniel, delighted with itself and wagging its tail in glee. It looked out of place here, I thought, like some elderly lady's lapdog. An army corporal emerged after the spaniel, and was hauled into the light by his comrades. He spat dirt. Someone gave him a canteen and he drank from it and hawked and spat again and began talking quickly in Spanish, gesturing as he talked.

'He says there is a tunnel under the church,' the interpreter told me. 'It is not so long. He has left a marker tape. The dog found a man...' he paused to listen to the corporal's rapid speech. 'He thinks just one. An old man, he says.'

'A dead man?'

'No, no. Talking. Praying, maybe. Trapped. Perhaps it is Father Rafael. The soldier could not go closer, he says. The tunnel is dangerous. There is water. And he says he felt the rocks move.' The interpreter gazed at me and kept his eyes expressionless. 'I think he was afraid to go further, the soldier.'

'Tell him I think he's a hero.'

The interpreter did as he was asked, but the corporal merely ducked his head and knelt to make a fuss of the dog. He knew it didn't make an ounce of difference whether he was a hero or not, and I felt a fool for having spoken. I stepped through the little ring of soldiers and villagers and crouched by the hole. The sun was high now and it glared off the broken masonry. The mouth of the tunnel was velvet black and a faint wisp of dust rose from it. I heard the grind and rattle of digging machinery start up not far away, and, very faintly in the distance, the rotors of a chopper socking the air as it beat its way up from the city. But I was aware that the men and women around me were silent. I heard footsteps behind me and Stella's hand came to rest on my shoulder.

'Maybe they'll be able to reach him from the top.' Her Scottish accent came across very clearly, cool, matter-of-fact, as if she were ordering drinks in the pub at home. It was almost comical to hear it here, in this place, discussing a man's life.

I said, 'Oh, yes?' I got to my feet and dusted off my hands.

'We don't have to do this, you know.' She was using her school-marm voice now. 'I'll tell you straight, Michael, my vote's against it. We're only the assessment team. We should at least wait for the truck. Wait for the others.'

But I could tell from her tone that she had already decided.

It was suffocatingly hot in the tunnel and the stench was so strong that I had to halt for a few seconds to get my stomach under control. Ahead of me the darkness was so dense I thought I could feel it against my face. I snapped on my helmet torch and it threw a white lance down the tunnel, touching ancient beams and bro-ken brick and a jumble of fallen slabs, canted at crazy angles. The corporal's tape led along the bottom edge of a tilted section of floor which had collapsed into what must have been the crypt. Brick vaulting held the rubble clear at one side, and a clutter of wood and concrete beams formed a rough ceiling. I scrambled forward on all fours. I had a spare few inches above me if I kept my head down. I began to tell myself that this might not be too bad, but each time I repeated the words in my mind they grew less convincing.

I could hear Stella panting behind me and my own breathing was harsh in my ears. I paused and forced my body into silence and reached back and motioned her to be still and checked the other sounds around me. A single clink from my harness as a buckle shifted. Water splashing somewhere close. Unconsciously I felt inside my clothing for the chain which held my talisman. The old Yale key was worn to smooth bronze in the years I had carried it, and I rubbed it again now, feeling the action steady my nerve. Then a new sound, a high, melodic note repeated over and over, like a birdcall. It took a moment for me to recognise it as a human voice.

I moved forward. The corporal's marker tape had run out. The tunnel narrowed so that I had to work my shoulders through and in doing so I dislodged a small runnel of crushed masonry and the sound of this was terrifyingly loud in the darkness. Grit filled my nose and eyes and I choked, and when my vision cleared I could see the dust coiling in the beam of my torch, turning the light sickly yellow. Three feet to my right a stone sarcophagus lay open, ruptured by the quake, and the shrivelled occupant lay laughing soundlessly at me through ivory pegs of teeth. I stopped and breathed hard.

Stella came up to me and as she saw the open tomb I heard her suck in her breath. 'That one's lost a lot of blood,' she said.

The voice came again from the darkness, thread thin but joyful, perhaps a chanted poem, perhaps a hymn of praise.

I said, 'I can hear him. He's singing.'

'That's all we need. Come all this way to dig out fucking Pavarotti.'

'If it's Pavarotti, you can carry him.'

She touched my arm. 'Michael, do you think this might be far enough?'

'How do you feel about it?'

'You always answer a question with another question. Why is that?'

'What makes you ask?'

'This is far enough, Michael,' she said in a different voice.

'I can hear him singing,' I repeated, as if this were sufficient answer. She did not reply this time. I said, 'Stay here and hang onto the line. I'll call you when you can help.'

The tunnel twisted and dropped steeply over the course of a couple of metres, and the space opened suddenly into a large chamber. I was standing in water – perhaps eighteen inches of surprisingly chill water – and the smell of the air had changed, had become dank and fetid.

I called, 'Father Rafael? Can you hear me?'

A pause. 'You are English?' The man's voice was clear and startlingly close.

'Yes. English. I'm a doctor.'

'So?' Astonishingly the disembodied voice started to laugh, a harsh wheezing sound. 'Welcome to my country.'

I had him now, a movement against the jagged wall of rubble, low down near the surface of the black water: the outline of his shoulder, his arm, his head, and now the whites of his eyes and teeth.

'Move carefully,' he said. 'There is a well.'

I edged forward and found firm ground underfoot. I took another step, and then a third. This time my leg vanished to the thigh in the blackness and the water was shockingly cold. I felt with my foot for the lip of the well and inched round it, dragging my pack behind me, until I could crouch in front of him.

In the torchlight I could see that the priest's face was black with dirt, streaked here and there by the dripping water, the eyes impossibly large and luminous. He was quite an old man, I saw, bald and with a creased and humorous face. I wondered if he was delirious. Both his arms were free and apparently uninjured and most of his upper body was clear of the rubble, but I could see no more. 'Can you move at all, Father? Can you feel your legs?'

'Show me your face,' the priest said, and groped in the dark and found my upper arm and gripped it with a hand like a claw. 'I should like to see another man's face.'

I took off my helmet and shone the torch beam into my own eyes.

Father Rafael studied me. At last, and very quietly, he said, 'You know what it is to have fear, young man.'

I said nothing.

'I also knew fear these three days,' said Father Rafael. 'But not any more.'

'There's nothing to be afraid of now,' I felt for my belt pack and unzipped it, glad to be occupied. 'We can help you now.' Yet I was conscious that it was the priest who was offering me comfort, and not the other way around. I felt a great need to keep talking. 'Now we've found you we can get you out.'

'The time for dreaming is past,' Father Rafael said. 'The water is rising. In one hour, maybe less, I will drown.'

'We can get you out,' I repeated.

'Young man, the church is on my legs. And even you cannot move the Holy Mother Church in one short hour.' Father Rafael wheezed his concertina laugh once more. 'The church is a rock, no? And now I know how heavy.'

Stella was splashing through the shallow water towards me, though I had not called her. I was very glad to see her dark shape and the spoke of light from her helmet, and my relief made me gruff.

'Watch out for the well in the middle there,' I told her. 'And get his vital signs. I want to see what's holding him.'

As if we were not there, the old man started to chant again in his thin voice, something in Latin, something joyful and ancient. I ran my hands over his body, from his hip down the length of his right leg. Most of the limb lay beneath the surface of the water. Just above the knee I felt the lump of what must be a fracture, though he made no sound when I touched it. I moved my hands along his left leg. It was twisted back at an impossible angle and where the knee should have been my fingers slid into pulped flesh and I felt sharp bone. The old man stopped singing then, though he gave no other sign of pain. I squirmed around behind his body and from this position I could see in the torchlight where the limb lay crushed under a great slab of masonry. The torn flesh was brownish and bloated.

'Pulse 130 and thready. BP eighty over nothing.' Stella folded the stethoscope away into her pack, keeping her voice neutral. 'Maybe we can get some pumps in. Hold the water level down until Patrick gets here with the truck.'

I looked around in the dripping darkness. I could have been imagining it, but the water seemed to have crept up even since I had arrived. I said, 'We're going to have to take the leg off to get him out.'

Stella said nothing, but I could read disapproval in her silence. I knew she was asking the old unspoken questions which always hung over marginal decisions like this: who stood to benefit from more pain? I said, 'It's a bit of a Houdini act but I can just about get to the crush site. With a bit of luck we can do it under IV midazolam and fentanyl. Get the stuff from the jeep. I'll stay with him.'

She hesitated for no more than a second, then turned and splashed away along the tunnel. That splashing was perhaps the loneliest sound I had ever heard. I wondered how the priest could possibly have survived for three days in this blackness, in this annihilation.

The bony hand groped out again. 'Why have you come here, young man?'

'It's my job.'

'To save me?' the priest persisted. 'Is that why you come? But you have already saved me – from dying alone, never to see again the face of a good man. This is not why you come. Not only for this.'

The force of his words made me stop and look at him. The priest's eyes caught the light, the whites shining like porcelain in the darkness. I had the weird feeling that this man knew more about me than it should have been possible for him to know. I felt the hairs rise on the back of my neck.

'We have a chance,' I said, trying to hold my voice steady. 'But I'm going to have to –'

'You cannot save us all, young man,' Father Rafael said. 'All the suffering and the sick and the trapped. All the victims.'

I could hear myself breathing in the darkness. 'But I have to try,' I whispered. 'Don't you understand? I have to try.'

The old man smiled, his few teeth glinting, and his grip closed like a nutcracker on my arm. 'My friend,' he said, 'we are both of us trapped.'

I heard Stella crashing through the water behind me and her voice came echoing down the tunnel, tight with fear. 'Michael? Did you feel that?'

I could hear nothing over the thumping of my pulse. Had there been something? A grumble in the earth more felt than heard? It was easy to imagine such things down here with this ancient goblin leering at me from the edge of death. Something flicked against my cheek. I looked up. The slab above our heads was flaking under the weight it carried, tiny chips of stone pinging off the surface into the water, against my skin, against my clothing. One hit me under the eye and stung like a wasp.

'Get over here,' I shouted at her.

She came up behind me, gasping, and then we were into the routine and I broke the fentanyl ampoule and filled the syringe, squinting at it against the light.

'This is going to take the pain away, Father.' I turned to Stella. 'Get in there behind him and tie off the leg.'

She moved to one side of the priest and shone her torch into the shadows. 'Michael, for Chrissake. It's under water. This is fucking hopeless.'

'Just do it, Stella.'

She grabbed my shoulder and pulled me hard against her, whispering. 'Listen to me. You'll get us all killed. Whack the needle into him and let's get out of here. It's the best you can do for him.'

'She's right, this one,' the priest said. 'She knows…'

I looked wildly from one to the other. Then it happened again, and this time there was no doubt. The ground shuddered. The water around my legs rippled in broken rings of silver.

'Michael!' Stella's voice cracked up an octave.

'Now go. Quickly.' The priest released his grip on my arm and shoved me hard, so that I stumbled back a step and lost my helmet torch and it splashed into the water and spiralled like a turning fish down the long dim shaft of the well. There was a gigantic crack above me and something heavy hit me across the arm and I dropped the syringe. Stella shouted and yanked me back on the rope so hard that I cleared the well without realising it and I was flailing in the dark and then I could see the light on her helmet and hear her shouting and sobbing and dragging at me and then I found my feet and we were scrambling along the tunnel with grit and the smell of death coughing out past us as the chamber collapsed.

Some soldiers were tipping cold water from a canteen over my head and into my face. All at once the sunlight blinded me and I

9

was hacking volcanically to clear my lungs. The men were fussing around me, shouting questions in my face, feeling my arms and legs for injury. I was scraped and sore and my arm was bruised and my chest felt tight with the dust and my pulse was skipping at an insane speed. But the light and the air filled me with a sinful joy.

'I'm OK.' I waved the men back. 'Truly. I'm OK.'

They exchanged doubtful glances but stepped away. A small cloud of dust hung over the entrance to the tunnel, a smudge against the hard blue sky. That was Father Rafael's marking stone, I thought, a cloud of grit drifting in the sun. It was more than most of these people would get. Behind me Stella was sitting on the flank of the rubble mountain with her face on her folded arms. Her attitude did not invite comfort. After a moment she rose to her feet and stumbled away down the slope without looking at me.

CHAPTER TWO

I leaned on the balcony rail and sipped Polar beer from the bottle. They had billeted us in an old army barracks twenty miles outside Caracas. The balcony looked out over a small beaten-earth parade ground and a clutter of outbuildings. Three jeeps were parked in the compound below and sentries with automatic rifles idled around the gate. It was almost dark and the neons of the city were springing on beyond the perimeter fence, quivering in the warm air. I could see the landing lights of planes dropping down into the international airport, with more lights stacked in the cobalt sky behind them. They would be carrying more food, more tents and shelters, more purification equipment, more search and rescue and medical teams. Perhaps soon things would be easier. Perhaps soon there would be no more Father Rafaels.

I heard the door open behind me. I caught the talk and clatter of people eating together in the canteen downstairs, but I did not want to join them. Stella moved up and put her hands on the rail a few feet away from me. Like me she carried a bottle of Polar beer. After a few moments she slapped at a mosquito on her bare arm. She did not look at me.

I said, 'Not hungry, huh?'

She didn't reply.

I said, 'Me neither.'

Down below a fourth jeep arrived with a change of guard, and both shifts of soldiers lounged around, cradling their weapons. They did not seem anxious to leave. They smoked and chatted and laughed for a while. The red points of their cigarettes moved in the darkness, and perhaps this prompted Stella, for she turned to rest her back against the railing and took a pack from the pocket of her shirt and lit up and blew the smoke gratefully at the sky. Without looking she held the pack out at arm's length to me.

'No thanks.'

'Are you afraid it might be bad for your health?'

'What was I supposed to do, Stella? I could hear him singing.'

She rounded on me, thrusting her face into mine. 'You know your trouble, Michael?' Her Scots accent sharpened. 'You don't know when to stop.'

'I'm sorry. I should have sent you back.'

'Sent *me* back? You should have sent your own stupid bloody self back, that's what you should have done.'

'I thought we could help, that's all.'

'Michael, we're the fucking assessment team, remember? We're supposed to assess, not go potholing after musical priests. For God's sake, we weren't even supposed to be there. We were supposed to be running a nice quiet surgical program in Caracas.'

'I didn't arrange the earthquake. We were just the bunnies on the spot, that's all.'

She flicked the cigarette half-smoked out into the black void. 'I'm out, Michael. This is it for me. My last mission.'

'You're not serious.'

'Oh, I'm very, very serious. I'm going home tomorrow, just like I'm scheduled to.'

'I thought you'd stay on,' I said carefully. 'I thought we both would. Work with the team for a while.'

'I'm going home and I'm going to damned well stay there.' After the smallest pause she added, 'I'm going to marry Gordon.'

'Does he know?'

'He'll do what he's told,' she said grimly. 'I'm going to marry Gordon and then I'm going to have four or five fat happy bairns. And I'm going to have a lot of pot plants. And a wee budgie.'

'You'll make gynaecological history.'

'Extremely amusing.' She glowered into the night.

I brought to mind a picture of Gordon: worthy, dark-suited, bespectacled. Gordon was an actuary. The rest of the trauma team at St Ruth's knew Gordon and were not kind about him. They joked that he had wanted to be an accountant, but lacked the charisma. I thought of the places I'd seen Stella working, at home and overseas – abseiling down a cliff face to reach an overturned coach in Morocco, wading armpit deep towards trapped survivors as floodwaters swamped an Italian village. The two of us had operated in a cellar in Bosnia once with an unexploded tank shell protruding from the ceiling.

'You'll die of boredom, Stella.'

'I can do boredom, after today.' She took a pull on her beer. After a while she turned her head and looked at me, and the anger seemed to have fled from her. 'You should think about it too.'

'I don't want to marry Gordon.'

'You're rising forty. You've a beautiful wife you don't see much of.'

'Cate understands.' I spoke a little abruptly. I did not quite understand why, but whenever Stella mentioned Caitlin I found myself resenting it.

Stella looked away. 'Michael, you're busy enough in London being Prof Curtiz's anointed son. Leave playing heroes to the younger ones, why don't you? Give yourself a break. Give us all a break.'

'You're very full of philosophy tonight.'

'It comes of being nearly squashed flat by five thousand tonnes of rubble.' She added, more quietly, 'You know something, Michael? It doesn't matter how many times you go back, you won't get them out. Maybe you should face that.'

I didn't answer.

She said, 'I'm going to get drunk. Want to come?'

'You go ahead.'

She hesitated, as if she might have been about to say more, then leaned forward and kissed me lightly on the cheek, and walked away through the door and down the stairs.

I watched the door swinging behind her. I had told her the story – most of it –one warm evening at a Kurdish refugee camp in Turkey. I don't know why. I'd never told anyone else as much, not even Cate. But I had told Stella how, at thirteen, I was not strong enough to resist Anthony's restraining grasp as hoses spouted and lights flashed and pumps roared and sirens shrieked and horrified neighbours gathered and desperate shouting rang down the sub-urban street. I didn't tell her all of it. I didn't tell her how hard Anthony had held me, painfully hard, and about the snorting noise he had made. I hadn't understood that noise at the time. I had never heard a fully grown man cry before. I didn't tell her about the figures in the window of my parents' bedroom, two taller figures and two little ones, silhouetted against the gathering glow, hand in hand. Nobody else saw them there, standing as if grouped for a family photo in which I would never again take my place. I suppose nobody else saw them because they couldn't have been there, being already dead by then. But that made no difference, because I saw them. I saw them still. I remembered thinking that I had expected trouble that night, for running out like that and coming home late. I had *wanted* trouble. But not this much.

Down in the courtyard one of the jeeps fired up and four of the guards climbed in. There was a chorus of shouted farewells and jokes and laughter, and the jeep bounced out through the archway and revved away into the hot night. I took a pull of my beer and found it was warm and realised I must have been standing here for an hour or more since Stella had left. The soldiers were going home, I supposed, and I wondered, did soldiers go home at night? Soldiers like these? I hoped so. I liked to think these men would go home to screaming children and stacks of tortillas and smouldering wives in dresses of faded floral cotton.

I wondered what time it was in England, and whether Caitlin would be at home now. I pictured her moving through the bright, ordered rooms of our Notting Hill house, busy with domestic things, humming to herself. Or perhaps she would be up in the attic room – her eyrie, she called it – listening to music, reading, whatever she did up there. Or shopping. I closed my eyes in the hot darkness and saw the striped awnings down Notting Hill Gate. And I saw her moving through this scene, tall and fair and slender, the bag over her shoulder, her sunglasses pushed up on her forehead, her newly-shorn hair shining. In my mind she was carrying daffodils wrapped in newspaper and laughing with the traders and shopkeepers who knew her – Stavros in the café, Julian the florist, Ivan who ran the fashion boutique. They all adored her, would do anything for her. Everyone wanted to look after Caitlin. I was filled with a rush of such tenderness for her that for a moment it hurt me.

To hell with it, I thought. And to hell with our 'arrangement'. The least I could do was call her up and tell her I loved her.

I left the balcony and went quickly downstairs. My route to the communications room took me past the bar. The room was noisy with drinkers, a mixed crowd of support staff and medics and aid workers from half-a-dozen countries. Someone had found a guitar and was making an attempt at flamenco and a chorus of drinkers were joining in, banging on the tables, clinking beer bottles together, whooping and shouting. As I passed, Stella backed out of the room with a beer in one hand and a cigarette in the other, shouting at someone still inside. She bumped into me and turned. Her eyes did not quite focus.

'Why hello, Doctor Michael.' She was swaying a little and a strand of her red hair was stuck across her brow. She pursed her lips and looked at me with growing intensity, her eyebrows lifted. I knew it showed in my face, all of it. I could see her sobering up as she watched me.

I nodded towards the bar. 'Quite a party.'

'They're just letting off steam.'

'That's good.'

'Go on in, if you want to see a naked Dutch anaesthetist singing Carmen.'

'Tempting, but…'

'You should see where he put the rose.'

'That settles it. Goodnight, Stella.'

She did not move out of my path. Instead she put her beer down on a window ledge and flicked her cigarette away. I brushed the strand of hair away from her forehead, kissed her quickly on the cheek and moved her aside. I had not reached the end of corridor before she called to me, as I suppose I must have known she would. When I turned she came up to me and locked her hands around my neck and kissed me hard. She tasted of tobacco and beer.

I broke away from her and tried to uncoil her arms from my neck. 'Stella…'

'I know all that, Michael, so save your breath.'

I held her at arms length. 'You know this won't work.'

'What's the idea?' she said. 'Guilt without sex?'

A memory leapt into my mind of the last time I had seen her naked, nine years earlier, at that same refugee camp in Turkey. It would only be a matter of days before I met Caitlin and my life changed, but I couldn't have guessed that at the time. All I had known at that moment was that Stella had a strong hard body, and she was completely unselfconscious about it, almost as if she were a model in front of an art class. She was, I couldn't help thinking, quite unlike Caitlin in every way. Caitlin moved like a lynx. She always carried with her the scent of mystery. There was nothing prudish about Caitlin, but some part of her always remained her own, remained to be discovered. With Stella, what you saw was definitely what you got.

'Come on, Stella. Let's not give ourselves problems.'

She saw that I meant it and looked away quickly. 'We nearly got our stupid bloody selves killed today. I just wanted to celebrate being alive, that's all.'

'I'm sorry.'

'You're always so bloody committed, Michael. Underneath you're hardcore Puritan, you know that? It doesn't make you many friends.' She must have seen the surprise in my face, because she relented. 'I didn't mean that exactly. But you're always on this bloody quest. You never let people get close to you.'

'I suppose I think I'm pretty lucky with what I've got.'

She looked squarely at me. 'If you're so bloody lucky with Caitlin, what are you doing here? Oh, well, maybe you come out here for the weather. All the best disasters happen in the tropics, after all. It's always bloody winter in London.'

Winter. I was dazzled by an intense vision of drifting London drizzle and black handprints of leaves on pavements and creaking ice underfoot. What *was* I doing here? Perhaps there was something in what she said. Perhaps I was drawn by the violent sun and the taste of heat, drawn to a world where the colours were primary and the choices stark. She was right. It was always winter in London.

'Let's drink to that, at least,' Stella stood back and lifted her glass to me. 'To the end of winter.'

She drank, handed the glass to me.

'To the end of winter,' I said, and I drank too, the sweet beer tepid in my throat. I made to hand the glass back to her, but she was already pushing her way back into the crowded bar. I put the glass on a window ledge and walked on.

On the ground floor Patrick had made a communications room out of a cell which opened onto the courtyard. Three steel desks were jammed into the space, cluttered with computer and communications equipment. If Patrick was surprised to see me he disguised it. He keyed in the number I gave him and passed the handset to me.

'Should go straight through,' he said, 'but make it quick. You've only got a couple of minutes before we lose the satellite.'

I heard the door close and realised that Patrick had left the room. I put the handset to my ear and Caitlin picked up almost at once.

Before she could speak, or I could change my mind, I said, 'Cate, you were right. You were right about everything.'

At first I could hear only the hiss of static.

'Michael,' her voice breathed across the world. 'Michael, this can't be you. Not now.'

'There's nothing wrong, Cate. I just had to tell you I've thought it all through.'

'There's nothing wrong,' she repeated in the same ghostly voice, as if in wonder.

'I'll tell you all of it, as soon as I get back. I've never told anyone all of it. You were right about that too. After that maybe we can start to find our way forward again. Start to find one another again.'

'Michael,' she said, scarcely audible, 'I so want to be found.'

The intensity in her voice brought me up short. I wondered if she might be a little drunk. I pictured her lonely and miserable with a bottle of wine and I felt guilty about that. Or perhaps it was the small hours of the morning in London and I had woken her. I said, 'Did I get the time wrong? Is it very late?'

'It's very late, Michael,' she said. 'It's very, very late.'

The link began to break up as the satellite slipped around the blue shoulder of the earth. Between the hisses of static I could hear the sound of her breathing. I called her name again and again, but I could no longer get her to hear me. And yet her breathing still seemed to come through to me, like the rhythm of the sea. Inexplicably I felt something cold trickle in my stomach at the sound of it. The line went dead.

CHAPTER THREE

S tella left for her flight in the middle of the following morning. From the window of my room I saw her loading her bags into a battered white taxi in the courtyard. She didn't like fuss and probably she had chosen her moment to slip away when no-one would notice. Especially not me. In a second she was gone. I could hear the vehicle banging and popping all the way down the rutted track to the main road.

I stayed for two more days. Probably I should have taken the same flight as Stella, but I felt bad about leaving before the field hospital was properly set up, even though this wasn't strictly my job. And I wanted to brief the new team leader, a young Dane who did not arrive until the following evening. And I wanted to hold a full briefing with Patrick and Julio. And there were a dozen other things.

I told myself that I wanted an orderly handover in every way. The truth was I wanted to clear my mind before I saw Caitlin again. And perhaps I also wanted not to acknowledge that anything could really be wrong with her – anything more than a few too many glasses of wine and a fit of the blues. I tried calling three or four more times over those couple of days but I got no reply each time, though there was nothing unusual about that. Eventually, and with a certain guilty relief, I gave up ringing. I did not want to hear that haunting cadence in her voice again.

I got a place on a returning aid flight the following night.

The folding seats along the sides of the fuselage were crowded with men and women, paramedics and emergency services people, already playing cards or reading or sleeping. From somewhere out of sight I could hear the excited whining of a sniffer dog belonging to one of the rescue teams, and for a second this and the dim interior of the Hercules made me think again of Father Rafael. I forced the thought out of my mind. A low hump of luggage and equipment was secured under netting down the centre of the fuselage. Through the open tail I could see the lights of the airport, and a black fringe of palm trees along the perimeter fence, until the ramp slowly began to rise. A little later the first of the big engines coughed and fired and in a moment the fuselage was booming. I could see pinpricks of coloured light up near the flight deck. The forms of the other passengers were dimly visible around me, hunched and sleeping in their seats. If the lights came on, I would not recognise a single face, but I felt a surge of companionship with them. I wondered what homes they were going back to, these resilient men and women. I wondered what memories had kept them going while they were far from the people they loved. The question was still rolling around my mind as I drifted away.

A summer night, nine years before. The fine Georgian façade of Morrow House, a marquee on the lawn, paper lanterns in the trees, a long sloping garden down to the gentle Gloucestershire Severn. The murmur of well bred conversation. A resident golden retriever barked and someone shushed it. The dog looked hurt at the rebuke, and shambled away. I leaned against the bole of an ancient cedar and sipped my drink, watching my friend Bruno with my usual mixture of amusement and admiration. Bruno, who had absolutely no shame, had taken the stage and seized the microphone. Now he was crooning his way through a Randy Newman number, and doing it with surprising skill. It was the sort of thing he did.

'Campbell told me about it,' Bruno had shouted over the din of his ancient Austin Healey on the M4. 'I think he actually got an invitation. Some rich bitch's birthday party. Kate – no, Caitlin somebody. Caitlin Hotly-Clambring. Something like that. You know the bloody silly names these people go in for. Daddy's in cement, and the best place for him.'

'It'll be black tie. We'll be thrown out.'

'Just say you're a friend of Caitlin's.'

'And what are you going to say?'

'Well, obviously, that I'm a friend of yours.'

'*That child done washed us away...*' Bruno finished on a long sobbing note and with a flick of his hand closed the band down at precisely the right moment. The applause was rapturous and there were several cries for an encore. The band's vocalist made a big thing of shaking Bruno's hand in congratulation and looked as if he meant it.

'I'd normally say something cutting right about now,' the girl moved up beside me, 'like your friend oughtn't to give up his day job. But actually I think he'd make out pretty well.'

She was tall and fair and I knew immediately that she was out of my class. My father hadn't had time to teach me much, but I had once heard him remark, with a kind of wistfulness, that there ought to be a law against the way some women looked. I saw now that this was the kind of creature he had meant.

'That's Bruno for you,' I said. 'Give him five minutes and he'll have a recording contract lined up and a tour of Scandinavia.'

'He's very good looking,' she remarked, archly.

I glanced at her. Had she slurred her words just a little? She looked back at me, or rather through me, with extraordinary directness. Her pupils were wide and black. I wasn't sure if she expected an answer, but while I was thinking about it Bruno jumped down off the stage and came backslapping and glad-handing through the crowd towards us. 'Tapster, there!' he shouted to a barman at a trestle table. 'A dish of your finest Alka Seltzer for my friends!'

The man beamed at Bruno and poured three glasses of Moet. If I had tried shouting for Alka Seltzer, the barman would have called security. Bruno swept up the tray and carried the sparkling glasses to us. He put the tray down on a tree stump and took two drinks from it and handed us one each and raised his own to the girl.

'Caitlin, my sweet. Such a wonderful party. And you're looking radiant, as always.'

'Why, thank you, kind sir.' She smiled winningly at him. 'But who the fuck are you?'

'Didn't Michael tell you?' Bruno sipped his champagne and looked reproachfully at me over the rim of his glass. 'Dear boy, we'd all be grateful if you spent just a little more time on the social niceties.' In one graceful movement Bruno set down his glass and plunged off again before she could ask any more questions.

'You're the two freeloaders who left that old heap in the drive. It drips oil on the gravel.' She pulled a face, hammed up the counties accent. 'Daddy's furious.' She cocked her head towards the terrace, where a tall and strikingly handsome man was chatting with guests. He was at least in his late sixties, but his very upright bearing and his trim moustache gave him a steely presence, like a Victorian general. Even from here I could tell that he was trying very hard not to look in our direction.

I pushed myself up from the tree and put my glass back on the tray. 'I knew this was a bad idea. A really bad idea.'

'You also told the man on the door you were friends of mine.' There was laughter in her voice now. 'Naughty, naughty.'

'And I thought I was so convincing.'

'You're the one who shouldn't give up his day job.' She opened her eyes wide at me, enjoying my discomfort. 'Daddy's sent me over to make sure you're quite pukka. He knows you aren't, of course.'

'This means the horsewhip and blunderbuss treatment, does it?'

'Your secret might be safe with me.' She took my arm. 'Let's go for a walk.'

'A walk?'

'You know the kind of thing. One foot in front of the other. Repeat several times.'

'Right,' I said.

'You can't go anywhere tonight in any case,' she led me through the long grass down to the riverside track, where the water shone like a silver plate between black trees, 'I filled your petrol tank with Moet.'

'Couldn't you have let the tyres down like anyone else?'

'Style,' she said, shaking her head. 'You've either got it or you haven't.'

The leaf litter was soft underfoot. The aisle of black trunks stretched away in front of us. The sounds of the party receded as we walked.

'Do you hear that?' she said, stopping me. 'It's a blackbird. I just love blackbirds, don't you? They look so ordinary and they sound so wonderful.'

We stood in the warm dusk, listening to the birdsong ripple between the trees. After a moment we walked on in silence.

'Here.' She stopped me with an upraised hand, and then led me through a screen of alder and willow. An old wooden jetty clambered away from the bank. I could see the gaptoothed slats of its timbers, black against the surface glitter. She held her hand out to me. 'Come on. It's more or less safe.'

We walked out and stood at the end of the jetty, beyond the reeds, where the deep water slipped past. It made me uneasy and excited to feel the river gliding all around me just an inch or two below my feet, murmuring darkly to itself, nudging at the timbers. A few yards away the weir rumbled in the darkness and a wraith of vapour hung above it.

'We own all this, you know,' she said, with a touch of derision. 'That is to say, Daddy does.'

'The jetty?'

'Not the jetty, stupid.' She giggled. I had not expected her to be capable of giggling: she didn't look the type. 'The river. This stretch of it, anyway.'

'How can you own a river? It disappears all the time. Which bit do you own? Today's or yesterday's?'

'Daddy thinks he can own all of it. He's filthy rich, you know. He's in line for the House of Lords.'

'So you'll be Lady Caitlin? Is that how it works? Only I lent my Burke's Peerage to the head gardener.'

But she didn't laugh. 'I'm not anyone,' she said. 'I'm just the rich bitch daughter.'

I cleared my throat and looked away at the vanishing river. 'I'm sure nobody says that.'

'They all do. And you know what? When people talk about you that way it makes you start to act that way. Somehow you get surrounded by all these chinless idiots with their Jaguars and their yachts and their villas in Davos, and before you know it, you're part of the set, and you don't know anyone else, and you can't get out.'

I kept quiet, wrongfooted by her change of mood and unsure what to say.

'After a while you start taking risks,' she said, 'just to make it bearable.'

'Risks?'

'Stupid stuff. Too much of everything, too often, too fast. Risks with people too. Just to break the tedium.' She glanced up at me. 'You haven't the least idea what I'm talking about, have you?'

I thought of the Kurdish refugees I had been treating until the day before. I wondered how many of the children I had tried to help were dead by now, for lack of the simplest drugs, or food, or clean water. I said: 'I didn't know being rich was so tough.'

There was a highly charged moment of silence. Then she reached her long arms up around my neck and drew me down and kissed me. After that, as if nothing whatever had happened, she slipped away and flung herself down on the black timber of the jetty and threw her head back so that the light from the sky lay along her face.

'I used to come down here as a little girl.' She lay back on the timber and spread her arms, crucified in the starlight. 'I wasn't allowed, of course, but I used to sneak down sometimes when they thought I was asleep in bed, and then I'd lie like this, for hours, just looking at the sky. Sometimes I thought I'd just blow away, fall away from the earth like a feather.' She opened her eyes. 'You never feel like that, do you, Michael?'

'Don't I?'

'Not you. You're a heavy man.'

'Is that right?'

'I don't mean that's bad. But you believe in an ordered universe. And you believe it's your job to keep it that way. You would never blow away from the earth like a feather.'

I sat down beside her. Nobody had ever described me in this way and I wasn't sure I liked it. It sounded a bit earnest and dedicated. And yet at the same time what really concerned me was not that she had misread me, but that she had read me too well, and that I had been in some sense found out. I knew, as soon as her words were spoken, that I would remember them forever, and that I would remember also the river and the jetty and the rush of the weir. I trailed one hand over the edge of the jetty and the sliding water caressed me until my wrist ached.

'I'll tell you what I believe,' I said at last. 'I believe there's just pain and joy in the world, and you can make more of one, or more of the other. You decide which.'

The murmur of the river seemed to gain in volume. A night bird cried somewhere close, very loudly.

I realised that I was kissing her, and that she tasted of wine, and that her hair was cold over the back of my hand where I cradled her head. I realised too that my loose change was escaping from my pocket and rattling between the slats into the river and that both of us could hear it and that both of us were pretending not to.

'Well, it's my birthday, isn't it?' She rolled her head back against the timber, smiling at the stars. 'That means I can have anything I want.'

I did not wake again until just after dawn when the Hercules touched down at Brize Norton. I had slept awkwardly and my shoulders and back felt locked and my mind was numbed by the hours inside the booming fuselage. But by the time I emerged from the terminal, blinking in the October morning, I was aware of an unexpected tremor of excitement. It was a new day, fresh and clean and with the smoky taste of autumn in the air, and I was about to surprise Caitlin. She was no longer used to impulsive gestures from me. I would put that right. I would put a number of things right.

I felt a rush of longing for her. I stood for a while in the sunshine outside the glass doors of the terminal, thinking of her, jumpy and nervous. Maybe I was still a little heady from the flight; the bizarre dislocation from chaos to order. I felt good. I thought suddenly: it would be all right. I had not been sure before, but standing here, in this glass-bright morning, I knew it was going to be all right.

The Red Cross had chartered a minibus for some of its people arriving on the same flight and I begged a lift with them all the way to Victoria Station. The trip took over three hours, most of it grinding through suburban traffic. I wondered about calling her on the mobile, but now that I was so close it seemed like a failure of nerve to ring. I wanted to startle her, to make an entrance. I pulled my jacket around myself and tried to sleep, but found that I was too keyed up.

By the time I climbed down onto the pavement outside the coach station it was not far short of midday. London smelled of diesel and of the yellowing leaves of the bay trees, awaiting some signal to fall. Despite the lateness of the season the city was teeming and vibrant. I felt a little high: the buses were a violent red, the parks splashed with garish flowers. The whole place seemed electric with energy, like a vast turbine churning out power and noise. I walked up to Victoria Tube Station, dug out my Oyster card and took the Circle Line to Notting Hill Gate.

Twenty minutes later I was standing at the railings opposite the house. I saw that the skylight in Caitlin's eyrie was open, which meant she was almost certainly home. I crossed the street and climbed the steps and quietly let myself in. I closed the door behind me. It was cool and peaceful inside the house after the din of the city. I stood for some moments in the hallway savouring the familiar pattern of light and shade and the friendly smells of the place – herbs, coffee, cut flowers from the market.

'Cate?'

My voice echoed up the polished hall. She did not answer. The house was silent. More than merely silent. It was mute. I stood quietly for perhaps half a minute, trying to deny what I already knew, that something was out of place. The house felt tense and watchful, as if it were observing me and not the other way around. I took a few steps and something on the floor at the foot of the stairs caught my eye. A scatter of pink petals, bruised and crushed. I stooped and picked them up. They were cool in my palm, not yet discoloured. A geranium, like the ones from the tub outside the front door.

'Cate?'

I walked to the foot of the staircase and went up three steps. The bare wooden treads were smudged and dirty. There was the slightest susurration from above. At first I thought it came from the traffic outside, but now I could tell that it was a faint lilt of music, drifting down from the attic. If there was music, she had to be in the house. My heart began to thump. I dropped my bag and ran up to the first landing, checking automatically in the bedroom. The room was clean and bright and normal, the bed neatly made, clothes folded on a chair. I came out onto the landing.

'Cate?'

A litter of broken glass and terracotta and earth and smashed chunks of marble and scattered CDs shining in rainbow colours at the far end of the little landing. The floor was sticky under the soles of my shoes. I stared at her and forgot to breathe until the pain in my chest forced me to. I was aware that an alarm was screaming somewhere in my mind, a purely mental alarm, and that there were well rehearsed responses to this alarm which I had made a thousand times before, efficiently and coolly. I was not responding now.

Caitlin lay with her legs splayed impossibly up the sweep of the stairs. She looked smaller than I knew her to be. Her dress was rucked up and under it her legs were bare and white, and this made her look coltish and vulnerable. Her head lolled over the bottom step and her face was turned towards the wall. A slick pool had gathered under her and had spread over the boards.

I knelt beside her and touched her neck, tentative, disbelieving. Her flesh was warm and there was the faintest pulse and this warmth and flutter threw the switch in me. I could not reach her properly on the stairs and I pushed the litter from the landing and moved her and settled her on the boards, knowing I had no choice and no time. Where my hand cradled her head I felt something like broken china move under her scalp.

I heard myself talking to her, baby-talking, crooning, my voice coming from further and further off as I worked – two breaths, fifteen compressions, two and fifteen, two and fifteen. The muscles of my upper arms began to burn with the effort, but she would not breathe. Twice more I felt for the flutter of her pulse. Once it was there, and once I was no longer sure. Two and fifteen. Again. Again. My movements were becoming clumsy, and sweat began to run down the line of my jaw and drip onto her, but she would not breathe.

The nearest phone was in the bedroom, not five yards away, but I dared not leave her for the time it would take to call help. Two and fifteen. Again. I could no longer find a pulse, but I did not stop. There was always the chance that she would start to breathe, for just long enough to keep her brain alive. Or that someone would call by, and I would be able to shout for help through the door at them. I knew that she would never breathe, and that no-one would call, but I had to believe in these things all the same. And after a while even this shred of faith ceased to matter. Nothing mattered except to keep working, in a delirium of exhaustion which no longer had anything to do with hope, just with a dogged refusal of one part of my mind to accept what the other part knew perfectly well.

I crossed a boundary at some point, I was not entirely sure when. But I knew that time had passed and that I was no longer labouring over her, but cradling her there, rocking her and stroking her cooling forehead. There was a flatness about her body that I recognised, a total relaxation which had begun to mould her flesh onto the boards of the landing and to smooth the small lines of her face and neck.

I got up then. I must have been there for a long while, because the muscles in my legs screamed. I took off my jacket and folded it and pillowed her broken head on it even though I knew she was dead. I stood back from her. My clothing was wet and heavy on my belly and thighs where I had held her against me. The wet cloth grew cold and I was distantly conscious that this was disgusting, and acting on some echo of training I walked quite calmly to the bathroom and stripped off and stuffed the soiled clothes into a linen basket. Then I washed myself and crossed into the bedroom and found some fresh clothes and dressed again.

Somewhere in this process I got lost for a while. I stood in the centre of the bedroom just looking around, perhaps for a couple of minutes, perhaps for longer. There on the wall was Caitlin's Grandma Lavinia in her sepia photograph from the 1920s, trying not to laugh as she perched on her bicycle. And Beamish the bear, his one eye fiery in the lowering October sun which fell through the double windows. I stepped across and sat on the bed and idly stroked his nose. Beamish had been Caitlin's bear since her earliest childhood and was worn bald by her affection. I stroked him again. I looked around again as I did so. The room seemed quite normal in its component parts, but it did not quite fit together. I could not place it, but I had the impression that there was something I had forgotten to do, something important.

Far across London a police siren wailed on its way to some more routine emergency. I stood up and crossed the room and snatched up the bedside phone.

CHAPTER FOUR

There was a crash from the corner of the room and the clatter of something broken and I leapt to face the sound. A uniformed constable, backing out of the photographer's way, had knocked one of Caitlin's maidenhair ferns off the dresser. It lay in a tangle of fronds and dark earth. A big shard of pottery rocked on the polished floor, clicking like a metronome. A momentary stillness settled in the busy room, and I felt people glance warily in my direction.

'Sorry, sir,' the constable said to me. He was absurdly young. 'Very sorry.' He got down on his knees and began ineffectually to brush the shards and the earth together with his hands.

'Leave it,' I said. 'It doesn't matter.' My heart was hammering.

'No trouble, sir. No trouble.' He kept his face away from me, in an agony of remorse. He was almost in tears. He kept brushing at the litter, making a little mound of humus and broken roots, patting it into place like a child's sandcastle, not knowing what to do next. Someone took pity on him eventually and brought him a dustpan from the kitchen and gradually the purposeful activity of the room resumed.

'Are you all right, Doctor Severin?'

The detective inspector was a neat, plump woman in her fifties. She wore a blue blazer and had a perm, and behind her thick glasses her little round eyes didn't miss much. I knew she had noted the way I had jumped at the crash. I could still feel the adrenalin fizzing in my blood and my pulse was taking a long time to settle.

She said, 'We can leave this a while.'

'I don't think that will make it any easier.'

'If you're sure.'

I looked around the room to avoid those keen round eyes of hers. They were strangers, these men and women at work in my house, serious, focused people, and those who met my eyes did so with a studied lack of expression. Their professional detachment began to make me feel foolish.

I said, 'I'm afraid I'm not being much help.'

'Dr Severin, this is an awful business for everyone. Awful.'

The inspector had a low, rasping voice which was at odds with her prim appearance. Sitting there in her neat blue blazer she reminded me of an accounts manager in some struggling but respectable manufacturing firm, a diligent, painstaking person. Her hand moved towards her tan leather bag, and then scuttled back. I guessed the hand had set out on a familiar errand, perhaps to find cigarettes, but had recalled itself at the last moment.

'There's no point putting yourself through this now,' Stella told me abruptly, as if she had been keeping this back under pressure. She was hunched on the sofa opposite, her hands locked together in her lap. Her red hair was all over the place and she was trembling, but there was no mistaking the fierce protectiveness in every line of her body. I could not adjust to her being here. The police had insisted on calling someone to be with me, and I had nominated Stella, but my perception of time was so distorted that she seemed to have got here miraculously quickly, and this disturbed me. When no-one answered her, Stella stood up and moved away a couple of steps and took a packet of cigarettes out of her bag.

'Don't smoke in here,' the police inspector told her, without looking at her. 'If I have to suffer, you can too.'

Stella put the cigarettes away and sat down again beside me. Talking to Stella in this way demonstrated the policewoman's authority to me more clearly than anything else I had heard her say. Her face was soft and her glasses flashed innocently, but she was not dull at all.

I became more precisely conscious of the bustle in the house. It was as if the scene around me were springing into focus, as if I had been drugged and was suddenly startlingly awake. Men and women in white coveralls were coming and going, the photographer was prowling around the room taking endless shots, blue light stabbed through the windows from a police vehicle drawn up on the pavement outside. The late afternoon traffic rumbled in the street, unusually loud through the open front door.

People with heavy shoes were clumping around on the boards in Caitlin's eyrie and on the spiral stairs that led to it. That was the weirdest thing of all, to hear strangers up there. The thundering footfalls made the metal of the staircase hum and ring. Every step surprised and distracted me. I had rarely heard anybody up there, hardly ever even Caitlin herself, who had moved as quietly as a cat.

The inspector was still watching me through her round little glasses.

I said, 'Forgive me, but what's your name? You've probably told me four times but I can't seem to recall it.'

'Maureen Dickenson. Detective Inspector Maureen Dickenson. We can arrange for a doctor. You probably should see a doctor.'

'I don't want a doctor,' I said. 'I spend my life surrounded by doctors.'

A big-shouldered man in a loud check jacket cruised into the room, flipping a notebook shut. The young uniformed constable paused guiltily in the act of carrying the broken pot-plant out to the kitchen.

'You do that, Watts?' the big man demanded.

'Sorry, Sergeant.'

'You dozy prat. Where's SOCO?'

'Upstairs, Sergeant, I think.'

'Make sure he knows you've been crapping up his crime scene. He'll love you. And then bag and tag that rubbish.'

'Sergeant.'

The boy fled and the big man caught sight of me and Dickenson in the window seat behind him. He lifted his chin to the inspector and then to me, and walked out to the kitchen.

'Can I call you Michael?' Dickenson asked me suddenly. 'We don't like to be too formal these days. I don't, anyway.'

I nodded vaguely.

She sat back, not taking her eyes from me. 'Well, when you're up to it, Michael, we'll have to take a formal statement. That would be easier at the station. And you'll understand there are a couple of medical bits and pieces for us to go through so we can eliminate your prints and DNA. They'll be all over the house, obviously. We'll be doing the same with Miss Cowan here and the neighbours and the cleaner and everyone else who's been in here recently. You probably know the routine – being a doctor yourself, I mean.'

She glanced around the room and her little eyes settled on my bags. Someone had moved them into the main room from the foot of the stairs where I had dumped them on my way in.

'You'd been away, had you, Michael?'

'In Venezuela. The earthquake.'

'You were at an *earthquake*?'

'Stella and I. We work for MSF. Médecins Sans Frontières.'

'You do that for a job?'

'No, that's voluntary. I'm on the trauma team at St Ruth's the rest of the time. We both are.'

'St Ruth's in Euston Road?'

'That's my day job.'

Stella chose that moment to take my right hand in hers. Perhaps she felt herself drawn in by the mention of her name. I didn't want her to hold my hand, but I felt that to pull away would be unkind.

'And how long had you been away?' Dickenson asked.

'Three weeks. Nearer four.'

The big-shouldered sergeant in the sports jacket came clumping over, calling instructions loudly to someone over his shoulder as he walked. He saw that he had interrupted us and stopped. 'Sorry, boss.'

Dickenson looked only a little pained. She reminded me of a woman with a Rottweiler, fond of it, glad to have it around, but a little embarrassed by its bulk and clumsiness. 'Dig, this is Dr Michael Severin.'

The man held out a broad hard hand and I took it. Perhaps he was a little over forty. He had scarred eyebrows with deep-set Neanderthal eyes tucked beneath them. I wondered what Dig could possibly be short for.

'I'm not going to say it, Dr Severin,' he told me. 'Everyone for weeks ahead will be telling you how sorry they are, how tragic it is. But no-one knows that better than you. Best the rest of us shut up and get on with trying to do our jobs. Sort this mess out. Far as it ever can be sorted out.'

'Yes,' I said. I found his physical presence overwhelming. I added, without quite knowing why, 'thank you.'

'This is Digby Barrett, Michael,' Dickenson said, 'he's my DS. Detective Sergeant. We work together.'

Digby. Could his name really be Digby? Could anybody's? I felt a slightly hysterical desire to laugh. I could not meet the brown gorilla eyes, but I sensed DS Barrett had picked up my thought all the same.

He said, 'Who's got keys to this place, Dr Severin? Apart from you?'

'I have,' Stella said. 'And he's got mine. In case we're away at different times.'

'And the neighbour on this side,' I added. 'Maybe others. One or two of Caitlin's friends, I expect.'

Barrett scribbled in his notebook and for a moment the sound of his ballpoint gliding over the paper was the only noise I could hear.

'Do you have children, Michael?' Dickenson asked.

'Children?' The question jerked me back to sanity.

'I thought not. Looking at the place.'

Barrett gazed around. 'Nice home. Used to be.' He pulled up a chair and sat down. 'You know the neighbours, Dr Severin?'

'Not very well.' I was finding it hard to concentrate. 'The house on the left's empty. It's been for sale for a month or more.'

'I'm not getting any reply from the one on this side either.' Barrett jerked his thumb. 'Out at work, are they?'

'That's Henry. Henry Kendrick. He's retired.'

'Maybe he saw something, then. Is he usually home during the day?'

'He's away now. He'd have been away when…this happened.'

'You're sure?'

'He's got a son in New Zealand and another one in the States. He visits them every year, for weeks at a time. He left before I did. He's not due back for – I don't know – a while yet.'

Barrett grunted.

'What did she do for a job, your wife?' Dickenson said.

'Nothing.' At once I regretted saying that. It sounded disloyal and I felt the woman's disapproval instantly, like a cold draught. I went on, 'Caitlin was involved with…' I struggled to remember, to be precise, '…with several galleries. Art galleries. She was interested in art. She spent a lot of time at the Tate especially. Tate Britain.'

'So she worked at the Tate Gallery?' She seemed anxious to fit Caitlin into some regular salaried occupation. Perhaps that made it easier to visualise her, to categorise her.

'Voluntary work.' I realised that I could not clearly describe what Caitlin had done there. I was not sure she had ever told me in any detail. I wasn't sure I had ever asked. 'She helped with tours. Exhibitions. That sort of thing.'

'Voluntary work,' Dickenson repeated. 'But she didn't have a job. As such.'

'Not in the sense…' I trailed off, embarrassed at my ignorance. 'No. No, she didn't.'

Dickenson was quiet for a moment, apparently thinking about this. Then she stood up. 'We won't go on with this now. You've got somewhere to stay, Michael, I assume?'

'I'll go to Anthony's, I suppose,' I said vaguely.

'Who?'

'Old family friend. Like a father to me.' I thought about this. 'Christ. How will he take it?'

'Don't worry about how anybody else takes it,' Stella said tightly. 'Anyway, Anthony's away. I tried to call him, but I haven't got a number for his mobile. Do you?'

'He's never had a mobile. You know Anthony.'

'For Chrissake. The message bank on his home number says he's at some antiques fair.'

'Amsterdam. He goes every year.'

'Whatever.' She stood up. 'Meanwhile, you're coming to my place.'

Barrett got to his feet too, and so did Maureen Dickenson. But I did not stand. I said, 'What happened here?'

Some of Dickenson's briskness fell away and for a second she looked less like a police inspector and more like a tired middle-aged woman who had had enough of this work. 'It's too early to say,' she said.

'The smart money would be on a break-in that went wrong,' Barrett put in, as if to relieve her of the burden of committing herself. 'Possibly drugs related, and possibly opportunist. That's just a guess. Most likely Mrs Severin was just unlucky to be in at the time.'

We were all quiet for a second, pondering from our different perspectives the inadequacy of language.

'I want to get this over with,' I said.

The two police officers glanced at one another.

'The statements and the DNA and all the rest of it.' I said. 'I want to be useful. I want to help.'

Maureen Dickenson said, 'If you're up to it we can do it all tomorrow morning. Get it out of the way.'

Stella threw my bag in the back of the car and opened the passenger door and held it for me. But I lingered, staring back down the street at the logjam of police vehicles and the snarled-up traffic trying to crawl past them. I didn't like to be pushed out like this, to be forced to leave my home in the possession of these anonymous professional people who tramped around in Caitlin's room and broke her pot plants. A quiver started somewhere far down in my belly, like the thrumming of a moth's wing.

'What is it?' Stella demanded, seeing me hesitate.

'You remember that cave? The priest? The way the ground shook?'

'What are you talking about now?' she snapped.

She stood there with the keys in her hand, her chest rising and falling. I knew she was pretty close to the edge, closer than I was.

'Do you want me to drive?' I said.

'You? Are you mad? Get in the car!' She pushed me in with such force that I tripped on the kerb and had to catch the roof of her battered red Golf to keep my balance. She banged the door behind me and walked around the front of the car, ripping the black-and-yellow penalty notice off the windscreen and tossing it onto the back seat as she climbed in behind the wheel. 'You're staying at my place until we can sort something out. At least until Anthony gets back. Gordon's still trying to get in touch with him.'

I was grateful to Stella, and to Gordon, but I didn't want to stay at her damp little flat. I didn't want to be shunted about like a sick patient. I said, 'Stella –'

'For once, Michael, will you just do what I say and not argue about it?'

She revved the car savagely and bucked off the kerb, half into the lane, blocking it. She paused there, her foot on the brake, and turned in her seat to face me. A car behind sounded its horn, and then another, but she ignored them, looking into my face. I could not trust myself to meet her eyes. The car horns grew to a blaring chorus behind, but she still sat looking at me, as if on the point of saying something more. She was very pale, and her breathing was rapid.

Finally she took her foot off the brake and swung out into the traffic. Once we were moving Stella drove fast and expertly, finding perhaps some relief in the concentration it took to accomplish this in the thickening traffic. We did not speak again for some time. As we turned up Edgware Road her mobile buzzed and she snatched it out of her bag and thumbed the button and spoke illegally into it without interrupting the rhythm of her driving.

'Yes,' she said. 'Yes, of course he is. Well, thank God for that. Please. Sooner if you can, Gordon. No, don't ask me. I'm hanging by a thread myself here. OK. I will.' She turned the phone off and tossed it onto the floor between her feet. 'Gordon's still trying to get hold of Anthony. He's calling the hotels right now, trying to track him down.'

'Poor Anthony.'

I gazed out at the evening traffic. I tried to imagine Anthony's reaction when Gordon ran him to earth and broke the news, and methodical Gordon would do that eventually. Anthony had adored Caitlin. I rested my head against the car window.

An hour later I sat just inside the sliding doors that gave onto the courtyard at the back of Stella's flat, a dim basement not far from Queensway. The tiny garden was unkempt. From the sofa I watched the autumn evening fade beyond the glass. A willow sapling in a tub hung like a fountain of gold in the dying light. The room around me was peaceful. There were theatre posters on the walls, and a Mexican rug, and beanbag seats against the walls. Yet the room smelt unused. Stella spent much of her time at Gordon's more spacious Pimlico home whenever she was in London, but even when she was here she was not a domestic person. The little flat was a mess, the single bedroom a slovenly tangle. I could hear her in there now, ripping the sheets off the bed, shoving the furniture aside. In a moment she marched back into the room.

'Take these.' She shook the pills into my hand and thrust a glass of water at me.

I swallowed the pills automatically, to please her, not troubling to look to see what they were. She stood back and watched me. She was a strong woman, I thought with a certain weird detachment, a strong young woman with definite lines to her face who had seen a lot of pain and grief in her life and always handled it well. But I could see she was breaking up under this.

'You're not supposed to drink with those, but to hell with it.' She stamped across the room to the kitchen and came back with two glasses of white wine. 'It's piss, but it's all I've got in the place.'

I took the glass and drank a little. The wine was cheap and sweet. Outside in the garden a blackbird started to sing. It surprised me that I should still notice these things and still recognise how pleasant and peaceful they were. Caitlin would never taste wine again. I crushed the thought before it could take root.

'That was Anthony,' Stella said, and set her drink down. I looked at her strained face. There were dark circles under her eyes.

'What was?'

'On the phone. Didn't you hear it?'

'No.'

'He's stuck at Schiphol. There's been some problem with the flights. He got Gordon's message, but he can't get back here until tomorrow morning. I told him you didn't want to talk now. I hope that was right.'

'Yes.' I drank a little more. I was relieved I wouldn't have to face Anthony. I didn't want to see anyone else right now, not even him.

'He wants to take you down to Richmond as soon as he gets in.' I could hear the resentment in her voice. 'I suppose he thinks you ought to be staying there with him and not here.'

'Stella. I practically grew up there. You know what he's like.'

Stella bit her lip to whiteness. She stood up and turned away and pushed her fists into her eyes. 'I'm so sorry. I know this can't help you much.' She breathed deeply a couple of times and turned back to face me. 'God, you wouldn't think I'd spent years in A&E. The things I've seen. The things we've seen, you and me. But it doesn't help, does it?'

'No. It doesn't help at all.'

'Oh, Catey,' she burst out. Her voice broke. 'She was so beautiful. So beautiful.'

Outside the evening blackbird was trilling again. Caitlin would never hear a blackbird sing again, I thought. Never a blackbird nor a Brahms lullaby nor a baby's gurgle. The lists of loss began to unwind in my head, spooling out, slowly at first then faster. Never see a Degas or a daybreak. Never smell horses or hawthorn.

Stella lowered her face into her hands and began to sob without restraint. I stood up and put my arms round her. Caitlin would never feel this, I thought. My arms around her. She was on some cold metal tray somewhere with pieces of her skull loose inside her head and nobody's warm arms would ever be around her again. She'd never be kissed or caressed. Would never wear off any more of Beamish the bear's shabby yellow coat. Never, never again.

'I swore I wouldn't do this. I *swore.*' Stella leaned against me with the heels of her hands in her eyes and I caught her and took her through into the bedroom. I put her in the bed and pulled the duvet over her and she curled into the pillow, blind with sobbing. I sat and stroked her hot shoulder for a while, and then I left the room quietly and pulled the door nearly closed and went back into the main room and stood in the dusk and listened until, after a long time, I heard her ragged breathing grow steady.

It caught me by surprise when it happened. I felt my legs begin to go, folding under me, and before I could react I sat on the floor with a bump. I managed not to upset the small table with the glasses on it, and I was glad about that, because I did not want to alarm her, did not want her to come running down the corridor to me, did not want any more of her anguished sympathy. I stretched my arms in front of me on the cold floor and let my head come forward onto them. Outside in the dark garden, the blackbird sang pitilessly on.

Chapter Five

The little basement room was filled with light and with the unmistakable sounds of morning – muttering pigeons, a jaunty radio in a neighbouring flat, the ringing of heels along the pavement above.

At some stage in the night I had stretched out on the sofa and covered myself with a blanket. I folded the blanket back now and moved my body experimentally on the couch, the way you might move after an accident. My shoulders and back were stiff and the skin of my face felt drum tight. My throat ached in a way I remembered from childhood. I lay back in the sunlight and allowed the warmth of it to trickle into me. After a few minutes I got up and showered in Stella's glum cupboard of a bathroom. When I came out Stella was at work in the kitchen, dressed in a bathrobe, her hair tied back. The percolator gurgled.

'That was all the wrong way round. You were supposed to throw the wobbly, not me.' She set two unmatching mugs on the table, poured the coffee and gazed at me through the steam. Her eyes were puffy and her hair looked brittle. 'I'm a sight, aren't I?'

I leaned over and squeezed her hand. 'I've seen you look better with your teeth in.'

She moved her shoulders and went into nurse mode. 'There's only coffee. I haven't got a scrap of food in the place.'

'I couldn't face it anyway.'

'I'll get you some fresh clothes later.'

I squeezed her hand again and let it go.

She said, 'Two calls while you were in the shower. Anthony was one. He's back in London.'

'And the other?'

'That Sergeant Barrett? He wants to come over at nine to take you for the statement. If you still think you can handle it.'

'I can.'

'Anthony says he'll pick you up when you finish with the police, if that's what you want.'

I knew she still hoped I would stay at her place. I said, 'It's best I go back with him.'

She kept her face neutral. 'Do you want me to come along? To the police station?'

'I'd rather do it alone, Stella,' I said gently.

She looked down into her cup.

DS Barrett led me up the steps to a dark green BMW parked in the street. A young black detective with a gold stud in his ear sat behind the wheel.

'DC Baz Ellis,' Barrett said, nodding to the younger man, and opened the back door for me.

As I slid in the back Ellis met my eyes in the rear-view mirror. 'Sorry for your trouble. Horrible thing.'

I nodded an acknowledgment. Barrett got into the front. The car pulled away. Barrett stared wordlessly out of the windscreen. He was wearing the same jacket as the day before and his heavy face was creased. I guessed he had been up most of the night.

We parked behind Notting Hill police station. Barrett led me in through a back door and we climbed the concrete staircase. The place smelled of disinfectant and the bare cement hissed under our shoes. Barrett swapped greetings with uniformed and plainclothes officers on the way, but he was curt with them, as if to discourage flippant banter in front of me. He pushed through some double doors at the top and led me down a short corridor and into a room filled with familiar medical smells, where he made some excuse and left.

Perhaps it took a couple of hours, perhaps longer. I spent some time in a cubicle while an Asian duty doctor took a swab and collected samples of my saliva. Later DC Ellis took me into a bleak interview room where he and a blonde woman detective I didn't recognise took a statement from me. The woman spoke to me kindly, as if I were a sick child. She stopped me every now and then to clarify or repeat and when she did she called me 'love'. At some point someone took my fingerprints, and apologised for the stain the ink left on my hands. Afterwards I could barely remember the sequence of events. I carried away with me only a general air of competence and weary sympathy.

'Treat you all right, did they?' Barrett led me along the corridor to the lifts. I told him they had.

The lift whispered up. Barrett squinted at the numbers above the door. We came out of the lift and he led me down a passage past a glassed-in area crowded with steel desks. There were computers on the desks and half-a-dozen men and women, mostly youngish, working at the terminals. Papers and cups littered every surface. There were cartoons and notices taped to the glass. One said, 'Drug Squad: Please Keep off the Grass'.

Barrett saw me looking at it. 'Comedians,' he grunted.

He knocked on a door and without waiting for an answer pushed it open and ushered me through. It was a well-lit office on the corner of the building overlooking a slice of West London. There was no-one in the room. It was raining outside and the drops speckled the glass. I was surprised to find it was raining. I seemed to have lost touch with the outside world over the past few hours. There was a large pine desk with a monitor on it and neatly stacked papers and bound reports. Inspector Dickenson's tan leather handbag lay there too, along with a plastic lighter and two packs of Marlboros. The window was open a little.

Barrett said, 'Take a seat.'

As I did so Maureen Dickenson came bustling into the room behind me. I guessed she had been in the washroom. Her lipstick was glossy and a miasma of freshly sprayed perfume hung around her. She was wearing a suit of lavender wool which seemed too warm for the office and a double strand of pearls. It was a long time since I had seen a woman wearing pearls.

'Thanks so much for coming in.' She stepped up to me and I took the hand she offered. It was soft and warm. She brought her other hand up and gripped my wrist with it. 'I won't ask how you are.'

'Your people have all been very good.'

She inspected me with concern through her round glasses. 'Sit down, Michael. You must be exhausted. I know we all are.' She did not look exhausted, not in the battered way Barrett did. She pulled out a chair for me next to a low table near the window and I sat. There was a plate of sandwiches on the table. She sat down opposite me and peeled back the cling-wrap. 'I don't know whether you can face eating, Michael, but for the record it's that time of day. Dig? You're going to stay for a bit?'

'Sure.'

Barrett moved a few paces to one side and positioned himself next to the desk, just on the fringe of my peripheral vision. It was as though these were rehearsed steps in a little dance they both knew.

I said, 'You've got no idea who did this, have you?'

A limp sandwich hung from Maureen Dickenson's fingers.

'I'm sorry,' I said. 'I didn't mean it to sound quite like that.'

'It's natural to want quick answers, Michael. It's as natural as anything can be in a situation like this.' She arranged a napkin on her lap and lay the sandwich on it and looked at it doubtfully, as if I had spoiled her appetite.

'What do they think happened to her?' I felt rather than saw them look at one another over my head.

'We'll know more when we get the PM report,' Barrett said. 'Day or two.'

'Tell me.'

He took a breath. 'It looks as if she was knocked down the stairs by a blow to the face. There's an injury. And there's some sort of big pot seems to have come down with her. Maybe she knocked it over, maybe it was thrown down.' He cleared his throat. 'Thrown down on her.'

'It was a bust,' I said.

Barrett looked blank, even a little startled and I realised that the word *bust* had other connotations for him, perhaps more than one. I suppressed a crazy urge to laugh.

'A statue,' I explained. 'Wagner. That was a sort of a joke. She hated bloody Wagner. She used to say Wagner was a racist pig.'

'Oh,' Barrett said. 'Right.'

There was an awkward pause.

'Look,' he said, 'I know what you want to hear. But there's no way of telling for sure whether this was a sexual attack until the post mortem. I'll say this much: it doesn't look like it. I won't go further than that at this stage. OK?'

I nodded.

'You told me yesterday you didn't call the ambulance right away,' Maureen Dickenson said.

'I couldn't leave her long enough to get to the phone. She wasn't breathing on her own. I've put it all in the statement.'

Barrett said, 'Just so I'm straight about this: about how long was it before you called the police? After you found your wife, I mean?'

'Fifteen minutes? Twenty? It felt longer, but I don't suppose it can have been.' I looked them both in the face. 'Can you explain to me what kind of a person could do this? I've been trying to make sense of it, but nothing seems to add up.'

'It may never add up, Michael,' Dickenson said, 'there's sometimes no rational accounting for these things.'

I thought about this. But *no rational accounting* didn't help.

'It's hard to get a handle on it,' Barrett said: 'but there's a percentage of the population who spend their whole lives just looking for the main chance. Some of them are junkies, some are professional villains, some are just sick. My guess is the same as it was yesterday: your Caitlin was just really, really unlucky. That's all.'

Unlucky didn't help either. I wanted a pattern, a cause and an effect. I tried to get the image to develop in my mind: a crazed junkie with stringy arms, a cold-eyed thug surprised into reflex violence. Neither picture seemed quite to fit. I leaned a little closer to the open window. The damp air was cool on my face.

'But we can't discount the possibility,' Maureen Dickenson said, with some delicacy, 'that Caitlin knew her attacker.'

I looked at her. 'What?'

'Recognised him, anyway. Well enough to open the door to him.'

'How do you work that out?'

'He didn't force an entry,' Barrett said. 'I thought yesterday, maybe a break-in, but there's no sign of it.'

'But there was glass everywhere.'

'Only upstairs. Neither door was forced, no windows broken. All the damage was done inside the house. And there's nothing obviously missing. Money and jewellery left in the bedroom, electronic gear, mobile phone, TV – everything left untouched.'

'You seriously think she let him in?'

Barrett shrugged. 'Maybe. Thinking he was a tradesman, or delivery driver, or whatever.'

'It's also possible he knew you were a doctor, and thought there were drugs in the house,' Dickenson said. 'He could have been watching while you were away. Waiting until she came home, and then pushing his way in as she unlocks the door. Perhaps he intended to rob the place, but then it all went horribly wrong, and he panicked.' She paused. 'I'm sorry. I know it's not pleasant to think about, but we have to account somehow for what we find.'

I tried to process all this, to work out what it might mean. I could not seem to get it to keep still in my mind.

Maureen Dickenson said, 'Michael, you told me yesterday that you go away fairly regularly with these MSF people.' She lifted her sandwich and nibbled it. I was so thrown by the shift in tack that she had to look questioningly at me: 'Michael?'

'Maybe once a year with MSF. But there were other trips. Conferences, meetings. The usual.'

'For weeks at a time?'

'Sometimes, yes.'

'Caitlin was all right about all these absences, was she?' Her round little eyes locked on mine from behind her glasses. 'She understood?'

I realised only then what she was driving at. 'You're on the wrong track.'

'We're not on any track, Michael. Not yet. But I'll be honest with you. When my other half thought I was becoming obsessive about *my* work, he developed – how shall I put it? – interests of his own.'

I met her eyes. 'No.'

'Please don't be offended.'

'I'm not offended. We were close. You know what I mean by that? Whatever potholes we hit in the road, we both knew about them.'

'We're all human.'

'No. Absolutely not. We didn't have that kind of a problem.'

She watched me as I said this, but after a few seconds she seemed to come to a decision and she relaxed a little. 'Yes. Well.' She put her paper napkin and half-eaten sandwich back on the table. 'Michael, let me just say this. Everyone tells me that you were happily married, that you were made for each other. But you understand that I have to ask. If it turns out we need to follow anything up, anything at all, the quicker we do it the better.'

None of us spoke for a few seconds.

'You came back early?' Barrett said at last. He reached past me and took some food in his paw, shedding scraps of lettuce onto the carpet. 'Mrs Severin wouldn't have been expecting you?'

'It was meant to be a surprise.'

'There was a special reason for that? For wanting to surprise her?'

'I called Caitlin the other night,' I said. 'From Venezuela. She sounded odd, that's all.'

'Odd?'

'Vague. A bit...upset.'

They looked at one another and back at me.

I said, 'A fit of the blues. I wouldn't put it any more strongly than that. I think my call caught her off guard.'

'Why would it?' Dickenson asked. 'Wasn't it normal for you to call?'

'I hardly ever did. It was a kind of deal we had. It wasn't always easy for me to make contact, so we agreed we wouldn't make a habit of it. That way she didn't worry if she didn't hear from me for a while.'

'But this time you were worried about her,' Barrett said. 'Worried enough to call. And to come home early.'

'I'd been away a while. We'd had a rough day. I missed her.'

'And she sounded odd. Vague. Upset.'

'I decided to come back. That's all.'

Outside the rain fell steadily. I became aware that my voice had risen a little.

Dickenson said, 'We're just trying to build up a picture, Michael.'

'Yes. I see.'

She said, 'And you're right to feel the way you do. Angry, confused. This thing is tragic. Obscene. The whole world's going mad, I sometimes think. We get angry and confused too. People think we don't. But they're wrong.'

'You got to see our problem here,' Barrett's hand came past me like the grab of an excavator and enveloped another three or four of the dainty sandwiches. 'The way it looks now we've got nothing. No break-in. Nothing seems to be taken. We've got pretty obvious signs of a violent struggle, but nobody notices or hears anything suspicious. Neighbours, I mean, or passers-by. None we've found yet, anyway. We've got no signs of panic as this character flees the scene. We've got no distraught junkies turning up at the nick desperate to confess. We've got no word on the street.'

'I don't know how I can help you. I wish I could.'

I discovered that I was ravenously hungry but I did not want to take any food. It seemed indecent. And yet I could not keep my eyes off the plate.

'You any idea where she was going, Dr Severin?' Barrett asked.

'Going?'

'There was a suitcase in her room. Packed. It looks as if another bag was thrown down the stairs, around her, or over her, maybe.'

I stared at him.

'You didn't notice all that stuff on the stairs? Clothes, books, bathroom stuff?'

'I didn't notice much at all.' I tried to think. 'But yes, now you mention it. A suitcase, you say?'

'Like I said, one case and one hold-all, by the look of it.'

'I expect she was going to visit friends for the weekend,' Dickenson suggested. 'Or family, maybe.'

'Not family,' I said. 'Friends, perhaps.'

'Why not family?' Barrett asked.

'We didn't get on with Caitlin's parents.' I stopped, corrected myself. 'We thoroughly disliked one another, I'm sorry to say.' And a guilty thought struck me. 'Jesus, I should have called them. It never so much as crossed my mind.'

'We called them,' Dickenson said. 'Her parents are away on a cruise, but I imagine they'll have had the news by now, poor people.'

'Their only daughter,' I said.

'Puts it all in perspective, doesn't it?' she said. 'Family squabbles.'

CHAPTER SIX

A few minutes later I walked out of the police station and round
to the car park at the back. The rain had stopped, but water
lay in mirrors on the asphalt. I spotted Anthony immediately, a
funereal figure in his rumpled black suit, mooching slowly up the
aisle between the cars, staring down at his shiny shoes. He didn't
see me at once, and I allowed myself a moment or two to observe
him, partly to let my mind settle, but partly because some tangle of
associations led me back to another time when Anthony had come
to collect me.

It had been the day after the fire. The morning was bitterly cold
and frost lay as white as sugar on the parked ambulances. I had
noticed the way they looked like wedding cakes, and the way the
cold made my hands ache under the dressings. And there Anthony
had been, just as he was now, portly and muffled and bouncing
nervously on the balls of his feet while his maroon scarf blew behind
him like a pennant in the raw wind.

'Action,' he had told me, 'that's what's called for. *Action téméraire!*'

He had taken my bag from the nurse and avoided looking at
my hands. His eyes were watering. He pretended that it was the
east wind which caused this, but even then I knew better. I had no
idea at that time what happened to kids whose families had been
swept away, whose homes had burned to nothing. Maybe Anthony
would take me to an orphanage. I pictured somewhere like my
hated boarding school, the smell of boiled vegetables in stone corridors. I didn't care much what it was like. I didn't care much about
anything.

But Anthony hadn't taken me to an orphanage that day. Instead he took me to a street market, a long roadway crammed with stalls and with people. The people behind the stalls were loud and boisterous and some of them were strangely dressed and they shouted and laughed a lot and called out incomprehensible things to each other. Their tables were set out as if in a bazaar: porcelain figurines, and books with leather covers, and framed pictures, and ornate jewellery, and glassware, and antiquated toy aircraft in tin and enamel, and trays of coins, and military badges, and caskets of dark wood and ivory. The sunlight was crystalline and a thin sky soared above the awnings. There was something surreal about being in such a place at such a time with dull Anthony as my guide. For this place wasn't dull at all – it was magical – and in this fairytale landscape Anthony wasn't dull either. Elsewhere he might have been bumbling and a little ridiculous, but here he was a wizard, a prince, and he was greeted with deference at every turn.

'It's a first edition, Mr Gilchrist. Right up your street.'

'Some Meissen pieces in by next week, Mr Gilchrist. I'll put one or two aside.'

'Nothing up to your mark this time, Mr Gilchrist. But I'll keep you posted.'

Anthony had nodded and smiled in a vague fashion as he processed through the street, like royalty dispensing favour, but he stopped nowhere and bought nothing. I learned later that this was Portobello Road. I was to go there many, many times with Anthony and in fact Caitlin and I were eventually to live not more than a mile away. At the time I could not have imagined any of this, but even then I was fascinated by the colours and the energy and the noise of the place.

'You are not in any way to blame, Michael,' Anthony had announced quite suddenly, as we drifted between the stalls that day.

I stared up at him, but he did not stop walking and he did not look at me.

'I've been talking to the police and the fire brigade. It might have been that damned cigar which started it all.' Anthony seemed to notice something high above the rooftops, which required him to turn his head away from me for a few moments. 'So if we're to talk about blame, then it was my fault for buying him cigars. Or his own for smoking one and not putting it out. See how silly it gets? But in any case, you were not in any way responsible.' He had placed an uncertain hand very gently on my shoulder, and let it rest there. His touch felt awkward but I did not want to pull away from him. I knew he meant to be kind, even though what he said was, obviously, untrue. 'Best not to think about it at all, old chap,' he had said.

I realised that we had stopped. Immediately in front of us was a trestle table set out with mechanical contrivances – carriage clocks, pocket watches in plush cases, musical boxes, wind-up toys. Against the brick wall behind were ranked longcase clocks standing in an uneven row like sentries ill-matched for height. The stall was busy with ticking and clicking and the rattle of escapements and occasionally doors would fly open and birds or redcoat soldiers or ballerinas would appear and chirp or strut or twirl, and then vanish again. A tiny man with an earring and a trilby hat was peeping at me across the table.

'Who's this, then, Mr Gilchrist?' the man's quick eyes registered my bandaged hands and then flicked away, 'the Sorcerer's Apprentice, would it be?'

'This is Michael.' Anthony bounced on his shiny shoes. I could see he was pleased and relieved to see the little man. 'Michael, meet Mr Harry Judah. Harry is a very bad man indeed. Outrageous prices. Have nothing whatever to do with him.'

Harry Judah swept off his trilby. 'Purveyor of pre-loved cuckoo clocks to the gentry, at your service.' He had very black hair, and without his hat I saw that he was quite young. 'I am benighted to meet you, Mr Michael.'

I had no idea what he was talking about, but I felt his warmth and his teasing humour. I could tell that Harry Judah did not know what had happened to my family, but I saw the way he looked at my bandaged hands and I knew he guessed some part of my tragedy.

'You are planning to sell the lad as a chimneysweep, Mr Gilchrist?' Harry went on, replacing his trilby. 'I would get a wriggle on if I was you, before he grows any bigger, and before the whole town goes over to central heating.'

Anthony had started to lift his hand from my shoulder, but he changed his mind at that moment and let it stay there. He even squeezed a little. He said: 'Michael is coming home with me.'

Harry Judah kept his face neutral. 'You'll be taking care of the lad, then?'

'From now on,' Anthony had said, and there was a catch in his voice, 'I shall take care of everything.'

I came back to the present. Anthony had still not seen me, and I walked across the police station car park towards him. He was so deep in thought that I was only a few feet away from him before he lifted his mournful boxer-dog face to me.

'Hello, Anthony,' I said.

'My dear boy,' he said. 'My dear old chap.'

Anthony was sixty-four or sixty-five. No great age. But today he looked like an old man, beaten and spent. I had never seen him look like that. It was desperately cruel that he should be called upon to play a part in yet another hopeless tragedy. I felt irrationally responsible because both tragedies were mine.

'You look bloody awful, Anthony.'

'I do? Good God. *I* do?' Anthony whipped out his breast pocket handkerchief – crimson this time, I noted, with big white dots. He flourished it as though flapping the raindrops from his coat. He looked at the sky and then at the ground in a jerky fashion, as though surprised in turn by different things he saw in each place.

I said, 'Thanks for coming so quickly, Anthony.'

He took a deep breath, looking over my shoulder. 'Well, obviously. The moment I heard. I called in on your friend Stella. She gave me some things for you. They're in the car.' He tucked the handkerchief back into the breast pocket of his suit so that it flopped there like a large soft flower. We hovered for a few seconds, neither of us certain what to say next. At last Anthony said: 'How could this be, Michael? Hasn't there been enough pain?'

He was on the point of tears, but strangely just then I did not feel that way. It was a relief of sorts to take charge.

'Where's the car, Anthony?'

He took a deep breath, steadied himself. 'Just over there.'

'Let's go, then.'

We walked a few yards to where a new maroon Volvo lay beaded with raindrops. He fumbled for a while with the key fob before he managed to unlock the doors. I couldn't help staring at the car. I had never seen it before. Anthony owned an aged white Rover which years ago we had christened The White Lady – in my mind he had always owned it – and the sleek new Volvo did not suit him at all.

'Monstrosity,' Anthony muttered. 'The White Lady's at the garage. Bloody nuisance.'

I could tell that he was embarrassed about the alien car. I knew he felt that he had failed by not bringing the comfortable old Rover on this day of all days, for not surrounding me with every last vestige of tradition and familiarity. It was absurd for him to feel this way, but it was very Anthony. I couldn't think of any way to ease his distress. I walked around the Volvo and opened the passenger door, but then we both hesitated, looking at one another over the shining roof.

'I shall take care of everything,' Anthony said, and squared his shoulders. He got into the glossy car and clunked the door closed behind him.

The house where Anthony lived alone was a large dim place built in the 1920s and set in an unkempt garden full of shrubs and poplar trees. The paint was flaking from around the front porch, and the driveway was in need of resurfacing. Anthony never seemed to notice. During my school holidays this air of careless decay had intrigued me. The house would have been merely boring and suburban without it, like the upper middle class homes along the street, reclining behind their privet hedges and gravel drives. Instead, neither Anthony nor his house quite fitted here, in this time and place, and though I did not then understand what this meant I knew it to be significant.

Inside, the rooms were musty and encumbered with dark furniture. Books and paintings and statuary covered every wall and shelf. There were a lot of clocks in Anthony's house, including a handsome longcase in the hall and an ormolu carriage clock on the dining room mantel. They were all a few minutes slow. Anthony wasn't precise about time, but he had a real talent for repairing and restoring mechanisms: the locks of antique firearms, clockwork toys, musical boxes. He would sit at an old deal table under the conservatory windows, the only space in the house with good natural light, the tabletop around him littered with tiny brass cogs and springs, wheels and flints and weights.

None of this had interested me much when I was a teenager until one day Anthony had brought home a magnificent pair of duelling pistols by Wheelers of London. He had even let me handle them for a few minutes before locking them away in their fine rosewood case. I could still remember the cool kiss of steel and the smooth burr of the walnut butts. The pistols were so finely balanced that they seemed to be weightless. Anthony had looked at me blankly when I suggested we might load and fire them in the garden. I had visions of crows exploding in thunderclaps of black feathers, cartoon style. His failure to see the attraction of this idea was frustrating, but all the same it was deeply impressive that he should own such mystical weapons at all, and even more that he should have the skill in his fat little fingers to make them function again. I had felt differently about him after the duelling pistols arrived.

Anthony and I carried his bags into the house. The place was cold and dim after his few days away. It smelled of dust and old polish, the way I remembered it smelling from years ago. I had a keen sense of stepping back into the past. Though I had visited Anthony here regularly over the years, I had not stayed in this house since my teens.

I took Stella's plastic bag of new clothes upstairs to the front bedroom I had always occupied as a child. It was a narrow room with a sloping ceiling, smaller than I remembered, but in almost every other respect just as I had left it. I could still trace the holes made by the drawing pins which had held my map of Brazil to the cupboard door. My old desk was there in the corner, so small I could no longer get my legs under it. It still sported the slightly off-centre hole I had hacked through the surface, much to Anthony's horror, to take the cables of my first primitive computer. I didn't know whether it was my butchery of the desktop or the presence of a computer in the house which so shocked him. I doubt he had ever seen a computer before. He had not even owned a television. He still didn't.

The room was musty and it made my nose prickle. I sat on the familiar single bed and then stretched out on it. The light was fading outside. I had dreamed a lot of dreams on this bed, with the light fading as it was now, dreams of escape and adventure. In the old days, when the leaves of the old maple which overhung the window began to turn - as they were turning now - I knew that I would soon be back at school. I was nearly always impatient to be gone. I had always loved Anthony, but this strange old place was quiet enough for a young boy. Through my teens my visits here had become shorter and each time I stayed at the house I grew more and more anxious, more and more quickly, to get back to the real world, to distance myself from Anthony with his lugubrious expressions and his spotted bow ties. Yet here I was again, and here he still was. I wondered how long it would take me to find my way back to the real world this time.

When I was next aware of my surroundings the room was chill and the leaves outside the window were black against an evening sky. I sat up on the bed. The air was slate blue and in the corner the elderly radiator gurgled biliously. I rubbed my face and got up and turned the bedside light on and walked out onto the landing.

Downstairs I could see a line of amber light under Anthony's study door and I could hear the soft lament of a woman singing. I went into the bathroom and showered and shaved and came back into the bedroom and emptied Stella's bag onto the bed. She had bought new underwear and a sweater and stiff new jeans. I pulled on the unfamiliar clothes: they fitted approximately. I walked out of the room and down the dark stairs to Anthony's study.

He was sitting in one of the leather armchairs by the hearth. The room was full of plangent lament. Anthony was hunched in his dark suit on the edge of his chair, staring into a tumbler of brandy. He looked quickly away as I opened the door and then back at me, and although he arranged his face into a smile of greeting I avoided looking directly at him. He held up his glass for me to see.

'I know where it is, Anthony.'

I crossed to his elderly but magnificent Bang and Olufsen system which reclined in the corner under a cloth, like an altar, and lowered the volume of the keening soprano. The room was dimly lit and cool. I noticed that the fire had been set in the hearth but that he had not put a match to it. I went to the drinks cabinet and poured myself a scotch.

Anthony nodded at the blue squares of the window. 'Once it's October you can smell winter. The start of winter.'

I circled the room, pulling closed the dusty curtains, switching on a brass reading lamp, turning the volume of the stereo down another shade. This was Anthony's favourite room, a cluttered lair full of small mahogany tables with things of brass and pewter on them, of glass fronted bookcases and display cases of moths and beetles. It smelled of age and of wood smoke and of the sap in the pine logs by the grate.

In the old days Anthony would bring me into this room for his most intimate chats, typically to reproach me sorrowfully for some act of rebellion against another idiotic school regulation. I remembered sitting half-digested by one of those enormous chairs, scowling at him as he explained how necessary to the triumph of good over evil were order and discipline, and why it followed from this that I should always wear my cap outside the school grounds. I remembered too when, a year or two later, he had brought me in here to listen to Callas singing La Bohème. This introduction to high culture had not been much more effective than his lectures on discipline, but I had been aware even at the time that something special was being offered, something more even than music, and I had sat through the whole of it, a little awed by the half-understood honour being done me.

I noticed now that he had arranged a number of framed photographs on the coffee table beside his chair. I imagined him lifting them and examining them and setting them down again while I had been sleeping upstairs – polishing the glass, perhaps, with his spotted silk handkerchief. They were not, as I had feared, photographs of Caitlin. They were pictures of my father, lounging against the bonnet of a Landrover in some tropical place with a stand of palm trees behind him, grinning in that raffish way of his. And pictures of my mother, sunglasses pushed up into her hair, looking younger even than I remembered her, suntanned and slender in a striped tee-shirt. And pictures of Paul and Deborah, soft unformed faces full of light, my brother just six years old and my sister not yet four, the ages they would keep forever. And just one picture of me, glaring importantly at the camera, fierce in my responsibility as the oldest child.

I found some matches and knelt on one knee on the hearthrug in front of him to light the fire. And as I knelt there he placed his hand on my shoulder, as if I were a penitent receiving a blessing.

'You know, Michael,' he said, 'I was never much good at anything.'

His hand on my shoulder was the gentlest touch, but I found that for the moment I could neither move nor speak for the weight of it.

'Oh, I had all the right connections. Public school. Cambridge. So forth. But I was always, well, twelfth man. Even in Chambers. Sound enough. Willing enough workhorse. No real…spark, d'you see?'

With an effort I struck the match. I touched it to the curl of newspaper in the hearth and yellow flames flickered up. I sat back on my haunches and his hand fell away. The fire cracked and popped and we both watched it.

'Your father was such a dear friend to me, Michael,' he said. 'Extraordinary, really. I wasn't a bit like him. Good heavens, no!'

His heavy face lightened at the memory. 'Duncan had no social advantages at all, but there he was up at Kings with all of us public school wonders from Winchester and Rugby, mixing it with the best of us, bolshy, argumentative, taking no prisoners. We didn't know what had hit us. Duncan would have been a soldier, you know, in another life. I've often thought that. Touch of the T.E. Lawrence. Somewhere wild and remote.'

The light of the fire flickered across the picture of my father and brought the colours to life – palm trees of hectic green and behind them a glassy sky. It struck me that this photograph must have been taken just before my father's death, when he was my present age. And that was odd, because throughout my life I had always been approaching him more nearly as time passed, but from now on, he would stay young and I would grow older. With every year I would grow steadily further away from him.

My father had been an engineer, but Anthony was right, in another life he would have been a soldier. You could see it in the sun-creases of his face, in his smile and in the jaunty angle of his head. A tall man, a confident and capable man with intelligent eyes and decision in the very angles of his body. Everyone said I had grown to be like him. The comparison had nearly always pleased me, but I had never really known what it meant. He was away so much that I had never truly known him. And then I had irrevocably lost him just as I moved out of childhood. Lost him and lost the others. Lost all reference, all framework. This could not be repaired.

'Always Sancho Panza to his Quixote,' Anthony was saying. 'Loyal squire to the champion. Couldn't be otherwise. Chap like me. But I'd have done anything for him. Anything.' He looked at me. 'And then that damned stupid fire. Not in Sarawak or the Congo or somewhere. Surbiton. Good God! A mean suburban house fire in Surbiton.'

Down all the years we had never spoken of this so directly. I had a sudden longing for the hot wild places I had so often sought out and my father had sought before me, the harsh places where the choices were stark.

'But in a way, do you see,' Anthony continued, 'Duncan gave me my one chance to do something really special. To look after you. Oh, I don't claim much credit. Just a little. Just enough to be able to say, I could do something useful after all. I hope in some small way I may still be allowed to.'

I waited but he was silent after that. I looked down into the fire so that he could no longer see my eyes. It was an irony indeed. This soft little penguin of a man meant what he said. I was supposed to be the intrepid one, a man of decision like my father. I was the rescuer, used to facing choices of life and death, able to handle myself in a crisis. But when it came down to it, it was portly Anthony with his bow tie who had the steel in him.

CHAPTER SEVEN

I lay back on the slats of the jetty, cradling Caitlin against me. The summer moon hung above like a pantomime lantern caught in the trees. A couple of inches under my head the Severn muttered to itself against the timbers on its dark way to the weir. Somewhere a world away the decorous sounds of the party tinkled in the night, gentle music, well bred laughter. Behind us something splashed in the water like a dropped stone: a fish, hunted or hunting. I imagined it flickering through the dim channels beneath us.

She reached up and stroked her fingertips over my face, like a blind girl trying to read a message there. Her hand slid down the curve of my throat. I could smell myself on her fingers. My shirt was open and her hand brushed over the key, stopped, returned to it, lifted it in the moonlight.

'What's this? The key to your heart?'

'It's to remind me.'

'To remind you to do what?'

'To keep the universe in order,' I said, and kissed her hair.

'O heavy man,' she breathed in my ear, mocking. 'Don't you know it's in chaos?'

I thought of the refugee camps, all the desperate people, the abandoned people. 'No,' I said, 'the chaos is in us.'

Back through the woods I could hear Bruno singing again in his malty voice.

That child done washed us away, he sang. *That child done washed us away.*

When I next opened my eyes it was day.

'Did I wake you?' Caitlin was bending over me, smiling a little. I was aware of the water sliding past a few inches below me and the dank smell of mud. She said: 'You looked so peaceful there.'

'You didn't wake me.' I didn't know why I lied about this.

'I tried hard enough.' She laughed. 'This is terribly romantic, but I'm freezing to death here.'

'I'm sorry. I seem to be able to sleep anywhere.'

She pulled a funny face. 'Don't tell me. Your SAS training.'

'Right. I did the jetlag and champagne course. It was hell.'

'Did that include sex with strange women, hanging by a thread over a waterfall?'

She gave me that quizzical look I was to come to know so well, the look that always left me feeling she was just half a step ahead of me. The early light was in the sky and in the river and shining along the curves of her face and this changed everything, put everything in the hazard. It made me fearful, as if all of this might vanish like fairy gold, and so I said nothing, in case it might be the wrong thing. Our clothes were tangled inelegantly around us. My jacket was trailing one arm in the river. There was a light mist rising from the water. In the dove grey dawn it had grown very cold. She was holding the neck of her dress closed and I could see she was shivering. I sat up and wrung cold water out of the sleeve of my jacket. I could feel the slats of the jetty shift beneath me as I moved.

'Let's find some coffee,' she said, and stood up.

I followed her up the track beside the river. She bent to take off her shoes and she moved through the white mist that rolled off the water, shining like a ghost in her pale gown. We came through the screen of trees and onto the back lawn of the house. The low sun struck across the grounds and made the grass blaze with dew and made the wings of gauzy insects flare. Three grey rabbits sat up in the grass as we approached, surprised to find humans about so early, and then bounced casually away.

Walking after the girl, watching her straight back and her shining hair, swinging through the grass with her shoes hooked nonchalantly over her shoulder, it came to me that I had entered a place I had never been before. It came not as a shock but as a calm realisation. It was unknown territory, but I recognised it unmistakably as somewhere I belonged.

Caitlin turned to face me at that moment, as if at a signal, laughing in the cool light, her arms spread and her shoes dangling from one hand and the other stretched out to me. I walked up and took her hand, and stood looking at her, and her smile settled. She was quiet for a long time, breathing gently against me. I didn't know precisely when it was agreed, but I knew that it was agreed during those few moments, and without a word spoken. She hooked her arm around my neck and kissed me, and I kissed her in return. We were clumsy, like teenagers, as if we had both forgotten how to do it and would have to learn all over again. She kept her eyes open.

After that she took my arm and we moved across the lawn, through the debris of the party – stacked white plastic tables and chairs, wire baskets of wine bottles, glasses crowded onto trays on the trestles. In some of the glasses doomed mayflies circled in champagne, their wings puckering the surface. We must have looked like disreputable Victorian lovers, if there had been anyone to see us, Caitlin barefoot in her long dress and me in my dark dishevelled suit, kicking through the buttercups. Morrow House was utterly silent above us, a great cliff of buff stone with imperious Georgian windows and pillared porte-cochere.

'You really live in this place?' I gazed up at the tall façade, the leaves of ivy and Virginia creeper shimmering in the light. It was easily the grandest private house I had ever seen. 'It's like a castle in a fairytale.'

'Oh, yes,' she said, 'complete with resident ogre.'

I glanced at her. It should have been a joke, but it wasn't.

Several cars were still parked along the drive, a Jaguar and two Porsches and a regal silver Bentley. Beside the Bentley was Bruno's battered Austin Healey. Bruno was asleep across the front seat, smiling beatifically with a champagne bottle in his arms and his feet stretched out of the passenger window. He was wearing expensive suede boots and his legs were elegantly crossed at the ankle.

Caitlin led me around the sweep of gravel drive, past an Edwardian iron-framed conservatory which ran down one side of the house, and to a small group of outbuildings set back among the trees. She pushed open the door of the nearest one, a long redbrick shed with timber-framed windows and a slate roof heavy with creeper. I ducked inside through the low door. At one end of the shed stood a bank of ancient switchgear, brown bakelite handles and ivory painted dials with tall lettering, the whole assembly swagged with cobwebs in the slanting light.

'It used to be the generator house in the old days,' she said, brushing in past me. 'And then it became a…retreat of mine. Still is, sometimes.'

I caught her hesitation and looked curiously towards her, and I saw that the other end of the low building, a space about the size of a large sitting room, had been converted into some kind of a studio. There were corkboards fixed to the walls and drawings pinned to the boards. A trestle bench stood under the window with stacks of paper and spiral bound sketchbooks on it and jars with pencils and brushes in them. There was an easel in the middle of the floor and she was standing beside the easel, and as she stood there I could sense an awkwardness about her that I had not seen before.

'Coffee?' She spoke briskly and crossed to a small sink in the corner. She ran water into a pot. 'I can do coffee. The real thing. I put a camping stove in.'

I stepped up to the easel. There was a watercolour clipped to it, a landscape of rolling sedge greens and brilliant cornflower blue. It was bold and strong. In the low light it gripped my attention like a stained glass window in a church, pure and luminous, as if the sun shone through it from behind.

I said: 'Did you do this?'

'I haven't got any milk. There's some sugar if you can chip it out.'

I looked around the drawings and paintings on the walls: old farm buildings, flowers and trees, a churchyard with crosses and headstones, a herd of cows in a rain-swept pasture. Most were in pencil, some few in charcoal or pastel, a handful in watercolour.

'These are wonderful,' I said.

She put the coffee pot carefully onto the gas ring and kept her back to me. 'Like you'd know,' she said.

I blinked. 'What did I say?'

She did not answer and kept her face away from me.

'Cate, you shouldn't be embarrassed. These really are beautiful.'

'Yes?' She swung around, her hands behind her against the edge of the bench. Her face had changed. 'And how do they stack up against whatever you've been doing for the last couple of months?'

The question threw me.

'Don't be coy,' she said. 'You didn't get that suntan on a package deal to Ibiza, did you?'

'I've been working in a refugee camp in Kurdistan.'

'I thought it was something like that. Doing what?'

'I'm a doctor. I was with the relief operation.'

'Saving lives. Right? While I was doing...what? Ski-ing in Aspen with friends. I can't quite remember who now. I think we managed to get through an entire fortnight without anyone uttering a single coherent sentence. Oh, and then of course I had to go to Paris for a wedding, and I stayed on there for ten days, crawling around a few galleries and the odd concert when I wasn't just *too* hung over. And in between I was back here, painting pretty pictures, just waiting for someone like you to tell me I was the best thing since Matisse.'

'Am I supposed to feel sorry for you?'

'Feel what you want.'

'Caitlin, if you don't like your life, bloody well change it.'

'Just like that?'

'There are few enough people who have the freedom, or the talent. You do.'

'You think so?'

'Yup.'

Behind her the coffee percolator gobbled explosively and it cut short our exchange like a referee's bell.

'Well,' she said, and the tension between us fled as rapidly as it had blazed up. 'It didn't take us long to have our first argument, did it?'

She took the coffee pot off the stove and poured two mugs and brought them across to a wicker sofa against the wall. She put the mugs on an upturned planter pot, sat down and patted the seat next to her. I sat and she stretched her long body across me and kissed me.

'Michael, how old are you?'

'Twenty-nine.'

'Did your people bring you up to be independent?'

I thought about that. 'You might say so.'

'Mine didn't.'

'It sounds to me as if you do pretty well what you like.' I hadn't quite recovered my equilibrium.

'Yes,' she said. 'I can do anything I want. It's just that none of it matters.'

'Who says it doesn't matter?'

'He hates me doing this.' She pointed at the paintings and drawings around the room. 'Daddy, I mean.'

'Why?'

'Because I'm good at it. Because through it I can escape. Get away from him and into my own space.' She saw my face and laughed. 'You think this is all neurotic bullshit, right?'

'I didn't say that.'

'You didn't have to.' She reached across for her coffee and nursed it. Her dress rustled in the quiet room. 'I don't expect you to understand. You see a problem, you deal with it. It's the way you're wired. But I've got to twenty-four without knowing how to do anything worthwhile.'

'Does he tell you this isn't worthwhile? All this work?'

'You're very sweet,' she said. 'Daddy would never dream of calling it work.'

'Does it matter so much what *Daddy* thinks?'

'It's not so easy to change the way you are, Michael. The way you've been taught to be. Even when you don't like it much.'

That struck a chord with me and I could find no argument. I picked up my cup.

She said abruptly: 'You know what loneliness is, don't you, Michael? I can see it in you, that you know.'

'Yes. I know.'

'Well, then you know that loneliness takes away your will. That's something I discovered here, in this house. That without other people you have no power. And childhood's just the loneliest time of all. That's why I'll never have kids.' She put her coffee down and nestled back against me. 'Never. Never. Never.'

I felt her body mould itself against mine. Outside, the birds were singing in the cool morning. I thought again of the children I had seen in the last few weeks, their eyes luminous with accusation, fading out of life from malnutrition or disease or simple neglect. She didn't have in mind the same sort of suffering as I did, but it was suffering just the same. She didn't want kids. Why had she told me that? Did she think it would shock me, that I would think her strange? If she did, she was wrong. If deprivation was all the world had to offer them, kids were better off unborn.

I rolled my head to look at her. She was so quiet I thought she had drifted off to sleep.

'You got a white charger anywhere?' she asked suddenly. 'Only I could do with breaking out of the enchanted castle.'

'You mean I have to polish up my armour? I hate that.'

'I'm a bit of a handful,' she said, and grew serious. 'And my life's a mess. I mean, if you did feel like rescuing me.'

'That's my job. I'm in the rescuing business.'

She got lightly to her feet and stood in the mackerel light and put her hands behind her neck and let her dress whisper down to the floor so that it formed a shining pool around her bare feet. She stepped out of it and bent over me and unfastened the buttons of my shirt and slid her hands over my chest and down over my belly, watching me gravely as she did so. She sat across me and I let my hands rest on the cello curve of her waist and I kissed her and pulled her close to me.

'Rescue me, then,' she breathed, her mouth against my ear. 'Rescue me.'

I came awake peacefully, stretched out with my head on the arm of the sofa. I heard the sound of it even before I opened my eyes, the smallest hiss and tick of pencil on rough paper.

'Don't move,' she said. She sat a few feet away on a straight-backed chair, the drawing board across her knees. She was frowning with concentration. 'Don't you dare move.'

She was wearing my shirt, the sleeves rolled up to the elbows. Her eyes flicked up, followed the lines of my body, flicked down again to the paper. I kept very still, so still that I could hardly feel myself breathe. The sun fell in a bar across the studio. The light was warm on my skin, and it burned on her hair, and where it touched the material of the shirt it was so bright that it was hard to look at. She worked with intense focus, the pencil flickering across the paper. Occasionally she would narrow her eyes and squint rapidly from drawing to me and back again, the pink tip of her tongue gleaming between her teeth. Then she would pause to soften a line, stroking the paper with her fingers. It filled me with peace to watch her work, and with a sense of the most profound privilege. I had the strangest feeling that no-one had ever truly seen me before. I did not want her to stop.

'There,' she said at last. She looked critically at her work, adjusted one final line. The tip of her right forefinger and the ball of her thumb were shiny with graphite. There was a small smudge of it along her cheekbone. 'There.'

She turned the board so that I could see it. I sat up on the sofa.

'Cate, that's incredible.'

She shrugged. 'It's just the way your body fills its space in the world.'

I opened my mouth and closed it again.

'Hey,' she laughed, 'you're blushing!'

I found my voice. 'I just wish the real thing was that good.'

She put her head on one side. 'Other people's eyes are mirrors. It's only in them that we see ourselves.'

I stood, and leaned over her and kissed the smudge on her cheekbone. 'Thank you,' I said, and kissed her again. 'Thank you.'

The door opened with a crash and I heard Caitlin draw in a sharp breath and I instinctively stepped back from her. Caitlin's father stood in the doorway. I had a confused impression of tweeds, blue shirt against brown skin, a trim iron-grey line of moustache.

'Well, now, Catey,' he said, 'you're still entertaining.'

His eyes moved over me. I realised that I was still naked and I snatched up some part of my fallen clothing and held it over myself. The situation was so preposterous that I almost laughed.

But then I looked at Caitlin. I'm not sure what I expected. The scene was so bizarre that it was hard to know what to expect - perhaps embarrassment, perhaps indignation. Or even laughter, like the laughter rising in my own chest. But she seemed to be in the grip of something altogether more powerful.

I opened my mouth to speak, to say I don't know what - to apologise, I suppose - but in that moment her father looked at me and smiled. It was quite a warm smile, I thought, but it made me hold my tongue. Irrelevantly, I could not help noticing again how very handsome he was.

'Get out,' he said to me, still smiling.

I said, 'Mr Dacre, surely -'

He ignored me and turned to Caitlin. 'I want to see you in the house.'

Before either of us could say more he stepped out through the door and I saw him striding away across the lawn in his country tweeds.

When I looked back, Caitlin had stripped off my shirt and tossed it aside and was struggling into her dress.

I found my voice. 'Cate?'

'I'll have to go. You too.' She fought with a loop and eye at the neck of her dress. 'The bastard,' she muttered. 'The bastard.'

'Cate,' I said, 'come on.' I took her hands away and fastened the dress for her, and smoothed her hair and held her against me. 'I guess he's old-fashioned. He'll get over it.'

But she pulled away and walked quickly to the door. She stopped there, as though fighting an urge to run after her father. It was as if she had suddenly become an insecure teenager again. She hovered for a few moments, and then she came back into the studio and tore a scrap of paper from a sketchbook and scribbled a number on it and thrust it at me.

'Ring me,' she said. She stretched up and kissed me quickly on the lips, and fled.

I dressed slowly, calming myself, determined not to hurry, half hoping she might return. I left the studio and walked around the house and across the drive to where the old Austin Healey still waited. Bruno was leaning across the bonnet, languidly smoking a cigarette in the sunshine. He looked impossibly spruce, the way he always looked, as if he had just dressed for a cocktail party instead of having spent the night stretched across the front seats of a sports car.

'I was wondering where you'd got to,' he said. 'Not that I couldn't guess. Hop in.' He vaulted over the door and into the driver's seat. 'Next time perhaps you'll show a little more enthusiasm when your old pal Bruno lines you up with an upper class bonkfest.' He smiled dazzlingly and reached for the starter.

I said: 'Will this thing run on champagne?'

'Only if it's Moet.' He turned the key and the car started at a touch.

I climbed in and we clattered away down the long drive, the engine coughing. It was only when we had reached the iron gates that I remembered the drawing. I was on the point of stopping him and going back for it. But after all it was not mine to take, and I did not like the idea of returning uninvited. I seemed to have caused enough trouble. So I let him drive on and I left it there.

It was a decision I was to regret a great deal.

CHAPTER EIGHT

It was a clear cold morning, two days after I had moved into Anthony's house. I had taken a mug of coffee into the overgrown garden and carried it to the bench beside the pond. The pond had been neglected for years and the water was half-choked with lilies and duckweed. I liked the tangled wildness of it, and the bench had always been a favourite spot.

I paid no attention when I heard the car pull up at the front of the house. I assumed it was Stella's: she had taken the day off and she had been in and out all morning on uncharacteristically domestic errands. She had even bought flowers, although I was certain she did not know one from another. So I was surprised when Anthony opened the French doors and showed the two police officers out onto the terrace. Maureen Dickenson stepped down onto the back lawn with Barrett behind her and they walked towards me through the long grass. Her smile had a quality about it which I did not recognise. It made my stomach clench.

I said, 'What's happened?'

'Sorry we haven't been in touch, Dr Severin.' Barrett had a peculiar heartiness about him. He stuck out his hand so that I had to take it. 'You know how it is.'

'No. How is it?'

Anthony appeared behind them at that moment with a couple of folding garden chairs and there was a fussy little ritual as the chairs were opened and brushed down. Dickenson and Barrett sat down and Anthony slipped silently away, looking like a dutiful butler in his dark jacket. I could not be sure, but I had the impression he was avoiding my eyes.

'What's happened?' I said again.

'Full post mortem results,' Barrett said. 'She definitely wasn't raped.'

'It always looked that way,' Maureen Dickenson put in, 'but we've taken a day or two to be completely sure.'

My thoughts had gone clattering away like a flock of startled birds and for a moment or two I could not call them back. While I was trying, she spoke again.

'Michael, there is something I want to ask you. Just to get the picture absolutely clear in my head. I'm wondering if this is the moment to raise it.' She seemed embarrassed.

I recalled myself with an effort. 'Go ahead.'

'Then let me just ask this and get it out of the way. You were dropped off by the Red Cross bus at Victoria at eleven twenty-eight. The driver made a call to his base station just as you walked across the road to the tube. His call was logged.'

'Yes?'

She frowned, as if trying to solve a difficult equation in her head. 'There's seventy-eight minutes, Michael, between the time you got off that bus at Victoria and the time you rang the police. Allowing time for you to get home, I'd say you must have been in the house for forty minutes before you raised the alarm.'

'As long as that? I'd no idea.'

She watched me, assessing my reaction. 'Michael, have you any idea what you did for forty minutes?'

'You know all this. I've told you.'

'Tell me again. Please.'

'I tried to resuscitate her. I went on trying for a long time. I had to: if I'd left her for more than a few moments, she'd have died.'

'She died anyway,' Barrett said.

I looked at him, but his eyes gave nothing away.

'I kept trying anyway,' I said. 'Wouldn't you?'

'And afterwards?' Dickenson persisted.

'Afterwards I sat on the stairs with her.'

'And then?'

I thought back, trying hard to focus. 'When I knew she was gone I did...drop out for a while, before calling the police. I assume I went into shock. That's in the statement too.'

'And all this took forty minutes?'

'If that's how long you tell me it was.'

'You told us fifteen minutes,' Barrett observed. 'When I asked you on Saturday, you reckoned fifteen minutes from finding her to calling the ambulance. Max twenty. That was wrong, was it?'

'It must have been.'

'Strange, isn't it?' Maureen Dickenson said, 'the things we do when we're in shock? Because then there was that business with the clothes. The way you changed your clothes. Bagged the soiled ones.'

'Yes, I did do that.'

'Why?'

'I assumed the police would want them for forensic. Was that wrong?'

'No, I'm sure it wasn't wrong, Michael.' She seemed puzzled by my choice of words. 'But it strikes me as a very rational thing to do if you were paralysed by shock.'

'It just seemed right at the time. I can't explain it.'

'You're a surgeon,' Barrett suggested, and his sudden helpfulness surprised me. 'Some sort of automatic pilot? You get cleaned up after operations, don't you? Maybe it was a kind of a reflex.'

Dickenson said, 'Of course that must be it.'

Barrett leaned back in his garden chair. 'The only explanation.' He seemed to have lost interest in the discussion. He locked his hands behind his neck. 'Don't worry about it. I wouldn't.'

I was aware of a sense of relief that the matter was apparently closed, and was at once annoyed at myself for feeling this way.

'She was pregnant,' Barrett said, his face to the cool white sky. And when I said nothing, he dropped the front legs of his chair down onto the turf and leaned forward to look me straight in the face. 'You hear what I said?'

My mouth was dry and I could not at first form the words and when I did they boomed oddly inside my head. 'That can't be true.' I said. 'That is not true.'

'Ten weeks.' His face stony. 'Give or take. So she was three or four weeks gone before you even left for Venezuela.'

'That's impossible.'

Dickenson leaned towards me. 'Why is it impossible, Michael?'

'Do you think I wouldn't know a thing like that?'

'Oh, the kid wasn't yours, Dr Severin,' Barrett said lightly. 'The DNA people did tests.'

I searched for my voice; couldn't find it.

'No secrets, you told us.' His expression changed and he fixed his hard eyes on me. 'Absurd, you said it was, the idea of some other man. Bloody paragon of a marriage, yours was. But this isn't just a little fling we're talking about, is it? Your wife was carrying another man's child. For over two months. For one of those months you were at home. And you tell me you didn't know? You're a doctor and you're telling me you never so much as picked up a hint?'

The daylight in the garden seemed to flare and in my eyes the trees and ragged lawn shivered and jumped. 'There was never anyone between me and Cate.'

'I'm a Catholic, me,' Barrett said. 'I have enough trouble getting my head around one Virgin Birth. I can't handle two.'

He got up from his chair and walked away among Anthony's apple trees. I watched him in a daze. He bent down and picked up a late windfall from the long grass and knocked the dead leaves off it with his big hand, and spun the apple shining in the light and caught it.

'This is something you're going to have to come to terms with, Michael,' Dickenson was speaking very directly at me. 'She was pregnant. And the child wasn't yours. I'm afraid there's no possibility of doubt.'

Barrett had bitten into the apple and even from here I could hear him munching on it. I took my eyes from him with an effort. 'I don't know what this means. I don't understand any part of it.'

She stood up, gathered her bag and tucked it under her arm. 'I don't understand it either, Michael. Not if you've been completely open with us. But I'm going to take it from your reaction that you knew nothing whatever about Caitlin's pregnancy. That you knew nothing whatever about anyone she may have been seeing. And that you knew nothing whatever about any movements of hers which might be of interest to us. Is that right?'

I tried to take this in.

'Is that right, Michael?' she demanded. 'Or is it not? Because it's extremely important that if you have any more information than you've given us so far, you let us know right now. For your own sake. You do understand that, don't you?'

'Yes,' I said.

'Good. I want you to call me right away – and I mean right away – if anything comes to you. Anything you might have... forgotten.'

'Yes,' I said again. I passionately wanted her to be gone.

She hesitated a moment longer, as if about to say more, then turned and strode away across the garden.

Barrett stood watching her retreating back, still munching on his apple, and when she had gone into the house he walked the few steps back to where I sat. He took a last bite and examined the core in his hand, standing over me.

'There's nothing like a Cox's. My Auntie Violet used to grow them at her place in Basildon. Takes me right back.' He shied the core away into the bushes, and then stood there looking at me, thoughtfully picking a sliver of apple peel from between his front teeth with the nail of his little finger. 'I don't do this for fun,' he said.

There was a weight to his words that made me glance up at him. 'No, I suppose not.'

'You wouldn't be the first bloke who's been cheated on by his wife. Or to be in the dark about it.' He peered at the scrap of peel clinging to his fingernail. 'In fact, if your marriage really was as good as you say it was, you'd be in a minority that ain't hardly visible to the naked eye.'

'I don't want to talk about this right now.'

But he didn't move. He sucked the inside of his mouth. 'She didn't deserve what happened to her, Dr Severin, no matter what she'd done to you.'

'Of course not. I wasn't thinking about what she'd done to me.'

'All the same you'd better understand something very clearly.'

'What?'

'The difference between now and the first time we met. Then, you were the bereaved husband. Now, you're the betrayed husband. Very different things. Then, Mrs Severin was as pure as the driven snow. Now, we know she was a human being like the rest of us. So it would be a really good idea if you made sure that from here on in, everything you know, we know too.'

When Barrett had gone I stayed on the stone bench by the pond, watching the secret life of the water. After a while Anthony stepped out onto the terrace from the French doors. He had taken off his jacket and with his braces holding his big dark trousers up over his paunch he reminded me of a sad old clown. He sat down beside me on the stone seat, rolling between his chubby palms a stem of lavender. As he rolled it the brilliant florets whipped and blurred like the colours on a child's spinning top. A gust of wind sent a bright yellow drift of poplar leaves across the garden and made the branches rattle like bones above us.

'You heard,' I said.

'It might have been better if this particular truth had remained undiscovered.' He paused. 'I feel I should have known.'

'*You* should have known?'

'I saw her two or three times while you were away. Rather more often than I usually do, in fact. She never gave me the least clue that anything was amiss.' He stared into the dark water of the pond. 'I feel so sorry for her, Michael, the poor child. What could have driven her to behave in such a way?'

'I don't know.'

I looked up through the bare branches. I knew Anthony would take what Caitlin had done as a betrayal, not just of my trust, but of everything he believed in. I could not bear the thought of seeing that in his face. I said, 'I can't stay here, Anthony.'

The spinning flower stopped in his hands, reversed its rotation. 'But where will you go?'

'Home. I'll give the police a few days to clear up. But then I'm going back to the house.'

He did not look at me. 'And after that?'

I stood up. 'After that I'm going back to work.'

'Give yourself some time, old chap.'

'I need to work, Anthony.'

'Action, is it?' he said ruefully. '*Action téméraire?*' He crumpled the lavender in one hand and let it fall onto the paving stones at his feet. 'You must go where you need to go, my dear old chap. And do what you need to do.' He stood up and rested his hand on my shoulder. 'I never could keep you with me, Michael, could I? Even when you were a boy. I'm sure you felt you were a burden. I never was quite able to explain what it meant to me, having you here.'

I looked at the mossy paving between my shoes.

'I should like you to remember,' he said, 'that wherever I am, that place will always be a home for you.'

He walked quickly away across the lawn, his head bowed. I noticed that the rough grass had soaked the turn-ups of his trousers, and for some reason this weakened me almost to the point of tears.

CHAPTER NINE

I climbed the steps and let myself in and closed the door behind me. I had wondered what it would be like to be back here. But though I waited in the quiet, I felt nothing except relief and the comfort of familiarity.

I heard the first drops of rain slap against the stained glass behind me. I hung my jacket near the door and walked down the long hallway. I paused at the foot of the stairs, looking up into the shadows. Presumably they had returned Caitlin's things to her eyrie. I could not face going up there right now, but even from here I could see that the stairs had been scrubbed and I could faintly smell bleach and disinfectant hanging on the cool air in the stairwell. Who cleaned up after murder? I imagined a team of overalled workers clumping up the stairs, tut-tutting at the sight, then getting down to it, and ultimately sharing a flask of coffee and even a joke and news of the kids and the football while sitting on the steps where Caitlin had died. It seemed odd not to know who these people were, these workers who had done such an intimate service for us.

But then, there was a great deal I didn't know. Somewhere up on those stairs Caitlin had fought with some man. I didn't know much about that. And this was not just any man. It was a man she had allowed into her home, into her body, and I knew nothing whatever about him. I tried to picture their fight, tried to picture Caitlin tearful, hysterical, her hair flying. What had started it? She was packed to go with him. Perhaps he had come to fetch her. And what had gone wrong at this last of all possible moments? Had she only then told him of the pregnancy, and did he lose his nerve? Did she change her mind?

I walked slowly through the dining room and into the kitchen beyond. I could see that Filomena, our Sicilian housekeeper, had been in today, undoubtedly on Anthony's instructions. Filomena had left everything fragrant and polished: floors washed, tulips in a vase, crystal flashing in the dresser. She had left no sign of the police who had stamped around, their lumpen shoes in white plastic covers, moving the furniture, brushing dust onto surfaces, taking their endless photographs.

I picked up the phone from the corner table and rang through to the message service. There were several calls from people at the hospital, shocked at the news, tongue-tied or tearful. There was a message from Professor Curtiz himself, telling me I should take all the time I needed, reassuring me that the team could manage, no matter how long it took. There were two calls from journalists, several insistent messages from a victim support organisation, and one from a vicar in Kensington, in whose parish Caitlin and I had apparently lived for four years without knowing it. I erased all the messages, replaced the handset and unplugged the phone from the wall.

I opened the door which led into my study. It was dim in here and I switched on the green-shaded desk lamp. The room was snug and secret, with the rain beating down against the window and a rising breeze stirring the overgrown bushes outside. I crossed to the desk and unlocked the drawer and took out the framed photograph of Caitlin. I held it face down, only slowly turning it in my hands. I stared at her for a long time, and then carefully set the picture on the desk, facing out into the room with the desk lamp shining on it.

I went back to my chair, moving my head so that I could see Caitlin smiling at me from the picture as if from the other side of a small bright window. It was my favourite picture of her, catching that fragile smile of hers. She had never liked it: I could still see her turning up her nose and telling me the portrait made her look lost and vulnerable. I had denied it, but of course it was true. That was why I loved the picture, and it was part of the reason why I had loved

Caitlin. Whenever she was lost she had always allowed me to find her. This time she had at last moved beyond my searching.

'Why couldn't you tell me, Catey?' I asked aloud, my voice echoing in the dim room. 'What were you so afraid of?'

'I'm afraid of him, if you want to know,' Caitlin snapped, breaking the silence in the car.

I glanced across at her warily. Until this moment she had not spoken a word since we dropped down off the M4 and had begun the long meander through the Gloucestershire countryside towards Morrow. Now she held her face away from me, gazing out at the darkening shapes of the trees as they slid by.

'Afraid of your father?' I asked at last.

Tonight was to be that pantomime night, the night I would be formally paraded before the parents. After the farce of the last encounter with her father I expected some awkwardness, but it didn't worry me much. In the end Caitlin's people could think what they liked, and if a stiff evening with the county set wasn't likely to be a lot of laughs, it didn't rank very high on my list of calamities. Caitlin, though, had been increasingly tense as the day wore on. I thought she was overreacting. I thought this talk of fear was over the top.

'Maybe we should call it off,' she said suddenly, keeping her face turned away. 'We could ring them and make an excuse.'

'Cate, it's only a party. It can't be that bad.'

'You don't know.'

She stared out at the passing hedgerows, wordless again. I decided not to pursue it. In a sense, I reminded myself, I hardly knew her. We had met a dozen times in the four weeks since her party. There had been two weekends in country hotels, one on a friend's houseboat on the Cam, and in between a series of snatched nights during the week in my sparse Dulwich flat. I no longer thought of our meetings as separate events. I already saw them as a vivid continuum, and her absences as unnatural interruptions to it. I resented those absences more and more fiercely, and I was quite well aware of what this meant. But all the same, I hardly knew her.

'He's a Fascist,' she said. 'My father. He's a bigot and a bully.'

I glanced at her. I had heard her talk a little about her father. I thought it entirely likely that he was an overbearing old tyrant, but it was hard to take Caitlin's vehemence quite seriously. I said, 'Cate, are you sure he's not just a bit overprotective?'

She folded her arms and glared out at the dark trees.

I was reminded at once of what an impressive man Edward Dacre was. He was as tall as I was, and his flecked hair was thick, and he moved with an easy grace when he stepped across to shake hands.

'I do apologise for all this, Michael,' he said, 'drinks with father in the library. All terribly Victorian, I know. But you can't move for caterers in the rest of the house.'

His handshake was strong, but not one of those ostentatious bone-crackers favoured by men who want to appear dominant. With our last meeting filling my mind, I was relieved that he was prepared to be affable, more relieved than I cared to admit to myself. But I didn't know what to expect next. So I kept quiet, leaving him an opening – to do what? I was not sure. To crack a joke, perhaps, or utter some awkward admonishment. To refer in some way to what had happened, if only in order to dismiss it. But from his demeanour the whole ridiculous incident might never have happened. Perhaps that was to be his strategy. I could live with that.

'Caitlin says you're a scotch man? I've got some Glenlivet somewhere.' He hunted around among the decanters, making a game of it, until he found the right one. 'Water with it? Or are you a purist? You look as if perhaps you are.'

I wasn't certain how to take that. I said, 'Straight will be fine, thanks.'

I glanced across at Caitlin, sitting on the edge of the sofa. I gave her what I thought was a comical look, making fun of all this, but she made no response at all. She held her hands locked in her lap and stared straight ahead.

'Hadn't you better get changed, Catey?' her father said, holding up the scotch and peering through it.

The words had a certain authoritative weight, as if he were speaking to someone else, someone younger than Caitlin. It put me on edge. I remembered how she had become a child in his presence on that last occasion. I tried to dismiss it: I supposed this sort of thing happened between father and daughter.

She stood up and walked across the room. At the door she turned to give me a glance I could not interpret, and quietly left.

I looked around me with a mixture of wonder and amusement. The room made me feel as if I had strayed into a period drama. The dark shelves were crowded with bound volumes from floor to ceiling and a magnificent mahogany desk with a green leather top stood across one corner. The lighting was dim but tall windows in the opposite wall looked out over a lawn dotted with lilac and hydrangea bushes. Low evening sunlight fell through the trees onto the grass. Caitlin's father handed me the scotch, waved me to a chair.

'Sit, please.'

I sat in one of the leather armchairs. I couldn't decide what to call him, so I settled for avoiding the issue. 'This is an incredible house.'

'Yes, isn't it?' he chuckled agreeably, like a man who cannot quite believe his own good fortune. 'It certainly impresses the bejesus out of me.'

'I suppose it's been in the family for generations?'

'Oh no, we're complete parvenus. My father started the family business back in the thirties and did rather well out of it, and bought this place. I took over the house and the business when I left the Army twenty-odd years ago. But they say it takes three generations to make a gentleman, so I'm still one short.' He sat down opposite me. He had very bright blue eyes in a lean brown face and his short pepper-and-salt moustache made him look like a forties film star. He said, 'So Caitlin will be the first of us to be gentry, by that definition.'

'She's gentry by any definition,' I said gallantly.

'You think so, do you?'

Again his tone gave me that tremor of surprise. 'Don't you?'

'They say children are a blessing, Michael. But you know, that's not always true. Rather more often they break your heart.' He regarded me thoughtfully. He put his drink down, stroked his moustache, smiled at me with his mouth. Something changed at that moment. It was as if a drop of cold water had trickled down my spine. He said, 'What are you, exactly?'

'Do you mean, what do I do?'

'I know what you do, Michael,' his smile did not waver, 'you're undertaking some kind of medical course.'

'I'm a surgeon,' I said, stung.

'Quite. But what I want to know is what you *are*.'

'I'm afraid I don't understand.'

'No? Well, let me put it this way. The old rules still apply around here.'

'What old rules?'

'I didn't bring Caitlin up to see her throw herself away on some penniless medic.'

I stared at him, dumbstruck.

'Now this is nothing personal, Michael. I'm sure you appreciate that. I do realise that people who come from nowhere can occasionally make something quite creditable of themselves. But the smart money isn't on it.' Again, that electric smile. He poured us both another drink. 'I have to protect her. It's what fathers are for. Caitlin is a highly intelligent young woman. She speaks several languages. She's academically quite clever. She's very beautiful. And of course she has all the social graces. But in many ways she's been a disappointment to me. And here she is, at twenty-four, without having achieved anything worthwhile. She has what my American business friends would call no *endgame*.'

I found my voice at last. 'Haven't you seen her art?'

He gave me a pitying look. 'Michael, please.'

'She's got the most extraordinary talent.'

'There is a weakness about her,' he went on, as if I had not spoken, 'a frailty. It's something her mother had too. Still has. It can make her prey to all kinds of passing fancies.'

'If that includes me,' I said, setting my glass down hard, 'I'd say she can make up her own mind.'

'Michael, understand this. I love my daughter.'

'So do I.' It was the first time I had given voice to this, and doing so made something leap in me. 'But I didn't come here this week-end to ask for her hand in marriage, if that's what you expected. If that ever happens, I won't trouble to ask anyone's permission but hers. Sorry if that violates some sacred tradition.'

'Do you think this is about tradition? Let's not be naïve. This is about power.'

I stood up. 'I don't want to talk about this any longer.'

'You're still quite a young man,' he said. 'So I hope you'll have time to learn that you can't act just as you please. Not when it affects me you can't. Not when it affects my people.'

'Your people?'

'There's a price to be paid for everything, Michael. Perhaps you'd forgotten that. Or perhaps you've developed a distorted picture of the world, after playing the Great White Chief among the niggers for so long.'

I got up to the bedroom somehow, blind and seething. I wanted to leave, to pack my bag and walk out now, make as grand an exit as possible. But I had not seen Caitlin since she had left the study, and I did not know where to look for her in the huge busy house, and I did not know what I would say to her if I did find her. And, I thought for the second time that evening, I didn't really know her. If I walked out now I was not sure what effect it would have on us: I had a great fear that I might lose her. I opened the bedroom window and looked out over the dark garden and gradually calmed down. After a while I went into the bathroom and showered, and when I came out again I had myself under control.

I had never been to a party in a place anywhere like the hall of Morrow House. It was a cavernous space with a long teak table and smoke-darkened oil paintings on the wall and a hearth big enough to roast an ox in. The hearth bore the date 1799 carved into the keystone. I walked in unnoticed and took a glass from a tray borne by a waiter and pretended to examine one of the paintings, trying to make myself inconspicuous. Perhaps forty people milled around in the enormous room, florid men in middle age and overdressed women. They were loud self-satisfied people and I instinctively disliked them, but I was glad there were so many of them. It made it easier for me to lose myself.

I looked around but I still could not see Caitlin. I did catch sight of her mother for the first time that evening, an elegant woman of sixty in a dazzling burgundy dress, and I watched her covertly as she moved from one group of guests to another. She had her daughter's colouring and fine bone structure and she moved through the crowd like minor royalty. It was hard to see her as the downtrodden wife I had pictured from Caitlin's words. She looked to me like a tough, intelligent woman, but I was no longer prepared to take anything here at face value. Without consciously deciding to do so I moved through the crowd to avoid meeting her.

I found myself cornered by a tall woman in a linen suit and crimson lipstick. 'I'm sure the Indian chap must have been simple in the head,' she was saying, apparently believing that I had heard the first part of this story. 'He just ran out into the road after a goat. Can you imagine? In the middle of an international rally! Poor George – my husband – had absolutely no chance of stopping.'

I tried to catch the eye of a waiter as he slid past bearing a tray of drinks.

'He was killed, of course,' she said.

I stopped in the act of taking a glass. 'Killed? Your husband? But that's dreadful.'

'No, no. The chap with the goat. George was doing nearly sixty, after all. The whole thing was appalling. George would have been quite well placed otherwise.'

Perhaps she saw my expression, for her mouth set sourly and she cruised away. I took my wine and made myself as unobtrusive as possible at one side of the vast fireplace, hoping not to be rediscovered.

'You're right, Michael,' Caitlin's mother moved up on my blind side with a hiss of her splendid dress. 'The lunatics have taken charge of the asylum.'

I supposed she had been watching the exchange. She had spoken in a fixed manner, her smile unmoving, as if painted onto her pale face, nodding and raising her eyebrows in acknowledgement to people who drifted past us. For an instant I was reminded of those old war movies where members of the escape committee exchange passwords out of the corners of their mouths while queuing in the camp canteen.

She said, 'I'm Margot Dacre. Obviously.'

'I'm sorry we haven't met before, Mrs Dacre.' I held out my hand but she ignored it. Perhaps this wasn't the way members of the country house set greeted one another. Perhaps she really did not see.

'Call me Margot. I dislike the surname. And you would have met me earlier if you hadn't been avoiding me so carefully.'

She was balanced like a fencer, her quickness like a blade before her, but she did not entirely fool me. I could see Caitlin clearly in her now, not so much in her sharp defence, but in what she defended, a certain vulnerability.

I said, 'I'm rather out of my depth at this sort of thing.'

'Nonsense. You've done terribly well in such a short time. My husband loathes you already.'

'Did he give you a reason?'

'Oh, he doesn't need a reason, Michael. And don't take it at all personally. You're in very good company. Edward loathes anybody who so much as looks at Caitlin, and quite a lot of people do rather more than look at her, as you can imagine. In fact, Edward hates a considerable list of people.'

'Imagine that.'

'He doesn't much approve of people, full stop.'

I put my glass on the mantelpiece. 'I'm not sure I could give a damn who he approves of.'

'Oh,' she smiled in a satisfied way, 'I believe this is anger.'

I hadn't realised I was losing my temper until that moment. I said, 'In fact I don't think I give a damn what anyone here thinks about anything.'

'Which includes me, no doubt.' She observed me over her glass. I had the impression that she was focusing on me, but detachedly, as if I were a specimen of some kind. She said, half to herself, 'I wonder if you really might be different?'

I was still trying to decide how to respond to this when Edward Dacre came striding into the room through the archway a couple of yards behind her. He stopped and stood there very erect, his legs a little apart and his hands clasped behind his back, surveying his guests milling in his magnificent room. Despite my flaring resentment I was struck by the sheer force of his presence. And then I saw Caitlin hurrying after him, moving around him to look up into his face. Her hair was tangled and I saw that she was still in the jeans and sweater she had worn in the car on the way down. I knew from that alone that something was very wrong.

She was pleading with her father and her voice was full of fear. I heard her say, 'Tell me that's not true. Please.'

He jerked up his chin, lifting himself away from her. His eyes had a hard glitter, and I could see he relished her confusion. 'Haven't you changed yet, Caitlin?' he demanded, as if he had not seen her before. 'You might at least try to look respectable.'

One or two of the nearest guests veered discreetly away, sensing a scene, but the hubbub in the rest of the room burbled on unabated.

I said, 'Cate?' and she turned her white face, searching in the crowd, finding me.

'My pictures,' she cried to me in desolation. 'He's burned them. All of them.'

'What?'

'And why not?' her father demanded, speaking to the ceiling, and this time the noise in the room faltered. 'It's pretty clear you never planned to come back here for them.'

Margot Dacre was still facing me, her back to the little tableau. Her expression froze and her fencer's poise deserted her. 'I tried to stop him.' Her voice was small and her eyes vacant. I wasn't sure she was talking to me at all. 'I begged him. But he has been unwell, you see.'

I moved her by the elbows out of my way, as if she were a piece of furniture. She did not seem to weigh anything. I stepped across to Caitlin, keeping my head down, not trusting myself to look at her father, at those glittering little eyes.

'Cate, that's enough.'

She looked up at me, distraught, uncomprehending, but I walked past her and down the dim hall and took the stairs to the landing two at a time. I left the door of the bedroom open behind me and dumped my bag on the bed and crammed in my clothes and my book and my wash bag and savagely zipped it. I heard her footsteps on the stairs and along the landing and when I turned she was standing in the doorway, her hands on the frame on each side, blocking it, breathing hard. Her face was pale and her blonde hair was everywhere. She looked about sixteen.

'Michael, you can't just walk out.'

'Has that old bastard really burned your beautiful drawings?'

'He started with my picture of you.' Her face crumpled. 'Then everything else. Books, sketch pads. All of them. Everything since I was a child.'

'And do you know why?'

'To punish me, of course. To hurt me.'

'Not just you. To hurt both of us. It's very effective.' I lifted my bag off the bed. 'Come with me, Cate.'

'I can't.'

'And I can't stay here and watch him do this to you.'

'You think it's all so simple,' she flung at me. 'But it isn't simple. Sometimes people can just be stifled, shut away from the light so they can't grow strong. It gets to a point when they're starved so thin they don't have any strength left at all.'

I stepped up to her and put my arms round her and pulled her hard against me, and then released her. 'Come with me. Please.'

But she didn't move. I took up my bag, stepped around her and trotted down the carpeted steps. At the bottom I paused for a few moments in the cool darkness of the unlit stairwell. It smelled of hyacinths and beeswax. In the main hall the party was building up again, men haw-hawing like a colony of walruses, a tinkle of glasses, a little shriek of delight as one woman was introduced to another after a gap of two or even three days. I walked to the end of the corridor and slid the bolts on the back door and slipped out into the darkness and walked around the flank of the great house in the mothy summer night. I had reached the car before I heard her feet scattering the gravel behind me.

She got in beside me without a word and I drove fast down the long driveway and out through the iron gates, afraid at every moment that her resolution would break and she would stop me and get out and be lost to me again.

'You can start afresh, Cate,' I said. 'Draw new things. Draw a whole new world.'

She stared out into the rushing night. 'I'll never draw anything again,' she said. 'Not ever again.'

It had grown cold and dark in the study and I couldn't decide how long I had been sitting here. I found a bottle of scotch and poured myself a very big one and then busied myself for a few minutes lighting the fire in the grate. I went to the stereo cabinet and put on Mozart and as the flames flapped up against the bricks I sat in one of the leather chairs which flanked the hearth and watched them and the wild shadows they threw. I remembered Caitlin's photo on my desk. There she still was, in the pool of golden light from the desk lamp, gazing sadly at me across the room. I lifted my glass to her.

The big brass knocker on the front door banged twice.

I dropped back into the present with the shock of stepping off a quayside into a winter sea.

Again. Two sharp, heavy, incredible knocks.

I got to my feet. I placed Caitlin's picture face down on the desk, and walked through into the hall, snapping the light on. I pulled the door open.

She gazed at me unspeaking, a slender woman, quite young, leaning against the doorframe. She straightened as I opened the door. She wore a fawn raincoat and the material was dark and wet. Her long black hair lay pasted in ropes across her face and across the shoulders of her coat and I could see she was shivering and trying to conceal it. She looked exhausted, but she held her head defiantly, as if expecting an argument and ready to fight back.

'You're Michael Severin,' she announced, as if I might try to deny it. She had a strong northern accent, Yorkshire perhaps. 'You're Dr Michael Severin.'

She was strikingly handsome, with a long aquiline face, and I thought it unlikely that if I had met her before I could easily have forgotten her. But there was nothing about her I recognised. It crossed my mind that she might be a journalist.

'I need to talk to you, Dr Severin. It's important.'

'I don't know you. And I'm not up to talking right now.'

I went to swing the door shut, but she put her foot against it and calmly resisted me, looking levelly at me as she did so. She had the fiercest eyes. I had not expected resistance. I did not know how to handle this and I found it impossible to decide what to do next. It was quite dark outside in the street and the wind was slinging the rain against her back and around her and in through the door.

'If you don't let me in, Doctor, you're going to get as wet as I am. And besides, I'll spew up on your doorstep.'

I found that without making any decision about it I had stepped back and let her move past me into the house. I closed the door behind her. When I turned she was leaning on the banisters at the foot of the stairs, her back to me, breathing hard. That was easier. I knew what my role should be when she looked like that, when anyone looked like that.

I said, 'Are you ill?'

'I've been walking. For hours, it seems like.' She sounded impatient, either with my question or with her own weakness.

'You'd better sit down.' I stepped up behind her and pointed at the lit study door 'Go through there.'

She nodded, pushed herself away from the banisters and her knees buckled. I caught her round the waist. She didn't weigh much and I held her easily. Her head rolled against my cheek and I smelled the rain on her skin and on her hair. I lowered her to the floor at the foot of the stairs and her black hair spread out on the boards like the hair of a drowned woman on a deck.

I turned her onto her left side and automatically checked her breathing and pulse. The pulse was a little fast. Her clothes were drenched and her face was marble to the touch. I brushed the wet hair away from her forehead. There was a small star-shaped scar on her right temple.

What I should do next was clear enough: get a blanket and cover her and then call an ambulance. Instead I knelt on the floor and watched her. It seemed improper to be watching this unknown woman as she lay helpless, but something about her would not let me stir. Perhaps the fact that her shoes had come off as she fell and her feet were a little muddy and her skirt was rucked up, and the careless angle of her legs made her look as vulnerable as Caitlin had looked.

She made a small noise in her throat and her eyelids flickered open and I saw her eyes focus on me as she came round. She swallowed and tried to push herself up on one elbow.

'Stay there,' I told her.

She ignored me and gathered herself into a sitting position. When I moved to help her she shook my hand away. 'I'm all right.' She was angry with herself. 'I just haven't eaten, that's all.'

I took her wrist and checked her pulse again. She sat there on the floor, her lips thinned to signal impatience, but she allowed me to do this. This time the pulse was steady. I said, 'Sit on the step and put your head between your knees and breathe deeply for a couple of minutes.'

She pulled a face. 'Yes, Doctor,' but she moved to sit on the bottom stair. Her skirt was up around her thighs and she tugged it down crossly. 'Sorry. I don't usually do this sort of thing.'

Her colour was beginning to return. She had very high cheekbones and that mass of tightly curled black hair. I couldn't place her age.

Maybe about thirty. She may have been a little younger but there was a toughness about her that spoke of experience and gave her gravity.

'Who are you?' I had not intended to be so brusque, but I felt jumpy and unsure of myself.

'My name's Angie. Angie Carrick.' She delivered this with some weight and watched me as if to see if it produced any reaction. When it didn't, her eyes shifted away. 'I knew Caitlin.'

'Were you a friend of hers? I don't remember you, I'm sorry.'

'What's happened is horrible. I just had to come to see you about it.'

'I haven't been seeing people much.'

'I can understand that.' She stood up carefully, one hand on the wall. 'It's probably wrong of me to be here. But I had to come, just the same.' She straightened her back. The strength was visibly flowing back into her. She took a deep breath. 'When it comes down to it, Dr Severin, we're all wounded by this thing. Aren't we? Everyone who knew her is wounded. You. Me. Everyone.'

Her tone was matter-of-fact, as if it should be obvious to me that we were fellow sufferers. I didn't know how to react to this.

'You're wet through,' I said at last.

'I walked from the bus station. Victoria.'

'You've come a long way?'

'From up north.'

It was pretty clear she didn't want to give any more details. I could not imagine why. 'There's a bathroom under the stairs.' I nodded at the door. 'Towels and so on. Don't lock it.'

'I shan't be having the vapours again, Doctor, don't worry.'

'All the same.'

She looked at me curiously, and I knew she had picked up something from my tone. She had very dark eyes. They were the kind people used to call black.

'I'll be back in a minute,' she said, almost as if she were concerned about me, and not the other way round.

When the bathroom door closed behind her I picked up her wet coat and her shoes and I carried them into the study. It was something to do with the dimness of the light that made me think I could hide in here, recover myself. I felt unsteady and I laid her things down and put both hands on the desk, one each side of Caitlin's face-down picture, and waited for my equilibrium to return. I wasn't sure how long this took. Five minutes, maybe. Perhaps ten. I could hear the girl in the bathroom, running water, clicking open the airing cupboard door.

I glanced across at my chair. On the table beside it stood my drink, still three-quarters full. I picked it up, and as I did so I heard the toilet flush and the bathroom door opened and when I looked up she was in the room behind me. She was wearing a thin black top and a flowered skirt, black with red swirling hibiscus blossoms, and she stood in the doorway shivering, rubbing at her bare arms with a towel to warm herself. She had taken off all her makeup and without it her eyes were even darker. After a second she walked across the room and sat in my own chair, ignoring the free one opposite, and rested her head back against the leather and closed her eyes.

'God, that's better.' That deep, no-nonsense voice. 'You know how you get, so buggered you feel sick? Well, you would know, I suppose, being a doctor.' She opened her eyes, shook out her mass of dark hair and lifted it and let it fall between her fingers. I could see droplets spray from it in the lamplight. She sat back a little and sighed and pointed to the drink I held. 'That's scotch, is it? I don't like to ask.'

Nothing in her voice suggested that asking was a problem to her. I poured her a scotch. She cupped the glass in both her hands and sipped gratefully.

'That's so good. So good.' She set the glass down on the side table and looked up at me. 'I want to thank you for letting me in, Dr Severin. I'm not sure I would've, in your place.'

'You didn't give me much choice.'

'There's always a choice.' She looked around the book-lined study and out past me through the open door into the dining room with its blond wood and Aegean blues. 'This is a beautiful, beautiful house. I've never been in one so beautiful in all my life.' She caught something in my expression. 'Do you think I'm joking?'

'No, I...'

'Because I'm not.' She shook her hair out again. 'And the music's lovely.'

'It's Mozart.'

'People don't write stuff like this any more, do they? What's it called?'

'It's the Clarinet Concerto.'

'Did they have clarinets back then? I never knew that. Or is it saxophones I'm thinking of?'

I could not for a moment decide whether or not she was serious. Before I could make up my mind about that she stood up abruptly and walked across to the wall where a cluster of framed photographs and certificates hung. She stopped in front of one that showed me and a Médecins Sans Frontières team, working in a tented first-aid post in Sierra Leone, surrounded by a crush of African refugees. I had always liked that photograph, and it had pride of place on the wall. We were all so full of purpose in it. Our frail tent was a raft in a heavy sea, the crowding Africans the survivors of a shipwreck. We looked like the only people in the world who knew what to do.

'This is you, isn't it?' She tapped the glass. 'They said in the paper you did this kind of stuff. I think I even saw you on the TV once. Would that be right?'

'Possibly.'

'Looks romantic, this work you do.'

'Romantic?'

'Being able to help. At least it must make you feel like you're able to help.' She looked frankly at me. 'Though I don't suppose you make much difference in the end, do you?'

'No. I don't suppose we do.'

She was peering closely at the picture again. 'Who's the woman? The redhead?'

'Her name's Stella Cowan. We often work together. She's a nurse.' I hesitated, puzzled. 'Why?'

'Nothing. It's none of my business, anyway.' She put her hands on her hips and looked around the room again. 'To live here, in a place like this. Did it really happen here?'

But this was a question too far.

'How did you know Caitlin?' I said. 'Where did you meet her?'

She picked up her glass and looked into it. 'I didn't know her well. I worked with her a few times.'

I could not imagine in what context this woman could have worked with Caitlin. They were so utterly different. 'At the Tate, was it?' I suggested. 'Or one of the other galleries?'

'What?'

'Where you met Caitlin.'

'Yes. At the gallery. That's right. Can I call you Michael?'

I ignored that. 'Do you often come down to London to work? At the Tate?'

Her mouth set into a thin line. 'What's this? The third degree?'

As if to forestall more questions she moved away from me and across to the desk. I thought she was going to fetch something from her bag which lay there, but when I looked again she was turning over Caitlin's picture in her hands.

'Please don't touch that.'

She gazed at Caitlin's face under the light. I stepped forward to take the photograph from her, but to my surprise her eyes filled with tears as she examined it and this stopped me.

'Oh,' she said, as if struck by a sudden physical pain, 'she was such a lovely woman. Such a lovely woman.'

'Give it to me.'

But she did not give it to me. Instead she carefully replaced Caitlin's picture on the desk, standing it up so that Catey smiled into the room at us.

'Why don't you tell me what you really came here for?' I said.

She seemed to consider this gravely enough. 'No. It doesn't matter. I'd best go. I should never have come.' She slipped her bare feet into her shoes, picked up her wet coat and slung it over her arm. 'I just had to see you. To tell you how sorry I am.'

'That wasn't the only reason.'

'No. I wanted to reassure myself about something.'

'About what?'

'It's personal. It doesn't matter now.'

'I don't believe you were a friend of Caitlin's. Did you even know her?'

'Leave it alone, Michael. I made a mistake. Just forget I came.'

The music ended and the room became quiet, except for the hiss of rain against the window. She stretched over to replace her glass on the side table.

'Caitlin had a lover,' I said. 'You wouldn't know anything about that. Would you?'

She froze with her fingers still touching her glass. Her hair had fallen forward and I could not see her face. 'I don't know anything. I can't help you.'

She made to leave and I stepped forward and gripped her arm, gripped it much harder than I intended, for I felt the muscle roll and slip over the bone. She winced and I let her go.

'I loved her,' I said. 'I loved her and she's dead. I want to know how that could be.'

She glared at me, hot-eyed, massaging her bruised arm. 'Men always need to invent some grand conspiracy, don't they? To explain away their mistakes. But maybe it's simpler than you think.'

'I don't understand you.'

'Maybe you were just too busy chasing your own dreams, Michael. You never had time for hers.'

I felt a tic start to jump in my neck. 'What do you know about this?'

'I know that you want to blame someone else for it. Anyone else will do.'

I saw her head snap back and I saw her stagger, stumble half over the arm of the chair and sit heavily on the floor. It surprised me that she should move in this way. She sat there for a second, fixing me with polecat eyes, and it was only then that I realised I had hit her. She turned her head to one side and moved her mouth and touched her lip with her hand and looked at her fingers. She got to her feet unsteadily and straightened her clothes, still sucking at her lip, her eyes never leaving mine. I could not speak. I could not believe I had done this: I could not believe I was even capable of it. I looked down at the hand which had struck her, as though it might have acted on its own.

'So,' she said, 'the fine house and the lovely music.' She rolled the back of her hand against her lip and it came away with a smear of blood on the pale skin. She looked at it and then back at me. 'None of that makes you any different, does it?'

I took a step towards her. 'Please let me –'

I didn't see her move. I had been slapped only twice by women in the past, once by a frantic mother in casualty, once by an outraged student lover. But this was something quite different. Her knuckles caught the top of my cheekbone and I felt my head jerk round and heard myself grunt at the force of it. I put my hand up to my cheek but it was numb and it felt like someone else's. She stood watching me, her eyes narrowed, massaging her right hand with her left, balanced and ready as a cat. I was twice her size, but she was not scared of me: or if she was, she was damned if she was about to show it. I stood there like a fool, rubbing my cheek.

She said, 'You never knew who she was, did you? You never even tried to find out.'

She walked away towards the door and left the room without looking back. I heard the front door close behind her, and for a second or two I could hear her steps ringing away down the wet London street into the night.

CHAPTER TEN

It was a relief to be in a suit again. I had not worn a suit since before Venezuela. It felt good to be striding through the gloomy morning rush hour with my important briefcase at my side. Men who dressed like this didn't have wives who were murdered by their lovers. Men who dressed like this didn't knock women sprawling for saying the wrong thing. It was another kind of man who did that sort of thing.

I nudged my way through the crowds on the steps from the tube, smelling the wet dog smell of winter coats, apologising to the people I jostled. My apologies were sincere, and I smiled as I made them, for I was grateful to these men and women. They didn't know a thing about me. They didn't even see me. They were thinking of how late they were for work, and of their mortgages and their kids' lousy school reports, of how long they had to wait till the holidays came and they could see some sun again. In their ignorance of me I could forget myself.

I walked down the hospital's driveway and past a couple of paramedics in green overalls who were smoking by a parked ambulance, and went in through A&E. It had always been a ritual with me to come in to work this way, and it was comforting to do it again now. The place still gave me a rush, even after all these years – nurses hurrying under the hard lights, a crackle of energy, astringent hospital smells, the clatter and bustle and hum of it all.

It was busy this morning. An ambulance was backed up outside Majors, and another was pulling in, its siren just dying away and its lights still flashing, onto the wet concrete of the forecourt. A boy was wheeled in on a trolley as I walked past, a motorcycle helmet resting on the blankets between his feet. A knot of trauma nurses and paramedics worked around him as the trolley rolled, adjusting a drip, talking to him, calling his name. *Paul! Paul? Can you hear me, Paul? You're going to be fine, Paul. I just need to give you something, Paul, to help with...* Confident, competent voices. The voices of experienced people who knew what they were doing. It made me feel good to hear them, and I knew instinctively that young Paul – whoever he was – really would be all right.

I recognised several of the nurses and paramedics but they were too busy to register me. Vernon Choudhury, a registrar I had played squash with occasionally, was at the door of the ambulance, speaking earnestly to a tearful woman who trembled on the brink of hysteria. He was deliberately blocking her as she tried to move past him. He did not see me as I walked in. Simon Somebody, a gay technician I knew from Radiography, hurried past with a clipboard. He saw me all right, but he was too surprised to speak, and stood gaping stupidly as I strode past him. When I pushed through the swing doors onto the stairs he was still standing there with his mouth open, and there he stayed until one of the nurses bumped into him and told him roundly to move his backside. The expression on Simon's face made me smile as the swinging door closed behind me.

I trotted up the stairs and strode along polished corridors towards Orthopaedics, moving into the original Victorian building with its cream paint and dark wood, past busy offices and knots of people hurrying about their morning business, talking, laughing, arguing. Phones rang. Pagers bleeped. Filing cabinet drawers screeched on metal runners. Computer screens glowed blue behind frosted glass. The corridors smelled of antiseptic.

In my office I shook out my wet coat and hung it behind the door and turned on the computer. The office seemed unusually bare to me. The desk had been cleared and polished, and the mail tray was empty. But there was something more than that. It took me a moment to place it, but I realised finally that my photographs were missing, the two of Caitlin I kept on the desk, and the bigger one of the pair of us which had been on the right hand wall. I could not quite connect with this fact. It puzzled me. I could not get it into focus. I tugged at my desk drawer – perhaps the photographs were in there – but the drawer was locked. I never locked the drawers of my desk. I did not even know they had locks.

The door burst open and Meredith Wren filled the space. Meredith was the department's senior secretary, though the title in her case was open to interpretation. She was fiftyish, large and powerful, and was about the least appropriate person to be named after a small and timid bird. She wore a violent scarlet and yellow cardigan and she looked belligerent. I could see that she had not expected to find anyone in here, though that didn't make sense. After all, it was my office. She hesitated just for the time it took for the door to rebound juddering against her foot.

'So tell me,' she demanded, 'what am I supposed to say to you? I've got an answer for most things, but I'm no bloody good with tragedy.'

I walked around the desk and put my arms around her warm woollen bulk and hugged her. It seemed the right thing to do. She patted my back awkwardly. Then she stepped back and cleared her throat noisily. 'And now tell me what you think you're doing here.'

'Meredith, I work here.'

She narrowed her eyes. 'And what's happened to your face?'

I tugged at the desk drawer again. 'Have you any idea where my pictures are?'

She closed the door behind her. 'Michael, look at me. Stop rattling around with that bloody desk, and look at me.'

I did as I was told. When Meredith commanded, it was not easy to ignore her. For the whole Department it was Meredith who filled the role of staff crisis counsellor, gardens overseer, and organiser of leaving parties. Meredith shouted down the phone when the cleaning wasn't done, Meredith ran to earth medical records in the NHS labyrinth when teams of dedicated searchers failed to find them, Meredith fed the fish in the Doctors' Mess aquarium. Meredith, in fact, ran the place.

'Now you listen to me, Michael. I'm going to make you a cup of staff tea. Is that a first? I think it might be. And you're going to sit right there and drink it.'

'I don't think I've got time, Meredith. There's the Fracture Meeting.'

'If I make you tea, you're bloody well going to drink it. In fact we'll both have one. And then I'm going to call you a cab. And you're going to go home.'

I laughed. 'Thanks, but I don't think so, Meredith.'

I thought I had spoken in a normal voice, but she looked at me sharply, as if some cadence had disturbed her. I knew that under any other circumstances she would have argued – or rather that she would have steamrolled me into submission. Instead she said, 'Tea. I'll be right back. Don't you move.' She marched quickly away down the corridor.

I could have used some of Meredith's tea, but it was out of the question to wait for her, with the morning's Fracture Meeting about to start. I checked my watch. It was a little after eight, which meant it was probably already under way. I went out and closed the office door behind me.

Ray Moore must have been consultant in charge the day before, because by the time I reached the meeting he was already at the X-ray box, taking down one set of shots and sliding a new set into place against the light. He was concentrating on his task, peering through his thick glasses at the images, and giving one of his sarcastic running commentaries at the same time. All fifteen people in the room were focused on him as I slipped in at the back. An Asian registrar smiled a greeting and moved aside for me. He must have been new because I didn't know him. No-one else noticed me.

Ray, his back to the audience, flicked the central X-ray with his nails.

'Our second trauma call of the day. Young Mr Jason Pratt. No comments please. Twenty-two years old. Spent the evening at a lager-tasting and then attempted to impress a young person of the female persuasion by driving at speed the wrong way up Gower Street in his extremely attractive lime-green Toyota. He then entered into an ill-judged contest with a garbage truck and came away with second prize. I'm glad to say his passenger escaped injury, and that in so doing she also escaped Mr Jason Pratt.'

There were a few comments and some laughter. I glanced around the room. I knew all of these people, some of them very well indeed, and it was odd to watch them and yet still to be unobserved. John Donohue and Fred Tanaka, fellow consultants with offices near my own. Dee Orville from Physio. A handful of SHOs and registrars – the names flicked up automatically: Don, Maggie, Patti, Jonathan. The Nigerian anaesthetist, Sam Okigbo. Over near the window, fearsome Carrie Iverson, the Scrub Sister. And just two rows in front of me, her red head bowed over her notes, Stella. She was so close that I had not at first seen her.

'The young Pratt,' Ray Moore went on with lugubrious emphasis, 'was conscious – not to say vocal – at the scene, with a GCS of 12. That's rather higher than I expect he normally manages. As you see here he proved on admission to have an isolated closed midshaft fracture of the right femur...'

He looked up at his audience. Saw me. His eyes grew wide behind his thick glasses. He said, 'Michael.'

The whole room heard those two syllables. The instant silence that followed had a farcical quality to it. Faces turned to me, at first curious, then in turn shocked and sympathetic and embarrassed. These looks made me feel like an alien, as if these people I knew so well could see in my face how utterly changed I was. It was not until that moment that I began to suspect it myself.

I said, 'Good morning, everyone.'

No-one spoke. I could not bear the weight of their eyes on me. I looked away, at the X-rays on the illuminated wall. I made a play of squinting at them. There was a rising murmur from the room, concern, alarm. A pager squawked and was not answered.

Ray Moore said, 'Michael, we're all so bloody –'

The pager squawked again.

I said, 'Why doesn't someone get that?'

Stella was the first one to move. She barged between two of the registrars and grabbed my arm and spun me round. 'Michael. Outside. Now.'

'Why?'

'Outside.'

Someone opened the door for us and she thrust me through it and followed me into the corridor and closed the door behind us.

'Stella, please don't start with the what-are-you-doing-here routine. I've just had all that from Meredith.'

She pushed back her hair. 'Michael. I haven't got time to deal with this now.'

'You don't have to deal with anything.'

'You should know better than this. You're not thinking straight.'

'I need to work, Stella. That's all. I'm a surgeon and I need to work. People need to do what they do.'

'Wake up to yourself, Michael. Do you suppose the Silver King's going to let you near an operating theatre. *This* week? You're in shock.'

'Why not let me decide how I am?'

'You're the last person competent to do that.' She peered at me. 'Have you been in a fight?'

'A fight? Don't be ridiculous. Of course not. Listen –'

'Hello, Michael,' Professor Curtiz said.

Neither of us had heard him come up, but he was at my elbow, immaculate in his pale grey suit, smiling genially. Curtiz, the senior surgeon and Head of Orthopaedics, was a small, perfectly groomed man of sixty. He had a permanent skier's tan and a fine head of silver hair - hence the nickname - and authority swirled behind him like the tail of a comet. Meredith hovered in his wake. She looked uncomfortable, like a prefect who has failed to handle a situation and has had to summon the headmaster to sort matters out.

The door of the meeting room opened and Ray Moore stood there, looking at us each in turn, all his banter drained away. I could hear the room buzzing at his back. He fumbled at the handle to keep the door pulled to behind him. He said, 'Christ, Michael. I just wanted to say... I mean, we all...' his voice trailed off. He tried again: 'We didn't know you were coming back so soon.' He looked at Curtiz in appeal.

Curtiz said, 'Michael, I think you and I ought to have a talk, don't you? Before we cause any more disruption?' He touched my elbow. 'My office?'

He began to guide me away up the corridor. I could see the relief on Ray Moore's face, and in a moment I heard him flee back into the Fracture Meeting and close the door gratefully behind him.

Stella said, 'I was just going to take Michael home –'

Curtiz glanced back at her, smiling pleasantly. 'I expect you're busy?'

Stella opened her mouth and shut it again.

Without turning, Curtiz called, 'And was there some talk of tea, Meredith? Or was I mistaken about that?'

It was characteristic of Professor Curtiz that somehow he remained untouched by National Health Service parsimony. His was a patrician's office, cool and light and with a very high ceiling. It smelled of cut flowers and of his own discreet aftershave. There were some abstract prints on the walls – Chagall and Picasso. High windows soared like columns of pearl. Beside an enormous desk a flat-screen computer stood on a credenza. Curtiz led me to the chesterfield between the windows and sat in the winged armchair opposite me. He rested his delicate and rather beautiful hands on his knees, the forefingers perfectly aligned with the creases of his trousers.

'Nothing in my long experience of life and death, Michael, has taught me how to make sudden bereavement any easier to take, let alone under these circumstances. You know that everyone here feels for you. I suppose that's not the slightest help.'

'Everyone's very kind. But that's not why I'm here.'

'No. You're here because you…need to work.' He cocked his head at me. 'That was the phrase, I think?'

'Yes.'

'That's not good enough.'

'I'm sorry?'

'Medicine isn't about what *you* need, Michael.' His voice was perfectly level. He glanced at his expensive watch. It flashed like a new silver dollar against his tanned wrist. 'I should be operating right now. I would have been if Meredith had not called. At this moment a young woman downstairs has had to wait for help from me, because I am here, dealing with you, and not there. You take my point.'

'There was no need for this, Professor. I'm all right. I'm fine.'

Curtiz' lips compressed. 'I can't imagine what you're going through, Michael. But whatever else you may be, you are not all right. You are not... fine.'

There was a tap on the door and Curtiz called 'Come!' Meredith bustled in, puffing, and set two thick mugs of mahogany-coloured tea on the low table between us. I could feel her glancing at me, but I avoided her eyes and looked out of the window. The winter sky was like watered silk and a few distant gulls soared in it, high over London.

'Don't leave the spoon in it,' Meredith said. 'It might dissolve.'

She was reluctant to leave. Curtiz smiled and waited while she fussed around. Finally, when she could delay no longer, she stumped away over his gorgeous blue-and-gold carpet and left the office.

'I want to work,' I said. 'I want to be of use.'

'You want to comfort yourself, Michael. I don't blame you but I can't permit it.'

'Just let me –'

'No.' He picked up his tea, sipped at it, made an appreciative face. 'You look a wreck, Michael. Is that eye painful?'

I stared at my mug in silence.

He set his tea down and brushed smooth his jacket in a neat cat-like motion. 'Do you want my advice, Michael? Get out of here. Bomb yourself out on every pill God made. I'll have something sent round. Sleep for a week. Two weeks. Don't be alone more than you can help. If you want I'll see that Stella Cowan gets time off.'

'That's not going to do any good.'

'Don't make me send you on compulsory leave.'

'You've got to give me something to hope for.' I could hear the pleading in my voice and I despised it, but I could not help it. 'Please.'

Curtiz stood up and moved around to stand behind me. For a few seconds he stood looking down at me. 'Michael, call me in two weeks. I'm not going to make you any promises, but if you still feel the same, we'll see what might be done. Perhaps some lecturing. I don't know.' He placed his small fine hand on my shoulder. 'Now go home.'

I didn't go home, not immediately. I walked for the rest of the day. For hours, until I could think again. Until my resentment and my anger were dulled. I walked clumsily, blindly, jostling people, jay-walking into traffic. Once I stepped off the kerb and collided with a bicycle courier and left him sprawled on the pavement. He was too shocked to protest. The city roared and pumped around me. The raw surge of it swamped the black energy I carried inside me, swamped it so thoroughly that, by the time I noticed the winter's day was failing, I felt almost calm again.

I got back at about six. The house was cold and dark. Some mail lay on the floor of the hall. Cards, letters, handwritten envelopes. I knew what they would say. I carried them in and put them unopened on a bookshelf. There was already a pile of unanswered mail growing there.

A package of some kind lay on the dining room table. A note from Stella and something wrapped in foil – food presumably. I had no conceivable interest in food. I opened the note and a foil strip of capsules rattled out onto the table. The note said: 'Diazepam compliments of the Silver King. I promised I'd drop them off. Michael – call me. Just let me know you're OK.'

I called her. When she answered I said, 'I'm OK, Stella.'

I was about to hang up when she said, 'I don't think you should be there. In that house.'

'Everyone seems to know where I shouldn't be, and what I shouldn't be doing.'

'Michael, eat something and take a couple of Diazepam. Sleep it off. I'm on shift right now, but I'll call round later.'

'You don't need to do that.'

'It's not just for your benefit,' she snapped. 'Eat something, Michael. Promise me.'

'OK.'

I hung up. I carried the foil parcel of food into the kitchen without opening it and dropped it into the bin. I toyed with the strip of capsules for a while and then threw that into the rubbish after the food.

It was only then, with the house quiet and dim, and the day's failure and rejection stretching out behind me, that I allowed Angie Carrick into my head again. I touched my cheek and found it was bruised along the bone. The flesh around my eye was puffy and it made a dark blur at the edge of my vision. I hadn't noticed this all day, nor the dull ache of the bruise. In my mind I saw the girl sitting awkwardly on the floor in her hibiscus-patterned skirt, her hair awry, rolling her hand against her lip, and a surge of shame washed over me. I wondered where she would be by now. I imagined her in a room somewhere, touching her cut lip with her tongue every few moments and cursing me. I didn't blame her.

I got up and walked through into the dining room and took the address book from the phone table and flicked through it. The entries were almost all in Caitlin's handwriting. There was no Angie Carrick listed. I had not expected that there would be. I stood there thinking about this for a long time, tapping the little book on the back of my hand.

I went into the kitchen and found a French Opinel clasp knife, walked quickly upstairs and up the spiral stairs, snapping on the lights as I went. The cleaning had been mercifully thorough. The stairs up here smelled powerfully of disinfectant.

I shoved the door wide and then I was inside, breathing hard. I sat down in Caitlin's chair by the small table and switched on the desk light. A broken pane in her window had been repaired with hardboard. Boxes of books and papers and files lay stacked on the floor, returned, I supposed, by the police. Her computer and the remains of her stereo were neatly packaged in bubble wrap. The bags she had been planning to take away with her were taped together and stacked with the rest. These things and the cardboard cartons which held her other belongings gave the place a deconstructed look, as though she had merely moved out, moved on, leaving the room to await the arrival of the removals truck. I had dreaded recognising Caitlin in the very position of things on the shelves, the pictures on the wall. Instead what I found was a nearly hollow space, stacked boxes, a bare floor. I opened the clasp knife, and slit the packing tape on the first box.

By nine in the evening I had opened all of Caitlin's boxes, set up her computer and checked her discs and files, gone through every one of her books and papers. After that I moved downstairs and took down the books and CDs from the dining room shelves. I pulled our photo albums out of the cupboard under the window seat and spent hours poring over them. I took out our personal boxes – insurance, bank statements, private letters. I sorted through all of it. I worked with a dogged intensity, the way a soldier might set out on a long march, without much thought of eventual success, but with a certain relief to be moving. I lost myself in the task.

It was close to midnight before I was sure that there was nothing to find. Nothing was out of place. No scribbled notes carelessly left at the backs of drawers, no cryptic references in desk diaries, no photographs of strange men I didn't recognise. I pushed aside the pile of box files I had opened on the dining room table and leaned back in the chair and stretched. I looked around me. In light of the desk lamp the mess I had made of the room looked destructive, as if I had ransacked it in a burglary. I was sorry about that. I did not feel destructive. I felt only a great urge to know, to understand. But for the moment, I could think of nowhere else to look.

I got stiffly to my feet and leaned for a while at the back window, my hands spread on the sill. I was weary and unshaven and hungry, but I could not focus on what to do about any of this. The door creaked behind me and before I even registered the sound I spun around so violently that I caught the wall phone with my arm and sent it clattering off onto the floor.

'There's nothing wrong with your reflexes, then,' Stella said.

I stood there with my heart bouncing. 'How did you get in?'

'Thing called a key?'

'I'd forgotten you had one.'

'I'd have knocked, but I was afraid you might be asleep. I did tell you I'd drop in.'

'You did. Yes.' My pulse began to slow a little. I bent to pick up the phone and fumbled it back onto the hook. 'Yes, you did.'

Stella nodded at the cluttered room. 'Clearing up, were you? Good idea, probably. Has to be done. The sooner the better, I suppose.' She paused. 'You look bloody awful, Michael.'

I saw she had brought three white Sainsbury's bags in with her. 'What's this?'

'We medical people know it as food, Michael. It's what you use to keep your body attached to your soul.' She picked up the shopping bags and carried them through into the kitchen. She called over her shoulder, 'I suppose you threw out the other stuff I left?'

'Sorry. Couldn't face it.'

'Uh huh.'

I followed her into the kitchen. She dumped her bags on the surface and unpacked them and opened the fridge and made a face at the smell. She took things out of the fridge and began to drop them into the rubbish, then frowned and reached into the bin and took out the foil strip of diazepam tablets. She held it up accusingly.

'Michael, if you're serious about getting back to work you'd better start doing what the Silver King says.'

'I'm serious about it, Stella.'

'He wants me to keep an eye on you, as if I wouldn't have done that anyway.' She put her hands on her hips. 'He wants you back when you're ready, but he won't take you if I go back to him and tell him you're slummocking around here pouring whisky into yourself and not eating. And I will tell him that, you understand me? I was going to go easy on you tonight. I promised myself I would. But -' She broke off, came a step closer, and peered at me under the stronger kitchen light. 'And how *did* you get that black eye?'

'It's just a bruise.'

'Aye, I know what a black eye is, thank you, Doctor.' She poked my cheekbone with her fingertip. The contact sent a spike of pain down into my jaw. 'How *did* you get it?'

I hesitated, thought about lying, decided not to. 'A woman called Angie Carrick did it. You ever hear of anyone called Angie Carrick, Stella? Supposed to be a friend of Caitlin's?'

'I wouldn't know Caitlin's friends. This woman belted you? When did all this happen?'

'Last night. She came here.'

'What did she sock you for, for Chrissake?'

'I asked for it.'

'How?' She poked my cheekbone again, rather harder this time.

'Will you stop doing that?' I moved out of range. 'If you must know, I hit her first.' It was the most immense relief to confess it.

'You?' She widened her eyes. 'You *hit* this woman? Why?'

'She said something stupid about me and Caitlin.' I thought about that. 'Maybe not stupid. Careless.'

Stella did not react quite as I had expected, with outrage, or perhaps with sympathy. Instead she said carefully, 'People say all kinds of things at times like this.' She moved back and crossed her arms. 'Where did you find this Brunnhilde, then?'

'She just turned up.'

'You invited her?'

'Of course I didn't invite her. I'd never heard of her.'

'She just dropped in?' I could see Stella was offended on my behalf at the intrusion. 'I bet you made her welcome. Well, obviously you did.'

'I feel a complete prick about the whole thing.'

Stella snorted. 'Well, it looks as if she got her own back. What did she use on you? An iron bar?'

I didn't answer.

She said, 'Maybe we could both do with a drink.'

She found a bottle of cheap red wine in one of her plastic supermarket bags and uncorked it. She poured two glasses and we carried them out into the dining room. She took hers to the window seat and sat down and kicked off her shoes and took out her cigarettes.

I said, 'You've only been in the place for five minutes and you're going to fill it up with fumes?'

'Och, bollocks to you, Michael.'

She lit up and leaned back to slide up the sash window a little, tapped ash out into the dark street and closed the window again. She squinted around her at the state of the room, and I noticed again how very littered and disordered I had left it. She blew some more smoke and eyed me through the haze.

'If I could just get back to work,' I said. 'Isn't that what we tell other people to do? Get back to some familiar patterns?'

'Aye. That's when familiar patterns don't involve sticking scalpels in people.'

'I'm all right. I know this doesn't look good, but I'm all right. I'll get it together. Truly. It's being useless that drives me mad.'

'What's the idea, Michael?' she demanded suddenly. 'You want to save somebody because you couldn't save poor Catey? Make it come out even? Nobody could have saved Catey. She was dead.'

'I thought you were going to go easy on me tonight.'

'This *is* easy. You want me to get tough?'

'No.'

It was stuffy in the room, or maybe it was the tone of our conversation which made it oppressive. I stepped forward and pushed the window all the way up. The hiss of the sleeping city floated in on a wash of cold air. Stella's cigarette smoke funnelled out past me.

'I can't understand how I didn't know,' I said.

'About the child?'

'About its father.' I faced her. 'How could a thing like this happen?'

Stella studied the tip of her cigarette. Once again, she did not respond as I expected. 'Come along, Michael. Something like this must have occurred to you before now. Caitlin was a stunning woman. Do you think other men didn't see that? She's bound to have been noticed.'

This shouldn't have shocked me, but it did. I got up and fetched more wine and poured it. As I tipped the bottle into her glass she reached up and took my wrist in her free hand.

'You know I wouldn't say anything to hurt you, Michael. You *know* that. But people send out signals when they're lonely. They can't help it. Not even Catey could have helped it. She didn't turn to ice, lovely pure Caitlin, when you were away – away with me, most of the time, bucketing around the Third World.'

'You make it sound like she just had a fling. That would be hard enough to take, but it was more than that.'

'Possibly. But -'

'Not just *possibly*, Stella. She was pregnant by this bastard. She had her bags packed so she could leave me and go with him. And then he killed her, for Chrissake. That's not a fling.'

'You don't know she was going away with this character. Not for good. You don't know she was leaving you.'

'What interpretation would you put on it?'

'I don't know. I'm just saying that this kind of thing happens when people are lonely. Something small triggers it, and it gets out of hand.' Stella pushed her hand tiredly through her hair. 'Somehow the wrong person picked up her signal. They were care-less. She got pregnant, and everything followed from that. It's awful, but it happens.'

'There's more to it than that. And this Angie Carrick knows something about it.'

'Oh, and I suppose that's why you hit her? Away with you, Michael!' She tossed her cigarette butt out of the window. 'This woman said something hurtful and you spun out. That's all. You don't have to dream up some big conspiracy to justify yourself.'

'She came here to check up on me in some way. Maybe to find out how much I knew.'

'Paranoid, are we now?' Stella got another cigarette out, clicked her lighter fiercely at it, then realised she was trying to light the filter and slung the cigarette into the fireplace.

I said, 'Are we having an argument?'

'I just think you'd be better to spend a little more time on this planet instead of one of your own creation.' She got up and stood in front of me. 'Michael, you do understand, don't you? None of us really knows anyone. *Really* knows them.'

I put my arms around her. 'You're a good friend, Stella. The best.'

'Aye. I know.' She held on tight. 'Too bloody good by half.'

We stood there for a few moments, clinging together. I said, 'And maybe it's time you left.'

'Maybe it is, too.'

She stepped back so abruptly that she trod on her wine glass on the floor behind her. I heard it tinkle and crunch under her heel. She did not even glance at it. She swept up her bag and strode down the hall to the front door and pulled it open. I followed her. She stood in the doorway and spoke without looking back at me. 'You know, Michael, we're two of a kind.'

'Yes?'

'We're awfully good at facing up to problems – just so long as they're a long way from home.'

Caitlin said, 'I already feel a long way away from home.'

'I hope that's good.'

She pressed herself against me. 'What do you think?'

We were standing together at the windows of Anthony's conservatory, gazing down the long ragged garden. The evening sun fell between the poplars and threw shadows over the little knots of people gathered on the lawn. For once, it was just possible to call it a lawn; in our honour Anthony had had the garden mown for the first time in living memory. The May evening was still sappy with the smell of mallow and nettles mashed under the blades a few hours before. There were still tufts of long grass and weeds around the untrimmed shrubs, and an impenetrable jungle of brambles at the far end, but the garden was broader and more open than I ever remembered.

There were more people too than I had ever seen here before, thirty or forty of them, friends of mine and Caitlin's, young, smart people, milling around the trestle tables with glasses in their hands. It was a fine evening and midges were swinging in domes under the trees. A string quartet on the terrace was taking a break from playing Haydn and I could see Bruno already chatting to the first violin. I knew he would be trying to persuade them to play something he could sing.

It was odd to see Anthony's house invaded by these revellers, his workbenches tidied away and most of the boxes of clocks and springs and flywheels shoved out of sight in his study and the door locked on them. The house had even been cleaned, after a fashion. But then, after all, it was a special occasion. Caitlin and I had been married four hours earlier at the Kensington and Chelsea Register Office. The event hadn't been without its strains – her parents had naturally boycotted it – and we had tried to keep the whole thing low-key. But for Anthony, the celebrations ranked with a royal wedding.

'He loves you so much, you know,' Caitlin said. 'You're the son he never had, obviously.'

I caught something wistful in her tone which I could not identify. We both watched Anthony out on the lawn, cruising from one group of guests to another, bottle in hand. He dispensed pride, goodwill, and champagne on all sides. He was beaming, resplendent in a new pinstripe bought for the occasion, a red rose in his buttonhole, a scarlet silk handkerchief blooming from his breast pocket. He was easily the most formal figure there, and probably the oldest, but also quite possibly the happiest.

'He's such a sweetheart,' Caitlin said, 'and he must have been quite a dish when he was young.'

'Anthony?' This took a little imagination.

'Well, not a dish, exactly. You know what I mean – that 1930s Oxbridge look. Sort of crumpled elegance. Terribly cultured, but begging to be looked after.'

'He was always just Anthony to me. Always there. I never thought about him living any other kind of a life.'

'He must be so lonely here in this big house.'

'He's got his clocks and his antiques and his music. The world just passes him by. He knows it's there, but he prefers to go on living in the one he's created around himself.'

'Oh,' Caitlin gave a sad little laugh, 'not like the rest of us, then.'

I watched Anthony as he bustled around the lawn below us, florid, avuncular, bursting with pride and pleasure, and for a second I glimpsed him through Caitlin's eyes. It was my wedding day, and all his happiness was entirely and unselfishly on my behalf. I wondered if I had ever seen him properly before.

'He loves you too,' I said.

'He must do,' she said, 'he really must.'

A girlfriend of Caitlin's arrived just then and there were excited greetings and embraces and Cate was dragged away. But I stayed at the window for a few minutes longer, glad of my few moments of peace, turning over in my mind what she had said. I had so very rarely thought of what I owed Anthony. Caitlin must be right, and in some ways I was the son he had never had. I had never thought of him as a replacement for my father, and yet in so far as it was possible for him he had filled that breach. It was far from a natural role for him, and I knew his inadequacies scared him. I was grateful for all he had done, but until today I had not considered that his sacrifice might have gone beyond pure generosity. That there might have been options of his own he had given up to honour his commitment to me and to my dead, natural father.

'Hello, champ.' Stella came up behind me, put her arm around my waist and squeezed me. 'I hope you're pleased with yourself.'

'I am, Stella. I truly am.'

'You should be. She's a doll.' She looked down at the little crowd on the lawn. Caitlin was out there now, laughing with her friends, radiant in the twilight. 'No,' Stella said. '*Doll* just doesn't do it. I think your Caitlin's the most beautiful creature I ever laid eyes on. The bitch.'

'Don't beat about the bush, Stella. Just come right out and say it.'

She turned under my arm and kissed me decorously on the cheek. 'You know I wish you everything good, Michael. Both of you.'

'Thanks, Stella.'

We stood there for a while longer. I knew she was thinking about how random it all was, how close we had both come, she and I. She was asking herself what would have happened if I had not left Turkey on that particular day, or if she had come back with me instead of staying on an extra twenty-four hours. Or if – in that tiny window of time – Bruno had not inveigled me into gate-crashing some unknown rich girl's birthday party in Gloucestershire.

'Let's go outside,' Stella said abruptly, and pulled away from me.

It was growing dark in the garden, but Caitlin saw me at once and walked across the lawn and put her arm through mine. Someone was lighting the torches among the trees and as the flames sprang up it became night. Blue clouds were piled in ramparts high up into the evening sky and the trees were black against them. The quartet had started playing again, but I seemed to hear this from a long way off. I put my arms around Caitlin and kissed her.

At some point as I held her the music broke up and died away, and when I looked up again I saw that Anthony had taken centre stage on the terrace. The musicians of the quartet stood back from him, smiling indulgently at his interruption. The leaping flames of the torches made him look like a portly Roman senator at a feast. The light flashed on his glasses and shone on his face and made brilliant his buttonhole rose and his scarlet handkerchief. He was slightly tipsy, and perhaps even a little ridiculous, but he had about him such an aura of innocent joy that no-one laughed. Instead they made a spreading space of silence for him, and in a few moments the very smallest of sounds had died away – the rustling of a dress, a cleared throat, the clink of change in a pocket.

'Every man has a duty in this dark world, a great duty or a small one.' Anthony gazed out at the still faces of the guests. 'I knew his father, you know. Michael's father. Duncan Severin – now there was a man with a great duty. But he was not spared to fulfil it. And when a man of the first rank is struck down, then a chap of the second rank must step forward and do his poor best to fill the gap. Action! That's what's called for. Bold action. And I did try. I did try.' Nobody moved. Perhaps nobody breathed. A bat flicked through the light and it was so quiet I could hear it twitter. Anthony's bloodhound eyes wandered over the crowd and sought me out. 'How well I succeeded, you good people can see for yourself. A fine young man. In the very image of his father. Stepping forward in the world to take his father's place.'

His gaze shifted from me to Caitlin and I felt her tense under my arm. The light from the blazing torches fluttered over Anthony's radiant face, painting it red and gold. 'But a chap cannot go through life alone. Not even a strong man, a man with a mission. To be alone is to be corroded. I know this all too well, and yet I never thought that I would meet a person worthy – you must forgive a fond old guardian – a person worthy of Duncan's son. Nevertheless, such a person has come to us. It seems like a miracle, but it is so.' He drew himself up and lifted a glass in the torchlight. 'So this toast, my friends, is not to Michael, who will win plaudits enough in his life. But to Caitlin, to whom I entrust my charge. And my hope. And my love.'

I gave it a couple of days, but the thought of Angie Carrick and her strange visit would not leave me alone. On the Wednesday morning I finally called Detective Sergeant Barrett on his direct line.

'Sorry, Dr Severin,' he said at once, 'I've got nothing for you yet.'

'It's not that. I wanted to ask you if you'd come across a woman called Carrick during the investigation.'

'Garrick?'

'Carrick. Angie Carrick. Late twenties. Northern accent. Attractive.'

'Doesn't ring a bell. Why?'

'She called in on me a couple of nights ago. Said she was a friend of Caitlin's, from work, but I'd never seen her before.'

He hesitated. 'Would you have? Seen her before?'

'What?'

'Well, only that you don't seem to have known a lot about your wife's working life.'

'All right. Forget it.'

I would have hung up, but he said, 'Tell me about her.'

I told him what little I could, omitting only the way our meeting had ended. I couldn't bear that Barrett, of all people, should know about that.

'I'll make some inquiries,' he said when I had finished, and rang off.

I stood by the phone for a while. I was quite sure DS Barrett would find nothing on Angie Carrick, and fairly sure he wouldn't look very hard. But I felt better anyway for having asked him, and at once the vision of that dark haired girl sprawled on the floor of the study, her hand to her mouth, began to fade.

Chapter Eleven

'Well, you look a bit better than last time. I will say that.' Professor Curtiz rose from behind his vast desk as I closed the door. He crossed the room and took my hand. 'How are you, Michael?'

'I'm doing all right. Seriously. Doing better.'

He looked at me with his silver head on one side and did not at once release my hand. I could see the doubt in his face. 'I rather hoped you wouldn't come back just yet. It's still very soon, you know. Very soon.'

'I just need something to do, Professor Curtiz.'

He sighed. 'I could hardly pitch you straight back in at the deep end.'

'I'd prefer it if you did.'

'Let's take it one step at a time, shall we?'

'I hear John Donohue's been off sick all week,' I pressed. 'He could be gone for a while.'

Professor Curtiz straightened. 'You've done your homework, I see.'

'And Bernie Driscoll will be going back in Dublin at the end of the month. It'll be pretty short-handed here.'

He pursed his lips in irritation. I knew he resented being corralled like this, and I thought perhaps I had gone too far. But at that moment a bar of winter sun fell from the high window across his face. The light died away again almost at once, but in its cruel brilliance I saw for the first time that Professor Curtiz was not after all a demigod, was not the immaculate Silver King of hospital mythology, but was in fact a tired and harassed elderly man. I could feel him wavering in the face of my assault.

'I'm very determined,' I said. 'Very determined indeed.'

'I know you are, Michael,' he sounded weary, 'but I also know that there's a difference between determination and desperation.' He walked a couple of steps away from me and leaned back against his desk, looking at me, still in doubt. 'All right,' he said at last. 'Here's what I'm prepared to do –'

Both Curtiz and I should have been used to the raw shrilling of the trauma call, but when it sounded it caught us both by surprise. He recovered quickly. He pushed himself upright and thumbed the pager at his belt. I could clearly hear the voice from the switchboard.

'Trauma Team to Resus Two and Three immediately.'

'Absolutely bloody wonderful,' Curtiz muttered. He glanced up at me. 'Do you know, Michael, I'm getting altogether too old for this.'

But he was already moving. I followed him out of the office into the anteroom where his secretary sat. He issued a string of rapid instructions to her as he strode through. Ring so-and-so. Cancel this. Reschedule that. He paused to shed his jacket and caught sight of me hovering in the doorway behind him.

'The fates seem determined to undermine me.' He unclipped his platinum cufflinks and tossed them to the secretary, who caught them deftly, as if from long practice. 'Come along, then.'

We hurried down the polished corridor. As we passed my office I saw Meredith inside, busying herself about some small task. I gave her a triumphant thumbs up, but to my surprise she did not respond. Instead she stood there watching us grimly as we passed.

The first of the injured were already coming in by the time we got down to A&E. I heard snatches of talk about a bus crash. One ambulance was backed up to the doors and another was wailing down the ramp. Behind the siren I could hear others.

Curtiz strode through the screens into Resuscitation Room Two, with me on his heels. The space was already crowded and buzzing – an A&E doctor I recognised and two nurses I didn't, Sam Okigbo the gasman, Vernon Choudhury the registrar, Carrie Iverson the Scrub Sister. Equipment was rolling in and people were busy with leads and switches. I felt the adrenalin spurt into my blood and my focus grew sharp and colours grew vivid under the harsh lights. It felt right. Just watching it and listening to it – the bustle, the clipped voices, the practised moves. It all felt right. Even the smell was right – cold, volatile, heady.

Curtiz stripped gloves out of the wall dispenser and tossed me a pair. I had already peeled an apron off the roll and tied it around me and now I tugged the gloves on, working my fingers into the skin-tight rubber. That felt right, too. Dressed in the kit I felt armoured, safe, up for anything.

'And how many do they think we can handle?' Curtiz was demanding of one of the A&E doctors. 'A dozen majors? They don't want much, do they?' For emphasis he snapped the rubber of his surgical gloves.

Someone pulled back the curtains and the trolley came trundling in between us pushed by a knot of nurses and green-clad paramedics. A woman, the straps rucking her city clothes, a face the colour of putty smeared with mud and dirt. There was some blood on one shoulder and dark spots were appearing magically on the floor below. Curtiz and I stepped back as the paramedics counted down and smoothly lifted the woman onto the table, still strapped to her spinal board. They began to release the straps. Sam Okigbo took his stethoscope from round his neck.

Curtiz called, 'So what've we got here?'

A paramedic glanced up. 'Head injury. Apparent chest injury. Deeply unconscious, GCS of 3. Intubated and ventilated at the scene. Pulse 120. BP 80 over 40.'

Curtiz made to step forward, and then he hesitated. 'Do you want to run this one, Michael?'

'Yes,' I said quickly. 'Yes. I want to very much.'

'Splendid.' He walked out past me with a great show of nonchalance. 'I'll be around. Just in case you need a hand.'

'Thank you,' I said to his retreating back. 'Thank you.'

I moved up to the table and the team parted for me. They had already set up one drip in the woman's right arm. As I approached a nurse was fixing a second one into her left. Sam Okigbo was bent over her chest. He straightened as I came up.

'No air entry to right side of the chest, Michael,' he told me.

He stood back, awaiting instructions, and I had a clear view of the woman's face for the first time. She was quite young – perhaps early thirties. Her face, what I could see of it, was fine-boned and regular. I thought she might have been pretty. Even beautiful. Her hair showed between the straps and the bandages. Short, blonde hair. Ash blonde.

'Michael?' Sam said.

I leaned closer. I needed to see her better. At that moment I needed it more than anything else on earth.

'Do you want a chest drain, Michael?' Sam prompted.

I was aware of the merest tremor of unease flitting through the room. I reached out and touched the woman's hair. It was matted with blood and dirt.

My paralysis probably lasted no more that a second or two, but it was long enough. I let my outstretched hand fall to my side and stepped back from the table.

'I can't do this.'

There was a bustle of released activity which moved around me like a current around a rock. There were some hushed voices, some hurrying steps. Someone – one of the trauma nurses – was murmuring to me and guiding me away and helping to peel the gloves off my hands. Once I was outside the screens Professor Curtiz magically reappeared beside me.

'Everything's fine, Michael.' His voice was infinitely gentle. 'No harm done. Go home now.'

He patted my arm and was gone. His kindness was more shocking to me than hot fury would have been. The nurse fussed with the fastenings of my apron. Someone found my jacket and handed it to me and helped me on with it. And then I was alone. Behind the curtains I could hear Curtiz giving instructions in his clipped voice.

I wandered away towards the exit through the hurrying nurses and the drip stands and the stretchers. Trolleys jingled and clattered around me. I seemed to pass through the urgent crowd unnoticed, like a wraith.

I walked out into the raw day between two shining ambulances. Their paintwork bloomed and faded with rose light, faded and bloomed. I found a bench and sat on it. The damp wood soaked through my trousers. I watched the ambulances come and go.

A car horn sounded, an impatient double beep. Stella had both nearside wheels of her battered red Golf up on the grass. She leaned across the seat and wound down the passenger window.

'Get in.'

She parked on the pavement just off Gordon Square and left her fake 'Doctor on Call' sign on the windscreen.

The pub's lounge bar was a cavernous place sporting a lot of timber and brass. On the walls hung the sort of hunting and angling prints the breweries supply in job lots. It was too early for the lunchtime crowd but green beans and glossy sausages and other food lay ready in a stainless steel bain-marie at one end of the counter. The smell of onions almost overpowered the reek of stale beer from the carpet. The barman was a pink balding man with a white jacket. He was polishing glasses and seemed surprised to see us.

Stella marched up to the bar and ordered a couple of double scotches without asking me, and pulled out bar stools for both of us and sat down. Irrelevantly I noticed she was wearing a blue and white striped dress which made her look crisp and practical. It seemed to fit her mood. She slid the scotch towards me and looked at me questioningly.

I said, 'I was a fool.'

'Yes, Michael, you were. But here's goodbye to all that until you've given yourself a deal more time to get your act together.' She lifted her glass and drank. She straightened her back as if loosening a crick. 'If it makes you feel any better I checked up on her. The patient.'

My heart skipped. 'And?'

'She's in IC but she'll be all right. Nothing you did, or didn't do, made any difference. Curtiz knows that. They all know it.'

I stared at my hands. 'If only she hadn't been blonde.'

'Michael.' She put her glass down and gripped my wrists and forced me to look at her. 'My dear, she wasn't blonde.'

My mouth went dry.

'She wasn't blonde,' Stella repeated, very precisely. 'She wasn't young. And she wasn't Caitlin. Now d'you see?' She shook my wrists as she held them. 'Now d'you understand?'

She released me and slid down from the stool and took a credit card from her purse and gave it to the barman. I heard her tell him to run a tab for us. She took both our drinks and carried them over to a table near the window. I followed and sat down obediently where she told me to. She returned to the bar and came back with two plates of steaming food, a bottle of Chilean red and two glasses.

'I can't eat,' I said.

'You're going to eat, Michael. Deal with it.' She sat down, tossed off her scotch and poured the wine. 'And then we're going to get a bit drunk. I've got the afternoon off.' She unwrapped her cutlery and attacked her food at once.

I took a deep breath, drank a little. 'I should have listened to you. To Curtiz. You were both right.'

'Agreed. But?'

'But I don't need you to ride herd on me like this from now on. I've not been behaving like the smartest man on earth, but I'm not an invalid.'

She filled both our glasses again. 'Don't fool yourself, sunshine. This isn't just in your honour.'

'What does that mean?'

'I'm leaving,' she said.

'*What?*'

'I've been offered a new job, and you're helping me celebrate.'

'You can't leave. You're the best theatre sister in the whole damn place.'

'Aye,' she said. 'And it's *senior* theatre sister to you, Doctor. Though surprisingly enough, I've discovered that St Ruth's doesn't legally own me. I do feel like it sometimes, but I'm not actually a fixture.'

'What sort of a job is this?'

'Head of Nursing Programs.' She cut off a chunk of sausage and put it in her mouth, chewed it and swallowed, using the pause for effect. 'At Mater Misericordia. In Caracas. That's Venezuela, you might remember.'

'Ah,' I said. That made some sort of sense, which in turn made it real: as real as it could be to imagine St Ruth's without Stella. To imagine London without Stella. Life without Stella, come to that. I struggled to get it all into focus.

'They liked what I did on the MSF mission,' she was saying. 'The clinical program. They liked it very much.'

'Yes,' I said. 'I know they did.'

'Now they want me to head it up permanently. Well, a one-year contract at first. It's a big chance for me, Michael. A move into management. A deal more money, of course.'

'You've accepted?'

'Not quite,' she said, with an emphasis which I missed at the time.

I remembered the conversation on the balcony in Venezuela, a hundred years ago. 'And Gordon? Those plans you had? The fifteen bairns and the budgie and the goldfish?'

'Dull bloody Gordon?' she cried, and tossed down her cutlery with a clatter. 'Gordon, the fucking corporate anorak, has found himself someone new. Can you believe that, now?'

'No.'

'I wouldn't mind so much if it was some mousy little female accountant from the office. She's a *dancer*, for God's sake. A dancer in some nightclub. Twenty-three and drop-dead gorgeous, apparently. Would you credit it?'

I said, 'A dancer. Gordon.'

'When did bloody Gordon ever go to nightclubs?' she demanded. 'He never bloody took me to bloody nightclubs. He never took me bloody *dancing*.'

I shook myself to clear the images from my mind. 'Stella, you're worth ten Gordons. I always thought he was a boring fart.'

'So did I. What pisses me off is that he wasn't, and I didn't know.'

She sat there staring furiously at me, breathing hard. I could see she was close to tears. I put out my hand and covered hers with it. She made a face and, perhaps as a distraction, went back to her meal, eating steadily and avoiding my eyes.

I watched her, and after a moment I ate too. The food was surprisingly good, and we worked our way through it in companionable silence for several minutes. The wine was beginning to sing in me and the bar was starting to fill up. There was some talking and some laughter. Suited men from nearby offices came in, a gaggle of hilarious girls celebrating a birthday, a lecturer from the university showing off to a tutorial group. It felt illicit to be here, sensing the first effects of wine in the middle of the day, but I was glad of the activity around us.

Stella finished and pushed aside her plate, poured us two fresh glasses. She looked directly at me. 'You should think about moving on yourself,' she said.

'Me?'

'You won't leave anything alone if you stay here. It's not just the work. You'll be forever turning that house upside down, ripping the place apart, like you were the other day when I found you. Going through her things, looking for anything – any little speck of dust – out of place. You'll never let go of the past. I just know it.'

A busy waitress arrived and scooped up our plates and we sat silently while she worked around us. When she had gone, Stella crossed her hands on the table in front of her. 'Michael, come with me. To Venezuela.'

I had lifted my glass to my lips. Now I lowered it again without drinking, and set it down carefully.

'You don't have to look quite so stunned,' she said. 'It's not such a crazy idea.'

'I didn't say it was a crazy idea.'

'There'd be no strings, obviously. It's not about that.' She leaned forward. 'But you'd be away from here. And they love you there at

Mater Misericordia. Juan and Alfredo and Pilar Gonzales and the rest of the team. They're always asking about you.'

'Stella, what would I do in Venezuela?'

'Does it matter right away? They've offered me a bungalow. One of those big places with a pool. Take it easy for as long as you want. Learn Spanish. Travel a bit. You know how beautiful the country is. Buy yourself a four wheel drive and piss off into the jungle. Just hang loose. Get your head together.'

'Stella –'

'Then when you're up to it – I don't know, in a few months – you could take on a bit of work. Only if you felt like it. They'd kill to get hold of someone like you at the Mater, you know they would. And Curtiz would be all for it. He'd understand. He'd let you go whenever you needed to.'

'After today,' I said, 'he'd probably drive me to the airport.'

'There's no huge rush for a decision.' She shrugged, acting nonchalant. 'I thought maybe… once the funeral's over we could talk about it.'

I had not thought about the funeral. I had not allowed myself to. This was all coming in too fast for me to process.

She saw this and backed off at once. 'Maybe that's too soon.'

'Maybe.'

'But then again,' she edged on, 'there'd be nothing for you to stay for after that, would there?'

'I thought you said no pressure?'

'Everyone needs a bit of pressure.'

The waitress reappeared beside us. 'Like to see the dessert menu?'

Stella said, without taking her eyes off me, 'Got any Venezuelan wine?'

The girl looked startled. 'I don't think so. I never heard of any.'

Stella picked up the empty bottle and showed it to her. 'You see that? Where it says "Produce of Chile"? Well, get us another bottle, cross out "Chile" and write "Venezuela". OK?'

'Whatever you say.' The girl looked doubtfully at the bottle, then fled.

'We could do this, Michael. We really could.' Stella reached out across the table and gripped my hands. 'And you'd be doing me a big favour. You know me – I'm all talk. I'd never have the courage to go on my own.'

'Give me some time to think about it.'

'If you ask me,' she said, 'thinking is just what you don't need.'

From the bar the waitress called across, 'How do you spell Venezuela, then? Is it like Venus?'

'Yes,' I told her. 'Just like that.'

CHAPTER TWELVE

The day of Caitlin's funeral was shockingly, disrespectfully, quite improperly glorious. I drove myself there, cruising westward into the Gloucestershire countryside, through winter woods and newly turned fields under a cold sun. The trip took a little over two hours, and I was sorry when it was over.

From the corner of the lane which led up to Morrow church I could see one flank of the building and people milling in the carpark. With the window down I could even hear them talking. I pulled over and got out and walked a little way into the woods. The trunks were mossy and the fallen leaves were soft underfoot and I took comfort in the dimness and the clean dank smell of the earth. When the slamming of car doors and the voices faded away, I walked back to the lane and up to the church. Standing apart from the other cars two black funeral limousines shone in the sun, next to a silver Jaguar which I knew to be the Dacres'. A uniformed driver leaned against the bonnet smoking a cigarette. Noticing my look, the man straightened and made a token gesture of hiding the cigarette behind his back.

I could hear the organ wheezing as I walked up to the door. The church was a cavernous brick pile built in the early 1800s for workers at the local tweed mills, and the three rows of mourners seemed lost in it. Perhaps there were fifty of them. Several heads turned as I walked quietly in. I did not look at the questioning faces but I could not fail to notice, right up at the front, Stella's red hair and Anthony's rounded shoulders. In the very front pew I saw Margot Dacre, her back still ramrod straight though she must now have been over seventy. Beside her, positioned at the end of the pew in a wheelchair, sat Edward Dacre.

The coffin lay on a trestle in front of the altar, heaped with flowers, bathed in coloured light from the stained glass. As I walked up the aisle the organ trembled into silence and mourners began to get to their feet and bearers in black suits started to remove the small mountain of blooms from the casket. The brilliance of the flowers hurt my eyes. I could hear my own heels ringing on the flagstones. I saw the bearers pause in their work around the coffin and look up to face me and I heard a collective ripple of breath from the mourners. The vicar, a thin, hesitant man, took a half-step towards me, but by then I had climbed the steps to the coffin and was brushing aside the last of the blossoms and placing my hands flat on the polished casket. The varnish was cold under my palms. I stood quite still with the light falling on me and the heady perfume all around. Someone shuffled, a pew clattered, a woman stifled a sob. I lifted my hands from the coffin. My palms left perfect prints of warmth on the glossy surface. The handprints faded gradually to nothing. When they had gone I walked down the length of the aisle and out into the cool sunshine.

The bearers brought the casket out, its ruby varnish flashing in the sun, and loaded it into the back of the hearse. People came streaming out of the church, grim faced, darkly clothed, bending close to one another. I looked away from them. Oaks and beeches stood beside the churchyard wall, skeletal against a duck-egg sky. Soft clouds piled up above the flank of the Cotswolds. A magpie hopped among the graves, its blue-black head on one side, impatient for us to be gone. I was impatient too.

By the corner of the church there was a bench under an old yew tree and I ducked through the branches and sat down. The little crowd mingled on the grass a few yards away, giving me my privacy. I recognised very few of these people. A woman who might have been a schoolfriend of Caitlin's, helpless with grief and supported by a man I did not know. An elderly, grey-haired lady whom I thought had once worked as a cook at the Dacre house. A scholarly man who looked like the family doctor. There were also two watchful young men in Marks & Spencer funeral suits, trying not to look like policemen. Just once I caught a glimpse of Digby Barrett on the fringe of the crowd, resembling an undertaker himself in his long black coat.

After a while I stepped forward into the sunlight and I let them move around me and speak their kind words into my face and shake my hand. Serious Patrick from Médecins Sans Frontières, tanned after some new assignment. Professor Curtiz, his silver head bowed and shining in the thin sun. Meredith, her face red and smeared, all her bolshieness fallen away, and her bright clothes bundled under a drab raincoat. There were other colleagues too, but most of the mourners were people who had been close to Caitlin rather than to me. I had met most of them at one time or another, but I was ashamed how little I knew about their lives and their work and how little I knew of the ways in which Caitlin must have touched them.

Somewhere in the middle of it all I found a short woman standing squarely in front of me. She was about forty, with cropped hair and no makeup, and there was something aggressive in her stance that pulled me up short.

'We're all gutted down at the Centre,' she announced. 'Staff and students. I want you to know that.'

I didn't know what she was talking about, but I said, 'Thank you,' and made to move on. She did not budge. I looked more closely at her, but she was in no way familiar to me.

'I know you weren't happy about her coming,' she blurted, as if this was something she had been determined not to say, but could not hold back. 'All the same, she did some good work at the Centre. Some really, really good work.'

'At the Centre,' I repeated.

The woman frowned, an expression between bewilderment and irritation. 'I'm Julie Clarke? The York Road Centre?' She spoke with great deliberation, as if I might be wilfully misunderstanding her.

I couldn't begin to imagine what sort of work Caitlin might have done in this place I had never heard of. But this woman's tone did not leave any room for contradiction, so I merely nodded dumbly and hoped she would move away. Still she did not.

'We loved her, Michael. That's all I wanted to say. I really don't want you to forget that.'

She strode away and I watched her push through the crowd. But then I was engulfed again by sorry and tearful people and I had no more time to think about it.

Over near the gate I found Anthony discreetly passing money to the undertaker, touching the man's elbow and thanking him while slipping the folded notes into his other hand. I didn't know if people normally tipped undertakers these days, but it was, like everything Anthony did, decorous and unobtrusive.

I walked up to him. 'I want to thank you for everything, Anthony. I'm a little late with that, I know. Cate would have wanted to thank you too.'

'My dear old chap. It's better to be busy at times like this. It's a privilege to be useful, in fact.' He squinted up at the rolling silver clouds. 'Stella has told me about this opportunity in Venezuela.'

'She's been offered a job there. She thinks it would be good for me to go along. Just…for a change of scene.'

'So she said. Well, perhaps it might lead you back to the path you have chosen for yourself. I know that has proven difficult for you here.'

'You think I should go?'

He lifted his lugubrious face to mine and drew himself up. 'I believe it might be worth serious consideration, my boy. A man needs something to keep him going. Anger and self-reproach will do for a while, but you won't find them sustaining in the long run. Believe me, I know.'

'Bold action,' I said. '*Action téméraire.*'

'That's the ticket, old chap.' He smiled briefly and moved away between the graves. He kept his head down and did not look back.

The two funeral limousines pulled past me, glittering in the sun, bearing Caitlin away. Their departure cleared an open space between me and the Dacres' Jaguar, and abruptly I found myself facing Caitlin's mother. Margot Dacre was standing beside her husband's wheelchair at the open back door of the car. She gave no sign of having seen me. The wheelchair was turned away from me, and the chauffeur stood on the other side of it, on the point of helping Edward Dacre onto the back seat. I did not want to approach them, but it seemed absurd not to make some gesture of sympathy, and I stepped forward.

'Margot?'

She moved away from me without a word, around the front of the car and across the gravel to the door of the church and in through the dark entrance. The chauffeur, still stooped over the wheelchair, watched her go in bewilderment, unsure what he was supposed to do next. I helped him lift Edward Dacre into the car. The old man said nothing at all as we moved him. His eyes were empty. The tall body was wasted and he was as light as an old leaf. He felt as if he would not even dent the leather upholstery with his weight. I leaned over him to fasten the seatbelt, avoiding that blank gaze. There was a sweet smell about Edward Dacre, a smell of breakdown and decay.

I walked across to the church and in through the door. Up near the altar an elderly man was sweeping up flower petals in the rainbow light from the window. The bright vacancy of the place swam in front of me and drifting dust motes burned like fireflies. The organist was working the pedals of his instrument, perhaps looking for some fault, making wooden knocking noises which boomed through the nave. It was a strange feeling, to walk back into the church now that the service was over. The echoing space felt like a theatre when the audience has left and the actors have gone, a place draining of its magic.

Margot Dacre was sitting halfway down the aisle, her back to me. Her black figure reminded me of a silent and watchful bird. The sweeper's broom hissed against the flagstones. The organist laughed, exchanging a comment with someone out of sight, and then he realised we were in the church and he closed his music and hurried away. The man with the broom glanced up at us and left quietly through the vestry door. Margot rose as she heard my footsteps and stepped into the aisle to face me. She lifted her veil and beneath it her face was clenched. She locked her gloved fingers together in front of her. I was startled by the hostility I read in her eyes.

'I know what you want, Michael,' she said. 'You want absolution. But I'm not going to give you that.'

I put my hand on the back of one of the pews to steady myself. Her eyes were bright and alert, and there was no pity in them. I was having trouble controlling the muscles around my mouth.

'Margot, you must know I'd give anything if I could change things.'

'Really?' Her eyebrows arched. 'I wonder why you didn't do that earlier.'

She walked past me and away down the aisle, her heels clicking on the flagstones. When she reached the last pew she stopped.

'We shan't be at the cremation, Michael,' she said without turning. 'We've said our last farewells. All of us have, I think.'

She pushed open the heavy door of the church and walked out and the door swung shut behind her and banged like a cannon. Through the diamond paned windows I saw the birds rise in clouds from the bare trees.

I waited inside the church, listening to the exchange of muted farewells outside, footsteps on the gravel, the clump of doors. One by one the cars drew away. I heard them move quietly down the lane and take the turn at the bottom and accelerate gratefully away into the living world beyond. I let perhaps ten minutes pass in this way, until it grew still outside, and then I left the church, stepping out into the brilliant afternoon. The wind was rushing through the trees and flattening the grass against the ground.

Only a few people migrated from the service to the crematorium, and the room was half empty. Baroque organ music floated from the speakers. I sat in the third row of seats with my head against the pale wood of the row in front. I heard the curtains whisper open. I heard the whirr of machinery. But I could not convince myself this had anything to do with me or with Caitlin. I kept my head down and did not watch.

Outside they had heaped Caitlin's flowers on a green bank. It was sheltered here but even so the wind made the blooms shiver. Petals were scattered like confetti all around and the cellophane wrapping of the wreaths rattled. The sound irritated me, an insistent buzz like something caught in the spokes of a child's bicycle wheel. I stooped to rearrange the heap of blooms in the hope of quietening the noise.

One small tribute drew my attention, made up of wildflowers gathered in a posy. I unpinned the handwritten card and stood up to read it: 'From Julie and all the team at York Road – Catey, we will never EVER forget you XXX'. I had almost forgotten the encounter, but now I thought again of the square dark haired woman I had met among the mourners. There was something about this schoolgirl note which did not sit well with my memory of that brisk and impatient woman. I tried to remember what she had said. I thought it might be important, but my mind was a tangle.

'She was well thought of, your missus,' Digby Barrett said from behind me. 'Nice to know. It's something, at least.'

I slipped Julie Clarke's note into my jacket pocket. He was standing a little back from the heaped flowers, and the dark clothes made him massive in the winter sunlight. He left a gap for me to speak, but I could not think of anything to say.

'I'll go if you want,' he said. 'Say the word.'

'I was just leaving myself.'

'Right.' He pulled his flapping coat around himself and buttoned it, but gave no sign of moving. 'No luck with that Carrick woman, by the way. No-one seems to know her.'

'I don't suppose it matters.'

'You're probably right.' He still didn't move. 'Could you use a drink at all? There's a pub down in the village. Looked a nice little place. I thought maybe a stiff one wouldn't go amiss.'

'I was about to drive back to London.'

'One won't hurt and I won't tell. Besides, there's something I want to show you.'

'Something like what?'

He shook his head. 'We can leave it. Probably you're not up to it right now.'

I gave up then, and he saw that I had, even though I said nothing.

'The Nag's Head,' Barrett said. 'Follow me there.'

It was the kind of genteel low-beamed place that passes for a country pub in the south of England, all copper pans on the walls and horse brasses on leather straps and an enormous fake log fire that would have required a small gas field to power it. There was a cappuccino machine behind the bar and a gourmet menu on the blackboard. The room was packed with the new country aristocracy of the wealthy retired – their pristine Range Rovers crowded the carpark – along with a few smart young professionals from Gloucester or Cheltenham, impressing their clients or their lovers with lunch in the country.

Barrett led me to a table near the window. He was carrying a large leather case with important steel catches and a shoulder strap. He must have taken it from the car. Without comment he placed it on the table, where it was large enough to cover almost the entire top. Next to it he put a plain wooden box, probably mahogany, perhaps an antique. I had never seen either of these things before.

'What can I get you?'

'Half of something. It doesn't matter what.'

He thrust his way through the crowd and I sat down at the table. I had to shift the leather case aside slightly to make room for myself. I glanced up and caught sight of Barrett at the bar, half turned towards me. He smiled and nodded and lifted the drinks as if to show that he was on his way, but I knew he had been watching me. He was at my elbow in a moment, carrying a pint of some cloudy bitter for himself and a half for me. He set my beer down, moving the leather case onto the floor and propping it against the table leg on my side, leaving the box on the surface.

'I thought I might as well return all this to you now. We've finished with it.' He raised his pint to me. 'Cheers.'

I left my drink on the table. 'What is this?'

He tapped the case with his shoe and affected surprise 'Your wife's pictures. Lovely they are too, ain't they? Bloody tragic. Talent like that.'

'This portfolio isn't Caitlin's.'

Barrett placed his glass carefully on the table. 'You don't recognise it? Nor the box neither?'

'If this is some sort of a riddle, I'm not in great shape for it right now.'

'You take a good look, Dr Severin.'

'I don't need to. They're not Caitlin's.'

'They were in her room. Among all her other gear.'

'They're not hers.'

He took the mahogany box in his square hands and slid back the lid and showed me the contents: pencils, graphite sticks, a small penknife, a putty rubber black with use. He looked at me inquiringly.

'It's the sort of stuff she used to use,' I said. 'But she hasn't drawn anything for years.'

'Open the portfolio.' He moved the box and our glasses aside and hefted the case up onto the table for me. 'There's nothing so dreadful in there. I wouldn't bugger you about. Just take a look.'

I flicked back the catches. I could see at once that the drawings were Caitlin's. I recognised her work as I would have recognised her voice. Many were mere sketches, some pencil and some pen-and-ink – a preening pigeon in a square, the bole of a tree, the figure of an old man, hunched under an umbrella and leaning against the rain. Several studies of buildings, some astonishingly detailed and precise, and others, captured in a few fluid lines, as if they might have been sketched from the top deck of a passing bus. Some were London scenes. I recognised the landmark buildings: St Paul's, the Albert Hall, Hampton Court. But there were many others, a confusion of images I could not take in.

'You never told me your wife was an artist.'

'She wasn't. Not any more.' I turned the heavy pages. 'Not for years.'

'You mean maybe, not a *professional* artist,' Barrett pressed. 'Doing this was, like, a hobby of hers?'

Buildings I didn't recognise, a few others that looked familiar, a spray of blossom, a bird on a fence post. I stared at them without really seeing. There had already been a lover I didn't know about. A child I didn't know about. A bundle of drawings I didn't know about shouldn't have counted for much against such things. But it did.

'Because she pretty certainly drew these, didn't she?' Barrett persisted. 'She's signed and dated every last one of them.'

'Yes. She drew them.' I closed the case deliberately. 'But I've never seen any of them before. As far as I knew she'd never drawn anything since we were married. Since before that. I wanted her to start again but she never would.'

'Something made her start again.'

'Apparently.'

Barrett pursed his lips and thought about it. 'OK,' he said. 'Here's what I want you to do, Dr Severin. I want you to take that portfolio with you. And I want you to take a good long look at those pictures. And when you've looked at them, you let me know if anything springs to mind.'

'I never even knew they existed. What could I tell you?'

'Anything odd about the dates, any of the locations that mean something to you. There's a few drawings of her parents' bloody great mansion, and some of St Paul's and the Tower and suchlike. But it's the other ones I'm more interested in. Just look at them. You'll do that?'

I rested my hand on the cool leather of the portfolio.

'Right.' Barrett said with decision, as if I had answered. He got up and buttoned his coat around him. He took his time over this. Finally he said, 'When it comes right down to it, there's a good few things you didn't know about your wife, aren't there?'

I looked up sharply at him. He jerked up his chin in a gesture of farewell and walked across the low bar to the door.

CHAPTER THIRTEEN

There were several drawings of Morrow House, as Barrett had said. And other buildings – a ruined mill, a college I thought I recognised as Magdalen in Oxford, a row of terraced houses.

But the last dozen were different. A simple brick building, a farm cottage, drawn from several different angles. A woodland setting – she had caught the scatter of light through leaves, a path climbing a steep ferny bank, a stream with stepping stones across it. The house was not especially picturesque. It looked a little run-down, with the door of a lean-to outhouse hanging loose and one or two slates missing from the low roof. There was a water butt by the door. A rusting piece of farm equipment, a harrow perhaps, lay half submerged in bracken under the front window. This was a real cottage, I knew that, not some construct of Caitlin's imagination. It was a place with an existence in space and time, a building of bricks and mortar and wood. The path outside would be muddy and the door would creak and probably the roof would leak. A modest place, even a shabby place. And yet it was a place she knew intimately, perhaps a place she loved.

I closed the portfolio gently on the pub table and ran my thumb over the edges of the sheets of cartridge paper inside so that they buzzed – there were more than a hundred of them. How many hours of concentration did that take, how many hours of immersion in a world I knew nothing about, a world in which I did not figure?

I slid open the mahogany box. It smelled of shaved wood and reminded me of primary school. Her pencils lay inside, worn down, their paint grubby with graphite. I picked one up delicately. It should smell of her, I thought. It should have a message for me, something she had used so well. But I could not even remember how she had held a pencil, how the lines of her face had settled in concentration, how she had rested the pad on her knee. Presumably she had had characteristic ways of doing all this, but I had only ever seen her draw once, and it was so long ago. It left something hollow inside me, that I could not even imagine her at work. I put my elbows on the table and rested my head in my hands.

An evening gallery opening at the Tate a couple of years before. It was the middle of winter. Caitlin had helped to organise the event, and I was late. With the trauma team, I had worked all afternoon on a seventeen-year-old Swedish girl who had stepped under a bus in the Strand. At first we had hopes for her, but in the end we could do no more than stand aside and watch her slip away. She was quite lovely, particularly as she died, and it had touched all of us to watch the life fade out of her. I had found it impossible to put her out of my mind as I hurried down wind-swept Tottenham Court Road, failing in the rain to catch one cab after another. I arrived at the Gallery cold and wet and tired and ready to pick a fight.

The room was full of elegantly emaciated women and middle-aged men with pony tails who wore expensive suits over black tee-shirts. Waitresses kitted up like Victorian chambermaids bore trays from which these people ate decorative food and took glasses of Sancerre. Most of the guests were already vocal and rubicund. I took a glass from a tray and drank it greedily. I attracted a few glances, perhaps because I looked so crumpled, but more likely because my foul mood was so obvious. I could not see Cate, and rather than be forced to talk to any of these unjustly healthy people I pushed through them to the wall and stood looking at the work on show. They were bleak drawings in charcoal, shanty town street scenes with elongated figures, bent in despair. A mother and child, a stick dog gnawing at something in a gutter.

'Hello, stranger.' Caitlin moved up beside me and stretched up to kiss me.

'I'm late. Sorry.'

She glanced at me. 'Bad day?'

'Sorry again.' Before I could stop myself, I glanced at my watch.

She caught a passing chambermaid and took a glass of wine from her tray and gave it to me. She squeezed my arm. 'I know you hate it. We'll be out of here soon.'

'I don't hate it,' I snapped. 'Why do you say that?'

She let a moment pass. 'So what do you think of the work?'

'Why did you stop drawing, Cate?'

'All right, we'll go now.'

I tried to protest but she took the glass out of my hand and replaced it on a waiter's tray and steered me towards the exit. She spoke quickly to a colleague and collected her coat. In a few moments we were out in the cold night on the steps above the Victoria Embankment. I was immediately remorseful.

'Cate, we can go back. Let's go back.'

She led me down the steps and we crossed the road and stopped, leaning on the parapet, looking out over the black river sliding past in the night.

'Michael, if you think the work I do is meaningless, if you think it's trivial, you have to tell me now.'

'I just don't understand why you work for these wankers. When you've got such talent yourself.'

'The world needs doctors. It doesn't need another second rate artist.'

'What does that mean?'

'It means I live this way for you, Michael. For us, of course. But mainly for you. Because there has to be a balance. It seems that I can't help with the important things. I can only help with this bit, so that's what I do. It's not much, I know. But I can't do even this if you don't value it at all.'

I had the sense, at least, to put my arms around her and hold her with some desperation while the numbing wind whipped down the river.

The landlord cleared his throat.

'Was there anything else, sir? Only we normally close at three.'

He stood over the table, a hearty man with a beer-gut bulging under an Arran sweater. He carried a tray loaded with dirty glasses. I became aware that the pub had emptied around me and that the pumps behind the bar had been draped with dish towels and that a girl in an apron was wiping down tables.

'I lost track of time.'

'Absolutely no problem, sir.' He swept away my glass, still half full of tepid beer, the same beer that Barrett had bought me. He nodded at the portfolio, open on the table in front of me. 'Lovely work, sir, if I may say so.' He took a couple of steps away and stood beaming at the door, holding it open, until I walked through it. 'Look forward to seeing you again!' Deftly, he locked up behind me.

Less than half an hour later I drove through the iron gates of the Dacres property. I idled the car down the long drive with its cedars and cypresses. The trees stood like dark cut-outs against the November sky and threw bars of shadow which flickered over me like a strobe. The buff stone house appeared around a bend in the drive, that imperious façade and the iron-framed conservatory running the length of one flank. I slowed almost to a halt, just rolling forward.

I remembered Morrow House on the evening I had first set eyes on it, when Bruno and I chugged up this same sweeping drive in his decrepit Austin Healey. On that occasion the place had been floodlit, fans of light up the warm stone. Bruno and I had guffawed at the sight and punched one another and made jokes about Castle Dracula and wondered what breed of creature could call such a place home. Now, ten years later, I drove past the Dacres' silver Jaguar and pulled up in the precise spot where Bruno and I had parked on that day. I drew a deep breath, tucked the portfolio under my arm, and got out of the car.

Edward Dacre was partly hidden by the columns of the porte cochere, and so it took me a moment or two to spot him sitting there in his wheelchair in the last of the winter light. He looked to me like a piece of spindly old furniture put outside to air. I had never been reconciled to him, but I found it pitiable now to see his proud presence so reduced. His frailty made me feel offensively strapping. I wanted to apologise for it. I could see no sign of Margot.

'Hello, Edward,' I said.

The yellowed eyes flicked up towards me. I could see no recognition in them, only a faint puzzlement. There was a chair set out on the gravel beside his wheelchair, with a pair of secateurs and a folded newspaper on the seat. I moved the paper and the secateurs and sat down. He had a blanket over his knees and a book under his folded hands, though he no longer looked to me as if he were capable of reading. Perhaps Margot left the book there as a matter of form. The wind brought down some twigs and leaf litter from the beech trees, and a corner of the old man's blanket lifted and I caught it and folded it back over him and tucked it in.

There seemed no point in holding grudges now. The light had gone out of his eyes. I tried to imagine him in his prime, a fine, powerful young man, resplendent in his uniform, striding ashore on some foreign beach with an enormous revolver at his hip. How hard it must have been for him to adapt to the drab grey world of fifties and sixties Britain after that. To live just long enough to know that the world he cherished had gone forever, despite the rearguard action he had fought for most of his life. I hoped that at least he was past understanding what had happened to Caitlin. What a waste of time it would all have seemed to him if he knew that.

The conservatory door opened behind me and I stood up. Margot Dacre was wearing a maroon tracksuit and gardening gloves and she carried a large terracotta pot full of dark soil in her arms. It was as if she had meticulously discarded every trace of the funeral of just a few hours before. She stood looking at me with her eyebrows raised.

I nodded at the pot. 'Can I take that for you?'

'No.' She didn't move. 'You shouldn't have come.'

'Margot, I had to see you.'

'Why? In the hope of finding out whose child she was carrying?'

'You know about that, then.'

'Only because the police told me.'

I had no doubt she was telling the truth, and I saw for the first time that she, too, had been deceived. 'I'm sorry, Margot.'

'Are you?' Then she softened a little. 'Well, for the record, I knew nothing about her life away from here. She never told me about any other liaison. She never hinted. You can believe that or not as it suits you, but it happens to be the truth.' She took a breath. 'I'm not aware that we have anything more to say to one another.'

I lifted the black leather portfolio onto the chair and opened it at random and showed it to her. She set the pot down on the gravel and brushed her hands together and glanced at the folder. Her face was blank.

'Am I supposed to react in some way?'

'This house features in half-a-dozen of these drawings. Several of the sketches are dated in the last few months.'

'She came here. Try not to look so surprised, Michael. We are her parents.'

'Why would she come here without telling me? Why would she take up her art again and not tell me that, either?'

'I was not my daughter's keeper. Unfortunately.' She took her eyes away from mine and looked up at the sky. A cloud shadow darkened the front of the house and then raced away across the lawn. She seemed to be thinking something through. 'Come with me,' she said.

I hitched the strap of the portfolio over my shoulder and followed her into the hallway I remembered so well, a long panelled passage smelling of dried flowers. Margot stalked ahead of me into the vast dining room. Nothing had changed here – the high ceiling where darkness floated, the great hearth, the tall windows onto the brilliant garden. Margot moved to the head of the long table, her arms crossed.

'You kept her from me,' she said, 'year after year, you did everything you could to discourage her from coming back.'

'I didn't have to keep Caitlin away from here, Margot. I'm only surprised she came back at all. But evidently she did.' I slapped the portfolio. 'She loathed this place with a passion, loathed the emptiness, the arguments, the way her father treated her, the way he treated you, the way you stood by and let it happen.'

'This is righteous indignation, is it?'

I unslung the portfolio from my shoulder and let it fall with a crash onto the table. 'Indignation doesn't cover it, Margot. I'm a shade more than fucking indignant. What right do you have to accuse me? It was you who condemned her to grow up in this prison with that bigoted old bastard bullying her for year upon year. You never had the courage to break out – not even for her sake. And you blame *me*?'

In the sudden silence the echo of my shouting fled among the roof beams. Before I could say anything more she walked around the table and seized my hand. It was the first time Margot had ever done such a thing and I was too surprised to resist.

'There's something I want you to see,' she said.

She led me through the dining room and up the back stairs. Her grip was as strong as a claw, and at times she seemed almost to be towing me along. We emerged onto a broad carpeted corridor with windows on one side and plain wooden doors on the other. She opened the first of these and stood aside.

'This was Caitlin's bedroom. When she was a child.'

I was suddenly aware of how much I did not want to see this room today, but there was no possibility of retreating now. A bright plain chamber, quite small, with a narrow cast iron fireplace and a sloping ceiling. An old single bed, neatly turned down. A wicker basket filled with soft toys. A school swimming trophy on the mantel.

'You can see the river from the window,' Margot said. 'She used to love to watch the river.'

Yes, Caitlin had done that. She had told me. I saw her now, a little blonde girl with big eyes, sitting up in that bed for hour upon hour in the night, staring out at the moonlight flashing on the water, lost in the big dark house like a princess in a tower. I took a step towards the window and stopped. There were three framed photographs on the sill, and on the wall to one side of them a calendar with blocks of days marked off in coloured felt-tip.

I became aware of a discomfort that I could not place, something low in my belly. It was distinct and physical, like the jumping of a nerve. The photographs were all of me. I picked up the first of them, a recent shot taken on assignment in Greece. I was laughing and wearing sunglasses, hanging out of the cab of a truck, waving at the camera. The other two shots were also of me on overseas assignments, both taken in the last couple of years. I looked at the calendar on the wall. The blocked-off dates marked my stays overseas. The original return date for the Venezuela trip had been crossed out and a question mark replaced it. The fluttering in my belly grew stronger.

'Every time,' Margot said. 'Every single time you went away in the last two years she would come and stay here, for a night or two. Sometimes longer. And I would hear her, you know. I would hear her sobbing in here. This wife of yours who understood why you had to leave her.'

I stared down at the picture in my hand. 'She never told me any of this.'

'Well, of course not, Michael. It was her duty not to tell you.'

Outside, battlements of cloud were forming over the wooded slopes beyond the river. The cloud was dark grey above and fleeced with gold at the base where the sinking sun touched it.

'You crush us,' she said. 'You stifle us.'

'Crush *you?*'

'Me. Caitlin. You crush the very life out of us. Men like you and Edward. You suffocate us with your endless bloody protection. You go off on your crusades, and you leave us like chatelaines. Pay the servants. Keep the home fires burning.'

'It wasn't remotely like that between Caitlin and me.'

'It's always like that. With Edward it was Italy and Korea and then Malaya. With you it was Turkey, Africa, South America – these god-forsaken holes you're always flying off to, so you can play saviour.'

She turned away and stood looking past me, out of the silvered window.

'Do you know, Michael,' she said in a different voice, 'when I was a girl I wanted to teach.'

I looked up at her.

'History and English. Yes, really. I'd done my certificate. I had a job lined up. A little village school in a place with the ridiculous name of Barnes Wittering, down in Kent. It would have been my great adventure. No woman in my family had ever had a job. I'd never been anywhere on my own. Barnes Wittering might have been somewhere near Singapore for all I knew of life outside London. I'd even bought my ticket. I still have it somewhere.' She paused. 'And then I met Edward. Of course he wouldn't hear of it. And I couldn't prevail against him. He was a good deal older than I was, and much more wordly wise, but that wasn't the reason. The reason was that I loved him, and that's why I couldn't win. Because I loved him I couldn't even *fight*. Just as Caitlin couldn't fight you.'

'I'd never have stood in Caitlin's way, whatever she wanted.'

She turned to face me. 'What she wanted was to *live* with you.' Perhaps unconsciously she touched the counterpane on the bed, stroked its nap with the flat of her hand. 'Not to be treated like some geisha.'

'Margot, I would have done anything for her. Anything at all.'

'Yes,' she said, 'except need her.'

I put the photograph back down on the windowsill. I could not take my eyes off my own face in these pictures. In every one of them I was laughing. In every one I was completely, revoltingly happy.

'She loved you more than the moon and the stars, you know,' Margot said in a matter-of-fact voice. 'Don't ever forget that, Michael, or it will all have been for nothing.'

I heard her walk away along the wooden corridor and down the stairs. I knew she did not intend me to follow. When the silence had fallen again I moved quietly around the room, touching things, handling things – dusty rosettes Caitlin had won at gymkhanas as a girl, a faded snapshot tucked into the mirror frame. Perhaps,

I thought, she could be summoned by my touch. I pictured her drifting into the dim shadows of the mirror, pale as flax, reaching for me. I hoped that she would. I prayed that she would. I sat on the narrow bed and closed my eyes.

After a while I left the room and closed the door softly behind me. I walked along the corridor to the back stairs and down into the cavernous dining room. Margot was not there, but dried plants lay on the long table, and a cut glass vase stood nearby, as if she had been arranging the display but had been called away before she had finished. The musty smell of dry leaves hung in the room. The portfolio lay on the table precisely where I had left it. I slung it over my shoulder and let myself out of the back door into the gathering evening.

It was going to be a wild and blustery night. The wind was already making the trees groan. I paused at the corner of the house, and looked back along the rear terrace. Yellow light splashed onto the black lawn from the windows. Her father would be sitting in there somewhere, trying, perhaps, to reassemble the scattered fragments of his memory before they fled from him utterly, whirled away on some wind even more powerful than the one that pressed against me now. I felt a pang of fellow feeling with the old man as he struggled to make sense of a world that was losing its coherence around him even as he watched.

At that moment I saw another light in the trees ahead of me. It came from the old generator house, from Caitlin's studio. I left the path and pushed through the wet shrubbery. The door of the studio stood ajar. I swung it open and stepped inside. The space was much as I had last seen it, the one and only time I had seen it, with Caitlin's easel in the centre of the floor and drawings and watercolours pinned and taped to the walls all around. I let the door close behind me. It was secret and secure in here, in the gold light, with the branches scratching against the roof and the rain slapping the windows.

Margot said, 'Caitlin never brought anyone else here, nor even spoke of anyone else. I was as deceived as you.' She was sitting on a stool by the window bench. She looked older and smaller than she had appeared to me in the house. 'I shouldn't like you to be in any doubt about that.'

'Thank you.'

I stared at the drawings and paintings, delighted by them as I had been then, by their boldness and their strength.

'This is all new work,' Margot said. 'Edward really did burn everything that day. But she started after Edward's second stroke. That was nearly two years ago. I don't know what started her working again. I didn't want to ask in case I frightened her away.'

'She never told me.'

'There were a great many things Caitlin didn't tell any of us. She didn't tell me about our own grandchild, for heaven's sake. Our only grandchild, who is now smoke and air and ashes. Just as she is.' The image shocked me, and perhaps she saw that it had, because she added, 'I don't mean to be cruel, Michael. But you're not alone in this.'

I let my gaze wander across the drawings again: an old man hunched over a pint at a pub table, ducks on a pond, a spinney of fir trees.

'We had Caitlin quite late in our lives, you know,' she said. 'It was my idea to have a baby. Edward was already in his mid-forties. I was afraid of his reaction, so I didn't give him the choice. I so desperately wanted something of my own. Something important. Someone who would need me.' She looked at me.

I could not easily meet her gaze and I turned my head away. If I had not done so I might have missed the picture altogether, tacked to the wall beside the door. I stepped up and looked closely at it, not quite sure why at first, except that it was so different from all the others. A scrawled child's picture in blue crayon. A house with two approximately square downstairs windows, divided into panes like Battenberg cake. Smoke curling from a tottering chimney. Stick trees with cottonball foliage. Something – some machine with wheels and spikes – out the front. A cottage. The brick cottage I had seen in Caitlin's drawing, but a childish version of it, endearing in its clumsy energy.

I tore it roughly off the wall. The drawing had been scrawled on an A4 sheet of copy paper. I turned it over. Written on the back in crayon, in crude infant school capitals, were the words: *I have tassted your absense and it is bitter.* It had the air of a quotation laboriously but inaccurately copied out of a book, the letters ill-formed. And beneath it an awkward signature of sorts, in barely joined-up script: B. Carrick.

I placed the picture on the bench top in front of Margot and smoothed it flat.

'I don't know where she got that,' she said. 'I suppose it was a gift of some kind. It must have meant something special to her.'

I flipped the paper over and pointed at the signature. 'Who was this B. Carrick?'

'I wouldn't know. It looks like the sort of picture a child gives a teacher. Doesn't it?'

'How about Angie Carrick? Have you ever heard that name?'

'Michael, I'd tell you if I knew.'

I folded the drawing and slid it inside my jacket. As I tucked it away my fingers touched a scrap of paper in my pocket. I moved away from Margot and pulled out the paper. It was the scribbled message which had been pinned to Julie Clarke's flowers. Julie Clarke at the York Road Centre. Students, she had said. Young students? Kids?

'What will you do now, Michael?' Margot asked.

'What?'

'With your life?'

'I don't know,' I answered her distractedly. 'There is an opportunity overseas. A job, I mean. Not an assignment. I'm thinking about it.'

'Where?'

'Another godforsaken hole where I can play saviour.' I was surprised at the bitterness in my own voice.

'You'd probably be wise to go,' she said quietly. 'You can't do anything for Caitlin now.'

I touched the folded picture in my jacket pocket. 'She wanted me to find her,' I said. 'She so wanted to be found.'

CHAPTER FOURTEEN

I left it until the following morning to drive to the York Road Centre. It had taken less than ten minutes to find the place on the computer. It was in Streatham, apparently, a part of south London I didn't know well. There was a website, but it was down for maintenance and I could learn very little more about it.

Cross-city traffic meant that the journey took well over an hour. But I found the York Road Centre easily enough, a low L-shaped building in liver-coloured brick just off Streatham High Street, in a network of drab streets not yet touched by gentrification. It was set behind a breezeblock wall which someone had backed into and half-demolished. There were bars on the windows and there was graffiti over the brickwork, and in the drizzle the place looked like something out of the old Eastern Bloc, grim and institutional. I pushed through the double doors into a hallway flanked by notice boards and fire extinguishers.

Inside, the atmosphere was cheerful and busy. The boards were covered with flyers and notices offering language lessons, legal advice, rooms to let, yoga classes, drug rehab. From a room to my right I could hear the sounds of an exercise class. The floor bounced a little underfoot and even here in the lobby there was a faint smell of sweat and stale towels. The female instructor was calling the moves in a rhythmic and high-pitched chant. The voice sounded familiar.

On my left, another set of double doors opened into a canteen. I walked in. It was a barn-like room set with laminated tables and lit by a row of roof windows pearly with grime. I could smell fresh coffee and ginger and chicken. A soccer match was showing on a wall-mounted TV in the corner. A West Indian woman in an apron banged around behind the counter, preparing food and humming to herself. There was a chopping board in front of her with a ragged pile of green herbs on it.

'You want somethin', sweetheart? Only strictly, we ain't open yet.'

'Julie. I was looking for Julie Clarke.'

'That's Julie's class you hearing right now.' She jerked her head towards the sounds of effort and exercise and then looked me very directly up and down. 'But you don't look like you up to no exercise today, sugar.'

I had forgotten to shave and I realised I looked shabby and unkempt.

'I'll wait.'

'You do that. You use a coffee?'

'Thanks.'

I sat at one of the tables and she brought me coffee, bustling round the counter flap and setting down the mug in front of me. I had a sudden almost irresistible urge to ask her about Caitlin. Maybe Caitlin had leaned on that counter and joked with this generous woman, and had drunk her coffee, and had eaten her ginger and chicken for lunch, here in this other life I knew nothing about. For a second I felt an almost unbearable sense of rejection.

The West Indian woman hovered near the table. 'You OK there, sweetheart?'

But before she could offer any more of her dangerous kindness the doors burst open and the room was crowded with panting middle-aged women in garish gym clothes, chatting and jostling and pushing towards the counter. The West Indian woman retreated through the flap and lowered it like a drawbridge. I caught a glimpse of Julie Clarke on the far side of the throng in blue tee-shirt and shorts. The black woman signalled her over and I saw the two of them look in my direction, one concerned, the other startled. Julie Clarke pushed through the crowd to my table.

'Michael, you're about the last person I expected to see here today.' She paused 'Ever, in fact.'

'There's something I need to ask you.'

She stood staring at me in a manner which was both troubled and aggressive. Her tee-shirt was darkened with sweat around the neck and armpits and I could feel the heat given off by her short heavy body. She dabbed at herself with a towel slung around her shoulders.

'You look pretty done in,' she said. 'Are you all right?'

'Can we talk?'

She glanced at her watch. 'Let me take a shower.'

'Now would be good, Julie.'

She was irritated by my insistence but was unable to deflect it. 'All right. Come along.'

She marched away through the crowded room and I followed her out into the lobby and through a door opposite the gym. It was a tatty little office with a scarred metal desk wedged between two green filing cabinets. The desktop was clinically neat. There was a brass model of a Bugatti on it and a soft-focus picture of a brown-haired woman with doe eyes. A photocopied sign on the wall read: "The floggings will go on until morale improves." She moved behind the desk and sat down, rubbing at her spiky hair with the towel. She motioned me to the only other chair in the room.

'We're completely torn up about Caitlin,' she announced. 'All of us. I probably spoke out of turn yesterday, but I just wanted you to be clear about that. I can't begin to imagine how you must be feeling.'

'I appreciated you coming.'

She pursed her lips. 'Even when you didn't know who I was?'

'That's why I'm here. To work out how it could be that I didn't know about you, about this place. About what she did here.'

She stopped rubbing her hair. 'You were never interested before, apparently.'

'I'm interested now.'

'What good will that do?'

'Some, I hope. I hope it will do some good.'

She slapped the towel down hard on the desk. 'Maybe if you'd shown any concern at all with what we do here, then you'd have known what a very special person she was, without having to dig around now, when it's too late.' She caught herself and sat with her chest rising and falling, aghast at what she had said. She started to rub furiously at her hair with the towel again. 'I don't want to make life any harder for you, Michael. But to come here *today*. She worked here for two years. In two years you never once came. Never once.'

'I'd never heard of this place until yesterday, or of you.'

She was silent for some moments, apparently trying to convince herself that I was telling the truth. 'She came here to teach,' she said at last. 'She started with a couple of literacy classes a week, mostly for migrants. That was about two years back.'

'She taught English?'

'Literacy,' she was impatient with my ignorance. 'To anyone, but mainly migrants. She wasn't very good at it at first. In fact she was never very good at it. I don't think she'd ever actually met anyone who couldn't read or write before she came here. But she so wanted to help that it was… infectious. It affected all of us. Later she started coming out with me or one of the others. Old people, the women's refuge, hospitals, prisons.'

'She did that?'

'Yes, Michael, she did it all. She wasn't much good at any of that either. It would get to her too much. She'd had a sheltered upbringing. I suppose you know that much. But she learned. And she never, ever, stopped trying.' Julie pushed her hand through her short hair. 'There are people around here who thought she was a saint. They'll never feel that way about me, no matter what I do. But there was something special about Caitlin. And you know something else, Michael?' She lifted her square face defiantly to me to show she was prepared to admit her own mistakes. 'I never thought she'd stick at it. The surgeon's wife, all Harvey Nichols and good intentions. But you should have seen her.'

'I wish I had,' I said. 'I wish very much that I had.'

Perhaps she took this as an apology, or perhaps it had relieved her to get her resentment off her chest, because some of her aggression fell away. 'I didn't think we'd ever get over it when she left.'

'She stopped coming?'

'Well, yes.' She looked at me doubtfully.

'When?'

'Six, eight months ago? Maybe a bit more. She still dropped in, helped out every now and then. But she said things had got too busy at home.' She hesitated, as if deciding whether to say more. 'Actually she said you didn't like her coming here. I don't know why she'd say that, if you really didn't know about this place.'

'Neither do I.' I took the folded drawing out of my pocket and spread it on the desk in front of her.

'What's this, Michael?'

'Just look at it.'

The lines of her jaw hardened. I could tell she did not like being interrogated, but that she thought I might be too near the edge for her to protest safely. I thought she might be right. She glanced without recognition at the drawing. I turned it over but kept the signature covered with my hand so that she could see only the message: *I have tassted your absense and it is bitter.*

She frowned. 'What am I supposed to make of this?'

'This drawing was among Caitlin's things. I had thought it was the work of a child, but could one of the students here have done it? Given it to her?'

She raised her eyebrows, already seeing where this might be going. She opened her mouth to reply but before she could speak I uncovered the signature. She said, 'Oh.' She took the drawing from me and turned it to the light.

'Who's B. Carrick, Julie? And for that matter, who's Angie Carrick?'

'I don't know about any Angie, but I remember him all right. Barney. Barney Carrick. He came to classes here. Eighteen months ago or so? A bit longer. A northern lad. He was a piece of work, if you like that kind of thing. Good looking men, I mean.'

'Is he still around, this Barney Carrick?'

'He only stayed for a couple of months. He did a few classes, but after that he did hang around for a while. Helped out about the place.'

'Doing what?'

'He gave us a hand around the Centre with anything that needed doing. For free. We were glad of it too, having a useful character like him to call on. He could fix most things, and he was easy on the eye. A bit of a tough guy too, which can be an advantage around here from time to time. I remember wondering why he was here, exactly, working for charity, when there didn't seem to be much he couldn't do. I got the impression he was kind of lost. Like he'd been in trouble and was trying to find his feet. We get a few like that.' She handed me back the drawing.

'Did he go to one of Caitlin's classes?'

'I think he did, yes.' She caught on at that moment. 'Oh, look, Michael - people from the classes are always giving the teachers stuff. Little gifts. Tokens. They're like kids, some of them, so proud of what they've learned. It doesn't mean anything.'

'Caitlin didn't keep anything else from here. No other little gifts and tokens.'

'It doesn't mean anything,' she repeated. 'This Carrick guy just came and went. They do. People drift in and out of here all the time. I only noticed him because he was helpful, and the girls in the office kept drooling over him.' She got up and pulled out a filing drawer and started flicking through it. 'Here.' She extracted a yellow cardboard file and spread it on the desk. There was a computer printed class list in it. 'Bernard John Carrick. The April before last. He signed up for Catey's course, all right. That lasted a term. Like I said, he hung around for a few more weeks after that, but then he left and didn't come back.'

'Did you get an address?'

'We have to, for the funding.' She traced a line across the register with her finger. She grunted. 'Not that this one would have been much use to us.'

She turned the paper so that I could read the scribbled address and tapped it with her finger. *The Indian Mutiny, Mason Park, Bradford.*

'A restaurant he'd been to, probably,' she said to my puzzled look. 'Some of these guys are really secretive. Dodging tax or the police or whatever. They'll put down the first thing that comes into their heads.'

I left the Centre and crossed the wet road to the car. I spread the crude drawing on the passenger seat beside me. The rain drummed on the Audi's bodywork and turned the windscreen silver. I called directory on the mobile and got a number for the Indian Mutiny restaurant in Bradford, and without much trouble found the street name too, and then I called the number. It was answered by a mid-dleaged man with a Peter Sellers accent.

I said, 'I'm trying to contact a Mr Carrick.'

'She is working.'

'She?'

'Angela. She is working today. Coming here about four o'clock.' The man paused. 'Who is, please?'

'I'll call later.' I disconnected while he was still speaking.

I sat there for a while, cooling my palms on the wheel, staring at the wavering windscreen until I was startled by a sharp knocking on the window next to my ear. I caught a flash of the slick black and yellow of a parking officer's uniform and saw a woman's ill-tempered face under a dripping peaked cap. I started the car.

CHAPTER FIFTEEN

I drove off the slip road and down into the industrial wasteland to the south of Bradford. I was lost at once in a clutter of factory estates. The concrete block roads were flanked by low shabby buildings with roller doors, trucks parked on derelict land, a bus depot behind a chain link fence, here and there a tall brick chimney from another age. The late afternoon was chill and a whitish haze hung over the high moorland to the east. The distant hills appeared to be smudged on a backdrop, as if they might exist half in myth. Down here the air smelled of diesel and wet garbage. I came out onto a long straight road which followed a railway line past endless sidings of rusted boxcars scrawled with graffiti. I turned right, away from the railway track, and drove under a viaduct and into the network of shabby streets beyond.

The terraces were Victorian redbrick, narrow houses with tiny front yards overgrown with privet and long grass. Derelict cars lay outside the houses and household junk was piled against the front fences. A group of ten-year-olds were kicking a football across the road ahead. I heard the ball thud off the Audi's rear wing as I passed and when I looked in the rear-view mirror the kids were standing in the road behind me, their hard little faces bright with malice. The street climbed to a T-junction with a wider road running right and left. A street sign said that this was Mason Park Road. I had no idea where to go, but it looked like a main route, and I turned right into it.

I had somehow thought the Indian Mutiny restaurant would be obvious once I got into the estate, but it wasn't and I did not know what to look for. There was a pub on the left and a few yards beyond it a small crowd milled on the pavement. I heard a glass smash in the gutter, and two men started swapping clumsy punches, backing into the street so that I was forced to pull up to avoid them.

While the awkward flailing fight went on, all curses and haymakers, a police patrol car came up the road from the opposite direction. Four officers climbed out of it and the crowd retreated jeering towards the pub. The police did not follow them, but they did not leave at once either. One of them caught sight of the Audi, inspected it thoughtfully for a moment, and then walked over towards me. I lowered the window. The man stopped and stood back a little and looked in at me. He was stocky and middle-aged and wore a high-viz anorak. I could see him taking in the car's obvious newness.

'You sure you're in the right place, sir?' He used his heavy accent to make the 'sir' sound like an insult.

'I'm looking for a restaurant. The Indian Mutiny.'

He put his hands on the edge of the window and bent down. 'That's Hukum's place, the Mutiny. First on the right and a couple of hundred yards down.'

'Thanks.'

I moved my hand to raise the window again. But he stayed where he was, looking over the rich leather interior of the Audi with contempt. Or perhaps it was me he was looking at.

'If I were you,' he said, 'I'd give the Pakki grub a big miss for tonight.'

'Why's that?'

'Just take my tip and drive your nice shiny car a long way away from here. OK?' He tilted his head at me in dismissal and walked away.

The restaurant lay in the centre of a drab parade of shops set back behind a wide pavement. An enormous Asian man in traditional clothes and plastic sandals was standing in the street outside the place, unlocking slatted steel shutters. I stopped the car and got out and the man turned to look at me and at the car with the same expression the policeman had worn. He was gigantic, at least a full head taller than me, and his blue-black beard glinted in the afternoon light. As I stepped up to speak to him he walked away from me as if he had not seen me, and went on with his work, leaving me standing on the pavement.

'Yes? What is?' The second man was older and much smaller, a clerkish figure in a shiny jacket. He had a round face and wore horn-rimmed spectacles, and he stood in the doorway of the restaurant drying his hands on a tea-towel. I thought I recognised the Peter Sellers voice on the phone.

'Are you the owner?'

'This is correct. Hukum, yes.'

'I'm looking for Angie Carrick.'

His expression did not change but I saw his eyes flick over me from head to toe. I noticed the big bearded man had not moved far and was rattling at one of the shutters, pretending that it was jammed. Hukum said, 'And you are, please?'

'I'm a friend of hers.'

He looked at me doubtfully and tossed the tea-towel inside.

I said, 'She came to see me in London.'

The bearded man finished with the shutters and padded over and stood very obviously beside me, over me, planted like a tree. Hukum spoke to him briefly in Urdu, rather as a man might send a suspicious dog to its bed. The giant moved past us and into the restaurant. I noticed that he made no sound when he walked.

'Angela is like a daughter to me,' Hukum kept his eyes on me through his horn-rimmed glasses. It was obvious he didn't like what he saw.

'I've come a long way to talk to her. Can you just tell her I'm here?'

Still he hesitated. 'She is at the Wharf Street canal,' he sighed at last. 'Looking for the old gentleman. Her uncle, Mr Stanley.'

'How do I get there?'

'It is not good for her to go there. I have warned her many times. But she is stubborn.'

'I can believe that.'

'There is trouble all the time here. Gangs and fighting and thieves.'

'I'll go and fetch her. Tell me where the canal is.'

Hukum did not trust me. Perhaps I had sounded too keen. But the early dark was drawing in and I could tell he was worried about the girl, and in the end his fear for her won out. He gave me rapid directions.

'I'll bc right back.'

'If you are not,' he told me, 'I am myself calling the police.'

I drove across the estate. There was a strange watchful atmosphere about the streets and very few people were out. A woman in a blue sari hurried three children along, splashing colour across the pavement, but in a second or two she was gone, like some exotic bird which had taken flight. An old man pushed an ancient bicycle down a side passage and locked the gate after him. Some of the street lamps came on and it was suddenly evening, a bleak winter evening.

I turned into Wharf Street. Brick houses, fronting straight onto the road, stumbled down a steep slope towards the canal. Half of them were boarded up, and in all the rest the front windows had been broken. I could not tell if they were inhabited or not. Across the bottom of the street stood a barrier of corrugated iron, spray-painted with obscenities. Some of the metal sheets were loose and through a gap I could see the sheen of water and the brick cliff of a factory wall on the far bank.

She was standing with her back to me on the edge of the canal, her hand shading her eyes, looking first in one direction and then the other. She was wearing jeans and a leather jacket and her hair fell down across her shoulders, making her look younger than I remembered. I could sense her tension from her stance. I pulled up at the bottom of the street and got out of the car and pressed the key fob to lock it. The alarm tweeted and she swung round sharply at the sound, and as she saw me she stiffened and crossed her arms over her chest. I stepped through the gap in the corrugated iron and onto the overgrown towpath in front of her. A cold wind prowled down the canal and ruffled the surface of the water and lifted her hair.

'You shouldn't have come,' she said.

'I wanted to apologise.'

The line of her mouth hardened. 'And?'

'And we've got to talk, Angie. You know it.'

'How did you find me?'

'That's not important now. It's important that we talk.'

'I can't. Leave me alone.'

I stepped closer to her. 'Angie, who's Barney Carrick?'

Her face locked. The wind moved a strand of her hair across her mouth and she brushed it away. 'You tell me,' she said. She zipped her jacket and turned away and I put my hand on her elbow.

'Who is he, Angie? Tell me that much.'

She shook her head and took a few quick steps down the tow-path. The wind was rising. I saw her put her head down against it and gather her hair with one hand.

'I have tasted your absence,' I called to her retreating back. 'And it is bitter.'

She stopped and faced me slowly.

'What is that?' I said, coming up to her. 'A saying of his? One of those pet phrases people use?'

'Just go away, Michael.'

I took the drawing out of my pocket and held it up for her to see. Her mouth opened a little.

'Why did he send this to Caitlin?' I asked.

She stood speechless for some seconds, her eyes moving from my face to the drawing and back again. It was the first time I had seen her look helpless.

'Angie, I'm not blaming you for any of this. For anything that happened. I just need to know. Who is Barney Carrick? Your hus-band? Your ex-husband?'

'He's my brother,' she said quietly. 'Barney Carrick's my brother.'

'And this?' I held the drawing up again. 'What does it mean?'

'You know what it means,' she said.

'OK.' I folded the paper and put it back in my inside pocket. 'OK.'

At once her spirit returned. 'It's no good, Michael. I can't help you any more. You have to go now.'

'You expect me to turn around and go home, as if nothing's happened?'

'It's best you do.'

'I can't leave this alone, Angie. You know that.'

She bit her lip, undecided. Suddenly she gestured down the towpath with one outflung arm. 'My Uncle Stanley's down there somewhere,' she cried, as if her uncle's absence were my fault.

'So we'll go and find him. And then we'll talk.'

'No, Michael,' she said. 'Don't you understand? I can't have anything to do with you.'

'I'll go to the police right now if you won't help me.'

'Do it then. Do what you have to do, but leave me be.'

She turned and hurried away along the canal bank. I knew she heard me start after her but she kept her head down and did not look back. The towpath led along the backs of tiny gardens choked with bricks and nettles. A barge lay half-submerged, its rusting iron shell slumped in the mud. A cold wind slung a few drops of rain into my face. The canal lay milky with reflected sky. Up ahead a bridge blocked the view down the towpath. I followed her under it, and as I emerged on the other side I saw the old man. He was sitting on a stack of railway sleepers at the water's edge, puffing on a pipe. He wore an old ginger coat and a greasy flat cap. He was tall and spare and had white hair and a white moustache stained with nicotine. I noticed that he had no socks on under his shoes and his bare ankles were knobbly and bluish.

'You old rascal,' she said, going to him. 'I was worried about you.'

'Was yer, lass?' He looked at her with wide blue eyes.

She sat down next to him. She hooked her arm through his and squeezed with some desperation and turned her face into the cloth of his coat as if she could blot out my existence if only she could not see me. I stood back awkwardly.

'You'll get yourself lost, you old devil, you.'

He gazed across at the clutter of derelict workshops on the far side of the canal. 'Been coming here for near seventy years, lass. Ought to know me way by now.' He looked past her dark head and surveyed me as I stood there in the rain. I had the impression his flat blue stare missed very little. He knocked his pipe out against the sleeper he sat on and pointed the stem at me as if I were a horse in a market. 'Who's your gentleman friend?'

'I didn't come to cause any problems.' I said, and could hear at once how melodramatic that sounded.

'Oh, aye?' He inspected me with new interest. 'So what did you come for? Sightseeing?'

'I've come to give you a lift home,' I said. It felt like inspiration.

'You've come from the Big Smoke?' he said, cocking his head at my accent.

'Yes.'

'Well, that's grand, that is. Come all the way from London just to give a broken-winded old bugger like me a lift.'

'I did have other reasons.'

'Fancy,' he said.

I could feel his eyes on me.

Angie stood up. 'We should be going back now, Uncle Stanley.' She pulled the lapels of her jacket together. The rain was falling steadily now, gusted by the wind, and the drops lay shining in her dark hair. She still would not look at me.

'You'll not melt,' Uncle Stanley told her. 'Not unless you're con-stroocted entirely of salt, like Lot's wife.'

Uncle Stanley, I guessed, was not a man who could be easily hurried.

He pointed at the canal. 'It's the frogs,' he announced. 'That's what I come here for, mostly.'

I followed the line of his outstretched arm. The rain stippled the water like pewter. The wheels of a sunken Tesco trolley stuck out above the surface. Its mesh had trapped waterlogged litter – chunks of polystyrene, plastic bottles, beer cans and food containers. 'Factories come and go,' he was saying. 'The screw works and the wire-drawing shop and the drop forge. But frogs? Frogs come back every year, just like nothing's happened. This canal were built in 1798. Did you know that? D'you think there's frogs in here 200 years old? That'd be long in the tooth for a frog.' He thought about it. 'If they had teeth, that is.' He looked at his pipe, as if surprised to find it in his hand, and put it away in his pocket. 'But mebbe I'm getting confused again.'

Angie reached down and took his arm. 'Come on, Uncle Stanley. Let's go home now. We shouldn't be out at this time. It's not safe down here any more.'

She helped him to his feet, and we walked at the pace of his slow shuffle for ten yards or so back the way we had come. Then the old man stopped and looked back at the stagnant water and the crumbling buildings beyond, where he must have worked for half a century or more.

'They manage things better in Peru,' he said, shaking his head.

'Peru?' Angie was impatient, but she humoured him. 'How do they manage things in Peru, Uncle Stanley?'

'I don't know, lass. But I bet they manage them a fooking sight better than here.'

I let them move on and then I followed a few paces behind along the darkening towpath and through the gap in the corrugated iron and up the street. When we came close to the car I walked ahead and unlocked it and opened the back door and stood in their way. Angie stepped up close to me.

'Why won't you listen, Michael?' she hissed. 'We don't want you here. We don't want any help from you.'

'You can walk if you want, lass,' Uncle Stanley said, and before she could stop him he slid into the back seat. 'But it's a fair hike back to Hukum's.'

'Is that where we're going?'

'Aye. That's where I stop. Hukum's.' He pronounced it with a long vowel: *who-comes*.

I helped him buckle himself in. I caught Angie watching me as I did this, but by the time I got behind the wheel she was already in

the front passenger seat, curled hard up against the door, her face
turned away. I put the car into gear.

'Nice wagon,' Uncle Stanley remarked in the tense silence as we
moved off. I could feel him bouncing a little on the upholstery. 'A
Super Snipe, is it?'

'A what?' I looked at the old man in the mirror. He was caress-
ing the leather. He seemed to be enjoying himself.

'A Super Snipe. Monty had a Super Snipe in Tobruk.'

'Now Uncle Stanley,' Angie said wearily, 'just don't start.'

'Lovely set of wheels, the Super Snipe,' Uncle Stanley
mused.

'It's not a Super Snipe,' I said.

'Monty's one were done all in camouflage paint,' Uncle Stanley
went on after a moment. 'His Super Snipe, that is. Looked right
gradely in camouflage paint, it did.'

'It's not a Super Snipe,' I said more loudly.

'No?' Once again the innocent stare in the mirror.

'No. It's an Audi.'

'Oh?' Uncle Stanley looked around him with renewed interest.
'A Yankee job, then?'

I pulled up outside the restaurant. The windows were lit and I
could see that the place was already filling up. Angie got out without
a word and opened the back door of the car and took the old man's
arm and hurried him inside. I tried to follow but on the threshold
she spun to face me.

'You stay away, Michael. I'm warning you, now. There'll be
trouble.'

She didn't wait for me to argue, but shoved open the door and
hustled Uncle Stanley between the tables and through a door which
led into the kitchens. I caught the door before it swung shut and
stepped inside. The restaurant was long and dark and smelled of
onions and hot spices. It was a shabby enough little place sporting
a takeaway counter and a clutter of tables with white cloths marked
with saffron stains, but the soft wall lights and the piped sitar music
made it welcoming after the bleak street.

It was half-full already and the atmosphere was noisy with languages I didn't understand. On the far side of the room Hukum, in his shiny lounge suit, was serving from a trolley stacked with small silver dishes. He glanced across at me and I could see the same mistrust in his face as before. I walked quickly across the room the way Angie had gone, but out of the corner of my eye I caught a movement from Hukum – a signal, perhaps – and a young Asian waiter blocked my path.

'She doesn't want to talk to you, my friend.' His accent was broad Yorkshire. He had a shaven head and a combative smile. 'Do you get the picture?'

I took another step and he placed the flat of his hand on my chest. He was a good deal shorter than I was but solidly built. I could feel his aggression through the palm of his hand, like electricity. I shouted over his head, 'Angie!' The room fell instantly silent. 'Angie, you've got to talk to me! You know you've got to.'

'No-one likes a sore loser, pal,' the waiter said, shoving me a little, 'so let's just keep it nice and friendly. OK?'

I walked forward into him so that he stumbled back against a table. I was surprised how easily he moved. There was a jingle of cutlery and a glass smashed and a woman squealed and there was some confused movement behind me.

I shouted again, 'Angie!'

I had almost reached the door she had gone through. There was a porthole window in it through which I could see a steamy kitchen and men in white aprons and caps glancing towards me, towards the noise. The waiter regained his balance and grabbed my arm and I shoved him again and there was scuffling and indignant shouting and someone else got hold of my jacket from behind. I stretched my hand towards the door but before I could touch it the porthole window darkened and the door banged open and the enormous bearded man I had seen earlier ducked through it and seized me by one shoulder and turned me round and pushed me hard down the length of the restaurant.

I cannoned into an unoccupied table and went down on my knees among the chairs and clattering china, wood splintering

under my weight. I could hear Hukum crying out in Urdu in a high
pitched voice, telling me to get out, maybe, or telling his people to
go easy. Before I could get to my feet I felt myself lifted from behind
like a sack and the front door opened before me and I was floating
effortlessly through it. I hit the side of the Audi hard enough to
knock all the wind out of me and I slid down it and skidded onto
the wet pavement and huddled there for a moment, gasping like a
fish. The giant stood in the doorway with his arms crossed and his
face expressionless. Faces crowded at the restaurant window.

I sat up against the car. The breath whistled in my throat. The
young waiter ducked under the big man's arm and came out onto
the street and stood in front of me. Before I could gather the
strength to move he kicked me in the ribs, not too hard, almost
experimentally.

'Warned you, pal. You wouldn't listen.'

He kicked me again, harder this time, so that I toppled over side-
ways and lay flat on the cold paving stones, wondering detachedly
how hard the next kick would be and where it would fall.

A clatter of footsteps and I heard Hukum's voice again,
berating the waiter. I dragged down half a breath. The waiter
and Hukum were arguing, Hukum furious, the waiter surly and
resentful. I drew down another breath. I felt vague and distant.
In my line of sight I could see their feet now, the waiter's thick-
soled boots, Hukum's worn black lace-ups, and in the doorway
the bearded giant's blue plastic sandals encasing huge feet with
horny nails. There were pieces of glitter in the plastic sandals
and they seemed remarkably beautiful to me. A pair of trainers
appeared on the step, and they came lightly down into the street,
and the argument stopped. The trainers came to rest in front of
me.

'Are you all bloody mad?' Angie demanded. 'Just what do you
think you're doing?'

'The fellow was causing a disturbance.' Hukum said. 'This is
undeniable.'

'So you beat him up?'

'I regret the violence,' Hukum conceded with majesty, 'but I do not think the troublemaker is gravely injured.'

'Get inside, the lot of you!' she commanded.

Hukum said, 'Angela, I do not recommend –'

'I don't think he's much of a danger to anyone any more, do you?'

'Very well,' Hukum said huffily, 'but Big Iqbal will stay.'

Hukum and the young waiter stalked back into the restaurant, still muttering at one another. I pushed myself into a sitting position against the car, at last able to breathe almost normally. Big Iqbal stood like a cigar store Indian in the doorway, his arms still folded, staring out into the middle distance.

'I told you to leave me alone, Michael. I warned you.' Angie hunkered down in front of me. Her voice changed. 'Are you all right?'

I could not answer at once. I felt childish and humiliated.

'Do you need a doctor?'

I found my voice at last. 'I am a bloody doctor. What I need is for you to talk to me.'

'Don't you ever give up?'

'Would you?'

I started to haul myself upright against the side of the car. One of my ribs hurt a bit but I could tell, a little to my surprise, that nothing much was wrong. She took my arm and helped me stand. Perhaps this small gesture reminded her of the last time we had seen one another, when the roles were reversed, and that was what decided her. She let go of my arm and stood back a step.

'We can't talk here. Can you drive?'

'Yes.' I dusted myself down and tried to gather some dignity around me. I walked around the car and got behind the wheel. She slid into the passenger seat beside me. I said, 'Where to?'

She clacked her seatbelt into place. 'Down to the corner and turn right. We'll go to my place. It's quiet there.'

I drove as she directed me. The familiar actions of driving calmed me and following her directions I drove out of the estate and down a main road and then onto a straight ruler of motorway lit like an airport runway. The green-and-white signs told me Leeds was six miles away. I realised the butts of my hands were grazed where I had hit the pavement. I had not noticed this before, but now they stuck to the wheel and stung me when I moved them. I took my hands off the wheel one at a time and flexed them and cooled them and she noticed me do it but did not comment.

'How did you find me?'

'Your brother left this address at the community centre.'

'Silly bastard.' She stared out of the window at the night. 'We both used to come to Hukum's when we were small. It would be Barney's little joke to say he lived here.' She flipped open the arm-rest compartment and sorted through my CDs and selected one and held it up. 'This any good?'

I glanced across. 'That's Vivaldi.'

'I can read,' she said. 'Is it any good?'

'Sure.'

She slid the CD into the player and settled back with her eyes closed as the intricate music swelled through the car. I glanced across at her and saw that the motorway lights were riding the strong planes of her face. I drove on in silence. But after a moment I glanced again, and this time her eyes opened.

'Left here and under the bridge,' she said. 'Follow the signs towards the city and I'll tell you.'

She directed me onto the Leeds ring road and then off at a roundabout and through a maze of suburban roads. We pulled up finally in a steep street in Kirkstall, lined with tall and handsome old houses which had the raw look of places recently renovated. We climbed a flight of stone steps between shrubs. A security light sprang on and the branches became black claws against the glare. The hallway was bright with neon and an alarm monitor blinked in the corner. I followed her up four flights of carpeted stairs and she opened the door and ushered me in and through to the main room. It was a pleasant roof-space conversion, open plan and airy, with big windows at the back which looked down on a black void of parkland and on the lights of the city beyond, trembling in the cold air.

A desk stood under a skylight with a computer and a white adjustable lamp on it and a collection of Open University CDs and workbooks on a shelf above. A packed bookcase covered one entire wall of the room and more books were stacked on the floor. A mini-stereo system sat in a blond wood unit and four speakers were mounted high up in the corners of the room. There was a single armchair under a chrome standard lamp and papers were piled beside it, documents marked with coloured highlighter, files of newspaper clippings, letters bearing official crests.

She spoke carelessly over her shoulder. 'It's a mess. I don't have visitors.'

A thick report of some kind lay on the floor at my feet near the chair. I stirred it with my toe as she dumped her bag, keeping her back to me. I couldn't see what was printed on the cover without bending down and picking it up, and I did not want to seem that curious. But I was curious all the same. Perhaps she heard the rustle of the document as I moved it.

'I work in housing.' She stepped across and stood in front of me. 'Not that you'd know, looking at the tip this place is in. Still, the cobbler's kids are never shod, eh?'

'I thought you worked at the restaurant.'

'At The Mutiny? Hardly. Uncle Stanley has a room there, that's all. Hukum's an old friend.' She took both my wrists in her hands and turned my grazed palms up and inspected them. 'Big Iqbal's protective about me. I didn't know he was going to get physical.' She jerked her head down the hallway. 'Bathroom's through there. Go wash and I'll find something.'

I did as I was told, standing at the little sink and picking out road grit and scrubbing at the grazes so that they stung. After a moment or two she came in after me and in a businesslike fashion took each of my hands in turn and dried them and spread some antiseptic cream on them. The act brought her bowed head close to my face.

'They're better left uncovered,' she said.

'Yes. I know.'

'You can do it your bloody self, Doctor, if you'd rather.' But she went back to her task, and I was glad that she did.

At length she straightened and flicked back her hair.

I said, 'Thanks.'

She did not immediately release my hands: instead she stood there, holding them, as if the touch brought her close to saying something more. But the moment passed. She said, 'I'll put some coffee on,' and walked out of the bathroom.

After a moment I followed her. I could hear her filling the coffee percolator in the kitchen. I looked idly through the books on her shelf. Some heavy textbooks on gender, globalisation, sociology and a triple rack of CDs. I counted three Vivaldi collections and four Mozarts, including the Clarinet Concerto. I caught myself smiling. She came back into the room.

I said, 'Housing? You're an estate agent or something?'

She poured the coffee. 'I work for the Leeds Development Agency. Or at least, I report to them.'

'Doing what?'

'I'm in the Mason Park Regeneration Project. We're supposed to be turning the estate around. It's a police no-go area and you pretty well need a visa to get in there if you're not a resident. So it shouldn't take more than a century to make it fit for humans again. You know what they call it in the Agency? The Toilet Bowl. Now, there's a challenge for you.'

'You're on the team?'

'I'm team leader.'

I could see she was pleased to have surprised me.

'It's not exactly Microsoft, Michael. Still, it's more than you expected of a gobby northern scrubber. Yes?'

She nodded at the armchair and placed the coffee on a table next to it. I sat. She jerked her thumb at the window, back towards the decaying estate we had left. 'We grew up back there in Mason Park, me and Barney. But even though he left, I'm the one that got away. More or less.'

I picked up my cup. It had hand-painted flowers on it in bright colours. I had not expected this. Coffee in a pretty mug. The clean sounds and smells of domesticity. The bright busy room. Nothing about Angie Carrick was what I had expected. She set her mug on the tiled hearth and knelt on the rug and tucked her legs under her and held her long hair back while she lit the gas fire. It ignited with a soft plop and touched one side of her face with magenta light. She held her mug between her palms and looked up at me over the rim of the cup.

'Your call,' she said.

'I think Caitlin and your brother were lovers.'

'I think so too,' she said. 'I expect that hurts you. I'm sorry.'

'You know I've got to go to the police with that.'

'Michael, having sex with another man's wife isn't yet against the law.'

'Murder is.'

'Is that really what you've talked yourself into?' She shook her head. 'Just because he sent her a little drawing, with a silly quotation on the back? That means he killed her, does it?'

'Not just that.'

'What else?'

'She was pregnant. Not by me.'

Angie opened her mouth and closed it again. 'Oh,' she said. 'I didn't know.'

'I didn't know either. But I found out. And a couple of days later, you turn up at my place with a lot of questions and some half-arsed story about being a friend of hers.'

'I didn't like to lie about that. I hate to lie. I just had to –'

'And then I find that Caitlin and your brother were…connected. That they knew one another at some community centre she never told me about. That he sent her drawings and messages. That it had been going on for maybe two years.'

'But this doesn't prove anything. Not even London coppers bang people up for murder on evidence like that.'

'They'll want to know where to find your brother. So do I.'

'And you thought you'd find him tonight? And just what were you going to do then? Make a citizen's arrest? I wouldn't advise trying that.' She put down her mug. 'Anyway, I don't know where Barney is right now.'

'You must know.'

'I don't. He works overseas a lot.' She saw my puzzlement. 'He's a soldier. Kind of. A soldier of fortune, he calls himself.'

'He's a mercenary?'

'He doesn't use that word.'

'I'll bet.'

'You think he's some ignorant thug, don't you?' she flashed out. 'Some retard who can't even read and write. But Barney's nothing like that. He was a decorated soldier, medals for bravery. He was in the Paras for six years, in Kosovo and Afghanistan and Iraq. He was a sergeant.'

I could not quite come to grips with her defiance. I felt as I had on my doorstep that first night, when she had pushed past me into my own home. I was unused to resistance and did not know how to deal with it.

'Angie, it would be better for everyone if you took this to the police yourself. Tell them whatever you know. Your brother's in trouble.'

'If he is,' she said, 'don't expect me to drop him in any more of it.'

'Then I'll have to.'

'So go ahead,' she snapped, losing patience, 'if you're so bloody sure it adds up. But I'll tell you this for nothing – it'll need more than a bunch of London bobbies to find Barney. He's trained. Very bloody well trained. There's only one person who can get to him, and that's me. And then only if he lets me.'

'If he's not guilty of anything why would he hide?'

'Because people like you think the way you think,' she said, 'and people like him have no other choice.'

She did not move as I got to my feet, but stayed curled in front of the fire, glaring fiercely up at me. She was framed by shadow like a woman in an oil painting, the light from the gas fire red along the line of her jaw and shining in a rose sash where her jacket had fallen open over her shirt.

I said, 'I loved her. Caitlin. I need to know. I need to understand.'

The fierceness faded out of her eyes. 'I didn't know about any child, Michael. But I do know that he loved her too. Really loved her. It wasn't like you think. I don't know whether that makes it better or worse.'

'How could you know what it was like between them?'

'Because I know Barney. Nobody else does. Nobody in this world.' She stood up to face me. 'I don't have the answers you want, Michael. But I do know he'd never have hurt her, I promise you that. And if she was carrying his child? Hurting her is the very last thing he would have done.'

I made a dismissive noise and she stepped close to me, into my space.

'He had this thing for women, this protective thing. It came from the way we grew up, him and me.' She could see I did not believe her. 'You wouldn't understand. It's not your fault, but you wouldn't understand, with all you've had in life.'

I wanted to leave then. I could have brushed her aside, but I could not bring myself to do it, and in my moment of hesitation an idea seemed to come to her. She said, 'Wait,' and crossed the room and went into the bedroom and came back with a photograph and held it out to me. 'That's him. That's Barney. It was taken a while back, but that's him.'

The picture showed a tall young man of nineteen or twenty with an open, laughing face. Perhaps she guessed the effect the photo would have on me, because, before I could control the thought, it leapt into my head that I would like him, that he would be competent, intelligent, humorous, somebody I would want to have on my team. And something else, something she could not have guessed. He was in jeans and a blue denim shirt, leaning back against the wing of a four-wheel-drive, with some exotic building in the background, a mosque, perhaps. There were hard black shadows in the dust at his feet. The picture looked remarkably like the one of my father which had stood on Anthony's table – the sun-creases, the louche pose, the whole attitude of self-containment.

It derailed me for a moment. The face in the photograph should not have been attractive, open, confident. Just as this room should not have been so bright and busy. The picture should not have looked like my father's picture. I turned it in my hands, and as I did so my fingers brushed a sheaf of four or five prints wedged into the back of the frame. I glanced down at flashes of burnished sky and groups of men in khaki. I gave her back the photo and as she turned away I slipped the spare prints into my jacket pocket.

'He's a good man,' she said, still gazing at the picture. 'Barney's not a saint, but he's a good man.'

'Things happen to people, Angie. I've seen some of the results. People who might have been ordinary, even decent people. Something snaps, and before they know it they've hurt someone.'

'Not Barney.'

'Something triggers them. I don't know what.'

'Not Barney, Michael. I'm telling you.'

'I'm not a psychiatrist. I'm going to let the police sort it out. We should both do that.'

I walked past her across the room.

'You've condemned him,' she said to my back, following me. 'You don't know him. You don't know anything about him. But someone broke into the castle and killed the pretty princess and now the prince wants blood money.'

I rounded on her as I reached the door. 'That's not the way it is.'

'Oh, yes. Some poor peasant's got to swing for it. And when it comes down to it, it doesn't much matter which peasant you pick. Isn't that right?'

I could not get the picture of her brother's face out of my mind – smiling, hopeful, spit-in-your-eye. I could feel the photos rustle in my pocket. I thought: no wonder she loves him, loves the colour and the vitality of his life, his happy-go-lucky good looks, his confidence. Growing up where they did. No wonder she loves him so. I met her eyes. They were clear and dark. She was as tense and poised as a panther. I reached past her and opened the door and stepped out onto the landing. As I turned to close the door behind me I could see her framed there, her face lifted and her eyes bright. I felt sorry for her, forced to defend her rotten handsome brother. It was the first time I had felt pity for Angie. And perhaps she read this in my face, for at that moment her shoulders went back and her eyes hardened.

'Damsels in distress turn you on, do they, Michael?' she said. 'Well, fuck off and look somewhere else for one.'

CHAPTER SIXTEEN

My ribs hurt and I knew I should probably find a hotel for the night, but I felt jagged and wakeful. I drove back to London with sleet slicing into the headlights.

Back at the flat I found the remains of Stella's food in the fridge – some ham and cheese and a stale roll – and I ate this standing by the kitchen window. The wind was rising, a hard wind which slung ice like gravel across the glass. I poured a glass of white wine, carried it through to sit at the dining room table, and took the photographs from my pocket. It was very quiet in the house, and the wind outside made it seem quieter still.

The light over the table made garish the colours of the prints. There were seven of them, six shots of men in uniform and one odd one, which looked like a poor quality holiday snap of Angie and Barney Carrick together. I put that one aside. The other six had evidently been taken in two different countries, or at least at two different seasons. In four of the shots the soldiers were dressed in green camouflage anoraks and were standing in some forested place. They held their rifles in the crooks of their arms, and stood around an army truck parked in a muddy clearing with a backdrop of pine trees and farm buildings.

The other two photos had been taken on a sun-blasted plain under a sky of startling blue. The men threw indigo shadows on the stony ground. Their camouflage clothing was sand-coloured and the sun struck off the angles of a tank which squatted in the background like a steel ziggurat. Even in the photograph the metal of its armour looked painfully hot.

Barney Carrick was easy to spot in all six pictures. Dark-haired, smiling from a lean brown face, his weapon cradled comfortably in his arms. In every shot his eyes were directly on the camera: the other men were caught glancing at the lens, or grimacing at it, or pretending to ignore it. But Carrick looked right down the barrel of the camera every time, as handsome and defiant as his sister.

It disturbed me to think of Angie standing at her door, her shoulders squared and challenge in her eyes. It was an image that wouldn't quite leave me alone. I was sorry I had sneaked the photos away from her like some pickpocket, but I could not deny it made me feel good to have them. I wasn't about to fool myself I was getting ahead of the game, but holding these pictures at least made it seem that the game had stopped getting away from me.

I put the prints back on the table and moved them around like solitaire cards. Barney Carrick stood smiling out at me from this wild and vibrant place, wherever it was. The hard sunlight caught on his teeth, on the barrel of his rifle. I sat and stared at the pattern of light and colour for a very long time. Eventually I took out my wallet and found the photo of Caitlin that I carried there and I set it down among the pictures of Carrick. Sleet lashed across the window.

Spray drove into my face and I was half-blinded by it and deafened by the squall. I used the camera one-handed because my other hand was clutching the wheel of Ben Friedman's boat. The wheel was twisting in my grip like a living thing and I really needed both hands to control it. It was only mid-afternoon but the bronze light was already so low that the camera flashed automatically as I pressed the shutter. The unexpected glare dazzled in Caitlin's eyes and sparkled on the spray and rainwater as it ran off her clothing.

I thought it was a waste of time taking a picture, and perhaps that was why it turned out to be such a fine shot. Her blonde hair was blowing everywhere and she was laughing with delight – actually laughing aloud, like a child. She hung with her hands hooked through the forestays, crucified there, swinging with the wild motion of the boat.

Behind her I could see the bow butting grey ridges of swell, while the horizon canted and plunged.

'Is this incredible?' She was shouting at me. We were only six feet apart but the wind snatched at her words. 'Or is it fucking *incredible?*'

'You better get down off there, Cate!'

But she threw her head back and let the saltwater stream over her face as she laughed again.

I didn't feel like laughing. I was wet and cold and a little worried. I didn't know Ben Friedman well – a heart surgeon at Bart's – but he had repeated his invitation to go sailing with him so many times that it would have been rude to refuse again. I wished now we had accepted in the summer. It was October, bleak and windy, and Ben turned out to be a fanatic of the worst kind. He was not very experienced, and his boat was not very large and not very well-equipped. Once clear of the shore the sea was so high and the rain drove down so hard that we quickly lost sight of land altogether.

I didn't much care for sailing at the best of times. I had assumed Caitlin would hate it, especially in this weather, in this boat. But she didn't hate it. She swung there, shouting with the thrill of it as the wind and the spray whipped her and the boat yawed and bucked.

Ben Friedman sat crestfallen at dinner that night in the yacht club, guilty about his misjudgement. I didn't feel merciful. I could still see too clearly the grey seas lurching all around us, and I could still hear the engine's impotent putter over the blast of the gale as we crabbed towards the jetty at last. But Caitlin was not angry with Ben. She was impatient with me.

'God, Michael, don't be such an old fogey! That was the most fun I've had in years.'

'Great,' I said.

'We weren't in any danger,' Caitlin waved her glass. 'Well, not much, anyway. Just enough to make it interesting. Do you think I've never been in a boat before?'

'Never one that small.'

'They're all small compared to the deep blue sea,' she said airily. 'Even the Titanic.'

I could not help noticing that she was glowing, and that she was drinking a little more than usual, talking a little more loudly.

She said, 'Loosen up, Michael. Life should be a bit risky.' She leaned across the table and gave me a look which I could not interpret. 'Yours is. Don't you think mine should be?'

We got back to the pub after midnight. There was a rowdy late night crowd in the public bar, but we came in through the saloon, which was empty and dim, with the bar shutters down and the chairs stacked on the tables. It was an old coaching inn with narrow passages and odd corners and I could not find the light switch and I had to grope my way along the wall towards the stairwell door, edging round the shrouded billiard table.

'This is like sneaking back into the dormitory after lights out,' Caitlin whispered. 'You feel kind of illicit.'

She giggled and pulled herself close to me in the darkness. She was breathing fast. I could smell the wine on her breath and feel her excitement through her touch. It took me a moment in the dark to find the door to the stairs. I reached it finally and pushed it open for her and as she edged past me she suddenly clutched me and kissed me hungrily, kissed me so hard that I heard our teeth click together.

The small mewing sounds she made in her throat seemed to echo in my own head. I put one arm under her buttocks and half-carried her up to the room. I had time only to kick the door closed behind us before we were in the big bed with its cool-damp seaside sheets and she was drawing me inside her and the whole length of her belly was thrusting up against mine. She hooked her hands in my hair and her long legs locked over the small of my back and her body gave a convulsive sob and gripped me hard, and her eyes sprang open and she gave a single desolate cry and we spun away from the world, holding on to one another as we fell.

Outside, I could hear the sea booming and dragging at the pebbles and the tinkling of steel halyards on the yachts in the marina.

I said, 'I thought that was going to happen on the billiard table.'

'It would have, if you'd taken any longer to find the way up here.'

I could hear from her voice that she was smiling. I was a little awed by the intensity of her need. She nuzzled my neck.

'You're very straight, sweetheart,' she said, and laughed gently. 'I like you just the way you are. But you *are* very straight.'

'We can make love on billiard tables whenever you like.' I was a little hurt.

'Oh, yes, right.' She kissed me. 'Tell me, Michael. Do you ever get the urge to do anything really dangerous, really wild? Something that scares you half to death?'

'I've just got back from bloody Somalia. That'll do me for this week.'

'Oh, I know you're the big hero at work,' she touched my face in the dark with her forefinger. 'Everyone knows that. But you can do that precisely because it *doesn't* scare you.'

'Cate, I'm terrified the whole time. I'm a professional coward. A devout coward. Trust me.'

'I bet I could make a list of things that would scare you a lot more than Somalia.'

'Try me.'

'Well, let's see. Learning to salsa?'

'Ah.'

'Or giving the keynote speech at the local comprehensive.'

'Hey. Dirty play.'

'Or me getting pregnant.'

The room wobbled and jumped back into focus again. I said, 'Are you?'

'No.'

I sat up a little and gathered her head in the crook of my arm. 'Our little adventure on the high seas churn you up a bit?'

'I guess it did.' Her voice had grown small in the darkness and lost its mockery. Outside the wind gusted and kicked a beer can clattering down the street.

'Have you been thinking about this a lot?' I asked.

'Not a lot. It just hits me sometimes. When you're away, mostly. It frightens me a bit, too.'

I rocked her against me, my mind spinning.

'I know how you feel, Michael,' she said. 'And I know what we agreed at the start. I'll not try to pretend otherwise.'

'But?'

'But I think we should make the space in our lives to talk about this. Go away somewhere. Just for a break. Italy, maybe. We haven't had any time away in years.'

I said, half to myself, 'You'll be thirty-three next week.'

She rolled her head to look at me in the dark. 'Oh, that's the explanation, is it? My biological clock.' She was suddenly waspish. 'Well, that's convenient. There's no reasoning with a bunch of hysterical hormones.'

'I didn't mean it that way.'

'You should have been a gynaecologist, Michael. You're a natural.'

I lay in the dark for some moments, unsure of myself, trying to decide upon the safest thing to say. But before I could speak Caitlin leaned across and lifted the bronze key which hung on its chain around my neck.

'Are you ever going to tell me what this is really about?' The hostility had left her voice as suddenly as it had come. She caressed the key. I caught the gleam of its polished metal in the dark and also the gleam of her eyes.

'It's my talisman,' I said. 'You know all about that. It brings me luck.'

'Good luck?' she said.

'So far.'

I could see her blonde hair shining in the shadows and I reached over and stroked it. I loved to feel the warm curve of her skull in the palm of my hand. She arched against my touch like a cat.

'I'm not so sure about that,' she said. 'I'm not so sure it's been good luck for you. Or for us.'

I stopped stroking her hair. I dreaded her saying anything more. I sensed she was on the point of breaking some taboo, as if a dangerous spell were about to be uttered and the very form of words would bring disaster. I did not know where this dread came from. Or perhaps I did know, but I did not dare articulate it, nor even let the memory form in my mind.

She said softly, 'Talk to me, Michael.'

'What about?' My voice was hoarse.

She tugged at the key. 'Talk to me, Michael. Don't get angry. Just talk to me.'

'But I don't know what you want me to say.'

'I want to know what hurts you.'

'Why?'

'So I can help stop it hurting.'

'It doesn't hurt, Cate. Not any more.'

'We're together,' she said. 'We've been together for six years. We're married. We're an item, as they say. Aren't we?'

'Of course we are.'

'Not two items.'

I ran my finger down the notches of her spine. 'That doesn't mean we can't keep back some things. Bad things.'

'Those are just the ones we shouldn't keep back.'

'Can we drop this?' I realised I was breathing rapidly. I wondered if she could feel it; of course she could feel it.

'I'm not a child, Michael, who can't carry the heavy weights.' She pushed herself up on her elbows. 'And this isn't some kind of a territorial treaty we've entered into. You can't set boundaries just where you feel like it.'

'It all happened a long time ago, Cate. It's over.'

'Over? It's what drives you. Every day. I don't know how, but it drives you. That means it drives us. And you're saying it's over? You're saying it's none of my business?' Her cool hair swept across my chest.

'How will it help to talk about it?'

'Because I think the two things are connected.'

'What two things?'

'This,' she lifted the key again so that I could see it shining in the half-light, and then guided my hand down and placed it low on her belly. 'And this.'

My mouth was dry. 'How could that be?'

'I think maybe if we could face one fear, then some others wouldn't be so terrible for us.'

A drop of sweat rolled down the side of my neck and it must have trickled against her arm, and perhaps she took pity on me at this, for she sighed and she rested her head against my chest.

'Michael, we love one another. And part of that means that I don't want us ever to fool ourselves that life is unchangeable. Safe. Under control. Because it isn't like that.'

I sensed that the exchange was over. I was relieved that it was, and gradually I felt calm settle on me again. It seemed ironic that she should be saying this to me. After all, I was the one who knew only too well the fragility of things, the randomness of disaster. Wasn't I? But though I could still hear her words in my head my rational mind was already working to convince myself that this was code, Caitlin-speak. That she meant merely I had been away too much, and had been inattentive and preoccupied when I came back. That was all true enough. And it was more easily mended than the other thing. Yes, I preferred to believe that. I stroked the inside of her thigh with the backs of my fingers.

She cried out in the dark in a strange voice as I did so, a plea or even a protest. It was almost as if she did not want my touch at this moment, as if she knew a chance was passing that might never be recaptured. But then I felt the nerves flutter under her skin and heard her draw in a small sharp breath, and her head rolled back and I felt her stir and clench. The inn sign groaned like a gibbet in the night wind and halyards tinkled above the black water.

I stretched back in my chair until my spine clicked. The photographs lay like icons against the dark wood. Catey laughed out at me from the past with her wet face shining with spray and with joy and the horizon was lumpy and tilted behind her. I had got it all wrong that night, of course. She wasn't putting on a brave face: she simply was brave. The lovemaking was passionate because she was passionate. I might be the beneficiary, but it wasn't for my benefit.

All at once I was dog tired, weary to my bones. I put Caitlin's picture back into my wallet and the other photos in an envelope. As I did so I noticed the holiday snap of Angie Carrick and her brother. I had almost forgotten about this one, but now I moved it under the light. I saw that the edges of the print were softened with handling and I realised that it was not, as I had thought, merely a spare photo, but a picture Angie had treasured, as I treasured my photo of Caitlin, a picture she took often from its hidden place to gaze at. I held it up, looked closely at it.

Angie was younger in the photo, perhaps twenty, and her brother a couple of years younger still. They were squeezed together on a park bench. He was in uniform and he looked stiff and self-conscious, as if he had not long been wearing it. I was puzzled by his awkwardness until I saw that she was laughing at the camera and perhaps at him. I guessed he had come to her to show off after leaping some important hurdle: getting through basic training or winning his wings – whatever they did in the Paras. Her long hair was loose around her lifted face and her eyes were bold and black. Brother and sister looked very much alike in the picture: fierce, proud, young, intensely alive. And they looked more than simply alike. They looked united, joined. They might mock one another or themselves, but no-one else had better try it.

The photo troubled me. I could sense in the image of Barney Carrick's face a vulnerability I did not want to acknowledge. I did not want to think that Caitlin could have seen this. I did not want to admit the possibility of any depth in their relationship. And Angie's face in that photo unsettled me more still, and because I understood the root of this I became angry with her. I turned the picture face down and pushed it back into the envelope, but the petty denial of hiding her face made me still angrier with myself than I was with her.

CHAPTER SEVENTEEN

In the morning I called Barrett.

'Tell me all that again,' he said, 'slowly.'

I repeated it for him while he took notes. I said, 'There are photos too.'

'You have been busy,' he said, in a flat voice. 'You'd better come in. Give us a couple of hours and I'll see what I can dig up by the time you get here.'

Maureen Dickenson turned the envelope in her hands and shook the photographs onto her cluttered desktop. She spread them out in a fan and moved them around a little. Her silence began to make me uncomfortable. She took her glasses off and squeezed her eyes closed and opened them again. The pouchy lines of her face had set hard. She did not invite me to sit. I could feel an atmosphere building in the office, but I did not understand why. I had expected energy, excitement, even congratulation. Dickenson moved the photos some more. Carrick's crude crayon drawing lay on the desk beside them. She tapped it with her nail.

'You say he drew this?' The question was for me, but she did not meet my eyes.

'He's signed it.'

She puckered her mouth. 'And do you recognise this place he's drawn? Assuming it's not just make-believe?'

'It's real. I don't recognise the house, but there are half-a-dozen sketches of the same building among Caitlin's drawings.'

'And what do you make of that?'

'I'd say it was somewhere they'd been together. Somewhere special to them.'

She grunted.

Her scepticism puzzled me. I said, 'That's just my guess.'

Dickenson put her glasses back on and said: 'I don't go in for guesses, myself.'

I looked from her to Barrett and back. 'Is there a problem here?'

She said, 'So this is the man we have to find, is it? In your considered opinion?'

'Isn't it obvious? They were lovers. Caitlin was carrying his child, for God's sake.'

'We don't know that yet,' Barrett cut in from behind me. 'Maybe the child wasn't his.'

I swung on him, 'How many men do you think Caitlin was sleeping with? I mean, just approximately?'

'And even if he was the father,' Barrett went on, unperturbed, 'that wouldn't necessarily make him the killer. Would it?'

'Are we going to play games at a time like this?'

'Well, in a way we have to. And we find jumping to conclusions isn't the way to win them.'

'Just what did you think you were doing,' Maureen Dickenson demanded suddenly, startling me, 'pursuing this on your own, without informing us? Behaving like some sort of cowboy?'

'I wanted some answers. You weren't giving me any.'

'And you think it's your job to look for them?'

'I told you about Angie Carrick,' I said. 'I told you to check her out.'

'You didn't say nothing about a brother,' Barrett said levelly, 'or about signed drawings, or about some community centre where your missus worked with this bloke without telling you.'

'I didn't know.'

'You knew before you called me this morning. If you'd told us when you discovered all this, maybe we'd have got somewhere.'

I made an effort to rein in my anger, but I was losing the struggle. I said, 'I'm going abroad. Maybe for good. It would be something if

I could take with me just some ghost of a reason for why this fucking awful thing should have happened.'

'We don't schedule our investigations to fit in with your career moves.' Dickenson's voice was harsh. 'This is a murder enquiry.'

'Did you think I might have forgotten that?'

'Maybe you'd forgotten we're all supposed to be on the same team.' She took her glasses off again and tossed them onto the photographs. 'I gave you every chance to talk to me, Michael, about this or anything else. But instead you go freelancing on some quest of your own. You confront this woman, who might have been a witness. You get yourself knocked about.' She pointed at my scraped hands and I quickly hid them. 'I don't like it when people go freelancing. Freelancers are a bloody nuisance. They don't know what they're doing. They muddy the waters. They never get a scrap of evidence that's admissible and they stop us from getting it ourselves.'

'This is the man you need to find,' I thumped the photos with my closed fist. 'I know it. You know it. And we're having a demarcation dispute?' I was goaded to fury by her tone, by the injustice of it all, and by the gathering knowledge that she was, of course, right.

'Maybe we should all take a chill pill,' Barrett said brightly. 'What do you think?'

I stepped back from Dickenson's desk. She glared at me across it. Her colour was high. But then her expression changed. I suspected she did not often lose her temper and that she disliked herself for it. I felt the same way myself.

Barrett said, 'I've been onto the West Yorks force and Social Services. Why don't I fill you in on what we've got on this character?'

'Yes.' Maureen Dickenson busied herself moving papers about so that she did not have to look at us. 'Yes, Dig. Good idea.'

I said, 'Maybe I was out of line.'

'Fine.' She shuffled some more papers. 'So let's move on.'

Barrett sat down at the end of the desk and opened his file and found some heavy-rimmed glasses and put them on. 'Bernard John Carrick,' he read. 'Barney Carrick, as he's known, apparently. Born Bradford, father unknown. His mother was a gutter junkie and part-time hooker. She died six months back, age of forty-four. Carrick's only known surviving relative is the one sister, Angela Jayne, twenty-eight. She works for Bradford Council or some such.'

'Leeds Development Agency,' I said. 'She's a team leader.'

He glanced down at his notes, then back up at me. 'Quite right.' He lifted his eyebrows and turned a page. 'Well, we'll be speaking to her pretty soon. She's his half-sister, in point of fact. They had the same mother, different fathers. Barney Carrick is twenty-seven, by the way.'

Twenty-seven. For some reason I had not worked this out before, and now that I heard his age stated aloud it seemed impossibly young to me. He was nine years younger than Caitlin had been.

'He did six years in the Paras,' Barrett said, 'so the Army will have psychological profiles and so on. I already spoke to some Colonel. It seems our boy had a bit of a reputation. Made sergeant twice. Lost his stripes once after some trouble – assault – but got them back. I suppose the Paras like them a bit rough around the edges. Finally got himself into serious strife in Aghanistan. He killed a woman and a couple of kids in some cock-up, and it sounds like they gave him the boot after that. More or less.' Barrett pushed his glasses up his nose. 'He owns a flat in London, in Brixton, has had it for the past four or five years. Pays the mortgage regular. The last couple of years, since his discharge, he's been working from there as a security consultant. Hired heavy, in other words. There's no reply from his phone and no-one's home at his flat, though neighbours say that's not unusual.' He flicked the pages. 'Motorbike freak. Keeps a low profile. Long spells abroad.'

I thought of the self-conscious youth in the earliest of Angie's photographs, and of the lean, hard soldier in the later pictures. Father unknown. Mother a prostitute and a drug addict, dead at forty-four and probably looked eighty. Rubbish was what we had called them when I worked in A&E, no-hopers like Barney Carrick's mother. Rubbish, we said, when they came in for the tenth or twentieth time in a month, catatonic or raving, until finally, inevitably and to everyone's relief, they came in dead.

'He's got no form down here,' Barrett was saying, 'but the Yorkshire lads know a good deal about him. He's been in trouble since the age of eleven. Mostly minor drugs and public order, but then at fifteen he all but killed a bloke in a pub up in Liverpool. Very nasty. Fractured this character's skull with a bar stool. Apparently it took four bouncers to pull him off. He should've gone to a Young Offenders for a couple of years for that, don't know why he didn't. There's nothing much more until he went into the Army.' Barrett closed the folder and took his glasses off and laid them on the cover. 'Is that roughly what you expected, Dr Severin?'

'I don't know what I expected,' I said.

Barrett folded his glasses away. 'None of this proves anything, of course. But we'd have to admit it doesn't look good for our Mr Carrick. Not good at all.'

A little later Barrett walked me up the corridor towards the lifts. Maureen Dickenson stood at the door of her office watching us go. She still looked troubled by our earlier exchange.

When we were out of earshot Barrett muttered, 'You don't muck about, I'll give you that.' I had the impression the meeting had somehow amused him. 'But don't get ahead of yourself, eh?'

We walked on in silence.

After a while he said, conversationally, 'Going abroad again? Where to this time?'

'Maybe back to Venezuela. It's not definite.'

'Back to saving the world?'

'I suppose it's something like that.'

'On your jack?' He corrected himself. 'On your own?'

'No. Stella Cowan's been offered –'

'Oh, right,' he said quickly, as if anxious not to pry into some delicate matter.

I looked at him curiously, but he didn't pursue it.

We turned a corner in the corridor and he stopped in front of a door, his fist on the handle. 'This is the incident room. Want a quick look?'

Before I could answer he pushed the door open. It was not much bigger than a large sitting room, jammed with steel desks and cluttered with computers, phones, faxes. Cabling lay in tangles across the floor. Desktops overflowed with empty coffee cups and takeaway food cartons. There were only three people working in the room, two plainclothes men talking on the phone and a woman constable in uniform at a filing cabinet. All three glanced at me curiously. The woman nodded some sort of acknowledgment, then she realised who I was and I saw her look at Barrett in alarm.

'There'd be more warm bodies about, but everyone's out hitting the streets,' Barrett said. 'Fifteen full-timers on this right now. And then of course there's all the forensic, and people checking the phone records, and the house-to-house, and all the rest of it.'

He stopped beside a large whiteboard which covered most of one wall. Names and codes in coloured felt-tip were scrawled on it. Barrett tapped the whiteboard with his knuckle.

'Sarge?' the woman constable called anxiously.

Barrett ignored her. 'Now here,' he rapped the board again, 'these here are the names of the investigating officers.' He seemed keen to explain. 'And these little bits of gobbledegook underneath, that's the computer code for whatever lead they're following up. Dozens of them, see? We've had people out all over since it happened, door knocking, asking questions, poking around in dark corners. There'll be more of them out today, what with this new stuff you've turned up. That'll go on till we get this thing sorted. And it will get sorted. Trust me.'

'Sergeant?' the woman said again, the concern plain in her voice.

Beside the whiteboard, I realised now, an untidy display of photographs had been pinned to the wall. They were photographs of Caitlin. Caitlin as the medics had left her, sprawled on the landing among the blood and the litter, her clothes torn away and her breasts bare. Caitlin, blue on a steel tray somewhere.

'Don't let it go to your head,' Barrett said as I stared at the photos, 'you had one lucky strike. But the hard graft's done down here, by these poor sods at the coalface.'

He walked me back out into the corridor. I felt sick and dazed.

'I'm going to have a chat with your friend Angie Carrick,' Barrett told me, as if nothing had happened. 'Meanwhile we'll put the word out about her low-life brother. When I get anything, I'll drop around to the house and fill you in. That might be a few days.'

I turned to go, but he touched my arm.

'Just so's you don't think we spend all bleeding day sitting on our arses around here. OK?'

It was already growing dark by the time I got back to the house. Through the back window the winter garden lay bedraggled, with a carpet of dead wet leaves flattening the grass. The rose bush against the left-hand wall had blown loose and lay like a tangle of barbed wire. The garden had always been Caitlin's territory, but now I could not escape how forlorn it looked. In my mind I promised her that I would tidy it all up sometime soon.

Her portfolio lay on the table where I had left it after the funeral, as black and heavy as an old family bible. I hefted it up and carried it through into the study and slid out a sheaf of the drawings and propped the thick sheets of cartridge paper behind ornaments and books on the shelves where I could see them. I sat down on the far side of the room and looked at them, from one to the other. They were startling drawings, better for the small distance my new perspective gave me, bold shapes and aggressive tones. The blacks were so solid that the layered graphite shone.

Outside, clouds rode the rough winds above the rooftops and the last of the chrome light shifted over the wall and over the images propped there. Images of an unremarkable brick house tucked into a wrinkle of land with a rusting harrow out the front, and a cracked window, and tiles coming off the roof. But of course it was not unremarkable at all. Not for them. For them it was an enchanted place, and the life lived there was magical, charged. It excluded me utterly.

Caitlin skipped down the last couple of yards and tossed her back-pack into the fat grass and sat on the wall and poked her tongue out at me like a naughty child.

'We could always get into the van with the baggage and be done with it,' I suggested. 'Put a stop to all this walking nonsense.' I slung my pack beside hers and settled on the warm stone next to her.

'You can make a route march out of it if you want,' she said. 'I'm on holiday.'

It was a game we played, only half in jest. I acted the team leader, plotting the route, setting the pace. It was my job to know where we were going and when we had to be there. Caitlin, meanwhile, would make detours to look at pretty Umbrian farmhouses, or to feed grass to a donkey in a field, or just to follow some byway that attracted her. I would try to insist on walking the whole of the day's march. She would as likely flag down a passing tractor and hitch a ride. Caitlin was not really so reluctant to be led, nor I so very reluctant to be led astray, but there was truth enough in this little charade to keep it interesting.

Since breakfast the track had taken us for four or five miles over the stony hills, through vineyards and fields green with new corn. It was nearly noon and the sun was high and it was warm and the shade here was delicious. I tilted back my head and stretched the muscles in my shoulders. I could hear water running. At the bottom of the slope behind us a stream ran between polished boulders towards a stone bridge a hundred or so yards away. Beyond the bridge the road ran in a sandy ribbon up the valley between stands of cypress. There was no sign of traffic. It was hard even to believe in traffic. Some low tiled roofs shone between the trees and a dog's faint barking floated from the blue distance. The ruins of a mill lay tumbled on the far bank between us and the bridge. Quern stones were scattered in the shallows like a giant's counters.

Caitlin got up and stretched and stepped over the wall and walked down the slope through the soft grass and the wildflowers, trailing her pack by its straps. When I came up with her she was standing by the edge of the stream, one hand against the trunk of a myrtle which overhung the water. I could hear the clucking of the current. A red and yellow hornet droned over the sandy margin. It settled and drank and then, with some new purpose, angled away low and fast over the water.

Caitlin sat on a boulder and unlaced her boots and began to take them off. 'We could have a place like that,' she said, nodding at the jumbled blocks of the ruin across the stream.

'Oh, yes?' I took my boots off too. The temptation to bathe my feet in this clear water was irresistible. 'And what would we do with it?'

'Live in it, Michael.' She put a small emphasis on the verb. 'Together.'

'Right.'

She took off her socks and the leather pouch where she kept her passport and her money and placed it on a rock. 'It's a thought,' she said.

She pulled her shirt over her head and shook out her blonde hair. She unbuckled her belt and slid her jeans and her panties down over her hips and stepped out of them, unclipped her bra and faced me, smiling, backing into the shallow water, each foot feeling behind her as she went, a graceful, dipping ballet. She spread her arms, knowing she was lovely, the chill water tensing her muscles and her breasts, her hair shining. She lifted her face to the sun, laughed aloud, dancing back, and I stripped and followed her. The water had run down from the mountains and it was shockingly cold.

By the time I was halfway across she had found the deep pool against the mill wall and she let herself fall back into it and then bounced up again, gasping and throwing bright water in a dazzle around her. I went under and could think of nothing for a moment, the chill of it driving everything out of me except an impression of greenish shapes under the surface and an explosion of silver bubbles and a roaring in my ears. I broke surface and shook the water out of my hair.

She was six feet away, seated in a few inches of water on one of the flat quern stones, her knees drawn up and her arms locked around them. She twisted a strand of wet hair round her finger and looked at me like a siren tempting a mariner. I swam two strokes and rested with my elbows on the flat stone she sat on, my hands under her calves. I could feel the current swaying my body beneath the surface.

'Other people have them,' she said, and I knew at once she was no longer talking about farmhouses in Umbria. 'Even quite ordinary people make a success of it. Some of them actually enjoy it.'

'Do they, Cate? How do they manage that?'

'They choose simpler lives for themselves. Less pure lives, lives which aren't always driven by some higher purpose.'

My spirits fell. I knew we had come on this trip for this very discussion, but I didn't want to have it now. I felt ambushed.

She reached out and stroked my hair. 'Do you know how lost I feel, Michael? I feel as if I've taken a wrong turn in the forest and now I can't find my way back. I feel as if only you can find me, but you're not looking.'

'We'll sort it out, Cate. Don't worry.'

'I'm afraid,' she said, 'afraid. I'm afraid of a life without milestones, of one good time after another, but in between the good times, these great spaces of emptiness. And no pattern to it all, no point to it. You're afraid too, Michael, but you won't admit it. You're afraid of stopping.' She was still stroking my hair. 'You're afraid of failing, of being found out for being human. Afraid of not being able to change things.'

'That's quite a lot to be afraid of.'

'There's something else, something I don't know about. Maybe it's those poor kids you see, the sick ones, the starving ones. But I think it's even more than that.'

I put my hands on her waist and looked up into her face. 'What's changed, Catey? I thought we had it worked out, you and I.'

'I dream sometimes of a quiet place somewhere, a space in our lives, some peace.' She smiled to herself, as if at a memory. 'Of going back to the beginning.'

'The beginning?'

'It's something my mother used to say. It had some special meaning for her. I just mean we should take some time to get to know one another. Do you think we have ever really taken that time?'

'And a child,' I said. 'You dream of a child, too. Suddenly.'

She leaned forward and put her arms around me and pulled me against her cold breasts. 'I used to think,' she said, 'that we would just be repeating mistakes. That I wouldn't wish childhood on anyone. And then I came to see that exactly the opposite could be true. That this is our one chance to break the cycle.'

'All this is just taking me a while to get used to, Cate. That's all.'

'No,' she said sadly. 'That's not all.' She reached out for the key and held it up and showed it to me, accusing me with it. She dropped it back against my skin and slid into the water like a seal, with hardly a splash, coming to rest with her arms around my neck, looking up at me. 'An adventure, Michael. Our adventure. Of course it's an untravelled road. That's the point. Going somewhere unknown together. A new way ahead for us.'

'I can't work like that,' I said. 'Not at a moment's notice.'

'We could wait for the day when you think you've done enough,' she said, 'but I don't think that day will ever come.' She held my face in her hands. 'Michael, I don't want you to stop doing what you do. I just want you to stop being a slave to it. To stop us both being slaves to it.'

I said, 'Give me some time. Maybe I can get there, but I need some time.'

'All right.' She stood back from me, her hands behind her on the flat stone. Her eyes grew large. 'But don't push me away, Michael. Please don't push me away now.'

There was the toot of a motor horn from the bridge and I looked over her shoulder and saw a tractor pulled up there, its trailer full of standing men in work clothes, waving and shouting their approval. Caitlin made a wry face at me, and then waved and smiled at the men so that they shouted some more and whistled in admiration. She looked back up at me, and despite the laughter and the sunlight I saw that her eyes were full of sadness.

CHAPTER EIGHTEEN

I laboured for two or three hours, stretching myself, turning the soil and clipping the dead branches and pinning back the tangled coils of the fallen rosebush. I had waited three days for the weather to clear, and even now it looked unlikely that the rain would stay away for long enough for me to finish my work. Right now it was clean and cold out here, with frost furring the dead leaves, and it was good to work, good to drink in the pure air.

I became aware quite suddenly that I was hungry. I drove the tines of the fork into the ground and leaned on it and tried to remember if I had anything left in the fridge from the supplies Stella had brought.

As if my thought had summoned her, Stella's car came zipping down the cobbled mews and squealed to a halt a few feet away. I could see its maroon roof over the fence, still patchy from where she had gone over it one creative weekend with an old paintbrush. I remembered that weekend. She had decided, unaccountably, that she was bored with the original colour. I didn't really want visitors right now, but at the sight of the VW I was filled with an unexpected rush of affection for her – Stella with her dodgy old heap of a car she so unreasonably loved, with her lousy parking and her uncomplicated loyalty. She opened the gate. She had a raincoat thrown over her green-and-white uniform. She hadn't expected to find me working outside, and when she saw me she stopped.

'Nobody expects the Spanish Inquisition,' she said.

'Did you bring any food?' I asked. 'It's about all you're good for.'

We walked to an Italian cafe behind the tube station at Notting Hill Gate. It was steamy and loud in the lunchtime crush, smelling of coffee and garlic. It was a place from before the area's gentrification, with red check tablecloths and plastic lobsters in nets. We ordered at once from the laminated menu, whitebait for Stella, pasta for me.

'No booze this time,' she said. 'I'm on duty at three. This is a bit of a flying visit.'

'Oh yes?'

'I just wanted to show you this. It came today.'

She opened her bag and took a large brown envelope from it and handed it to me. The envelope had big gaudy stamps on it. I opened it. The card inside showed a group of smiling men and women, mostly young, sitting at an outside table in the sunshine. I recognised most of them, the surgical team from Mater Misericordia in Caracas. Inside someone with extravagant handwriting had scrawled, 'Michael – we want so much that you come – we need you!' and under that a dozen of them had signed. Squiggles, smiley faces, kisses, little comments in Spanish with multiple exclamation marks. I turned it over in my hands.

'They're good people,' I said. I was unexpectedly moved. 'They're very kind.'

'It's just that I'm going to have to get serious with the dates sometime soon,' Stella said. 'I don't mean to hassle you.'

I turned the card over and over in my hands. 'It would be wonderful, wouldn't it?'

'It will be,' she said. She started to smile and then stopped. 'What have you done to your hands?'

I looked at them stupidly and saw again Big Iqbal and the steamy windows of The Indian Mutiny. 'Gravel rash. I fell over.'

'You *fell over?*'

'In the street. I tripped.' I felt my colour rise. 'It happens.'

'Were you pissed?'

'Stella - just a little accident, OK? For Chrissake.'

I knew she wanted to ask more, but did not quite have the nerve. She lifted her eyebrows. 'Well, I'm going to have to give the Mater some kind of an answer, Michael. They won't wait forever.'

'March,' I said, pulling the word out of the air.

'March? March is three months away.'

'Well, early March. A few weeks. God, Stella, I don't know. I just have to wait for the police to come up with something.'

She sat back, watching me. 'The Venezuela idea was supposed to make life easier, not more difficult.'

'It does, Stella. To have this opportunity. It does help. I just need to get some ends tied off here.'

'OK,' she said thoughtfully. 'March, then.'

She didn't speak much after that. When the meal was over I walked her back to the car, kissed her goodbye, and when she drove away I went in through the back gate. I thought again of those smiling Venezuelan doctors and nurses. I was looking at the card again as I walked up the path to the back door, so I did not see Barrett until I almost collided with him.

'Why, Dr Severin. I was just about to give up on you.'

I stood with my keys hanging in my hand. 'You've found Carrick?'

'Early days. Let's have a quick talk inside, shall we?' He nodded at the keys still in my hand. 'Inside would be more comfortable.'

I let him in ahead of me. He walked through the rooms looking around him like a tourist, as if he had never seen the place before, saying nothing. I found his silence oppressive and I put the radio on: it was tuned to a classical station.

'Do you want coffee?'

'If you're going to have one.'

'It'll have to be black. I keep forgetting to get any milk.'

'No problem.'

Barrett was wearing a long black coat that made him look a bit like a nightclub bouncer. He took this off and slung it over the back of a chair and sat at the end of the dining table where we could see one another as I worked in the kitchen.

I made the coffee and carried it through to him.

'Before I forget, here's your photos back.' He dropped an envelope on the table. 'We're hanging onto the drawing for a while, but I'll send you a copy if you want.'

'That's OK. Whenever.'

'And we'd like to do a reconstruction. You know, make a little film? Put it out on Crimewatch or whatever?'

'What is there to reconstruct? No-one saw anything.'

'We've turned up some CCTV of Caitlin in the shopping centre that morning. The boss thinks it might be worth doing a mock-up of her coming home. Maybe someone saw her let herself into the house. If we're real lucky, maybe someone saw this character hanging around, even coming to the door.'

'You mean Carrick,' I said.

'Very likely.' Barrett kept his tone flat.

'When do you want to do this?'

'Friday. We'll have to close half the street for a bit, but it's best to do these things on the same day as when the crime was committed. People follow patterns. Come into town on the same day every week, that sort of thing.'

'I see.'

'You won't have to be in it or anything, Dr Severin. Just watch. Tell us if we get anything wrong. Your wife's clothes. The way she walked. The order she did things. You'll do that?'

'If you think it'll help.'

'I don't put much store by reconstructions myself. But it's worth a try.'

There was a silence.

'You've no idea at all where Carrick is, have you?' I said.

'For my money he's off overseas. He's got the contacts and the experience. But he'll turn up eventually. They always do. Someone spots them, or they have to see their dear old Mum one last time, or they get homesick for fish-and-chips or a pint of IPA. Stupid things.' Barrett dropped a lot of sugar in his coffee and stirred it noisily. 'And meanwhile we've had the pleasure of a nice long chat with young Angie.'

'You have?'

'A real stunner, she is, by the way. You didn't mention that.'

'Is it relevant?' I picked up my own cup. 'So you went up to Bradford?'

'She saved us the trip. She's come to London.'

'She has?' I couldn't keep the surprise out of my voice.

'She's with that nutty uncle of hers. Moved into her brother's place in Brixton.'

'She can do that?'

He shrugged. 'Rent's paid. She's got a key. We've already had a good look around in there.'

'But what's she doing down here?'

'She wants to be near the action, she says. What she means is, she wants to be on the scene against the day we catch up with brother Barney, in case he needs her.'

'Can you give me her address?' I asked, after a moment.

He looked at me curiously.

'I want to return the photos. I took them from her place. I feel bad about it.'

'The address isn't a secret.' He scribbled on the back of a business card and slid it over to me. 'But I bet she wishes she'd stayed up North now. We gave her a bit of a going over. Figuratively speaking, of course. Had her down the nick for four or five hours. Middle of the night. The usual routine. Put the frighteners on her.'

'I see.'

'She's tough as old boots, our Angie, I'll give her that. She wasn't about to tell us anything about her brother.' He chuckled in grudging admiration.

'Maybe she doesn't know anything,' I said.

'Oh, sure.' He chuckled again.

It affected me oddly to hear him talk about Angie in this way. I could imagine Barrett prowling around her in some dim chamber, sneering like a B-movie heavy, and I felt bad about bringing this down on her. I looked at the packet of photographs, the photographs I had sneaked away from her. I felt a great need to speak up for her now, if only to make some sort of amends in my mind.

'None of what's happened is her fault,' I said.

Barrett grinned. 'Get under your skin a bit, did she?'

'I'm sorry?'

'Young Angie. Lots of spirit. Fine looking girl. Bit of fellow feeling there, maybe?'

'You are *not* fucking serious,' I said.

'Just a thought,' Barrett raised innocent eyebrows. 'Only she said something similar about yourself. About how cruel it all was. How it always worked out that the people who weren't to blame got to suffer. That's all.'

'Right. I see.' I dropped a sugar cube in my own coffee and realised I had already done this, possibly more than once.

'Plus, he was the father of Caitlin's child. Carrick was. That's official. The Army medical people kept some blood samples and we've got a DNA match. Makes you think, don't it? Lovely young woman like her. Low-life like him.' He watched me. 'You feeling all right?'

'I need some air.'

I stood up and opened the back door and stepped out into the winter afternoon. It was chill and damp outside and I was glad. I heard Barrett come out behind me and position himself by the door, setting his briefcase down on the paving at his feet. He had put on his coat and he stood there on the step, bouncing on his toes, surveying the little garden in the gathering gloom as if it were an estate. I noticed he had brought his coffee with him. He seemed in no hurry to leave.

'Bit of a gardener, are you, Dr Severin?'

'No.'

'Oh, I'm keen, me.' He pointed to the rosebush I had tied back up against the wall. 'You want to get some horse manure for that. Not too much, mind, or it'll burn the roots. I get mine from the Mounted Division. Nice to know they're good for something, eh? I'll see if I can bring you a bag.'

I began to wish very earnestly that he would go, but still he showed no signs of it.

'You know, this is a funny old business. Don't get me wrong. I've got no sympathy for a scrote like Carrick. But it looks as if he had a pretty bad time as a kid.' He paused. 'You had a pretty bad time yourself, didn't you? Don't look so surprised. I just had a squint back through the records, that's all.'

'Why did you do that?'

'Curiosity. You did pretty well, didn't you, Dr Severin? After a start like that. Losing your parents and your family and all.'

'I had help.'

'Maybe, but you've got to take some credit for yourself. You were smart and tough and resourceful.' He touched his case with his shoe. 'Not like this loser. Not like Carrick.'

He sipped his steaming coffee and warmed his hands around the mug. He nodded approvingly at the piles of swept leaves and squinted up at the dull sky. 'Just as well you're finished out here. I think it's just about to rain on your parade.'

'If you've got something else to say to me,' I told him, 'it's probably better you say it.'

Barrett set his cup on the outside window ledge and leaned back against the wall with his arms crossed. 'I'd be prepared to consider an accident,' he said reasonably. He nodded to himself. 'Yes, I could live with that.'

It was as if he were negotiating some minor transaction: buying a used car, perhaps.

'It's not so hard to understand,' he went on. 'You come home unexpected. You find your lady wife with her bags packed, you wring out of her what's been going on behind your back. There's some recriminations flying about. A bit of much-needed discipline results. Goes over the top. One-time fit of rage. Bang.'

I did not seem to be able to get enough air into my lungs.

'Oh, everyone's capable of violence,' he said easily, 'even you. And I just know Angie Carrick would agree.'

'What do you mean by that?'

'You were sporting a shiner last week. She gave you that, right? But only because you'd slapped her about a bit first. That's how it happened, isn't it?'

'This is all wrong.'

'Let's just call it a hypothetical for the moment, eh?' He closed his coat over and looked at the cold sky again. 'But I want to make a point to you, and I want to make it loud and clear.'

'And that is?'

'That there are things I just don't seem to be able to get straight in my head since we heard about this Barney Carrick. Now, for the boss, it's simple. You're a bit of a naughty boy for leaving us out of the loop, but that aside, Carrick's a nice neat prime suspect, and any day now he'll be sitting down at the nick saying how glad he is it's all over. But me?' He chuckled. 'Me, I think everything's changed since we heard about Carrick. I think all the cards've been thrown up in the air, and nobody knows quite how they'll all come down. Oh, I grant you our Barney's a mean bastard. He's more than capable. But then there's nothing to show he was ever near this house on that day, or any other. No DNA. No prints. No witnesses.'

'That doesn't prove he wasn't here.'

'It's some way short of proving he was, though, you've got to admit. There wasn't even a break-in. But you, on the other hand – we *know* you were here. You and your famous forty minutes.' He spread his hands, appealing for understanding. 'See how it adds up?'

'I don't believe this.'

'I think maybe you'd better. Because then there's the business of you and Miss Cowan. You're sleeping with her, obviously?'

'That's not true. That's absolutely not true.'

'It has been, though.'

'Not any more. Not for years - since before I was married.'

'So it's absolutely not true that you're planning to go and live overseas with her, then, like you told me?' He pointed back into the house. 'I see all your new foreign friends are already writing to you, planning your new life, as it were.'

'That's something entirely different.'

'Really? And I suppose you and Miss Cowan never enjoyed a certain – how shall we put it? – rekindling of old passions while you were away in South America this last time? Tropic moons, guitar music, long lonely nights? All that can do it to anyone.'

'No. We didn't. Not the way you mean.'

'Well, you might be telling the truth, but I'd suggest the difference between you getting it off with Stella Cowan, and you *not* getting it off with her, would go on a gnat's kneecap and roll about. And I'd further suggest that anyone who asks your Venezuela MSF team members about it, like I did, will come to the same conclusion. And that won't look good.'

I was suddenly close to tears. I was desperate he should not see this, but probably he did see it, for he ostentatiously avoided looking at me and instead put his head back and snuffed the chill air.

I said, 'You can't believe I would have hurt Caitlin. Even if I had known about all of it – about Carrick, about the baby – I would never have hurt her. Even if everything you say about me was true, I would never have hurt her.'

He observed me for a few seconds, speculatively. 'We're not very bright, you know, blokes like me. We wouldn't be coppers if we were. We'd all be brain surgeons like you, or whatever it is you do. So the way we work is really boring. One little piece at a time. You go on long enough, it makes a picture. It's not personal.'

It started to rain. Barrett shrugged himself into his coat and buttoned it.

'So far this is just what you might call a bit of private speculation on my part, Dr Severin. Meanwhile there's a full-scale hunt on for Carrick. Maybe they'll find him soon, and then there'll be another picture taking shape, and I'll be back here eating 'umble pie.' He paused. 'But some sort of an accident. Yes, I could live with that.' He walked down the paved path to the back gate, and turned there, with his hand on the latch. 'You might want to give it some thought. And meanwhile, don't take your trip with Miss Cowan without checking with us, will you?'

He lifted a hand to me in a farewell that was almost a salute, and let himself out into the mews. I heard his heavy footsteps clump away down the cobbles.

When I could hear his steps no longer I went back into the house. I went into the bathroom and stood there for a while, fighting down an urge to throw up, looking at the ghostly reflection in the mirror. I was sweating. I washed my face in cold water and the shock of it steadied me a little.

By the time I came back out to the dining room the house seemed dark and oppressive with the long winter evening stretching ahead. I felt trapped and not far from panic. Most of all, I felt alone. I picked up the envelope Barrett had left on the table. I didn't need to open it and look at the photographs again. I could see Carrick's face as clearly as if he had been sitting opposite me. Makes you think, Barrett had said. Low-life like him. Lovely young woman like her.

I slipped the envelope into my pocket. I didn't really feel calm enough to drive but I dug out my car keys anyway.

CHAPTER NINETEEN

It took me less than half-an-hour to find the place, parallel to Brixton High Street and not far from the railway line. There was an evening market in progress and the place was crowded with stalls and umbrellas and packed with people. Food was frying in woks on open stands and a steel band was playing somewhere nearby. The sound of it blared along the street.

The flats were above a short parade of shops within sound and smell of the market, built over an Asian store and flanked by an off-licence and a betting shop. All three places were closed. Through the Asian store's green canvas blinds I could see sacks of rice and millet and cartons of spices stacked along the narrow aisles. There was a passage down the side of the building and in a small parking area at the back stood a blue Fiat Bravo, with a Yorkshire Dales National Park sticker in the rear window. A door stood open under the angle of an iron fire escape. I stepped into a dim stairwell smelling of coconut and coriander and went quietly up the stairs.

For a few moments after I rapped on the flat door there was silence, and I was about to knock again when I heard her rapid steps and the rattle of a chain being released and the door swung open. I saw Angie's pupils dilate and her hand flew up instinctively to fasten the top button of her shirt.

'You've got a hide,' she said.

'Can I come in?'

'No. Piss off.'

She made to swing the door shut on me, as I had once tried to shut her out, but I put one hand against the wood, and held the envelope out to her with the other. 'I came to return this.'

She faltered. 'What is it?'

'The photographs I took from you.'

'Stole from me.' She snatched the envelope.

'That's right. And now I'm returning them. I wanted to do it in person.'

She looked from my face to the envelope in her hand and back again. 'Why are you really here?'

'You told me once that we were both injured by this thing. I've been thinking about that.'

I took my hand off the door, to give her the option of closing it in my face. She stood there a moment longer, glaring at me, then stepped aside. I walked past her into the flat. There wasn't much to the place: a room with a dining table in it, a kitchenette and a bathroom and two bedrooms leading off. It didn't seem to have been redecorated since the 1960s. A large window overlooked the car park at the rear of the building and gave an eyelevel view of a railway viaduct. I could smell Uncle Stanley's tobacco on the air, and pine scented cleaner.

'You've got a talent for finding me,' she said.

'They said this was your brother's place.' I looked around. 'What are you doing here, Angie? In London? You're going to get yourself into trouble.'

'What's it to you?'

'And you brought Uncle Stanley down here?'

'He wouldn't be left.'

'Where is he?' I said. I had expected the old man to be here and his absence made some sort of a difference which I could not define.

'He's down the market. Or maybe the pub. I'm not his keeper.' She tossed the envelope unopened onto the table. 'You look different.'

'I had a visit from the police today.'

'Well, that must've made you happy.'

'It didn't.'

'No, it didn't make me happy either, when they hauled me off in the middle of the night. Thanks to what you told them.'

'I didn't want any of that to happen, Angie. But you know I had to go to the police.'

'Do you know what they did to me?' Her voice was rising. 'They kept me in this fucking interview room for hours on end in the middle of the night interrogating me like some streetwalker. They didn't even let me go for a pee. The same fucking questions, over and over again. And that animal Barrett standing over me the whole time, just leering at me.'

She wrapped her arms around herself as if the memory made her suddenly cold, and I saw that she was shaking, and I realised how thoroughly they had frightened and humiliated her.

'If you know anything, tell them,' I said. 'Cooperate with them. Do everything they ask.'

'That's your advice, is it?'

'This thing goes beyond some twisted loyalty to your brother.'

'You don't know anything, Michael, and you understand less.'

'I know about his record.'

'Oh, yes. Sergeant Barrett has all the facts on Barney, hasn't he? Crippled a poor man in a pub when he was just fifteen. Violent, unpredictable, in and out of trouble. I know the whole mythology.'

'Are you saying it's not true?'

'It might be accurate. But that's not the same thing, is it?'

'Meaning?'

'Meaning things aren't the way you think. That Barney had reasons. He always had reasons.'

'What reason did he have for beating Caitlin to death?'

'He could never do that. Why won't you listen to me?'

'If you keep repeating that mantra long enough, I suppose it might come true.'

'Understand this, Michael. Barney was the only man who ever cared for me. If it hadn't been for him, I'd've been just like my mother: fucked at fourteen. And I mean totally *fucked.*' She was speaking more and more loudly now, and her eyes were growing wild. 'You can't sit in judgment on us. You can't even imagine what it was like for us.'

'Half the world had a lousy childhood, Angie. Do you think that makes this *right?*'

'You'd do anything to hang this on Barney.' She stepped up to me, her hair swinging. 'Why? Is it because you really think he did it? Or because he was screwing her? Is that what this is really all about?'

'Don't stop there, Angie. Why not go all the way and say I killed her myself? You'd not be the first.'

'Well?' she shouted, 'and did you?'

I gripped her by both shoulders, holding her hard, forcing her to stop. The strength of my grasp made her gasp but I didn't relax it.

'I sat with her on the stairs,' I said. 'I did everything I knew how to do. It was never going to be enough. Her heart was still beating. Just now and then I could feel it. In the end I had to wait for it to stop. Sit there and wait. It took quite a long time.'

Angie twisted as I held her, like some fierce animal I had pinned down.

'She didn't really want much,' I said. 'A life with some purpose to it. To be more than – what did you call her? - the pretty princess in the castle. But in the end she had to find someone else who could make her feel that way.' Something strange was happening to the coloured lights outside, something that made them wobble and run. 'And she wanted a child,' I said. 'Finally she had to go somewhere else for that too.'

I looked down into Angie's eyes. I did not mean to threaten her, but in my mind I was looking at Caitlin on the stairs, her bare legs crooked, and whatever Angie saw in my face at that moment terrified her, for suddenly she cried out and swung at me – right hand, left hand. I caught her wrists and held her but she writhed in my grip, hissing like a cat, her eyes huge and blazing.

I let my arms fall away from her and I stood back. She stood with her hands hanging at her sides, panting like a fighter who has broken away from a clinch.

The door opened.

'Well, excuse me all over the place,' Uncle Stanley said. He was carrying a cardboard box in his hands and it was full of tins and sealed foil packets and fresh vegetables. The smell of roast chicken floated on the air. The old man peered at us through a feathery asparagus top like some suspicious jungle animal.

Angie turned away, pushing back her hair, tugging down her shirt, trying to control her breathing.

'We had a problem,' I said, speaking in the old man's general direction. 'A small problem. We've worked it out now.'

'Oh aye? Algebra, was it? I don't remember algebra being that noisy.' Uncle Stanley gave me a keen glance. 'I'll go away again, shall I, before you start on logarithms.'

Angie stepped forward and seized the box from him. 'Give me that and shut the door before we all bloody freeze.'

'I'd better go,' I said.

She set the box on the table. 'You don't have to go.'

'It's probably best.'

Uncle Stanley looked from Angie to me and back again, his turning from side to side like a Wimbledon umpire.

'There's enough for three,' she said. She did not meet my eye and I could see her shoulders rising and falling.

'Well, make up your bloody minds,' Uncle Stanley said. 'No bugger'll get fed else.'

I sat down at the table.

Angie unloaded the box clumsily. She said to Uncle Stanley, 'Didn't you buy any wine, you useless old article? We can't drink that rotten brown ale of yours.'

'Wine, is it now?' The old man raised his eyebrows. He smacked his pipe down into his horny palm, making a noise like a small pistol, and then did it again, frowning at the result and blowing noisily through the mouthpiece. 'Well excuse me, I'm sure, but I didn't realise we were entertaining your gentleman caller. I didn't bring the dook patty neither.'

'I'll get some wine,' she said. I made to get up, but she waved me down. 'It's just downstairs. And I could do with some fresh air. Really.'

She put on her black leather jacket, keeping her face averted, and slipped out of the flat, leaving Uncle Stanley and me facing one another over the table. I was glad enough to sit quietly. The old man lit up and puffed contentedly for a minute or two, creasing his eyes whenever I happened to look at him, but he did not speak. A train rumbled past on the viaduct beyond the next row of buildings, heading out of Victoria or Waterloo towards the southern suburbs. Its trundling passage made cups rattle in the kitchen. We both watched as the carriages crawled past. It was strange to see the lighted windows so close and all those anonymous faces staring into this moment of our lives.

'They can see right in here,' Uncle Stanley remarked. 'Gives 'em something to do, poor devils.' He smiled out of the window and waved to the commuters in the crowded train. Incredibly, one or two waved back. 'And after all, that's the idea of a window, to be looked through. It'd be a wall else.'

He crossed his long hands on the table in front of him. Precisely set out on the surface were all his ceremonial objects: tobacco pouch, green-and-yellow Swan Vesta box, pipe cleaners, the short briarwood pipe resting in an ashtray on a nest of spent matches. He sat looking at me with his peaceful blue eyes. A calm descended on the room and, little by little, on me.

'You're a long way from home,' I said.

'I take as I find.' He looked around. 'It beats Tobruk in forty-two, I'll tell you that.' He picked up his pipe and inspected it. 'You know, Dr Seven, what happens in life has got bugger all to do with who deserves what.'

He lit the pipe, making a great play of it, ferociously shaking out each match. I tried to see his eyes, but they were lost in the smoke.

I got up and went to the window. The lights were springing on all over South London. I could hear the steel band in the market and the rumble of another train approaching, and I waited while the yellow-lit carriages rattled past. When I looked at Uncle Stanley the smoke from his pipe was curling around his eyebrows in a way that made him look like a wizard in a child's story.

I said, 'Tell me about Barney Carrick.'

'Ah.' He put the pipe down and folded his long hands over one another. He seemed to be looking into the past and it took him a moment or two to retrieve what he saw there. 'We think everyone starts with a blank sheet of paper, Dr Seven, don't we? All nice and clean and white. And we think that what they write on that blank sheet is up to them, up to them alone. Whether they write something rotten and low, or something fine and grand, it's their own fault, or their own credit, just as the case may be.'

I sat very quietly. There was something mesmerising about his voice. I did not want to break the spell.

'But it's not like that at all, is it?' he went on. 'Nobody's life is a blank sheet. Not even at the very start. It's already been scribbled on before we come to write our own story on it. Sometimes good things are writ on it, and sometimes bad. Bad things were scribbled all over Barney Carrick's sheet. And on young Angela's. And big important lad that you are, Dr Seven, I'll wager there were bad things on yours, too. Am I right?'

'Yes.'

He lifted his white eyebrows and sighed. 'But then again, mebbe that's no excuse. Barney did some rough things. Of course, our Angela thinks he learned his lesson since.'

'Do you think he's changed?'

'No, lad,' said Uncle Stanley. 'I don't think anyone ever changes. I think we just find out more about them.'

I heard the key turn in the lock and the door swung open and Angie came into the room with a couple of clinking plastic bags.

For half an hour we sat around the table eating chicken and salad and drinking cheap wine from a collection of odd tumblers.

We ate in silence. Outside the trains rumbled past and over my shoulder Uncle Stanley lifted his glass and made faces at the travellers and Angie scolded him for this and he carried on doing it anyway every time the carriages went by. Caribbean music drifted in. At some point I became aware that the old man, who had been carrying dishes into the kitchen in a relay of shuffling journeys, had not come back. I saw that the door of one of the bedrooms was closed, although I had not heard the latch click, and when I looked back at Angie she was sitting across the table gazing steadily at me.

'About earlier,' she said, 'I always had a mouth on me.'

'It's OK.'

'Michael, you've got to try to understand. By the time she was eighteen, our mother had me, Barney and the heroin to feed, and no getting rid of any one of us. It all happened in the same room, the needles and the sex and the beatings. We were like hostages, Barney and me. Sometimes I think it's still that way.' She threw back her hair. 'Me and Barney would go down to *The Indian Mutiny*, scrounging round the bins like a couple of starving puppies. That's how we got to know Hukum. It was Barney kept me out of strife. When I got old enough I worked all hours – three jobs and evening classes too. I had a knack for it, somehow. In the end I got myself into Leeds Met - the university. That was my way out. But while I had my head down, Barney got into one scrape after another. Finally, to keep himself out of more trouble, he came south and joined the Army. That was eight years ago. He bought this place early on. I used to come down to visit him here every now and then. Big adventure, that was.'

I glanced around the bare flat.

'It's not much now, is it?' she said, interpreting my look, 'not so much as a picture on the wall when Uncle Stanley and I got here. But when I used to come here it was full of stuff he'd brought back. Full of life, you might say.'

'What happened?'

'Iraq happened. I don't know the details.'

'You didn't ask him about it?'

'I haven't seen him for two years.'

It took me a moment to register this. 'You haven't seen him …?'

'Or even spoken to him, bar one time. I used to call him. Left messages. But he never replied.'

'But I thought –'

'Not a word for two years, aside from one phone call. That was the day of Mam's funeral, six months back. I don't even know how he heard she was dead, but anyway he rang me.' She hesitated. 'That's when he told me about Caitlin.'

'What did he say about her?'

'That she was lovely. That she was married.' She put her hand across the table and let it rest on mine. 'That she was special, and made him feel special too. And I know he meant it, Michael. I knew that was really why he'd called, to tell me that. When I read what had happened to her I thought he'd be bound to contact me, but he didn't and I couldn't find him. I was desperate to get in touch with him. I could hardly call the police. That's why I came to your house that night. In case you knew something.'

'And I knew less than you did.'

'I do have one other lead. Barney had an army mate. Chris Walker. Barney sent me pictures from places they went together. Bosnia, then Afghanistan. Other places too. It was in the Middle East he picked up that 'I have tasted your absence' line. He used to get Chris to scribble it on postcards to me. He couldn't write it himself, or not real well. But after Iraq, nothing. I heard he'd left the Army. I used to tell myself Barney'd made good, gone his own way. Met some nice woman, maybe. But I think the truth was that something happened in Iraq and he left because of that, and he was ashamed. I'm not sure, though.' She took a deep breath and looked at me. 'About the only thing I am sure of is that he didn't hurt Caitlin.'

'Angie, you haven't seen him for two years. You can't possibly know what he's become in that time.'

'But I know what's not his *style*. What it's not in him to do. Barney didn't skulk around after your Caitlin like some pervert. And he didn't hurt her like that and then run away and hide. That wasn't in him to do.'

'Somebody did those things,' I said.

'Yes. Some bastard. Some junkie, some maniac. But not Barney. If you knew him like I know him you'd understand that.'

'Believing can't just be an act of will, Angie.'

'And there's me thinking that's what faith was.'

Her conviction was unassailable. It had something pure about it, something almost religious. We both let the silence go on for a while. Her hands were still resting on mine and she seemed to notice this at the same moment that I did and she sat back and tossed her long hair away from her face. She turned her head and gazed out of the window as another train passed. I could see her looking at the coloured shopfront neons, the blue sodium along the streets, the yellow squares of a thousand windows in a thousand homes where ten thousand nameless people lived out their unknowable lives. Somewhere in the middle of all this, or in the darkness in between, her brother had moved – perhaps still moved – living a life of which neither of us knew anything at all.

She looked at me. 'Michael, I have to be here for him. Even if all I can do is to stand in the crowd in front of the gallows at the end of the day.'

I swallowed the last of my wine. 'I should go.' I stood up and put on my jacket and walked across the room to the door. 'Thanks, Angie.'

'What for?'

'I don't know. For talking it through.'

'Michael?'

I stopped with my hand on the latch. 'Yes?'

'Whatever happened between the two of them, that doesn't make you and me bad people. Not just because he's my brother and she was your wife.'

She sat in the window with the lights banked behind her and falling on her dark hair. Her face was fearful and defiant and hopeful all at once.

I smiled at her quickly and walked through the door and closed it behind me.

Chapter Twenty

M eredith Wren came powering around the corner from the
Strand, head down, plastic mac flapping, scattering shoppers
from her path. She clutched a worn leather briefcase to her breast.

I watched her from my seat in the window of the coffee shop. I
hadn't seen her since the funeral, but there was no longer any sign
of the crumpled and tearful Meredith of that day. I was glad about
that. It made my heart lift to see her hustling across the pedestrian
crossing outside the café. A motorcycle courier swerved and swore.
She gave him two fingers, barged open the door, and strode across
to me.

I stood up and gave her a hug. She seemed even more ample
than usual: my arms only just reached around her. 'Thanks for coming, Meredith. Let me get you a coffee.'

'Tea!' she shouted at the Italian waiter as he slid towards us,
'and not some bloody fruit cocktail, either. Workman's tea with two
sugars.'

The waiter made terrified obeisance and fled while Meredith
dumped her case on the table between us. She stripped off her raincoat to reveal woollen clothes in a startling combination of colours,
then sat, puffing, and opened her case. Coins and computer discs
and a packet of Bounty bars cascaded onto the floor. She scrabbled
for these things under the table and reappeared red in the face.

'Right,' she said. 'Mail.' She produced two thick bundles of letters with elastic bands round them and dumped them in front of
me. 'Don't read them now. Sign those.' She shoved a wad of forms
across the table so that the letters fell in my lap.

'What's all this?'

'Sick leave. Expenses. Insurance.' She waved an impatient hand. 'Just do as you're told and sign them.'

I signed. There were a lot of forms and she had marked with yellow stickers where she wanted my signature. It took a couple of minutes to scrawl on all of them. As I did so her tea arrived, along with another Americano for me. I gave her back the forms.

'Thanks for bringing this stuff, Meredith. I couldn't face coming in again just yet.'

She sniffed. 'The place runs better without you.'

'St Ruth's would fall apart without you keeping us all in order.'

'Of course it would,' she said, without a trace of irony. She stuffed the wad of forms in her bag. 'For the record, Michael, everyone asks about you.'

'Tell them I'm fine.'

'Are you?'

'What do you think?'

'I think it was a bloody silly question. But for my two bob's worth – get your arse on that plane to Venezuela, will you?'

'It didn't take long for that to get about.'

'Michael,' she said reprovingly, 'this is Meredith Wren you're talking to. Stop messing about with this private eye crap and get out of here. That's my advice. Get busy on something worthwhile.'

'It's Stella's job. I'm just going for the sunshine.'

She moved her mouth an inch to one side, but didn't say anything. She reached once more into her bag and slapped a green cardboard file down on the table and left it there for effect, while she slurped noisily at her tea.

'I'm not supposed to pass on this kind of stuff,' she said finally. 'Unless of course you tell me you're treating this man as a patient.'

'You might say that.' I couldn't take my eyes off the file.

'So say it, then.' Meredith was a stickler for procedure.

'Bernard John Carrick is my patient, Ms Wren,' I declaimed obediently. 'And I'm anxious to access his case history because I believe it may be relevant to his treatment. How's that?'

'Good enough.' She pushed aside her tea and picked up the folder. 'Who is he?'

'Someone in trouble. Maybe someone who *is* trouble.'

'Yes, well, he looks like bad enough news to me.'

I looked at the bulging file on the table. If you knew him like I know him, Angie had said. How much better would I know him after this? How much difference could it make?

'All this took a bit of rooting around, I can tell you,' Meredith said. 'Would you believe the Social Services files weren't even on computer? Not the ones from twelve years ago, anyway. They had to fax the damn things to me. Fax! I ask you. I had to hunt around to find one.' Among her other skills, Meredith was the only person who understood the Trust's computer system. 'Now then. The social worker he had at the time has retired, but I tracked her down. She's living in Arbroath. You know, where the bloaters come from? Or is it haddock? Whatever. We had quite a chat. Joy Parkes, her name. Nice woman. Breeds dachshunds.'

I sat very still, forcing myself to stay quiet. It was a big mistake to try to hurry Meredith.

'You can keep that, it's a copy.' She slid the folder over to me.

'Why don't you tell me the juicy bits, Meredith?'

'It goes right back to his childhood. Where shall I start?'

'I heard he was involved in a brawl when he was a kid. In Liverpool.'

'Ah, yes. That's a good tale.' She put her elbows on the table and clasped her big red hands. 'Your friend Carrick attacked a man called Dermot O'Neale in a pub, an unemployed merchant seaman, and got within a millimetre or two of killing him. Serious brain damage, lost an eye. Very nasty. Young Carrick was only fifteen at the time, and he would normally go into a Young Offenders for that, probably one of those high security ones. But there were extenuating circumstances, and that kept him out.'

'What extenuating circumstances?'

'Carrick's mother was on the game. O'Neale was a customer. Way back, when B.J. Carrick Esquire was a kid of eleven, O'Neale got violent and beat the mother up, and when he'd finished with her, being the prince that he was, he thought maybe he'd get his money's worth and move on to the daughter. I forgot to mention the daughter, girl of thirteen or so then, name of –'

'Angie.' A hollow space was opening in my stomach.

'Angela, that's it. Well, young Barney wasn't having any of this and he tried to protect his sister. Very plucky, you've got to say. But of course this O'Neale animal just broke him up, that little boy. Four broken ribs, punctured lung, concussion...There were no witnesses who'd testify. But young Master Carrick was prepared to wait four years for his chance. He traced this O'Neale creature back to Liverpool, found him in the pub. And got his own back.' Meredith rubbed her hands with satisfaction. 'The social workers made sure the magistrates knew the whole deal. That's why our Barney wasn't banged up for the assault. He got community service instead.'

'That's quite a story,' I said.

'Puts a different complexion on things, doesn't it? Knowing the whole script.' She closed the file and looked at me, her big face glowing. Her smile faded. 'But apparently that wasn't the story you wanted to hear.'

I'd been back home about an hour, flicking through the file at the dining room table. It was just before one o'clock and I was thinking about catching the news when the brass knocker on the front door echoed twice through the house. I suppose there are only so many ways you can use a door knocker, but perhaps she had a special method of doing it. Whatever the reason, I knew at once that it was Angie.

She stood on the doorstep, her skin gleaming in the winter light. 'You'll think I'm daft,' she said and shifted from one foot to the other.

'Come in.'

She moved past me down the hall. She had bought some new clothes, I noticed, a smart black woollen coat with a soft collar over a burnt orange top. In the dining room she stopped and faced me. I could see she was nervous.

'It's weird to be here again,' she said. 'Was it really just a few weeks back?'

'Give or take the odd light year.'

'I've found Chris Walker,' she said abruptly. 'Barney's Army pal.'

'Ah.'

'I called him. He's out of the Army. He runs a joinery business now, in Kilburn. I'm going to see him, Wednesday next. He keeps saying he doesn't know anything, but I want to talk to him anyway.'

'And you thought I'd be curious.'

'Are you?' She rested her fingertips on the table and in doing so she touched the green file. She must have seen her brother's name on the cover because she picked up the folder and looked at me very directly. 'Well. You're curious enough to do some homework. Learn anything?'

'A bit.'

'Enough to make a difference to the way you see things?'

'Don't let's get ahead of ourselves, Angie.'

But she went on looking at me speculatively for a long time.

'Buy a girl a drink?'

The bar was almost empty, a shabby old-style pub which didn't go in for lunches. I'd pointed out a café as we walked down Church Street – a bustling French place with a striped awning – but she had insisted on the pub. Perhaps she guessed it would be quieter. I got her a glass of dry white and by the time I carried it to the table she had taken off her new black coat. She was sitting at a table under the frosted glass window and her orange top burned like a flame in the delicate light.

'You didn't tell me about this man O'Neale,' I said. 'About what really happened.'

'You found out anyway.'

'You could have saved me the trouble.'

'You'd have thought I was making excuses for Barney. And besides, I don't much like to talk about it.' Her eyes grew hard, remembering. 'I heard Barney's ribs go. I can still hear that sound. I couldn't do anything to help him. That's where I got this.' She moved back her hair and touched the star-shaped scar on her temple, the scar I had seen on that first night. 'Can you imagine what that's like, not being able to help?'

'Yes,' I said. 'I know quite a bit about that. Look, Angie, I did learn some things I didn't expect to learn. I do understand him a bit better. You too, maybe. But at the end of the day, it doesn't change anything, does it?'

'He didn't have any reason at all to hurt Caitlin. He loved her. I keep telling you.'

'But it's not as if it stopped with O'Neale. Your brother was thrown out of the Paras. What do you have to do to get thrown out of the Paras?'

'I don't know. Neither do you. Maybe Chris Walker will.' She sipped her wine. 'Michael, I don't want to argue with you today. Let's talk about something else. Turn over a blank page.' She frowned. 'What are you smiling at?'

'I was just thinking of Uncle Stanley and his blank pages.' I could picture the old man, wreathed in pipe smoke in the dim flat, waving to the trains.

She pulled a face and hammed up his accent, 'Nobody has a blank sheet, my lass. Even at the start.'

'And he's right, too.'

'Oh, he's always right, is Uncle Stanley,' she laughed. 'He's not my real uncle, you know. He was just kind to us when we were little. He felt sorry for us, I suppose. He found us once, Barney and me, down by the canal. There were boats on it then. Barney was going to pinch one and row us away.'

'Where to?'

'He had it all worked out. Sneak through the locks with the canal barges, and down the River Aire to the sea. And then? I don't know. Africa or Australia, probably. He was about eight then. Rowing to Africa isn't a problem when you're eight. Uncle Stanley brought us back home, but when he saw what home was like I think he wished he'd let Barney row me to Africa. After that he used to take us walking up on the moors, just to get us out of the place. He'd have taken us in if he could've. In the end it's turned out the other way round.'

That would have been over twenty years ago, I thought. Uncle Stanley would have been getting on in years even then, approaching retirement, a man whose working life would have started in some factory after war service, a man out of another age. I wondered what he had made of the Carricks' sordid council flat, the litter of needles and soiled tissues, the wasted young woman with the bruises up her arms and on her ankles, the half feral children.

'I'm glad someone was kind to you,' I said.

She gave me a doubtful glance, but then she saw I was serious and for a second she could find no answer.

I cleared my throat. 'I've never been to the moors. I hear they're beautiful.'

'First time I went up there I thought it was fairyland. Like in a storybook. I'd never been anywhere like it. Nobody shouted at me. Nobody hit me. Nobody cried. Just this light and this clean air and that smell the earth has after the rain.' She turned her face to me. 'Have you ever heard a skylark singing, Michael?'

'I don't really remember.'

'I remember all right. They make this tinkle in the air. Sing while they're flying, they do. Uncle Stanley told me they were skylarks, or I'd never have known what they were. All birds that weren't sparrows were pigeons to me. I thought he was some sort of a wizard. He could name every bird up there and tell you incredible things about them – how that one could see a field mouse from the top of a cathedral spire, how this one hid her nest so cleverly in the heather that you could stand right over it and never know it was there. He showed me one once. These perfect little eggs. I wanted to take them home, but he wouldn't let me, though I begged and begged.'

'Did Barney go with you?'

'To the moors? Aye, once or twice.'

'What did he think of it up there?'

'He was a boy, wasn't he?' She laughed a little. 'He saw a bird, he wanted to shoot it.' She looked at me. 'What is it?'

'Nothing. That just reminded me of something.'

I was back at Anthony's for a moment, looking at the brass bound rosewood box and its red velvet lining and the steel and walnut duelling pistols nestled in it, and the brass plate reading: 'Wheelers of London, Firearms of Quality'. And the cartoon image formed again in my mind of crows exploding in bursts of black feathers, and Anthony's pained and comical bewilderment that I should want to see such a thing.

'I still dream about the moors sometimes,' she said. 'Of course I go back every now and then, pile Uncle Stanley in the car and drive up there. Takes twenty minutes now, not two changes of bus and an hour's walk, like it used to. But I can never quite find the same spot, you know? The magic place I went when I was a little girl.' She looked up at me. 'Is there somewhere like that for you, Michael? A secret place?'

'Ithaca,' I said, without thinking about it.

'That's in Greece, isn't it?'

'Yes and no. It's in another world. It's a place my father said he'd take me to. But he died before he got the chance.'

I must have laid some unusual emphasis on the words, for she put her head on one side, waiting for an explanation.

'There was a fire,' I said, not knowing why I was telling her. 'When I was a kid. They all died. Parents, brother and sister.'

'Well.' She pulled down the corners of her mouth. 'No monopoly on hard luck stories, then.'

'It was a long time ago.'

She nodded thoughtfully. 'You know what I think, Michael? I think maybe you should go there anyway.'

'To Ithaca? I'm not sure you can ever go back.'

'If you've never been there in the first place,' she said tartly, 'it's not going back, is it?'

I looked at her, the orange of her top warm in the pale light.

'What?' she said.

'OK, Angie. I'll come with you to see this man Walker. Hear what he has to say.'

She pushed her glass aside. 'Good.'

'But I don't promise anything,' I told her. 'Don't expect me to change my mind, no matter what he says.'

'I don't promise anything either, Michael.' She got to her feet and swung her coat around her. 'But I'll take the chance if you will.'

CHAPTER TWENTY-ONE

I waited until she had gone before I left the pub. I was not ready to go back to the empty house immediately. Instead I walked a few streets and crossed into Kensington Gardens, and wandered there for perhaps an hour along the sanded paths. Cloud shadows were chasing dead leaves over the grass and gulls soared in the up-draughts above the Serpentine. It grew cold and dull as I left the park, but as I walked my mind was still full of bright spaces.

I rambled as far as Vauxhall Bridge. I leaned on the railings for a long while there, looking at the sliding water, at the barges and the workboats thumping up against the tide, at the shining buildings on the far bank. A little further along I could see the very parapet where Caitlin and I had stood in the rain that night outside the Tate Gallery. I remembered Caitlin lifting her marble face to me in the cold wind. The wind was cold now, too. The sky was gunmetal and the branches of the bay trees along the embankment stood against it like cracks in ice. I stood there for a long time.

For some reason I was utterly spent by the time I got home. I put the chain on the door and climbed the stairs to the bedroom. I put Beamish the bear out of sight on a chair, avoiding the glare of his single eye, and set the white vacant mound of Caitlin's pillow on the floor where I couldn't see it. I opened the window to let in the winter air, and stretched out on the bed and for a while I watched the grey clouds sailing by.

The room grew cold. I wasn't sure if I really could still catch Caitlin's clean, slightly astringent scent: perhaps I dreamed it. From the wall Lady Lavinia's sepia image gazed at me from another century, uncertainly astride her bicycle as if it were a spirited pony which might take off with her at any moment. My weariness began to blur the room. Weariness and quietness. Lady Lavinia really did look astonishingly like Caitlin, I thought, my mind drifting. That faded image was just like Cate, in fact - graceful, passionate, finally unknowable.

The phone rang on the bedside table and I came awake as if I had been sluiced with cold water. I fumbled and groped, knocked an empty glass onto the floor, swore. I grabbed the handset and blurted, 'Cate?' into it.

'Michael, this is Margot Dacre.' The voice was so very close to Caitlin's that my hair stirred.

I sat up and rubbed my face furiously. It was dark and chill in the room and I found the light and switched it on. It blinded me. I could not tell for a moment whether it was night or day. I squinted at the clock through the glare. It told me it was seven in the evening.

She said, 'Edward has been taken ill.'

I took a breath. 'I'm sorry to hear that, Margot.' And as I said it I saw in my mind the old man's wasted body, and was surprised to find that I was indeed sorry.

'I felt you should know. I'm not sure why.'

'I appreciate it. What happened?'

'He's had another stroke. I don't think he knew much about it, which is a blessing. I doubt he'll know much about anything from here on. Which may not be very long.'

I said nothing for a moment. She misinterpreted my silence and her voice tightened a little. 'Of course I don't expect you to be over-whelmed with grief.'

'Where is he? Where have they taken him?'

'He was moved last night to a specialist unit at Guy's.'

'He's here in London?'

'And I'm staying at some dreadful marble and glass pile near London Bridge.' She hesitated. 'Michael, I hate to ask. But if you could spare a few minutes to see me... I'm at the hospital now.'

I had never heard her ask for anything before. 'Stay where you are.'

Margot rose as I came into the room. She was wearing a formal dress of grey silk. She was still a strikingly elegant woman, and her stance at that moment, in that dress, reminded me so sharply of Caitlin that it was painful.

'Thank you for coming, Michael.' She held out her slim hand and I took it. 'It happened yesterday. I couldn't rouse him after lunch. He normally has a nap, you see...'

Edward Dacre looked as brittle as glass. I took his pulse. It was unreasonably strong. I was not surprised. I would have been willing to bet that he wouldn't give up without a fight, although he was certainly going to lose this one.

Margot sat down in a chair on the opposite side of the bed and I sat too, so that we faced one another over the old man's still form like watchers at a wake. It was mid-evening by now, and peaceful in the room. The window was a square of black sky. I could hear the familiar sounds of a hospital meal-time from the corridor, the clatter of cutlery and trolleys, the bustle of activity, a burst of laughter. The laughter seemed inappropriate and I was glad when it died away and the corridor was quiet again.

'He's going to die, of course,' Margot said.

I didn't trouble to deny it. I didn't want to insult her.

'When I stood there, Michael, and I saw him slumped in his chair, and knew that the end was coming at last, I also knew I had to call you.'

'Margot, if there's anything I can do -'

'You aren't required to *do* anything,' she cut in, 'I didn't bring you here to ask your help. Possibly it's the other way around. I want to set the record straight. Straighter, anyway. About Edward, I mean.' She let a few seconds pass. 'I loved him once. Whatever happened later, I loved him at the start. I'm not going to deny that, with him lying here like this.'

I did not speak.

'He wasn't always the way you saw him, Michael. Edward was the most dashing man when I met him. We don't talk about women being swept off their feet these days, do we? But that's how it was. I was the most enthusiastic participant in my own fate, and when I realised I didn't much like that fate, I didn't do enough to change it. I can't sit here now and not accept my share of responsibility.'

'It couldn't have been easy, Margot,' I said carefully. I could tell now that she had summoned me here for some specific purpose. It worried me that I could not guess what it might be.

'I left him once, you know,' she said. 'And don't look so astounded. Oh, I didn't go for very long. A couple of weeks. That was when I was pregnant with Caitlin. I wanted you to know that. Because her baby haunts me, you see. That life inside her, fading out. The thought that it would have lived on within her for a little while, even after she was gone. So near to the light, and never to see it.'

I said nothing.

'But I'm not Caitlin,' she went on, more briskly, 'and she was not me. I don't pretend to know why Caitlin did what she did. But for what it's worth, this is how it was for me: I had an overpowering need to leave everything behind, to escape to my own place. To go back to the beginning. Barnes Wittering School was my beginning. The beginning I never made. So I went there.'

I struggled to remember. A village in Kent. A school. That's what she had said. 'Your teaching job?'

'I must have been slightly mad. I was in my mid-thirties when I was carrying Caitlin, and I'd been offered that job long before - when I was eighteen. When I got there I found the school had been closed for years. I ended up in a little bed-and-breakfast, trying to pretend I was free, whenever I wasn't prostrated with morning sickness. I'm afraid it wasn't a very dignified episode. Edward found me quite soon. I was relieved when he did.' She reached out and rested her hand on the sheet covering her husband's wasted arm. 'Surprisingly enough, he was very sweet about it all.'

I struggled for a moment with the image of Edward Dacre being sweet. 'At least you spread your wings,' I said. 'Isn't that the main thing?'

'Oh dear,' she sighed. 'You are making this difficult. The main thing, Michael, isn't that I flapped my pathetic wings. The main thing is that, despite his flaws, my leaving wasn't really a great deal to do with Edward. My leaving was my responsibility. That's what I'm trying to tell you.'

She flipped back the sheet and took her husband's still hand in both of hers and lifted it against her cheek, and gazed at me with defiance in her eyes.

When I left London the next day it was a raw white morning with a sky the colour of linen. The traffic was gridlocked along the M20 but by eleven I was driving towards Sevenoaks down Kentish lanes flanked by hedges of wet hawthorn. Driving gave me the illusion of more general progress, and the smell of the heavy land was good, and for a while I felt positive, like a man on track. When I reached Barnes Wittering I pulled up in a lay-by opposite the village green.

For all its absurd name the place had a substantial Norman church in grey stone which suggested that it had once been a bigger and more prosperous community. Now it was a pleasantly nondescript village, the kind of place which has an active Conservative Association, a retirement home, and a scattering of old thatched cottages being restored by people from the City. There was a war memorial on the green, some benches under a bare chestnut tree, and saplings protected by tubes of chicken wire. Flanking one side of the open space was a row of redbrick cottages with a post office and a shop and a pub. Behind them I could see an oasthouse with renovators' scaffolding up against the walls. No-one was working on it. No-one was in sight at all. On the other side of the road a sizeable Georgian house stood at the end of a gravel drive.

The GPS could take me no further without a postcode, and I picked up the map from the seat beside me. The village appeared as a tiny dot on a yellow country road, of no more importance than a few thousand other villages. I began to lose faith in my own mission as I sat there. Back to the beginning. They had both said that, mother and daughter. I had thought it important, this casual repetition of the same phrase, but now I could hardly imagine how I had convinced myself of that. In this cold grey morning, with the drab village all too real under the white sky, it embarrassed me to think that I had driven sixty-odd miles on such a whim. I put the car into gear and backed up, intending to turn for home.

'Oy!' An indignant man's voice. I braked sharply. I could make him out now in the rearview mirror, a Day-Glo anorak I should have seen before, a bicycle. I lowered my window. He was a man in his forties with a brown face and lot of smile wrinkles.

'You want to be careful.' The accent was Australian. 'This is a Royal Mail bicycle. It could have caused serious damage to your vehicle.'

'I'm sorry. That was my fault.'

'Fucken right,' he agreed cheerfully. He nodded at the map in my lap. 'You lost or something?'

'You might say that.'

'Whoa!' he cried, and raised one hand in the air, opening and closing the fingers to simulate a warning beacon. 'Double meaning alert!' He crossed his arms on the handlebars in a relaxed fashion and sat there looking at me. 'So what are you looking for, mate?'

'I came to find a house.'

'Well, I hope you've got heaps of money. Silvertails are thick on the ground around here.'

'This house.' I held up one of Caitlin's drawings.

He leaned closer to look at the sketch. 'Why?'

'Does that matter?'

He gave me a wry look, to show he'd registered my tone and didn't like it much. Once he'd made his point he peered at the sketch again, but quite soon he shook his head. 'I get around most of the local places and it doesn't ring any bells with me. That doesn't mean much, mind. I've only been living here twelve years. The local Taliban don't class you as a resident unless you've done your full twenty-five. You should try the vicar. He knows everyone. That's his job.'

'Thanks. But I don't think so. This was a dumb idea.'

'Suit yourself. But it's just across the green there. Can't hurt to ask.'

I followed his pointing hand doubtfully.

'Lonsdale, the vicar is. The Reverend Derek Lonsdale. Says so on all his letters. Youngish bloke. Looks like a Tornado pilot.' He slapped the roof of the car. 'Lots of luck, eh?'

I watched him pedal away.

I did not want to meet the vicar. I did not want to go on with this absurd quest. But I could not quite bring myself to drive away immediately after this exchange, so I drove around the green and down the lane beside the vicarage and pulled up. A tall man was standing a couple of yards away by the back gate to the vicarage garden. He held a furled Cinzano golf umbrella jauntily across one shoulder. He looked so pointedly at me that I lowered the window again.

'Were you looking for me, by any chance? Only I was just going out.'

He waited, and after a second I found myself holding up the file with Caitlin's drawing in it. 'I came here looking for a house.'

'Well, that's refreshing. Most people try the estate agents.'

'But to be honest I'm not sure any more what I am looking for.'

He smiled. 'Now you're talking my language.'

The postman had been right: Lonsdale did indeed look like a fighter pilot. He had a jaunty air about him and he had floppy hair and he wore a fashionable silver-and-white ski-jacket. He held his colourful umbrella at a rakish angle. He looked as if he should have had a pair of expensive shades pushed up into his hair.

'Come in for a second. Bring your pretty pictures.'

I got out of the car and followed him down a winding path through the cottage garden and into a conservatory at the back of the vicarage. It was comfortably shabby and had slatted benches and smelled of potting mix.

'The name's Derek, by the way. Derek Lonsdale.'

'Michael.'

'Take a pew, Michael, as chaps like me are supposed to say.' He waved me to a wooden bar stool near the bench. 'I can't offer you anything, I'm afraid. As I say, I'm just on my way out. Funeral, unfortunately.'

He didn't look like a man about to officiate at a funeral. He could have been a partner in some professional practice – an architect, perhaps – off for a game of golf.

'I'm afraid I'm wasting your time,' I said.

'Oh yes?' He took the plastic folder from me, gingerly drew out Caitlin's drawing, and held it up to the light. 'Well, I've never seen this place before, Michael. I can tell you that. Not to my knowledge anyway. Is it supposed to be in Barnes Wittering?'

'I'd convinced myself it might be.'

'I wouldn't necessarily know if it *was* around here, though. One could never be sure. There are thousands of little cottages like this around the countryside. Old farm workers' places and so on. Is the picture all you have to go on? No other clues?'

'I heard there was a school nearby. I even wondered if this might be a drawing of it.'

'Well, yes, there was a village school here once. The building's still there, in that street that runs behind the pub. It's a tea shop now. With stunning originality they still call it the Old School House. But it's nothing like this sketch. Sorry to disappoint you. This looks more like a farm cottage to me.'

I took the picture back from him. 'I'm afraid I'm just chasing smoke.'

'It's a beautiful piece of work, though, the drawing.'

'My wife.'

'I see.' He sighed. 'It probably won't help, you know, Michael.'

'What won't?'

'Going back. Doesn't usually help.'

I said nothing.

'She's not with you any more, is she?' he said. 'One way or the other.'

His voice was calm and unsentimental. I wanted to deny it, to tell him he had guessed wrong and escape further entanglement, but I found it impossible to lie to his face.

'She's dead,' I said. 'It's obvious, is it?'

'Fairly. Forgive me, but it rather comes with the territory, looking out for the symptoms. You get attuned to it. Did she grow up here, or something?'

'I thought maybe she had, in a way.' I lifted one hand and opened and closed it. 'Double meaning alert.'

Lonsdale smiled. 'And now you'd like to know where it all started. Do you think maybe it will come out differently if you play it through again?'

'I've given up on happy endings.'

'What do you hope for, then?'

'I'd like to know who she was. Apparently I didn't know. After nine years. Isn't that incredible?'

'Not at all.' He pursed his lips thoughtfully. 'It's a funny thing, Michael, but I'm constantly having to talk with sincerity about people I've never met, people I know nothing about. I have to do it again in a few minutes.'

'That can't be easy.'

I have a strategy. I like to speak quietly to a few people first. They may be quite casual acquaintances, or they may be people who had the most passionate involvement with the dead person. They all tell me some consistent things. How so-and-so had such a wonderful sense of humour, how they were generous or drank a little too much or loved their garden, or whatever. But what comes through most strongly to me is how *differently* they each seem to know the person. How much their stories are at odds with one another.'

'I thought I knew the real story.'

'But you did, Michael. My point is that the real story is the one you settle for.'

He got up and so I did too.

'I absolutely must be on time for funerals,' he said. 'You have to wonder why, really. It's not as if they're going anywhere. You're welcome to stay, of course. But I know you won't.'

'No, I won't. Thank you.'

I walked out ahead of him into the damp garden. A band of rooks were swinging in the bare ash trees beside the church, creaking like rusty nails. Lonsdale locked the door and we walked back up the garden path. At the gate he turned to give me his hand.

'The very best of luck on your journey, Michael. But try not to get lost yourself.'

He crossed into the churchyard and walked away between the gravestones, his jaunty umbrella over his shoulder, furled now so that it looked like a long stick of candy.

When he had gone I walked over to the tea shop which had once nurtured Margot's dreams. It was a pleasant little place built of sandstone from the Weald, and, as the vicar had said, it was nothing whatever like the cottage in Caitlin's drawing. The date 1857 was carved over the front door and a cast iron post-box was set into the outside wall with Queen Victoria's initials still visible beneath layers of red paint.

The lady who ran the place kindly showed me around. She was dressed in a mob cap and a checkered apron. She was the wife of an IT executive with Shell, she told me, and she ran the tea shop as a hobby. Her mustard Range Rover was parked in the cobbled courtyard. She showed me the single classroom, where Margot might have taught. It was crowded with round tables draped with chintzy tablecloths. There had been a lot of old school desks out the back, she had said. But they were terribly battered and marked, and she had had them burned.

CHAPTER TWENTY-TWO

Wednesday morning. Angie's shadow darkened the coloured glass of the front door and I surprised her by opening it before she could knock.

'Were you asleep on the doormat?' she said.

'I knew you'd be on time, that's all.'

I stepped out and locked the door. She had tied her hair back severely, all business, and in her black leather jacket she reminded me of a New York cop in a TV show. It was a chill morning and the cold made her skin glow. Her shiny blue Fiat Bravo was at the kerb. We got in and clicked on the GPS. Following its instructions we threaded through the traffic for half-an-hour and cut north up the Edgware Road.

Chris Walker's lock-up was on an industrial estate at the back of Kilburn. I saw his van first, a new white Berlingo with 'Christopher Walker, Joinery' painted in sober capitals on the side. It was parked outside a breezeblock garage with the shutter pulled down. A tyre repair workshop stood on one side and a paint distributors on the other.

Angie pulled up beside the van and we walked to the shuttered door. Someone in the tyre repair shop had a radio belting out rock music at full blast and the din was punctuated by the hiss and bang of pneumatics and the ringing of tyre irons on the concrete floor. Angie rattled at the shutter.

'Chris?' She kicked the bottom of the door. 'Chris Walker?'

The shutter rumbled up.

'Little Angie,' he said. Walker stood in the centre of the workshop, operating the door with a remote. He was a solid fair-haired man of middle height and he wore an army surplus khaki sweater with the sleeves rolled up and a carpenter's pencil shoved into the shoulder tab. His bare forearms were broad and tattooed. He examined Angie with approval. 'My, my – how you've come along.'

'Hello, Chris.' She stepped up and kissed him on the cheek. 'It's been a long time. This is Michael. He's a friend.'

He kept his eyes on me. 'And what does Michael want, when he's at home?'

'We both just want to hear about Barney,' Angie said, 'that's all.'

'You a copper?' he said to me. 'Or military?'

'Me? Do I look it?'

'Yes.'

'He's all right, Chris,' Angie said. 'He just wants to know about Barney, like I do.'

Next door the pneumatics banged again, louder now.

'Bloody din.' Walker finally took his eyes off me. 'When I first set up here I was diving under the table every time that went off.'

He pressed the remote and the shutter growled down and the workshop became a calm place. A bench with a vice and tools on it stood in the centre of the floor surrounded by half-completed pieces of furniture – chairs and small tables and a chest of drawers. There was an oil heater in one corner of the unit and the smell of it mingled with the scent of varnish and raw timber.

'I can't tell you anything much, Angie,' Walker said. 'I told you, I've not heard from Barney for two years or more.'

'Anything would help, Chris.'

'Anything like what?' He moved to the bench. 'You mind if I work? I think better when I work.' Without waiting for an answer he clamped a chair leg in the vice and began to sand it.

She said, 'Chris, the cops are looking for him.'

'I know that.' Carefully, lovingly, he stroked the grain of the wood with his square hands. 'But I don't know where he is, Angie. And I'll tell you something for nothing, the police won't find him if he don't want to be found. If anyone would know where he was, it'd be you.'

'I've hardly spoken to him since before he left the Army.'

Walker glanced up at her in surprise, but didn't stop working.

'You were his best mate, Chris,' she said. 'I'm desperate. Half the world thinks he did this thing. But he couldn't have. You knew him. He couldn't have. So why did he drop off the radar?'

He blew dust off the timber and began sanding again, but very soon put the block and sandpaper aside. 'Something happened to him, Angie, while we were in the Paras, and he changed after that. I tried to keep in touch with him after his discharge, but he never answered. He wasn't strong on reading and writing. You know that.' He banged his hard hands together to shake the dust from them. 'Still, that didn't stop him making sergeant twice. Nobody ever looked at me for sergeant, not even once.'

I said, 'Something went wrong in Iraq. Didn't it?'

He looked up at me again, slowly, a new light in his face. 'I know who you are,' he said. 'You're the husband.'

'Yes.'

He moved his mouth to one side. 'I've not been long married myself. Can't imagine a thing like that.'

Angie said urgently, 'Chris, I want Michael to know the kind of man Barney really was. And then he'll understand. Do you see? Then he'll understand.'

'And that's what you're here for?' Walker rubbed his jaw and went back to work with his sanding block, so that the hissing of it filled the unit and a twist of aromatic dust rose towards the light. 'I was in the relief patrol,' he said, without looking up. 'I got to the checkpoint a couple of minutes later so I didn't see it happen. It was in a little town outside Basra, on the main road in. About two in the morning. You watch the TV? They talk about the trouble there like it was organised, with sides and rules, but it's not like that. The whole place had just broken down. Packs of these headcases with AKs and RPGs and God knows what, roaming round, like bandits, like packs of mad dogs. Just out of control. Tanks, some of them had. Bloody tanks! I ask you. Different tribes would fight against one another, and the Shias would fight the Sunnis, and when they got sick of that, each group would fight among themselves. And, just for variety, every now and then they'd fight us.' He glanced up. 'Angie, Barney put forty rounds through that car. I'd love to tell you he didn't, but he did. A woman – girl, really, about seventeen – and two little kids. The mother was still screaming when I got there, but that didn't go on for long. Just as well. She'd lost her bottom jaw, poor bitch.'

I looked at Angie. She had one hand on the end of the bench as if to steady herself.

I said, 'There must have been a reason.'

'Oh, sure. A couple of ragheads had hijacked the girl's car. They come roaring up to the checkpoint, firing fit to bust. One of our lads gets all heroic, breaks the rules, steps into the road and fires back, and then his weapon jams, and he's left standing there like a spare prick. Barney's the NCO in charge. He sees this lad hung out to dry. And Barney's weapon doesn't jam. That's how it happens, this kind of thing. That quick.'

'But he couldn't know about the woman and the children,' Angie said. 'How could he know?'

'Of course he didn't know. No-one did till we pulled them out the car, what was left of them. The only consolation was that he also hit the two pricks who hijacked the car. So at least Barney could show justification. He might've been up for murder otherwise.'

Angie said, 'So the whole thing was a mistake, just a horrible accident?'

'We don't have accidents in the Paras, love. Not since Bloody Sunday we don't.'

Walker unclamped the chair leg from the vice and puffed dust from the surface and stroked the wood again and squinted down the length of it, checking for imperfections. It was a remarkably delicate piece of work in his big hands.

'But this wasn't the first trouble he was in,' I said. 'There was some assault. When he lost his stripes?'

He ran his fingertip along the smooth curve of the timber. 'That was in Bosnia. He broke a corporal's jaw. This lad had gone with a tart and knocked her about. Barney had a thing about that. I didn't like to ask him why, but he was sort of old-fashioned about women.'

Angie said, 'What happened after the Basra business?'

'He wasn't the same after that. Who would be? He wouldn't talk about it. He didn't even speak up for himself at the inquiry. Just let it roll over him. It broke something in him, I think. Not long after, he packed his bags and walked, just as quiet as a lamb. Like I said, I never heard from him after. I didn't stay in much longer myself.'

I said, 'So he wasn't actually discharged?'

'He was due to sign on again, but he just didn't do it. I think the powers that be were happy enough about that. Pity, though. All the lads looked up to Barney. He was a natural. You can tell. I'd already been in two years when he joined up, but I could see, soon as I laid eyes on him, there was something special about him.' Walker nodded at me. 'You know what I'm talking about, don't you? You say you're not army, but you know.'

'Yes.' I saw Carrick's picture in my mind and remembered my immediate response to it: that I would like him, that I would want him on my team. 'Yes, I know what you're talking about.'

Walker put his work aside and came out from behind his bench and stood in front of me.

'Angie here wants me to tell you that Barney couldn't have done this to your missus. Well, I couldn't swear to that. No offence, but I didn't know your wife, and I didn't know Barney's deal with her. One thing I do know, if you push anyone hard enough, they can do all sorts of mischief. But I'll tell you this – the way Barney was after Iraq, snow in August's more likely.'

Angie stopped the car in the mews behind my house and turned the engine off.

'Buy a man a drink?' I said.

'I want to come in for five minutes.'

I let her in through the back door. She walked through into my study and stood at the window with her hands on the sill, gazing out at the drab little garden.

'I thought you'd be pleased,' I said.

'After hearing what happened in Iraq? Barney killing those poor people?'

'But at least it was an accident. And Chris Walker backed up everything you said about your brother.'

'I didn't prime him to do that, if that's what you think.'

'Put your bristles away. I never thought that.'

She stood looking at me for a few moments. 'So what do you think now, Michael? Do you still believe Barney could have hurt Caitlin, after what you've heard about him? Do you really think he would have come here, to this house, and done this to her?'

I hadn't expected her to ask me so directly, and for the moment I could not answer.

'A deliberate act of murder? You must know he wouldn't have done such a thing. Even if he'd been capable of it – which he wasn't - do you suppose he would have come here, in broad daylight, when anyone could have seen him, and *killed* her?'

'For God's sake, Angie, I don't know. Maybe Iraq was what pushed him into it. How could anyone be sure?'

'Why is it so important for you to believe Barney's guilty? Is it just because he and Caitlin were lovers?'

'I don't know the answer to that either. But for what it's worth you're not the only one who thinks someone else may have done it. I told you that before.'

'They're not serious, Michael. They aren't really saying *you* could have done this, are they?'

'It's what DS Barrett calls a bit of private speculation. I expect he's just shaking the tree.'

'Bastard.'

She turned away from the window and wrapped her arms around herself and prowled around the room. There was something locked down about her, some repressed energy, and I found it impossible to take my eyes off her. She stopped by the desk. I had left Caitlin's drawings of the cottage there and she slid them carefully out of their plastic sleeve and onto the desktop.

'Caitlin must have had such talent,' she said. 'The police showed me copies. But these are more beautiful even than I remember.'

'Why did they show you?'

'Did I recognise this place? Did Barney ever talk about a place like this? That sort of thing. They thought it might lead them to him, I suppose.'

'I thought so, too. You didn't, obviously? Recognise the cottage?'

'Oh, no.' She touched the drawings reverently with her finger-tips, sliding the heavy paper over the desk so that several of them were displayed at once. I moved up beside her and clicked on the desk lamp and the drawings leaped out at us.

Angie had stopped at one in particular. I knew why this picture attracted her. It attracted me too, every time I went through the portfolio. In it, the front door was wide open. As if standing just outside that open door, Caitlin had sketched details of a room, a plain room with boarded floors and an iron grate, a rug and a suggestion of patterned paper on the walls. And an internal doorway through – to what? – a bedroom or a kitchen? Some other chamber in her life I had never seen. I knew that the objects I could see through that open door were real objects, things which Caitlin had touched and lifted. Furniture, paintings, books. And somewhere just out of sight, presumably, there would be pots and pans, plates and glasses and cutlery. A kettle and a teapot and maybe a couple of favourite mugs with Larsen cartoons on them. A patterned duvet, pillows, a bed.

I said, 'It was their place, Caitlin's and Barney's.' It was the first time I had linked their names out loud.

'Yes. I can see that it was.'

'It's like she had another world to live in, somewhere she preferred to the one we'd made together.'

'People make their own choices,' Angie said quietly. 'Sometimes they don't realise the damage they do.'

She moved the drawing and in doing so uncovered the road map which lay on the desk beneath it, with the village of Barnes Wittering circled in red felt-tip. 'Is this where the cottage is?'

'If it is, I couldn't find it.'

'But you went to this Barnes Wittering place?'

'I was hunting ghosts. I know it's crazy.'

'Did you find any?'

'No. That's the way with ghosts. You can only see them when they want you to.'

'Jesus,' she sighed, 'we're a pair, aren't we?'

She stood facing me, balanced there, one fingertip resting on the desktop between the drawings. I could sense her energy, like static, and in a moment I could feel it too, thrumming in the pit of my stomach.

'Do you want to punish me for this?' she said. 'For all this hurt they've caused you? For what you think my brother did?'

'Angie, of course I don't.'

'Good,' she said. 'That's good.'

She reached up and put her arms around my neck, and very briefly – before I had time even to draw breath - pulled herself up tight against me. Then she let go again, and stepped back, leaving her hands on my shoulders.

'There's enough pain around at the moment,' she said, 'and I won't add to it.'

The click of the back door lock sounded like a gunshot and we both started, and Angie let her hands fall away. There was the sound of a woman swearing and the door juddered open as someone kicked it and Stella backed through, staggering under the weight of half-a-dozen shopping bags. From one a potted purple iris sprouted and the bloom quivered over her shoulder. Stella set down her burdens on the floor and looked through the study door and saw us.

'Oh,' she said. 'I thought...' She put her shoulders back. 'I didn't think you were in, Michael. I meant to surprise you.'

'You did.'

Angie said quickly, 'I was just leaving.'

She walked past Stella, giving her a small nod as she went, stepped over the shopping bags and out through the back door. I hurried after her, out of the open door and down the little garden, and caught up with her as she was unlatching the back gate.

'It's OK, Michael. I know the way.'

'Angie –'

'Listen,' she said, facing me, 'I was probably well out of order in there. But I've never been much for play acting. Always call a spade a bloody shovel, or so Uncle Stanley says. But I just get so sick of it, you know?'

'Of what, Angie?'

'Of a step forward for me being a step back for you. You sink, I swim, and the other way about. It shouldn't have to be like that.'

My hand was on the edge of the gate and she let hers rest on it for a second, out of sight of the house.

'Don't you worry about this, Michael. We'll just let things ride for a while, OK? I won't call you, or anything daft like that. I won't bother you. We'll try and settle for doing one another as little damage as possible, one way and another.'

She let herself out of the back gate and closed it behind her, and I listened to her little Fiat buzz away before I walked back to the house.

'Well,' Stella said, and looked archly at me.

'Well what?'

'Who's the pre-Raphaelite with the accent and the attitude?' And as she said this, she must have realised. 'Oh, Michael. Don't tell me she's who I think she is.'

'Her name's Angie. Angie Carrick.'

I walked across the room and busied myself rescuing the potted iris which had fallen over, spilling soil on the floor. I was confused and embarrassed, and annoyed with myself for feeling that way.

'Michael, tell me you're not. Not really. Not with the prime suspect's sister?'

'I'm not anything, Stella. Not that it's anyone's business but mine.'

'Don't you dare tell me it's not my business!' she shouted and her sudden ferocity startled me. 'We're supposed to be friends, aren't we? And in case you'd forgotten, we're friends who are going abroad together in a few weeks. That makes it my business!'

'If you say so, Stella,' I picked up her shopping and dumped it on the kitchen surface.

'So how come I get the feeling there's another agenda running here?'

I rounded on her. 'I'm not running anybody's agenda but my own right now, OK? I haven't got space for anybody else's. Not hers. Not yours. Not anybody's.'

She blinked. 'Do you want me to go out and come in again? Or maybe go out and stay out?'

I got control of myself. 'I'm sorry, Stella. But you don't need to concern yourself about this.'

'I do though.' She sat at the table and got out her cigarettes and lit up. Perhaps this was a little act of defiance and she was challenging me to chide her about it, but I didn't have the heart. 'You don't make it very easy for us, Michael. For your real friends. For me and Anthony, for example.'

'Anthony.' I groaned. 'I've been neglecting him.'

'I've kept him posted, but he cares so much about you, you really ought to ring him more often.' She looked at the tip of her cigarette. 'I never thought I'd have much in common with the old buffer, but now I know just how he feels.'

'How does he feel?'

'He's worried sick, but he doesn't know whether he should ring, or come round, or whether that would make him just an interfering nuisance.'

'And that's how you feel too?'

'I felt that way three minutes ago.'

'I'll call him,' I promised her. 'You're right. We should all get together, like we used to.'

'He'd love that. Go back to his place for one of those gargantuan lunches. Let him cook. Make him feel useful.'

'Right,' I said.

'Michael, I think he would like us all to pretend for a while that none of this happened. To go back to the way things were.'

'Christ. Wouldn't we all.'

I caught myself hoping she would drop the subject. I was ashamed of myself, but at this moment I was wearied by the thought of one of Anthony's weekend roast lunches and his equally heavy concern. I knew Stella was trying to help, but I resented it all the same. I didn't want to go back, to make some empty pretence that the world hadn't changed. I couldn't work out what I did want, except right now that I wanted to be left alone.

'I'm free this Friday,' she said. 'We could do it then.'

'The police are filming a reconstruction. I have to be around.'

'Saturday, then,' she persisted. 'Portobello Road's on a Saturday, isn't it? Maybe we could all go to the markets together. Bores me shitless, but Anthony'd love that.'

'OK, Stella. OK.'

'Good.' She jumped to her feet. 'Saturday. Leave it to me.' She bustled past me, putting away the shopping she had brought, finding a plate on which to stand the iris in its pot. Almost as an afterthought she said, 'Besides, we'll need to have a talk about Venezuela, won't we?'

CHAPTER TWENTY-THREE

A uniformed constable brought us a couple of cappuccinos from Stavros' café around the corner, and handed one to Maureen Dickenson and one to me. I recognised the constable as the boy who had broken Caitlin's pot plant all those weeks ago during that very first interview. I remembered his anguish then and I gave him what I hoped was an encouraging smile. He returned it nervously and escaped as fast as he could. It struck me that if ever he got to be a grizzled superintendent, he would still be repeating the story of how he had screwed up his very first major crime scene. There was nothing he would forget about that day, the day of Caitlin's death. I wondered how far that could possibly be true of the hundreds of people who had passed the house on that ordinary morning, with no reason to suspect anything, and nothing unusual to see.

The police had blocked the road and a small crowd had formed behind the barriers. The film crew's minibus was parked up on the kerb and behind it stood three or four police vehicles. In my canvas chair I felt like a movie mogul. Busy men in anoraks were laying a miniature trolley track beside the kerb and mounting a camera on a dolly. There was a sound boom, and a small battery of lights, and a tangle of cables across the roadway.

I said, 'Is this really going to do any good?'

'You'd be surprised what people recall when they have a specific event to focus on, Michael,' Maureen Dickenson blew the steam from her coffee. She was doing her best to sound confident. 'It can bring back all kinds of things they didn't think were important at the time.'

Her answer sounded rehearsed to me. The whole thing was starting to make me nervous. The day was very cold and there was a little snow in the air. I shivered. I wanted to get this charade over with and go back inside the house and shut them all out.

The director, an unshaven man in a Burberry jacket, was shouting from across the street. 'A little quiet, please!' He clapped his hands for attention. 'We'll just walk through it one time, people, but let's make it as true as possible, OK?'

'Are they making a movie, then?' an elderly woman called over the barrier behind me. She had grey hair and she was wearing a plastic rain hat. The young constable asked her to keep her voice down. 'Well, what movie is it?' the woman persisted. 'Who's in it? Who's the star?'

'Quiet, please!' the director roared.

'Well,' the woman muttered. 'I only bleeding asked.'

The actress had already started her walk into shot, swinging along the opposite pavement towards the house. I had hardly ever seen the street empty and her footsteps rang clear in the silence, as if they were ticking off the seconds before some explosion. I found myself asking the same question as the woman in the plastic rain bonnet had asked: who was the star here? Some anonymous girl from an agency – someone who had always wanted to play Ophelia, maybe, and instead got her big break wearing a blonde wig and impersonating a dead woman. If ever she got famous perhaps she'd tell the story on some chat show about how she'd been Caitlin for fifteen minutes. *Quite a high profile murder*, she'd say. *You might even remember it.*

Maureen Dickenson leaned towards me. 'Michael, if there's any part of this that doesn't ring true to you it's very important you tell us so we can get it right. The smallest details could matter.'

The actress was wearing Caitlin's black Chinese jacket with red dragons on it, and Caitlin's red silk scarf which matched it. She had Caitlin's short hair, she was the same height and the same build. She even walked with something like Caitlin's high catwalk gait. She trotted up the steps to the house and opened her bag for her key. I tried to concentrate. Was there any part of this that didn't ring true? The question was absurd. A stranger was dressed in Caitlin's clothes, mimicking Caitlin's actions and about to let herself into Caitlin's home. How could any of that ring true? The girl had the keys out now and was fitting one of them into the lock. I had a great urge to leap up and demand to know what she thought she was doing, walking into my home, impersonating my dead wife.

'Very good, that's fine,' the director called, and the scene collapsed. 'Couple of minutes, we'll do it for real.'

The girl turned and came smiling down the steps and then realised that perhaps she shouldn't be smiling, not in this role. She ducked her head and walked back to her starting position behind the parked minibus. The crew got back to work on the camera dolly. A man unfurled a reflective screen and someone else paid out yet another electric cable from yet another reel. The lights sprang on in the dull morning and the scene became an amber stage. Someone tested sound levels in a low voice. Someone cracked a joke.

'Is it that blonde bit off *East Enders*?' the woman in the rain hat called to the constable behind us. 'Here, Young Mr Plod – get her to sign me Tesco's bill.'

'I can't do that, madam.'

'Don't you take that tone with me,' she snorted. 'It's not like you're a real copper. You're only in a bleeding film.'

I shifted in my seat. 'Maybe nobody saw anything.'

'Michael, there's always a chance,' Dickenson touched my sleeve. 'We're talking mid-morning on a Friday, on a busy London street. It's worth a try.'

I glimpsed Barrett on the far side of the road, prowling between the cars and minibuses, looking up and down the road, checking angles and vantage points. He was moving methodically, squinting up at the top floor windows along the street.

'Digby Barrett is a good officer,' Maureen Dickenson said, following my glance, although neither of us had mentioned him. 'But he does have a taste for the Gothic.'

Was this an apology for Barrett's *private speculation*? Did she even know about that? If she was playing some sort of a mind game with me, she had got it just right. An irrational fear was growing in me that out of the two or three million people who would watch this clip on the TV over the next few days there would indeed be those who had noticed Caitlin walk through that door, perhaps others who had noticed me come in a little later - but somehow no-one would have seen Carrick. Somehow he would have slipped past everyone, like some dark force, like a deadly gas.

'Stand by!' the director shouted, making me jump. 'Quiet please.'

The street fell silent.

'Rolling. Action.'

Caitlin's ghost came clicking down the street again, jaunty, carefree, the bag bouncing against her hip. She put one hand on the railings and her foot on the bottom step.

'Michael! Michael Severin!' The shout came from the back of the little crowd behind me. 'Let me through, will you! Let me through at once!'

For a moment I couldn't place the voice. Dickenson and I turned in our seats. There was some jostling and a few protests and raised voices. The woman in the rain hat said again, 'It's only a bleeding film.'

From the steps the actress glanced round at the commotion. The director said: 'For Chrissake,' in a tired voice, and then, more loudly, 'Cut!'

Behind us a small man was remonstrating with the young policeman. 'I live here! Do you hear me? I live here, and I have to speak to Dr Severin *at once*.'

'Henry?' I walked over to the barrier.

Henry Kendrick, my neighbour. He stood there in his blue blazer with its Air Force buttons, arguing with a knot of people. His neat tie was slightly askew at the neck of his check shirt, and he was a caricature of outrage and dismay.

'Henry?' I said again.

He heard my voice, looked up and found me through the crowd. His face filled with pain. 'This isn't true, Michael, what they're saying? About lovely Caitlin?'

'So you hadn't heard.'

'I've just come from the airport, for God's sake! Just this minute. Dropped my bags over there somewhere.' He looked distractedly behind him, and then back at me. 'And now they hit me with this. Say it isn't true, Michael. Tell me.'

He looked utterly stricken. I knew Henry only casually and I was surprised by the extravagance of his reaction.

I said, 'I wish I could tell you that.'

'But when did this happen?' He was nearly frantic. 'Exactly *when?*'

'Henry, you couldn't have helped in any way.'

'No, no, no, you don't understand at all, Michael. I've got this awful feeling. This *awful* feeling.' He swallowed, got himself under some control. 'Just tell me it wasn't on the fifteenth. Not the fifteenth of October. Not then.'

I opened my mouth but I could not speak.

Dickenson stood up briskly. 'We'd better all go inside, I think.'

In the kitchen I poured Henry a brandy and brought it through to him.

He was sitting near the window, pale and breathing rapidly. He loosened his tie. 'Forgive me. One doesn't expect this kind of thing. Next door, as it were.' He took the brandy from me and sipped it gratefully. 'Appalling thing. Appalling.'

The drink restored him a little and he shook himself. Henry was a trim sandy man in his late sixties. When he shook himself he did so literally, like a terrier. He breathed deeply in and out a couple of times, like a gym instructor leading a class.

'You have to be very sure about the dates,' Dickenson said, forcing him to focus on her. 'Very sure.'

'It was definitely the fifteenth, Inspector. Definitely. I'd hardly forget it, after all.'

I tried not to guess what he would say next. I didn't like brandy but I began to wish I had poured myself one too.

'There was some lash-up with the flights.' Henry was struggling to speak calmly. 'I've got two boys, you know. One in the States and the other in New Zealand.'

'Yes,' Dickenson was keeping her impatience under control with an effort, 'so you were away visiting them when all this happened.'

'Quite so. I'd booked to fly Auckland to Boston via South America, but bloody Air New Zealand cancelled the flight and the only connection was back through London – with a twenty-four hour stopover. They'd booked me into the Heathrow Hilton, but I thought I might as well sleep in my own bed. Water the plants. Pick up the mail. So forth. So I came back here for the night. The night of the fourteenth. That's why I was in the house the next morning.'

'And you saw Catey,' I said.

'I did, Michael.' Henry looked at me in renewed anguish, as if having seen her made him in some way responsible. 'I saw her come back from the shops, right down the street here, and let herself into the house.'

'You're sure of that?' Dickenson asked.

Henry bristled at once. 'There's nothing wrong with my eyes, dear lady. RAF observer's eyes. Like a peregrine falcon's.'

'Quite sure of the date?'

'It's on my itinerary. I have it here.' He took a folded sheet of paper from his jacket pocket and handed it to her.

She glanced at it. 'And how was she dressed?'

'Well, she wasn't got up like that young woman outside, I'll tell you that for nothing. Light top - cream or white - and jeans. She wasn't wearing a jacket and scarf at all. Oh, no. But listen to me -'

'She's wearing those clothes in the CCTV footage.'

'I can't answer for that. It was quite warm that day. Maybe she'd changed. Those bags she was carrying weren't Selfridges bags, either. They were Marks & Spencers bags. But you're missing the point entirely -'

'And you can be certain about the time?' Dickenson persisted. 'Think about it. It's quite important.'

'I don't need to think about it, dear lady. I was just getting ready to leave again for the airport - had a cab booked for 11.15 - and I saw the poor girl come back with her shopping. Saw her from my window, just above. It was 11.08. I logged it.'

'You *logged* it?'

'I keep a little book.' Henry made this sound perfectly natural. 'Keep an eye on things in the street, d'you see?'

'What point are we missing, Henry?' I prompted.

'Well, it's the young chap you should be asking about, surely to God! The fellow who came calling just after Catey arrived. Tall chap. Dark hair. Motorcycle gear.'

Within an hour they were all gone. Henry left with the police to make a formal statement. The film team packed up their equipment and the little crowd dispersed and the road was reopened and it became, once again, just a London street on a grey winter's day.

I went back inside and shut the door behind me. I had expected to feel relief but I was filled with restlessness. Henry's story would not settle in my mind. I kept seeing that dark figure on the front doorstep, and Caitlin's face as she opened the door to him. Henry's account made it real to me in a way that it had never been real before. But most of all I thought of Angie, and her unshakeable faith, and I didn't like to imagine how she would react when Barrett or some other heavy handed copper broke this news to her. For a while I convinced myself that I could resist, but in the end I let myself out, got the Audi out of the garage and drove to Brixton.

The street market was packing up, the dull afternoon full of the ring and clatter of steel frames from the dismantled stalls and the roadway was crowded with vans backing up to receive racks of clothes and boxes of books. I went down the alleyway past the Indian emporium. For a moment the smell of spices made the street exotic. In the betting shop next door men leaned on counters and gazed up with entreaty at TV monitors. The rising gabble of the race caller followed me all the way up the aromatic stairwell.

Angie opened the door. I did not remember knocking, and perhaps I did not knock. She was wearing a sweater with a colourful zigzag pattern, and her black hair was tied back and to one side, and at first glance this made her look very young. But her eyes were not young.

She said, 'They've found him, haven't they?'

'Not yet.'

'What, then?'

'There's a witness, Angie. Someone who saw Barney at the scene.'

'That's a mistake.'

'There isn't any mistake. A neighbour saw him arrive at the house.'

'And this neighbour only comes forward now?'

'He'd been overseas. But he was there when it happened. And he saw Barney. He's identified him. The times fit. Everything fits.'

She stared at me, silenced.

I said, 'Can I come in?'

She stood aside and I walked in. Uncle Stanley was seated at the table in a haze of blue smoke. He was reading a newspaper folded into a twelve-inch square.

'Well, if it isn't young Dr Seven. There's tea in the pot.'

'I won't be staying.'

The old man raised his eyebrows and went back to his newspaper.

'It must be mistaken identity.' Angie closed the door and followed me into the room. 'They happen all the time, screw-ups like that.'

'Angie, my neighbour is a man called Henry Kendrick. He used to be an RAF observer. He has eyes like a hawk. Henry can see straight down onto my front doorstep from his window. It's less than thirty feet. He identified your brother from the photo.'

She stood facing me, her jaw tense. I could see her desperately processing the information, computing and re-computing it, trying for a different answer.

Uncle Stanley began to gather his smoking paraphernalia.

'When?' Angie demanded. 'When is he supposed to have been there?'

'Caitlin got back to the house just after eleven. Barney turned up almost immediately, and nine minutes after that he left again, in a hurry. Looking distressed, Henry says.'

'Nine minutes?' she echoed, attempting sarcasm. 'Not seven minutes forty two-and-a-half seconds? I mean, couldn't he be a little more precise?'

'That's Henry. He's like that. When he's there he watches the street like an FBI agent, with a telescope and a stopwatch. He keeps a log, for God's sake. He's got a thing about people parking in the mews. He's got nothing else to do.'

Uncle Stanley shuffled to the window and peered up at the gunmetal sky. 'We've had a lot of weather recently, I reckon.' He went to the door and pulled on his long ginger coat.

'Well, and what if he *was* there?' Angie squared up to me. 'They were lovers, weren't they? So he came visiting her. You might not like it much, but it's not against the law. It doesn't prove he killed her.'

'So it's coincidence, is it? He just turned up at the house? And - what? - someone else happened along and killed her?'

'Maybe it happened after Barney left.'

'And before I arrived? And without Henry Kendrick or anyone else seeing anything? Come on, Angie.'

'I'm just going outside,' Uncle Stanley said majestically, and put his flat cap on his head. 'I may be some time.' The door opened and clicked shut, and in a second I heard the old man's shoes on the wooden stairs, and after that the little flat filled gradually with silence.

Angie was trying to meet my eyes, but for once seemed not quite able do so. She looked lost, like some hunted animal, running out of places to hide.

'I'm sorry, Angie. Truly.'

'Sorry?' she said bitterly, 'at least they won't be pointing fingers at you any more. You should be glad.'

'I'm not glad about any of this.'

The last of her aggression crumpled. She took a deep breath and let it out again. 'Jesus Christ, Michael. Why does it always come down to the two of us to sort this out? There's supposed to be a system, isn't there?'

'There's no system. In the end it's just you and me trying to make some sense of it all.'

Her mouth twisted, and she went to the window and stood gazing out over the endless brick and concrete blocks of the city. I stepped up behind her and put my hands on her shoulders and she did not pull away from me. Instead she closed her eyes, and rolled her smooth cheek against my hand and let it rest there for a moment. The branches of her collarbone were warm under her sweater.

'I can't take much more of this,' she said.

'I know.'

She turned quickly and put her arms around me and held on tight, so that I had to brace myself slightly to accept her weight. She seemed suddenly very small, clinging there, my arms around her and her dark head against my chest. I lifted her heavy hair and stroked it, and she let me do this, moving a little against me. I kissed her and her arms came round my neck and I could feel the whole length of her and smell her skin and her hair. She leaned back against my arms and put one hand up to my cheek and let it rest there. She held my gaze steadily. Then she pulled away and led me wordlessly through into the bedroom and pushed the door shut behind us.

She sat on the edge of the bed, looking at me. She was not smiling. As I watched her she turned away from me and drew the big sweater over her head and the pearl light from the sky fell in a bar across her, and shone on her pale skin and on her dark hair. She had a tattoo, a graceful tendril of vine leaves curling up from her waist and into the groove of her spine. I sat on the bed beside her and slid my arms around her waist and cupped her small breasts in my hands and she leaned back into me.

It was the middle of the evening when I woke. I could tell that she was awake beside me in the bed, though she had made no sound beyond the smallest alteration in the rhythm of her breathing. It was dark in the room, but we had not drawn the curtains and the glow of the city filled the sky and reflected a salmon light from the clouds.

Outside in the stairwell I could hear the door of an upstairs flat shut with a bang. Young people were talking excitedly as they clattered down the stairs, on their way out to a pub or maybe the movies. It was still early and they did not trouble to keep their voices down. They laughed and shouted at one another and pounded on the door of a friend's room, and then laughed and shouted some more, and finally they moved on down and away across the car park.

It was strange to be awake now, peaceful, full of a secret lassitude, while other people were going out, loud with energy, to start their evening. I wondered how long we could stay here quietly like this. I hoped it would be for a long time. I didn't want to think about tomorrow.

'What did you find when you went to that village?' she asked softly from the darkness. 'That place on the map?'

'A little bit of someone else's past, that's all.'

'You wanted to find the cottage. Their cottage.'

'Yes.'

'You hoped to find Barney?'

'I hoped to find Caitlin.'

She sighed. 'It was their place, Michael, that cottage. It belongs in some other time, like Barney and Caitlin do.' She drew me against her. 'He did love her. I know that and I know him. That's how I know he didn't kill her. I just want you to open your mind to that.'

'Love doesn't grant you immunity.'

I thought again of the photos of Barney Carrick, and the way I had felt his spirit radiating from them, a wild spirit, and the unexpected sympathy I had felt before I could arm myself against it. I wondered what Caitlin had seen when she gazed at this young man. I wondered who she had seen when she gazed at him.

I sat up on the edge of the bed. The window was a slab of ebony. I could hear the wind lean against the glass so that the fittings creaked.

'That Stella woman,' she said suddenly. 'The redhead?

'What about her?'

'Are you sleeping with her?'

'No.'

'Well, did you have – I don't know – some sort of an arrange-ment when you were overseas with her? Friends who fuck, that kind of thing?'

'No. Does that matter now?'

'Has there been anyone since you married Caitlin?' she per-sisted. 'Anyone at all?'

'No-one.'

'But even so you think you failed her, don't you?' She sat up behind me in the bed and rested the flat of her hand on my bare back. 'You think you let Caitlin down and it was all your fault. Don't you?'

'You said something like that to me yourself, once.'

'I know better now.'

'Do you, Angie?' I shook my head. 'We go to bed together once and you have all the answers?'

'I know this much. Whatever mistakes you made, it was Caitlin who broke faith with you, and not the other way round. Maybe you should think about that sometimes, Michael. Just to balance the books a bit.'

She moved against me and slid her arms around me from behind so that I could feel her breasts flattening against my shoul-ders. Her hair was cool against my skin.

I stood up quickly, pulling away from her, and walked to the window. I leaned my forehead against the glass, grateful for its cold kiss. 'I couldn't help her that day. When I found her.'

'She couldn't have been helped.'

'I'm in the rescuing business, Angie. That's what I do. If I can't do that I might as well turn out the lights.' Outside the jewelled city skyline shimmered in the gloom. 'I called her from Venezuela. I wanted us to have a new start. That's what she wanted too. But I'd left it too late to tell her.'

Angie sat up on the bed. 'So? There was plenty Caitlin didn't tell you. For starters she didn't tell you she was three months pregnant by another man.'

'How could she tell me that?'

'Why not? She's not the first woman it's happened to. And if she had told you, could things have turned out any worse than they did? At least you could have talked it through. But she never gave you that chance. Or herself.' She slid out of bed and padded up close to me, not touching. 'Michael, maybe you're right and you fucked up royally as a husband. But it's not a hanging offence. You didn't do this thing to Caitlin. It's not your fault. You're not a mind reader. And you can't raise the dead.'

'Christ, Angie.'

'Still, if you want to flog yourself, I can't stop you.' She reached out and held up the bronze key which hung around my neck so that it shone in the low light. 'And this? Is it to remind you of more people you couldn't save?' She let it drop onto my chest. 'Somewhere along the line, Michael, we all have to find time to save ourselves.'

I stared at her, full of resentment for what she understood and what she failed to understand. And yet we might have made our way through even then, if we had been granted just a little more time. But at that moment the front door latch clicked, and at the mundane sound of it the magic trembled and fled like smoke, and left us standing as if caught in a searchlight, two people in a mean little bedroom, wondering how we had got here and what we had done.

We both heard the old man close the door behind him with farcical quietness, and then creep across the main room, bump into a table in the dark, mutter a curse and let himself into the other bedroom. The springs of his bed twanged as he sat on it. He was trying so hard to be quiet, but he was puffing a little after his climb up the stairs and the sound of his wheezy breath came clearly through the plasterboard wall. I looked at Angie and could see it in her face too. It was as if this trivial embarrassment had shown us everything that would follow, the entanglement of it all, the twisted loyalties, the endless compromises.

I gathered up my clothes, not knowing what else to do, not wanting to look at her. Angie stepped back from me and sat on the bed. She reached behind her and pulled up the sheet and gathered it around herself.

She said, 'This was a mistake, wasn't it?'

'Angie –'

But she shook her head, a violent gesture to block out my voice. I dressed quickly in the darkness and walked out past her without looking at her again. I was still shrugging into my jacket as I emerged into the bitter night.

It was gone ten when I drove the car into the mews. A parked vehicle at the end picked up the glare of my headlights: a dark green BMW. Barrett had one foot on the bumper, bending to buff a black shoe with a yellow cloth. He straightened as I drew up. He wore a hound's-tooth sports jacket with a pattern so stark in the streetlights that it was hard to look directly at him.

'Hello, Dr Severin!' he boomed as I got out of the car. 'Tried the front, Baz and me. When you wasn't there, we thought we'd give it a couple of minutes out here, just to see if you'd turn up. You remember Baz Ellis?'

Ellis put his head out of the driver's window and lifted one languid finger from the wheel by way of greeting. I recognised the young black detective who had come here with Barrett once before. The gold stud in his ear winked in the light.

'What do you want?' I said. I did not want Barrett here and I made no attempt to disguise the fact.

'And here you are,' Barrett went on cheerily, as if I had not spoken, 'large as life. Baz? Get out of there, you idle sod, and give me a lift with this.'

Ellis sprang the boot open from inside and came reluctantly round the back of the car. He was a man who cared about his appearance, I saw, immaculate in tan slacks and tailored jacket and rather too much gold jewellery.

'Get hold of the other end, Baz,' Barrett was lifting a bulging plastic garbage bag out of the boot, gripping it by two corners. Ellis gingerly took the other end. 'If you just get the gate. That's the way.'

I did as I was told. The two men heaved the sack in through the back gate and dumped it on the wet brick path. Ellis stood back and beat at his trousers and smacked his hands together. 'Jesus, Sarge, I'll never get the pong out.'

'Prime Metropolitan Police horse shit,' Barrett told me proudly, ignoring him. 'And as you may have heard, there's plenty more where that came from. We get most of it from the executive floors, which is odd when you think they can't get the gee-gees in the lifts. I always wondered about that.'

I stared wordlessly at the shiny bag of manure.

'Don't you mention it,' he said to my silence. 'Now if you just spread some of that round the roses – not too much, mind, like I told you – they'll be up a treat, come next June. Like bleeding Chelsea Flower Show. Never fails.'

Ellis was clicking his tongue and prancing on one leg, trying to examine the soles of his shoes. He hopped his way back out of the gate and I heard the car door close behind him and the radio came on. Barrett let a few more moments glide past.

'I don't really want to talk right now,' I said.

'Well, that's understandable. But I'm not here to talk. I'm not even here to deliver horseshit, truth be told.'

'What, then?'

'I'm here to apologise.' He spread his hands humbly. 'I was wrong. Now that we can put Carrick at the scene, that's obvious. But you understand we sometimes need to fly a bit of a kite. It's not personal.'

I had been prepared to argue with him, to defend myself in some way, but this left me nowhere to go. I could not tell if he meant what he said, but at this moment I did not much care. I wanted him gone and I sought for the answer which was most likely to make him leave. I said, 'I suppose you were only doing your job.'

'Yes, that's true. But still.' He slapped his hands together. 'Anyway, all behind us now, eh? About the only thing Your Mr Kendrick didn't have was a home video.'

'Henry's very proud of how observant he is. He used to be in the RAF. Perhaps he told you.'

'Not above forty times. But anyway, it's thanks to him we know what happened. It's still circumstantial, of course, but I'd have to say it's pretty open and shut.'

Barrett prodded the black garbage bag with one toe, tugged up his trousers, and bent down to take a pinch of damp soil between finger and thumb. He crumbled it, smiling up at me.

'What did you really come here for?' I said.

'Lay down with dogs, and you'll get up with fleas.'

'What?'

'You've been seeing young Angie. More than seeing.'

I reached across and opened the gate wide. 'Thanks for the shit.'

He stood up. He ignored the open gate and moved into my space and let his smile fade. 'Your wife's been murdered. Just weeks ago. And you're sleeping with the sister of the prime suspect. You think that's clever?'

I did not want to admit it to myself, but his physical presence intimidated me. He saw this and relaxed a little, his point made, and moved back just a fraction.

'You don't know these people like I do, Dr Severin. Angie and her low-life brother. They're not like you and me. They're animals that run in packs, like stoats. They'll stick together through thick and thin.'

'Is this what you came to tell me?'

'Everything else comes way down the list for them. Right and wrong, other people's deserving. The law? That's hardly in it at all. Trust me, that little vixen will do anything to help her brother. Anything at all.'

'So you're watching her.' I imagined some shabby man in a raincoat, standing across the road, peering up at the window of her bedroom. I supposed I could be seen through that window, too. Maybe somewhere there were even grainy pictures in a file.

Barrett saw the distaste flit across my face. 'Get real,' he said. 'I'm a police officer.'

'She's guilty because her brother is? Have I got that right?'

'Well, well,' he shook his head, 'she's done a job on you already, ain't she?'

He brushed the crumbled soil off his hands, smiling unpleasantly. I realised that Maureen Dickenson's absence made me uncomfortable, which was curious, because her presence had always made me uncomfortable too. Yet, alone with Barrett, I knew that once again I had been led into an ambush, and it unnerved me to think how unprepared I had been for it.

'It's over with now,' I said. 'Angie Carrick and me. It was a mistake, and it's in the past.'

'I'm glad to hear you say that. If I were you, I'd keep it that way.' He nodded to me, and walked to the gate. 'Because the apple don't fall far from the tree. You remember that.'

Chapter Twenty-Four

I waited in the darkness until his car drew away, and finally let myself into the empty house.

The house was no longer welcoming. I seemed to feel the weight of the hollow rooms stacked around and above me. I didn't want to see the familiar spaces in which Caitlin and I had moved and laughed together. I felt as if I had been unfaithful to her, and was humiliated at being found out, especially by Barrett. It made no difference at all that these feelings were irrational. In the dark of the kitchen I poured myself a drink and took it straight upstairs.

I showered for a long time and came back into the bedroom towelling my body. I convinced myself for a moment that the shower made me feel better. But then I looked around the room. Beamish on the bed, Grandma Lavinia's picture on the wall, Caitlin's clothes in the wardrobe. I could not work out what had changed about these familiar things, but I was aware of something refracted, some perspective altered. It was as if everything in the room had moved a step back from me, had edged the first millimetre into another dimension. Into the past.

I sat on the bed. I did not want to feel them retreating from me, Beamish and Lady Lavinia and Caitlin herself. I could hear their fading voices, full of sadness and reproach. I stared at the floor between my bare feet, and then closed my eyes, pleading with Caitlin in my mind, summoning her face. But her image wobbled and dissolved. No effort could make her features coalesce in my mind. I opened my eyes again, for a second touched by panic. Caitlin's pillow was still there on the floor, tucked half out of sight under the bed where

I had pushed it so that I would not be too cruelly reminded. Now I wanted to be reminded. I wanted it desperately. I grabbed the pillow and shoved it into place on the bed and pushed my face into it, breathing hard, breathing in the last traces of her scent. But still her face would not come back to me. It seemed unkind of her not to come to me now, just when I needed her so badly. I had never known her to be unkind before. I hooked my arms under the pillow and folded it up around my ears, trying to block out the strangled sounds forcing themselves out of me, and which, despite the pain of their release, I could no longer hold back.

When I awoke it was close to dawn. I was cold, hunched uncomfortably on top of the bedclothes. I rolled over. Outside a steely light touched the slates of the rooftops. I got up stiffly and walked across to the window and opened it. The air was like iced water on my bare skin. It was Saturday, but between the houses I could already see the lights of early traffic moving along the high street. The morning was very cold and a sparkle of frost shone on the pavements. I felt calmer now.

I dressed and went downstairs, and as I got to the kitchen the phone rang. 'Did you sleep?' Angie said, as soon as I picked up.

'I suppose I did.'

'Good. That's good.' Her voice sounded tight, distracted. 'Only I couldn't. Oh, God. I didn't realise it was so early.'

'It doesn't matter.'

She hesitated. 'Michael, I didn't mean... I just thought we could comfort each other. For a little while.'

'We did, for a little while.'

'I didn't mean for us to make it worse.'

'There's just no room for you and me in all this, Angie. We forgot that for a moment, that's all.'

I stood holding the phone, looking out at the drab garden in the cold light, and in my mind I saw Digby Barrett again, lounging by the gate, giving me his sneering look and his contemptuous lecture.

'I'm sorry,' she said to my silence. 'I'm very sorry.'

'I'm not.'

I didn't wait for her to say anything more, but put the receiver back gently on the hook.

I went out after that. I did not think she would ring back but I did not want to risk being in the house if she did. So I walked for an hour or two around the West London backstreets, breathing the cold air, watching the city come awake. Lights were springing on in houses and flats. Eventually I stopped at a caravan selling bacon rolls and bought one and a mug of tea the colour of mahogany. The food and the awakening energy of the day restored me. At a little after nine I walked back to the house and let myself in.

Fitful sun fell in ramps through the dining room windows. The food sat warm inside me and I felt sleepy and vague. I spread myself on the windowseat on the far side of the room and gazed into the bright spaces, drifting. I should open my mind just a crack, Angie had said. Not much. Just enough to let the light in. I wondered if there would ever be enough light to show me what had happened that day, here in this house. If I had got back just a few minutes earlier I might have seen it for myself, but those few minutes were lost in darkness and confusion. I tried to picture the scene now. Perhaps we'd had it right all along, and Caitlin had refused to leave with him. I liked to believe that. I could see her in my mind, standing near the top of her narrow stairs, her bags at her feet. Perhaps she was tearful, perhaps shouting. And Carrick would have been standing over her, tall and dark in his motorcycle leathers, protesting or pleading, or simply begging her to be quiet.

I wondered what had sparked the violence. Maybe he had lost control and lashed out – a reflex, something from his training, maybe. Things like that happened. I knew that now. They happened even to people without training. And she had fallen, tripping over the cases, clutching at the ridiculous marble bust, bringing it down on top of herself. Had he even tried to catch her? Had he in his horror for once reacted just too slowly?

It might have been that way. Barrett had said to me that time that he could live with some sort of an accident. Yes, I thought. Maybe I could live with that too. I got to my feet and stretched in the thin light.

Stella's maroon Golf came bouncing to a halt outside the front window and my thoughts fled like drops of mercury. I got up and went to the door and watched as she parked in her usual slapdash fashion, jutting into the road. She got out but did not see me there at first. Under her coat she was wearing a neat jacket which looked a little formal for a passing visit. A hint of awakening memory began to stir in my mind.

'Hello, Stella,' I said, cautiously.

'Michael.' She stopped in surprise on the bottom step, her breath steaming in the cold. 'You're not ready.'

'Ready?'

Her mouth hardened and she put her hands on her hips. 'Michael, you bastard, you've bloody forgotten, haven't you? Anthony? The market? Lunch at his place?'

'Oh, Jesus, Stella. I'm sorry.'

She advanced threateningly up the steps. 'You've got precisely five minutes to get your arse into that car.'

By the time we walked into the market it was after ten. It was December now and there was already a Christmas atmosphere about the street, a Dickensian buzz and bustle. The roadway was crowded with stalls heaped with glassware and china and clothes and bric-a-brac and junk, and with bargain hunters picking over these things. The air was full of haggling, laughter, a certain determined cheeriness.

Anthony was waiting for us in a café in Bayswater Road.

'My dear old chap.' He rose to his feet and gripped my hand.

'Hello, Anthony.'

Now that I was here, it surprised me how glad I was to see his anxious, mournful face, the portly penguin figure with its conker-bright shoes. He stood there, smiling a little bashfully because he knew he could not disguise his delight at seeing me, his breast pocket handkerchief blooming. It was yellow spotted silk this time, and a bow tie to match, and a tweed jacket with leather patches, a concession to weekend informality. I saw then that there was something unchangeable about Anthony, and I realised how very important that had always been, and how crucial it was to me now. I might sometimes grow impatient with him. I might find his concern just a little claustrophobic. But Anthony would always be there, fighting my corner. For a second I could have put my arms round him as we stood there between the tables, and I might have done just that if I had not known how terminally such a display would have embarrassed him.

Perhaps he guessed what was going through my mind, for he announced suddenly, 'Action! Bold action is what a day like this calls for.' He fussed around finding his coat and his stringback gloves. He was the only person I had seen in two decades who still wore stringback gloves. 'Up and at 'em,' he cried. 'Steady the buffs. That sort of thing.'

We spent an hour wandering around the market. As always Anthony was greeted at every turn by the stallholders, and by dealers and bargain hunters in the crowd, people he had met at sales and auctions over the years.

'It's spelter, Mr Gilchrist. We don't see much of that about, eh?'

'Be seeing you at Bignor Manor on Monday, Mr Gilchrist? Some nice porcelain coming up, they tell me.'

'Signed copy, Mr Gilchrist. Absolutely bloody pristine.'

Anthony would stop and handle an ornament or a book or a miniature, click his tongue approvingly, exchange a word with the vendor, and then replace the piece. It was a ritual he went through again and again. Everyone knew that he never bought anything from the tables.

I could see Stella was bored by it all, and perhaps still miffed with me, but I didn't care. I felt light headed and distant. I enjoyed the familiarity of the place, the warmth of Anthony's pleasure, the sense that nothing very much was required of me except to be here.

A couple of hours at the market, and then down to Richmond and one of Anthony's legendary winter roasts. I could handle that today. Perhaps it was about all I could handle.

'Mr Gilchrist!' called Harry Judah. He was pushing through the crowd, half hidden behind a cardboard box of clocks which jingled as he walked. He could barely see over the box and his trilby bobbed comically above it. 'Were you planning on visiting us at the shop today, then?'

The shadow that passed over Anthony's face took me by surprise. His displeasure was so marked that I grew instantly alert and my peaceful mood evaporated at once.

'And young Mr Michael, too,' Harry rambled on innocently. 'It's been a while since we've seen you here. Couple of years at least.'

'Hello, Harry,' I said, 'it's good to see you again.'

Harry lowered his tinkling box to the ground and shook my hand, smiling broadly. He was in his mid-fifties now, I supposed, a creased little gnome of a man. I looked into his eyes as he shook my hand. I could tell from his expression that he did not know about Caitlin. Perhaps that was the cause of Anthony's discomfiture: he was afraid Harry Judah would say something clumsy.

Harry turned to Anthony, his eyes twinkling. 'We didn't see too much of you at the Amsterdam fair, Mr Gilchrist.'

I realised he was taking a shot at Anthony about something, but with the tension that was in the air he was on thinner ice than he realised. I wanted to warn him.

'But of course you saw me,' Anthony said testily. 'At least a dozen times, for God's sake. Don't talk nonsense.'

'Oh, maybe once or twice,' Harry winked knowingly at me, pleased to be getting a rise, 'but I think you must have found some fine pieces elsewhere, that's what I think.'

'Think what you damned well please!' Anthony snapped, with a flash of vehemence which made Harry Judah start, and then he added, a little bashfully, 'Good Lord, there were a thousand people there.'

'Just as you say, Mr Gilchrist.' Harry lifted his chin. He took up his box again, and from behind it pulled a face at me, a clown face which was meant to invite laughter, but instead betrayed how hurt he was. 'Another time, Mr Michael.' He nodded at Stella and moved away, his box clattering, his trilby bobbing over the top of it.

'What was all that about?' I said.

'Bit of a falling out, I'm afraid.'

'With Harry Judah? Over what?'

'It's nothing,' Anthony muttered. 'A piece he sold me turned out to be a fake. Of course I should have spotted it, but still.' He seemed to make a physical effort to regain his former bonhomie and banged his gloved hands together. 'Never mind! Come along, come along.'

He strode away, and we followed in his wake. But the episode continued to trouble me, and I hung back a little, turning it over in my mind. By chance, as we crossed the High Street, I glimpsed Harry Judah again a hundred yards away, loading his box of treasures into the back of a van.

'I'll meet you at the car,' I told Stella. 'I want to pick up a paper.'

Harry had loaded his goods and locked the van doors by the time I caught up with him.

'Young Mr Michael. Twice in one morning. What a pleasant surprise.' I could tell from his tone that he was still offended with Anthony, and by association, perhaps with me, too.

'What's the story, Harry?'

'Story?'

'I've never seen you and Anthony cross swords before.'

My directness deflated him at once and his face fell. 'My fault. I was out of order, ribbing him when you and the lady were there. Don't you worry about it, Mr Michael. He'll get over it, silly old tart. Time of the month, probably.'

I blinked. 'I'm sorry?'

'Well, I missed him once or twice during the fair, see? Truth to tell, he was probably off with one of them Indonesian cuties they have in Amsterdam. Everyone knows, of course, but we're all supposed to pretend we don't. Silly, ain't it? This day and age. But I suppose I broke the rules, teasing him about it in front of you.'

'Anthony? We're talking about Anthony Gilchrist?'

'I'll make it up with the silly old sod, don't you worry.' He shook his head in wonder at the absurdities of human behaviour. 'You'd better catch them up.' He turned to go.

'Harry, wait. Are you telling me he was off with some hooker?'

'Hardly, Mr Michael,' Harry laughed. 'Not with some *girl*.' Then he saw my face, stopped and pushed his trilby back on his head. 'You must have known. Come on. Gent like him? No lady friend in his life? Come on.'

'Harry, I'd no idea.'

'Oh, my good Gawd,' He was suddenly aghast at what he had revealed. He began to speak quickly, as if he could cover his indiscretion even now. 'A sweeter man you won't find, as you well know, Mr Michael. But Mr Gilchrist just has his little predilection, that's all. Only sometimes, when he's overseas. When it can't offend no-one. There's nothing wrong with that, is there, Mr Michael?'

'There's nothing wrong with it, Harry. I just never knew.' I focused on him. 'You must think I'm a complete fool.'

'Not a bit of it, Mr Michael, not a bit of it.' He spoke in an indulgent way that showed this was precisely what he thought. 'And what does it matter anyway? Just – don't let on I opened my big kisser, eh? I could bite my bleeding tongue off.'

'Don't worry about it, Harry.'

I walked away, leaving him standing by his shabby old van, watching me unhappily and tossing his keys in his hand.

I took a roundabout route between the market stalls to get back to the car. I hoped the detour would give me some space, but though I went over and over it in my mind I could not get a grip on this new knowledge. I had always thought of Anthony as a bachelor of the old school, eccentric, rather lonely, but at peace with himself. I had never considered any sexual dimension to his life at all. I found it grotesque to think of him with some streetwise rent boy in an Amsterdam hotel room. But most of all I felt sorry for him, that he had had to lock such an important part of himself away from me for all these years. And I felt an idiot, a blind idiot, for not having worked this out for myself years earlier.

'For Chrissake, will you move yourself, Michael?' Stella bellowed across the road. 'I'm freezing my tits off here. And where's the bloody paper, after all that?'

It was early afternoon by the time we reached Anthony's, and the cool sun slanted in through the windows at the back and fell into the dark interior of the house, making rods of light for the dust to dance in.

'First,' Anthony announced, leading the way into the kitchen, 'bold action is called for in here.'

His appliances – toaster, kettle, blender – all dated from the 1950s, heavy chrome and enamel units with rounded edges like Cadillac fenders. I had seen modern imitations of such devices make a comeback as fashion accessories, but his were the real thing, picked up in sales and auctions over the years and lovingly restored. Through the French windows I could see into his conservatory. He had cleared away his half-restored clocks and musical boxes and set the dining table, and I realised he had been preparing the house for hours. The roast must have been cooking while we were out, for the kitchen was already full of the savour of hot meat and herbs.

'Too many cooks!' he declared. 'Michael, you get the fire going in the study. Stella and I will handle things here.'

I glanced at Stella. She gave me a long-suffering look. We both knew Anthony would assign her some domestic task in the kitchen – something for which she was hopelessly unsuited – and then he'd find an excuse to slip out and spend a few exclusive minutes with me.

In his study the fire was set and ready to light. I touched a match to it and sat in one of the huge brown chairs while I waited for him. The logs were very dry and they caught at once, sending swarms of sparks up the chimney. I watched the flames and let them warm my face and hands.

It was all achingly familiar. And yet some perspective had shifted here too, just as it had shifted back at home. Here too something appeared to be retreating from me. Perhaps this was to do with my conversation with Harry Judah. Not to have known such a thing about Anthony made me wonder what other messages I had missed. I looked around at the antique clocks which kept only approximate time and chimed at unpredictable moments, at the crossed cavalry sabres over the fireplace and the stuffed caiman on the mantelpiece. It was certainly no ordered display of taste or style. It was a curiosity shop, as if the contents of Anthony's mind had been magically made real, so that the room was full of things from another age, strange things, whimsical things, but things redolent of continuity, of a simple wonder in the world, and – underneath the clutter – of solid and changeless values. Among those values was one that enjoined a man to keep his private weaknesses to himself, no matter the torment of loneliness it caused him to do so.

Anthony bustled into the room. 'Bizet, wouldn't you say? It feels like a Bizet sort of day.'

He crossed to his expensive stereo and whisked off the cloth which covered it and fiddled with the controls and in a second the sultry and passionate music was filling the room. He stood there with his eyes closed, silently conducting, comfortable in his market clothes, his leather-patched jacket and his mustard bow-tie and his corduroy trousers.

He said, 'I think we've probably got time for a tissue restorer before we eat, don't you?'

He fussed around the antique drinks cabinet and came over to me with an enormous scotch. I saw that he had poured himself an equally huge brandy and soda, and something told me that despite his joviality he was nervous. I wondered if he guessed I had gone back to speak to Harry Judah.

'To better times, old chap.' Anthony clinked his glass against mine.

I was full of affection for him at that moment, and full of remorse and sympathy. I would have liked him to know that I understood, that he no longer needed to hide, no longer needed to worry about my reaction or anyone else's. I thought that if I could somehow tell him this, it would be a precious gift to him, and some kind of recompense from me for all his sacrifice through the years. It could have been a moment of great meaning between us. It should have been. But it was precisely then, as Anthony's glass touched the mahogany of the table, that everything began to go wrong.

'Now,' he said, rubbing his hands together, 'I've prepared a few things you'll need.'

'Need? For what?'

'I've got it somewhere here...'

He got to his feet again and made a pantomime of looking around the room as if he had misplaced something. Finally he found a cardboard box near the window and lugged it over and set it on the floor between us. It was full of books and maps, some new, some clearly garnered from market stalls. On top of this jumble was an ancient solar topee.

'Now here's a prize exhibit!' Anthony lifted the topee and set it on his own head, so that he looked like some comic opera Victorian general. 'Isn't it splendid? I can't quite see you wearing it in the operating theatre, though.'

'What's this about, Anthony?'

He made round eyes at me. 'My dear boy, it's about Venezuela. Your trip.' When I didn't reply he bumbled on, sorting through the books in the box at his feet. 'Look at this, will you? A 1910 Baedeker for Latin America. I think the place has changed a bit since then, but maybe it will provide you with some amusement on the flight, at least. Some of this other stuff might be of rather more practical use. It's the best I could find, anyway.'

'Anthony.'

'Now about the Notting Hill house,' he powered on. 'Naturally that's going to be a difficult decision for you. My personal opinion? Put it on the market, old chap. That's my advice. I realise that will be a wrench, but you must feel free to leave me with power of attorney, and of course I shall take care of everything. We can have dear Caitlin's things...disposed of – for charity, perhaps, or in any way you see fit. Or we can put them in store until you feel up to coming back and dealing with them yourself. You must know that we'll all do everything to make this as easy for you as possible.'

'I'm not going to Venezuela.'

I was astonished to hear myself say these words. I had made no considered decision. But now that they were spoken I could feel the world shift around me, like a great boulder that had been poised, and now slides a little and lodges securely once more. Anthony stared at me in silence as the fire popped and spat in the grate.

'Nonsense,' he said at last.

'I'm not ready for that, Anthony.'

'But Stella? Her plans? Your plans?'

'I'll tell her.'

'I see.' He cleared his throat. 'I see.'

'I didn't mean this to come up now.'

He clasped his hands together and unclasped them. 'One has to go on, Michael. No matter what. Otherwise, one allows them to win, you see? The evil people who visit such tragedy upon us. And they must on no account be allowed to win.'

'I won't achieve that by going to Venezuela.'

'But it will lead you back into work! It will lead you back into life.'

I shook my head. 'I'm not sure that what I need right now is to rush back into work. Or life, for that matter. I did think that, but now I'm not so sure. I have to get things straight in my own mind first. And not in Venezuela. I have to get things straight here.'

He looked at me unblinking and the sides of his neck went white. I had not seen this happen since I was a schoolboy, sitting across from him in this very room. I could not remember what misdemeanour of mine had precipitated it then, but I recalled that it was so rare for Anthony to grow this angry that it had frightened me. Even now I could not quite suppress a flicker of that remembered fear.

'Nonsense,' he said again. 'You're a doctor. A fine doctor. You have a mission in life. You can never forget that.'

'I know you're trying to help. But I don't need my decisions taken for me. Not by you. Not by Stella. I'm sorry that it's taken me a while to see that.'

'This is about that Carrick woman.'

I looked up sharply at him. 'Let's not go there, Anthony.'

'I hardly credited it when Stella told me you'd been seeing her.'

'She had no business telling you anything.'

'We've never dealt in secrets before, Michael. Though I can certainly see why you'd want to keep this to yourself.'

I controlled myself with an effort. 'It's not a question of secrecy. It's just that it's my life, not anyone else's. And, just for the record, Angie Carrick has not done anything wrong. I get tired of reminding people of that.'

'Nothing *wrong*?' He startled me with the ugliness of his tone. 'For God's sake, have you forgotten what her brother did to you? To all of us? And she defends him? They're unspeakable, the pair of them!' He clutched his hand over his mouth and gripped his face hard and stared at me over his fingers, horrified at his own outburst. 'I'm so sorry.' His voice was muffled beneath his hand. At length he took his hand away. His fingers had left white impressions on his ruddy face and these took some moments to fade. 'That was unpardonable.'

Pain was stark on his face and it hurt me to see it. It came to me how very badly Anthony had been injured by the gross barbarism of it all, how completely his genteel world had been thrown into chaos. My world had never been genteel. That illusion at least could not be taken from me.

'It's not unpardonable, Anthony. But I'm going to make my own decisions, about this and everything else. And I'm just not ready to leave here yet. There are too many unanswered questions.'

Anthony took a couple of aimless steps across the room, his back to me. He pulled out his breast pocket handkerchief and flapped at himself. 'Michael, perhaps I have overstepped the mark, rushed my fences. But you don't seem to realise how important it is that you move forward on your life's mission.'

'I'm going to make my own decisions about this,' I said, more firmly. 'Now can we leave it alone?'

He swung round to face me. 'This is not a matter of your decision. You have a God-given gift. It's your *duty* to use that gift. Do you suppose your father would have hesitated for a moment?'

'Please don't lecture me about my father.'

'He would never have turned his back on such a call, no matter what personal tragedy he had endured.' His voice began to climb again. 'And you know quite well that you can't turn your back on it either. After all that's been done for you, Michael. The sacrifices that have been made for you!'

He was shouting, I realised with a sense of unreality, something I could not remember him ever doing before. I stood up. 'What's got into you, Anthony? I've told you, I have to sort things out here, or nothing else will ever make any sense. Now please -'

I put out my hand to touch his arm but he shrugged it violently aside.

'I never thought the day would come,' he said in a dead voice, 'when any son of Duncan's would turn his back on the great challenge of his life.'

I stepped back. I felt as if he had hit me. For a moment I did not think I could bear his contempt. I had never felt it before, and the blast of it now – at this precise moment – began all at once to tear away at a fog in my mind, a fog I had not realised was there. I felt unsteady. I put my hand on the mantelpiece, glad of the cold tiles against my palm. The photograph was there, a few inches away from my face, Anthony's favourite photograph: my father in his blue denim shirt, lounging against a Landrover with palm trees behind him and an inkblot shadow at his feet, laughing, handsome, sardonic.

Anthony watched my eyes. 'Michael,' he said, and now his voice had a falling tone, like the call of a night bird.

I lifted the framed photo and held it up so that in my line of sight Anthony and my father seemed to stand side by side, turned towards one another across the gulf of time which separated them.

And I saw Anthony's face, stricken and desolate, and at that moment I understood.

'You were lovers,' I said, 'weren't you?'

He closed his eyes. 'Ah, Michael, Michael.'

'You don't need to pretend, Anthony,' I said. 'Not any more.'

He was swaying a little, and I thought for a second he would crumple and I would have to catch him. But before I could move he whispered, 'He tried so very hard to do the right thing by Patricia and you and the other children. We both tried so hard. You must understand that.'

I set the photograph back onto the mantelpiece. I searched for something meaningful to say, but could find nothing, and instead I stood staring at the picture in silence.

'Please don't trouble with some liberal platitude.' Anthony gathered himself. 'I know quite well that love is not a crime. I am not ashamed of it. Indeed I am proud. But betrayal – that is a crime.'

'Betrayal? What betrayal?'

'Duncan had a wife and three beautiful children. He was unfaithful to them. We were unfaithful to them, he and I. But he did try so hard to resist. And I did my best to help him. I was prepared to do everything short of not seeing him. Even he wouldn't have permitted that. He didn't want to cause pain. But in the end, *we* were a problem he just couldn't face. A problem altogether too close to home.'

'All the travelling.' I said. 'All those overseas assignments.'

'I used to call him a faithless hound. Running away. But it was all he could do, do you follow?' Anthony gazed at me, his eyes pleading. 'I think he believed that if he could just keep moving, somehow he would stay free of the net, of the awful entanglement of it all.' His lower lip began to tremble. 'And in a way he succeeded. In staying free.'

'You've hidden this away all these years?'

'My dear old chap, what else could I do for him, but keep it from you? It was part of the promise I made to him whenever he went away, that I would keep you safe. From everything.' Anthony smiled at me, but there was the most profound sadness in his eyes. 'I did love him so very much.'

I pushed my hand through my hair. Through my confusion something jagged was breaking surface in me, and perhaps Anthony saw this in my eyes, for he added quickly, 'You mustn't be too hard on him. You must try to understand.'

I had the impression, from the way he spoke, that these were phrases he had repeated to himself a thousand times down the years. Ten thousand times. I imagined him alone in his gloomy bedroom, night after night, seated at the dressing table, the mirror relentlessly offering him back only his own dim reflection.

I said, 'This freedom of his cost a good deal, didn't it?'

'There's always a price to pay, Michael. I was happy to pay it.'

'You weren't the only one paying.' I pointed at my father's picture. 'Do you know why I thought he went away so often? Why he shunted me off to that miserable boarding school I hated, year after year?'

A great stillness came over him. 'You cannot have doubted for a second that your father loved you. That would be unbearable. After all the suffering. Unbearable.'

I heard Stella's quick steps in the hall and she shoved the study door open hard so that it bounced against the wall.

'OK,' she said, her hands on her hips, 'I'm through with the Upstairs, Downstairs routine.' And then she saw our faces, and dropped her arms to her sides and stood looking from one of us to the other. 'What?'

Anthony stood blinking at me, his eyes glistening. I couldn't take my own eyes off his face, though it wrenched me to see the anguish there.

I said, 'We'll talk about this again very soon.'

I touched the hairy tweed of his sleeve and squeezed his arm. I left a gap, but he did not fill it, and I walked out of the room past Stella and took my coat from the rack and went out through the front door and closed it behind me. I turned left down the short drive and out into the grey street. I didn't know where I was going in the raw afternoon and I didn't care.

I heard the door open again behind me, and Stella called, 'Michael?'

I ignored her and kept walking, down the hill away from the house, away from them both. I took a corner at random and strode on.

'Wait!' she cried. I did not wait, but in a few moments she came hurrying after me, her shoes clattering on the pavement, and then she was beside me, looking up at me, struggling to walk and question me and get into her coat at the same time, tenting it with her arms, tangling herself in the strap of her bag. 'Michael, for God's sake, slow down, will you? What's going on between you two?'

I marched on, hoping she would leave me in peace. I took another corner.

'Is it all that Venezuela stuff? Michael, it's his way. He's only trying to help.'

I turned to face her. 'I can't come to Venezuela, Stella. I'm very sorry. I didn't realise before today.'

I saw her jolt, but she recovered almost at once. 'OK. It's all much too soon, I can see that. I've rushed you into it.'

'Yes, it is too soon. But it isn't just that.'

At last she won her battle with her coat and dragged it on and settled it around herself. She said, 'You know very well I won't go if you don't.'

'I'm sorry, Stella, but I'm not responsible for that. I was wrong to let this go on for so long. If I had known earlier I would have told you earlier. But I'm not responsible for your decisions, nor you for mine. We're not joined at the hip.'

I looked around me, trying to get my bearings. I didn't know this street well, though it was only a few hundred yards from Anthony's. A suburban avenue with mock-Tudor houses and neat gardens put to bed for the winter and a few hardy residents washing their Fords and Vauxhalls in the driveways, in time-honoured weekend tradition, their soapy buckets steaming. There was a wine shop over the road and a bus stop a few paces from where we stood, with a glass shelter and a concrete lamp standard.

'Wait here while I get the car,' Stella said at last. 'We'll go somewhere and talk.'

'I don't want to talk. Talking's not going to help.'

'I'll get the car anyway. We can't stand here all day.'

But she didn't make any move to go back for the car. Perhaps
she was waiting for some sort of permission from me which didn't
come. Instead we stood in silence, locked together but not quite
touching. A red double-decker bus pulled up a few yards down the
street and a fat woman swaddled in beige clothing struggled to get
off with half-a-dozen shopping bags and a stroller with screaming
twins in it. The bus knelt at the kerb, its engine snoring, while the
woman puffed and cursed and the children shrieked.

'Michael. Just what are you trying to do to us all?'

The beige woman had got the wheel of the stroller jammed
against the bus door and was hauling at it, puce in the face, while
other passengers fussed around and the driver shouted advice. I
stepped past Stella and lifted the stroller clear and set it on the
pavement, the two children in it goggling at me as my face came
close to theirs. I could smell their new warm breath.

'Don't you turn away from me,' Stella cried.

But I did not trust myself to face her. I stepped onto the plat-
form of the bus.

'Michael?' she called from behind me. There was something
more than anxiety in her voice now, something like fear.

The doors hissed and clunked and as the bus drew away I saw
her standing on the grey pavement, her face tight with pain.

CHAPTER TWENTY-FIVE

For a week or more the world around me fell curiously quiet.
Barrett or one of his team called me every day or so, to
keep me in the picture. I could feel the hunt for Barney Carrick
sharpening by the day. They had a suspect, motive, opportunity,
and now they even had a reliable witness. Once a small team of
officers arrived at Henry Kendrick's place next door, perhaps to
interview him yet again, or perhaps to check angles and sightlines
from his window to my front door. I knew they were working with
other forces around the country, and it could only be a matter of
time before they found their man. Everyone seemed to know that.

Meanwhile, time stood still for me. For the moment there were
no more demands, and I was grateful for that. I let the midwinter
days pass formlessly over me. I went out as little as possible. I slept
at odd hours. I collected the mail each morning from the mat and
stacked it neatly, unopened, on the bookshelf. I read a good deal,
mindless stuff mostly. I listened to the radio late into the night. I
thought about nothing and no-one.

On the Tuesday evening while I was standing at the bedroom
window I saw Henry Kendrick come and knock on the front door
below, and then, when I did not reply, he walked all the way around
the block and up the mews to try the back. But I did not want to
talk to Henry. I didn't want his sympathy, and I didn't have the
reserves to offer him the reassurance I guessed he wanted - that his
evidence had been invaluable, that he had done the right thing. So
I waited for him to go away. He tried the same routine three days
running, but eventually even he gave up. Whenever the phone rang

I ignored that, too. After the first few days I recorded a message on the answering service telling callers that I had gone away for a while. In a sense it was true.

This time in limbo brought me peace: and perhaps that was why, as the days passed on, I became aware of the quiet voice speaking in my mind. It had, perhaps, been speaking to me for some little while, but my life had been too full of noise for me to hear it. This voice told me, softly but insistently, that I was neglecting something. That if I was to move forward, there was one pilgrimage I could no longer postpone. And when the command grew clear enough, I obeyed it.

I had never been back, not in all those years, and I had some trouble at first in recognising the place. The street was narrower than I remembered, and the bare maples and ash-trees in the front gardens were bigger. It took me a few moments to identify the house, but it was still possible to make out where the newer brickwork butted into next door's wall.

I got out of the car and stood on the pavement across the road. The street had moved up-market since my parents had rented here. Young professional couples had bought in, attracted by the proximity to London and by the area's lack of any cachet, which must have kept prices within reach. That much at least hadn't changed. To me it was still a drab and soulless street in a dormitory suburb, rank upon rank of featureless between-the-wars semis. I slipped my hand inside my jacket and felt the hardness of the key around my neck and traced its outline against my skin.

There were lights on in the house. A young mother stood in the yellow square of the kitchen window. She stooped to talk to a child too small for me to see. There were Christmas decorations strung around the kitchen, and the tinsel flashed in the light. My family hadn't stayed here long enough to put up Christmas decorations. And this kitchen wasn't even in the same place: ours had been at the back, with that door of ribbed glass and the chrome lock I remembered all too well.

I doubted I would recognise anything about it now, not even if I knocked on the door and somehow persuaded this young woman to let me in. I wondered whether she knew what had happened to that other family twenty-six years ago – a family perhaps not so very different from her own. I supposed she must have heard something. But after all, it was ancient history now, something that had happened in the dark ages before she was even born.

The sodium streetlights were on all down the road. One of them was faulty: it flickered and buzzed. The occasional car shunted around for a parking space or pulled into a concrete driveway. People were coming home on foot from the station or the bus stop, men and women hunched into their coats, hurrying against the winter wind as it sliced down the street. One or two of them glanced curiously at me as I stood there.

I had felt like a disembodied spirit that other night, fleeing down these black streets in my thin school jumper and flannel trousers, with the sleet driving horizontally between the houses and scalding my face. How cold it had been then. How cold even when I returned from my wild race through the dark, to stand there panting and bewildered as the flames roared from the burning house. Men shouted and ran, clumping in heavy boots. Policemen's breath plumed in the blackness. A fireman's hose coughed out ice which tinkled like glass bullets on the paving stones. Anthony had held me and tried to shield me, to protect me, but of course it was no good. I could not be protected. None of us could be protected, in the end. It was nobody's fault.

When I got home a thin December drizzle was weeping down. I parked the car in the mews and climbed the steps and felt for my keys. In that second of hesitation I heard Henry's sash window slide up, and I knew he had been waiting for me.

'I say, Michael?' he called. 'That is you down there, o'boy?'

Henry's habit of abbreviating phrases in this way was among the more irritating of his pseudo-military affectations. I badly didn't want to talk to Henry at this moment. I was tempted to ignore him even now.

'Michael?' he called again, rather plaintively.

'Yes, Henry,' I said wearily. 'It's me.'

'I don't mean to be a nuisance. Quick word?'

He was rarely so humble. I said: 'Shall I come round?'

'Just a tick, o'boy. I'll be right there and open up the back door.'

The window came down with a bang and at once his back garden light came on, and by the time I had walked around to his door he was sliding the bolt and swinging it open.

'Really appreciate it, Michael. Hate to impose. I know you must be absolutely sick to the back teeth of other people trying to… well, you know… trying to help. Go on up, please.' I did as he said and he scampered up the stairs after me like a squirrel. 'Awful business. Absolute bloody atrocity. Still can't believe it.'

Henry owned the whole house but lived on the first floor. He was a keen amateur astronomer and he would spend the evenings scanning the sky with his telescope from the back window. He claimed that he got a clear view of the heavens from up here, but my own theory was he got a clearer view of the neighbours' bathrooms. There was a nurses' hostel a block away and I suspected it came in for a good deal of Henry's star gazing. I supposed this was a harmless enough pastime for a lonely man approaching old age, and I did not feel as judgmental as once I had. The room was tidy and sad and over-decorated, the walls hung with prints of military aircraft cruising through azure skies. I recognised a Vulcan bomber in pride of place over the mantel and I remembered this was the aircraft in which Henry had served as observer during his years in the RAF.

'Drink?' He saw me waver and added rather pathetically, 'Do say you'll have one.'

'OK, Henry. Thanks.'

'I usually have a G&T about this time, but I've got –'

'G&T's fine.'

'Splendid. Splendid.'

He scurried off to the kitchen. I walked slowly around the room. An ugly lounge suite in butterscotch fabric. Silver trophies on the mantelpiece for billiards and darts. Framed photographs on the wall showing Henry as a younger man shaking hands with Prince Charles, leaning languidly against the nose of a camouflaged aircraft, standing with senior officers in Air Force blue. I moved across the room and stood for a moment at the back window, next to his telescope.

'I know how much the police valued your statement, Henry,' I called through to the kitchen, searching for something that would please him.

'It's a pleasure, I do assure you, as far as anything in this awful situation could be called a pleasure. Anything I can do to help to get that vile bastard caught and put away.' He chopped savagely at something on a board out of sight. 'This sort of thing makes you wish we still had the death penalty. Though that's too damn good for him.'

He came back into the room with two crystal tumblers the size of flowerpots. A quarter of a lemon floated in each. He handed me one. Even without raising it to my lips I could smell the strength of the gin in it.

'You seem to be the only person around here who keeps his eyes open,' I told him.

'One thing that isn't wrong with me – eyes like a bloody peregrine falcon, Michael, even at my age. Actually if I'd been half-blind I couldn't very well have missed him. The filthy bloody swine.'

He stopped abruptly and for some seconds the loudest noise in the room was the fizzing of the bubbles in the drinks.

'Point of fact,' he said. 'The thing is.' He moved his mouth to one side and looked at the carpet and then at the ceiling.

'Henry, why don't you tell me what's wrong?'

He drew himself up, as if to attention. 'Can't sleep. Keep thinking I should have done more. Feel I let the side down. Totally.'

To my astonishment his eyes filled with tears.

'Henry, we all feel like that. We all feel helpless. Me more than anyone. But what more could you possibly have done?'

'I saw this bastard come in, and I heard an argument of some kind. Shouting match. Walls are pretty thick, but still.' He looked at me in appeal. 'I think I may have heard the whole bloody horrible thing happen. I put it in the statement, of course, but I can't seem to get it out of my mind. I'll never forgive myself.'

'But for what, Henry?'

'I could at least have put my head round the door, once this chap had left. Checked up that Caitlin was all right.'

'Look, nobody expects -'

'But, you see, I thought you were in the house while this was going on.'

I stopped. 'Me? How could I have been in the house?'

'I didn't know you'd gone overseas. And when I saw your car out the back there – well, I assumed you were at home. I rather thought you'd given this young chap a piece of your mind, sent him packing. Perhaps even had words with poor Caitlin. I didn't like to interfere. Bit of a domestic, I thought. That sort of thing.' He gnawed his lip. 'And my cab arrived at that moment, so off I went to the airport, thinking everything was under control. Wish to God I hadn't.'

'Henry, you lost me somewhere there. You say you saw my car?'

'Thought I did. That maroon job of yours. Pulled up just out there in the mews. But of course I know now that it couldn't have been. Yours, I mean. And obviously you weren't in the house at all, but at the time…' His voice drifted away and he looked at me with spaniel eyes.

I thought back over what he had said, trying to make the pieces fit. 'Henry, just go through it step by step for me, will you? I want to get it straight in my mind.'

'Very well, o'boy.' He seemed relieved to be asked to give a precise report. 'First, I see Caitlin come home. A minute or two later, she lets this young chap in through the front door. He's clowning around with some flowers he's picked from the tub on your step. Acting the Romeo. Hamming it up. It's pretty obvious that they know one another, to put it mildly. Well, I didn't much like the look of this, so I took a shufti out the back into the mews, just to see if your car was there. To make sure you were home.'

'My car was in the garage the whole time I was away.'

'I know that *now*. But at the time I saw this dark red job, same colour as yours, just pulling in, as I told you. You can only see the roof from here so I couldn't do a proper ID. But it was right outside the back of your place, so I just assumed it was yours. Then after that there was the shouting match, and pretty soon this young fellow left again, rather more quickly than he came in, looking, well, pretty shaken. And I thought: good for you, Michael. You've told him where to get off.' Henry gazed helplessly at me. 'But it wasn't your car at all, was it? It must have belonged to some bloody shopper. If it hadn't been for that, I'd have checked. Called in on Caitlin. I thought you were home, so I did nothing, went off to the airport.' He shook his head. 'Never forgive myself. Never.'

It made me sad to think that the smallest of false assumptions could haunt him in this way. It taught me something, to see the futile pain in his eyes. Something about the fragile balance of all our lives, about the uselessness of asking what might have been.

'I want to tell you something, Henry.' I put my drink down and took his shoulders between my hands. I had never touched him before and I could see it startled him, but I forced him to look at me just the same. 'If you had called the police the moment Carrick walked into the house, they would not have been in time to save Caitlin. No-one could have saved her. I couldn't. Nobody could have. You're blaming yourself for her death because some shopper parked a red car in the lane? How crazy is that?'

He stood there for a minute, pursing his mouth. Then he said, 'Bless you, Michael,' and turned away towards the back window.

I knew I had taken a weight from him, and I was glad. But I was aware too that somewhere within me a much heavier and more ancient burden of my own had begun to shift, something I could not at once identify. I waited a moment, wondering whether to speak again, but Henry was still at the window, his back to me and his hands linked, his thumbs rapidly circling one another. I quietly left the room.

I had barely closed my own back door behind me when the wall phone shrilled in my ear, startling me so that without thinking I snatched the receiver off the hook.

'Why are you doing this to me?' The voice was strangled with fury and distress.

'Angie?' I hardly recognised her. 'What is it? What's wrong?'

'You're behind it, aren't you? You're sending her!'

Her tone frightened me. She sounded ill, tormented. How long ago had our last phone conversation been? Two weeks, now? Two short weeks and she seemed to have swung from melancholy to mania.

'Angie, you're not making any sense.'

'You listen to me, Michael. You send that Scottish bitch around to spy on me again and I swear I'll put a brick through her windscreen and drag her down the street by her hair.'

'Stella? Are you talking about Stella?'

'Did you think I wouldn't spot her? Her and that beaten-up heap she drives?'

'Angie, I don't know what -'

'An old VW,' she said. She read out letters and numbers, challenging me. 'Is that her registration, or isn't it?'

It was Stella's registration. I could not speak.

'Three times in the last week, Michael!' She was shouting now, close to losing the last of her control. 'What's the big fucking idea? Are you trying to send me some kind of a signal you haven't got the balls to deliver yourself?'

I leaned on the kitchen counter top and stared out into the night. I was silent for so long that she almost screamed, 'Michael? Are you listening to me, you bastard?'

'I'll deal with it,' I told her, and hung up.

Chapter Twenty-Six

Stella had always maintained that her life was too nomadic for her to settle permanently anywhere, and that was why she rented her Queensway basement flat. In fact she had lived here for years, ever since I had first known her. I could not count the number of times I had been here for parties or dinners, or to talk about our next trip or to hold post mortems on the last one. And this was where she had brought me on the day Caitlin had died. Stained concrete steps led down to the well where the dustbin stood, and a single desperate geranium struggled for life on the shelf outside the front door.

Stella must have heard me come down the steps for she opened the front door before I could knock. She was wearing a cheerful apron which bore a child's painting of the seaside with smiling sun and blue sea. But she was not smiling. She stood with her head thrown back and her mouth set. I had the strongest suspicion that she had been waiting for me.

'So she spotted me at last, did she?'

'For God's sake, Stella. What have you been doing?'

'Save your breath. If you're looking for an apology you won't get one from me.'

She tossed back her hair and walked away from me down the hall. I closed the front door behind me and followed her, picking my way past a tilting pile of nursing magazines, an old computer, boxes of books and garbage sacks with labels marked 'OXFAM'. There were a couple of big canvas grips, a backpack and six plywood tea chests in the living room. She had taken down the posters

291

from the wall, leaving pale squares on the plaster and little greasy marks where the Blu-Tack had been.

In the kitchen she turned to face me.

I said, 'We have to talk.'

'Yes, I've been trying to get you to do that for some time.'

'This isn't the way.'

'Do you want to eat?' she said suddenly, surprising me into silence. 'I've got some pasta left over from last night. You don't mind your pasta a bit dark, do you? It's not exactly burnt. Just a bit crisp.'

It was the kind of jokey exchange we had always shared, and yet now it was as if the lines were being read by strangers. She stood there in her colourful apron, daring me to object.

I said, 'Are you going to tell me what's going on?'

'Let's have a drink, for Chrissake. We could both use one.' She walked past me and unpacked a couple of tumblers and a bottle of Scotch from one of the tea-chests. She filled both glasses and handed me one, then clinked them so hard that I thought for a second mine had cracked.

'Stella, listen –'

'Yes, I went over to Brixton a couple of times to take a look at your little friend. Is that what you want to hear?' She raised her eyebrows at me.

I sat on the arm of the sofa. 'Why?'

'Honestly? Mostly to satisfy my curiosity. To see what she had over me.'

'For the record, it's over. It hardly even began.'

'She whistled, you jumped. I wanted to see why.'

'I'm sorry you've been so hurt by all this, Stella. I never meant that to happen.'

'Oh, don't worry yourself, Michael. I can see the attraction. She's got something, right enough. She's not exactly a Caitlin, but she's some way ahead of me, evidently. Despite all we've been through together. But I suppose a few years of friendship and shared history don't count for much in the end.'

'That's not fair.'

'You should try seeing it from where I'm standing.'

Her face did not betray any emotion, but I could feel her pain in the pit of my stomach.

She put her glass down on a packing case. 'I just had to see for myself, Michael. That's all. And now I have. I'll be out of your hair in a few days, anyway. Out of everyone's hair.'

I glanced around the cluttered room. 'You're taking the Venezuela job.'

'I think I knew all along that you wouldn't come. Like you said, we're not joined at the hip.'

'When's this happening?'

'The day after tomorrow.'

'You're not wasting any time.'

'Not any more of it. I've resigned from St Ruth's. I've cancelled the lease here. I've even sold the car.'

She delivered this last with a certain belligerence, knowing that this single piece of information must put her intentions beyond doubt. She had driven that beaten-up hand-painted Golf forever. I could not imagine her without it, nor anyone else driving it.

'You didn't have to resign. Curtiz would have held your job for the year.'

'I won't be back.' She found her glass and lifted it ironically to me. '*Salud, dineros.* And who knows? Maybe even *amor.*'

I got up and moved around the room, lifting items and putting them down again, avoiding her eyes. 'You once told me we were two of a kind,' I said.

'I did? That sounds very clever of me.'

'You were right.'

The smoke alarm shrieked. I saw fumes coiling out of the kitchen door, and in a moment I could taste it and hear the spitting of burned food in a pan.

'You weren't that hungry anyway, were you?' She got up and strolled into the kitchen.

I found the alarm above the door and turned it off. I opened the French doors and the front bedroom window to clear the smoke and collected the glasses and carried them in after her. At first I could hardly see her through the fug but I could hear her coughing and clattering as she worked over the stove. The room was still thick with smoke but she had opened the back door and thrown the pans out among the dustbins and the fumes were slipping quickly into the cold night and very soon the air was breathable again. I put the glasses on the kitchen table and filled them and set down the Scotch bottle between them. I noticed that a brown manila envelope lay there.

'Well, that's a couple of pans I don't need to pack.' Stella's eyes were watering, perhaps from the fumes. She squeezed them closed and rubbed them with her knuckles. When she had recovered she walked to the table and picked up her glass and sipped it and made an appreciative face. 'Grandad Macaulay always said you should be able to taste the smoke in it.'

I pulled out a chair and sat down and she sat opposite, gazing at me steadily. 'Are we still friends, Michael?'

'You need to ask?'

'Then I'm going to talk straight to you. Because I don't think there'll be another chance.'

The back door swung in the breeze behind her. It was growing cold in the kitchen and Stella leaned back and flicked it closed. She pushed the envelope over to me.

I said, 'What's this?'

'Call it a last ditch attempt. It's not very dignified, but I have to give it a try.'

I tore the envelope open and slid the plane ticket onto the table between us.

'It's an open return to Caracas,' she said. 'You don't have to use it at once. At all. But it will get you there. It will get you out of here.'

'Stella...'

'Just take it. Do that much for me.' She leaned across the table and opened my jacket and stuffed the envelope into my inside pocket. 'Michael, I know you don't believe it. But it's all going to go bad for you here. I know it is.'

She spoke with such conviction that the skin on the back of my neck began to prickle. I had the oddest feeling that until now we had both been reading from the same script, but that she had without warning switched to a different one. I had no idea what was coming next. She reached across and took my hands. Hers were warm and strong and her fingers gripped mine hard.

'Everyone's so shocked that this happened,' she said. 'But I'm not. It was bound to go wrong. Caitlin was mad to marry you, if she thought she could change you. I'd never have tried that. Father Rafael was right. We can't rest, people like us. We see this world the way it is – utterly fucking insane – but we're doomed to try to fix it just the same. So we really are two of a kind.' I made to pull my hands away but she held them tight. 'I never did like her much, with her cut glass accent and that fey way with her. I'm not proud of it, but when I knew she was dead, there was just a moment when I was glad.'

'Please, Stella.'

'It seems hardly fair that there should be something so attractive in weakness. I feel like I should be rewarded for being strong. But I'm not. Women usually aren't. We're penalised for it.'

'I loved Caitlin. I loved her completely. I still do.'

She held my eyes very steadily. 'So maybe I'm not the princess in the castle, Michael. But I can tell you this much: Angie Carrick isn't either. She doesn't need saving. It's you who needs saving from her. Excuse me if I get a certain unkind satisfaction from that.'

I wrenched my hands away. 'Don't say any more.'

'She's been stringing you along. She knows well enough where her brother is. Anyone but you would have seen it from the start. And I bet she found it pretty easy to distract you.'

'Give me a break,' my temper began to slip. 'What do you think she's been doing? Hiding Barney Carrick in the broom cupboard? Get real.'

'She knows where he is, Michael. If she didn't before, she certainly does now.'

I was struck suddenly by the memory of Angie's wildly altered voice on the phone. Had something indeed changed? I said, 'What does that mean?'

'She goes out all on her own. She doesn't drive. She takes the tube into London and stays away for six or seven hours at a time. Why would she do that? She never takes the old man with her. She never comes back with shopping or clothes or food. Twice last week she didn't come back all night.'

'Maybe she's met someone.'

'Nice try.' She smiled unpleasantly. 'I followed her once.'

'You *followed* her?'

'Aye. I thought I might shove the bitch under a train, and save everyone a lot of trouble.'

The remark was so deadpan that it was hard to be sure that she was joking.

'Och, away with your outrage, Michael! I followed her all the way through London. It wasn't easy. She changed tubes three or four times, jumped buses, all that. She didn't know I was there, but she thought somebody might be. Why would a woman do that, do you think, if she wasn't trying to hide something?'

'So what's your theory?'

'I think she was going to meet her brother. Or contact him, at least. She thought the police would be following her, so she didn't take the car. They'll have bugged it, obviously.'

'We're not getting just a little paranoid here, are we?'

Stella didn't trouble to answer that. She waited. She knew I would have to ask, and at last I did. 'Where did she go?'

'London Bridge station. She went all round the houses to get there, but that's where I last saw her. On the overpass, going off towards the eastern line platforms.'

'This doesn't prove anything.'

'Oh, you're quite right. Dreadful aspersion to cast. Sweet little Angie.'

She crossed her arms and opened her eyes very wide.

I got to my feet. 'You're right to go abroad, Stella.' I pulled on my coat. 'I'm really sorry it's come to this, but you're right to leave.'

I walked to the kitchen door, stopped and turned for one last look at her, sitting alone in her cheerful apron at the kitchen table with the bottle and two glasses in front of her. She lifted her face to me and gave me the merest ghost of a smile.

'Physician,' she said, 'heal thyself.'

From the alleyway beside the betting shop I watched Angie hurrying down the far side of the shining street. Her hair was tied back severely and her leather jacket glistened in the rain. She walked quickly, and above her the moist air swirled in halos around the streetlights. She passed me and crossed into the car park at the back of the Asian emporium.

I pushed myself away from the wall. I was cold and stiff. It was gone eleven at night, and I had been standing too long and at first my legs would not work properly. By the time I reached her she was already at the stairwell door, hunched over her keys.

'Hello, Angie.'

She leapt like a cat at the sound of my voice, spinning to face me, dark eyes blazing.

'You've been out a long time,' I said.

'Leave me alone, Michael' Her voice was hoarse, alien.

The rain pasted her hair across her forehead, and despite her wildness - or because of it - she suddenly she looked vulnerable to me, the way she'd looked the first time I had seen her.

'Angie, let's go inside and sort this thing out.'

'Get away from me!' She slapped aside my outstretched hand. She fought for some control, lowered her voice. 'Please don't make us play through this scene.'

'This isn't about you and me any more, Angie. You know where he is, don't you?'

She was breathing rapidly. 'Go away. Please.'

'You're going to get hurt. This thing's unstoppable now. If you try to stand in its way it's going to crush you. I don't want to see that happen.'

'What's the use of this?' she whispered. 'Neither you nor I could do anything different, even if we wanted to.' She turned away and fumbled with the lock, so that when she spoke again her pale face was in shadow. 'You have to go now, Michael.'

'I could believe it was an accident.' I realised I had echoed Barrett's words. The noise of her jingling keys stopped. 'Something out of his control,' I said. 'Out of anyone's control. Something that started a long way back. I could try to come to terms with that.'

She faced me slowly. 'Barney didn't kill her, Michael. I don't care what it looks like. That's the only thing you need to come to terms with.'

It was still there, in her voice and her eyes, that marble certainty. I did not know, as I had never known, how to scratch the surface of it.

I said, 'You know, Angie, I don't much care any more whether they find him or not. There are even days when I hope they don't, so that I won't have to go through the whole thing again and again, in some grubby courtroom. I know convicting him isn't going to change anything. But I have to know what happened in that house, what brought her to that. And Barney's the only one who could give me an answer.'

Her shoulders rose and fell, but she did not speak, and I knew she would say nothing more. I waited a few moments, but finally I turned and began to walk away. I swung back at the corner and saw that she was gazing at me, her mouth slightly open. Her face was wet and I realised she was crying. She stepped back into the shadows.

CHAPTER TWENTY-SEVEN

At seven the next morning I got up and went downstairs to the study. I set up Caitlin's picture in its familiar place under the desklight, so that she smiled into the room, and I sat and waited for the winter dawn to break.

I was not in a hurry. I had no doubt that it would be today, the end of my searching, and that I need not rush to meet it. A little before eight I showered, dressed in jeans and sweater, and took my time over breakfast. It felt for a while almost like a normal morning, a morning from the old time, with the radio news filling the room, and the smell of coffee on the air. When the rush hour traffic had died down a little, I locked the house, got the Audi out of the garage and drove eastwards across the city.

It took over an hour to crawl through the congested southeastern suburbs, but by mid-morning I was driving smoothly and fast, out through the opening country with London falling behind me. I left the motorway at the A20 junction. Not long after that I turned off again, this time onto a minor road, and then I was cruising towards Sevenoaks through the fat green countryside I remembered from that last trip, a country of farms and villages and handsome houses owned by the London rich.

There was much less traffic now and I was glad to be moving. I settled into the seat and let my mind drift back over the past twenty-four hours. I had a vivid image of Angie as Stella must have seen her, looking like a Cold War spy in her leather jacket, hurrying across the overpass towards London Bridge East, alert and wary of pursuit. Trains from London Bridge East ran into northern Kent. It hadn't taken me long to make that connection. They served not just the industrial regions along the Thames, but the small towns and villages deep in the countryside.

In copses by the roadside the oaks and beeches were skeletons, their upper branches drowned in mist. The fields were bare and here and there the soil was greasy where a farmer had ploughed in the stubble, the new furrows dotted white with scavenging gulls from the estuary.

This would be pretty country in the spring and summer, rich, drowsy, postcard Kent. The Garden of England. Perhaps they had swept out of London on Barney's motorcycle. I could picture the big machine grumbling down these same country lanes on a spring day, the heavy exhaust shaking blossom from the hedgerows. I could see Caitlin, her hands resting easily on the rider's waist, swaying into the curves. Caitlin on a motorcycle. I wasn't aware that she had ever been on a motorcycle in her life. I wondered where I had been when this adventure had started, not merely in what country I had been working, but in what other universe I had been living.

Just as I had the first time, I nearly missed the Barnes Wittering sign buried in the hedge, and I took the turn late, bare hawthorn branches squeaking against the car's bodywork. Almost at once I was there. The village green with its iron benches and chestnut saplings protected by chicken wire, the row of Victorian cottages, the pub, the half-timbered vicarage. I drove around the back of the vicarage and parked. From here I could see into the conservatory where I had talked to Derek Lonsdale, the vicar who looked like a fighter pilot. If there had been any sign of life I would have tapped on the glass, though it wasn't Lonsdale I wanted to see. But the house looked empty, so I walked back down the alley to the village green and across the wet grass which soaked my jeans, and took up my position on one of the benches. The cast iron was so cold that it stung me through my clothes.

I waited an hour. There were very few people about in the grey cold morning. An old lady came past, walking a small dog which wore a tartan waistcoat; she smiled at me. A beer delivery truck offloaded outside the pub, the aluminium kegs ringing like bells against the pavement. A builder's van drew up in a driveway. Two elegant women brayed gossip at one another for ten minutes outside the village shop.

I saw him at last, peddling his Royal Mail bicycle along the lane into the village, his Day-Glo anorak flashing. He caught sight of me almost at the same moment, stepped off his bicycle in the lay-by where I had first seen him, and wheeled it towards me across the grass. He leaned the bike against a tree a few yards away.

'Well,' I said, 'it's the Aussie postman who knows everything.'

He sat down beside me. He said, 'Double meaning alert, huh?'

'Could be.'

He smiled, reached into his anorak and found a tin and a packet of papers, and began to roll himself a cigarette one-handed. I hadn't seen this done for years and the dexterity of it distracted me. He lit up, sat back on the bench and blew a stream of blue smoke towards the white sky.

'I picked you as the jealous husband, see?' he said.

'That's right. I was.'

'Well, that's why I kept stumm. I've had a few problems with jealous husbands myself.'

'Did you know the two of them? Cate and Barney? Did you feel sorry for them?'

'I've never laid eyes on either of them. I don't think anyone in the village has. That's the first time I ever heard their names.' He tapped ash off the wrinkled cigarette. 'I just didn't want to be the one to blow it for them.'

'To blow it?'

'Listen. That old cottage was rented out, very hush-hush, by a young couple no-one ever saw. It was pretty obvious they wanted their privacy. I figured they had a reason. And maybe a right. Call me romantic.'

'I thought it was something like that.'

'So when you came round asking questions I flicked you on to Reverend Lonsdale. He's a good bloke. But he's new around here.

I thought he probably wouldn't know the cottage anyway. And – I don't know – I thought maybe he might be useful to you.' He dropped the last twist of his cigarette into the long grass where it smoked like a miniature marker flare until the dew doused it. 'There was something else.'

'Yes?'

He faced me frankly. 'Mate, I didn't like the look of you. There was something about you. I wasn't sure what you might do if I told you, and you went barging in there and found them. I didn't want to be responsible.'

'Is there something about me now?'

He examined me for a moment. 'No,' he said at last. He got to his feet. 'Maybe I made the wrong call. You never can tell, eh?' He zipped his anorak and walked over to his bike, then wheeled it back and stopped in front of me. 'Wittering Leas Farm, just beyond the crossroads. Don't be put off by the Tory dragon who lives there. The cottage is about a mile into the woods. There's a track from behind the farmhouse.' He squinted at the sky, as if assessing the chances of rain. 'She doesn't want to be found, your missus, does she?'

'Yes and no,' I said.

'Well, if you do find her, take it easy on her, eh? Maybe she had good cause.'

He lifted his hand to me, and wheeled his bicycle away across the green, leaving dark tracks through the silver grass.

I drove past the church and down the winding road out of the village between hedges of hawthorn and bramble which shut the lane in and hid the countryside beyond. The sky was heavy and the land was quiet under the weight of it. I had the impression that the Audi was the only moving object for miles. The gate was set far back in the hedge with a fingerpost above it, pointing to the farm. Beyond, a track led over pastureland towards an ugly modern bungalow with steel outbuildings. The car bucked along the track, fat tyres sending up jets of muddy water from the potholes.

As I drew close to the farm buildings a woman in a green head-scarf emerged from one of the barns and stood looking at me with her head thrown back. She was wearing a fashionably shabby Barbour jacket and she carried a bucket in one hand and a garden fork in the other. She put both these things down against the wall as I drew up and slapped her hands together. A large black Labrador came bounding up to her, skidding a little in the mud of the yard, its ears pricking up as it saw me. I noticed that under the muck, the woman's Wellington boots were the same shade of green as her headscarf. I opened the window. The dog bounced up and placed its muddy paws on the edge of my open window, smearing the paint-work and panting into my face in an ecstasy of welcome.

'James, for God's sake!' The woman cuffed the dog and it fell back from the window and sat gazing up at me in adoration. 'No manners at all, I'm afraid. No pedigree.' She looked hard at me. 'Was there something?'

'There's a cottage,' I said, 'behind the farm somewhere. How do I get there?'

My bluntness made her stare at me. 'Do you mean the old man-ager's house?'

'How do I get there?'

She stiffened, gathering dignity around herself. 'This is private property, you know. You can't just wander off down there.'

I got out of the car. The dog beat the ground with its tail.

'Look here,' the woman protested. 'You can't just leave that vehicle in the drive.'

'The keys are in it,' I said.

I stepped across to the fence. I could see the track now, a muddy path leading from behind the barn, crossing rough meadowland to the tree line.

The woman came bustling up behind me. 'I don't know who you are –'

'Did you see them?' I asked her.

'Who?' she stopped, confused by the question.

'The tenants. Did you ever actually see them?'

'No, as a matter of fact I did not.' She tried to put impatience and irritation into her voice, but I could see she was growing a little afraid of me. 'We don't live on the property. Now if you wouldn't mind –'

'Is that the way there? That path?'

'Yes, but –'

'Thank you,' I said.

I swung myself over the fence and strode away across the lumpy turf. After a few paces the Labrador came bounding up beside me, panting clouds of steam.

'James!' I heard the woman slapping her thigh for the dog, more and more furiously as it failed to return to her. 'James!'

The path led through an old orchard of apple and plum trees, iron-black now, the grass between them rank and sodden. Beyond the far wall the slope fell away, thick with alder and birch, leaf litter soft underfoot. It grew gloomy as I moved over the lip of the ground and down through the trees, slithering occasionally on the wet soil. The path angled down the side of the steep little valley. The air grew still as I followed the track. There was a cathedral quiet about the dripping trees and I moved silently, responding to the hush of the woods. After a while I noticed that the dog had gone and that I was alone.

The track snaked on through the undergrowth. I could not see more than a few yards ahead, but I was aware of the gentle rushing of a stream some way off to my right. I wondered if Caitlin had come this way, the twigs scraping against her borrowed motorcycle jacket, stepping over these roots, padding softly on these wet leaves. And Carrick with her, going ahead, pushing aside the branches and holding them back for her to pass.

The path twisted and then came up hard against a fallen trunk, a column of rotting timber shelved with fungus. It was chest high and I stopped behind it, the wood spongy to my touch. From behind it I could see the steep wooded slope drop down to the valley bottom.

And quite suddenly it was there on the other side of the stream, just a stone's throw away. A run-down brick cottage half-smothered in ivy, a water butt beside the front door. A lean-to with a loose door, some missing slates from the roof, and an old harrow rusting in the weeds outside. The windows were black squares. Trees hung over the house on both sides. The rushing of the stream over rocks filled the air. I could hear the jarring croak of a rook, somewhere in the upper branches. The valley was filled with watchfulness.

I waited for a little while, focusing myself, and then I stepped around the fallen trunk, and walked down the hill and across the stream.

The front door stood slightly ajar and it swung open with the softest of creaks when I touched it. The lintel was low and I ducked under it directly into a square room with a boarded floor and a single bright rug in the centre, blue and gold. A few dead leaves had blown in across the boards. The woodland light fell from two windows in the far wall and made the colours of the rug glow.

It was cold here and the air made my nose prickle, as though the place had been closed up for a while. I recognised at once the narrow iron grate, the cracked pane in the window, the floral pattern of the wallpaper. These details were so familiar from Caitlin's drawings that for a second it was impossible to believe I had never been here before, that this place did not in some way belong to me. And yet I knew in that same instant that the cottage was not at all as I had expected, and that nothing about it was mine.

The room was shabby and comfortable: a low table with a cheap reading lamp on it, two wicker chairs, and a slightly skewed bookcase holding perhaps a score of books. I glanced at them. Some collections of modern poetry. Several books on art and two exhibition catalogues, one Cezanne and the other Turner. A handful of biographies and some history. Caitlin's books. On a shelf under the window was a compact stereo system with a stack of CDs. Mahler. Stravinsky. Bartok. I picked up a sheaf of CD cases and turned them over in my hands. Caitlin had tried to introduce me to these composers, but I had found them hard work, and had never taken to them. And now here was the music she loved, in a world she shared with someone else.

There was a low arch on the far side of the fireplace. It led into a tiny kitchen. A cold wood burning stove. A shelf of tea and coffee containers. A stack of washed plates on the draining board. A miniature refrigerator with yellow post-it stickers on the door. I touched the slips of paper. Caitlin's cursive handwriting. Little notes to herself, the notes she had never returned to read. Reminders to buy the wine they would have tasted together, to bring in more logs for the fire that would have warmed them.

I walked out into the main room again and across to the bedroom door in the opposite corner. I stood in the doorway with my hand on the wall and looked in. The bedroom had a sloping roof and a single small window. Branches outside stirred and tapped against the glass in a way that reminded me of childhood and of shadow patterns on the wall, witches and dragons, of warmth and safety and a big bed. The big bed was there, and finally I looked at it; it nearly filled the little room, spread with an old-fashioned patchwork counterpane of many colours, neatly turned down. I stepped into the room and touched the bed with my fingertips. The sheet was cool on my skin.

The drawer of the bedside table was open a fraction and I slid it out. Inside was a comb, one of Caitlin's tortoiseshell combs, with a single bright strand of her hair caught in it. I sat down on the bed, heard the comfortable creak of springs. Caitlin's hair shone as I rolled it between my fingers. Every single cell contained the entire code for the whole human being, the scientists said. The whole human being. I wondered who would dare to claim they knew what that was. Outside the trees shivered and rattled in the breeze.

I did not see the portfolio for a moment. It was propped beside the bed, a leather case, the twin of the one back at the house, black with important steel clasps. I lifted it, rested it on the counterpane and opened it.

In her drawing Barney Carrick was stretched on the bed, on this bed, with his hands locked behind his dark head, gazing out of the frame, gazing at her, at me. He had just awakened. The sheet was rucked around him, his shoulders bare, one leg extended, unprotected, vulnerable. She had drawn the strong lines of his body, smoothly, cleanly. She had sat just over there to draw him, in that hard-backed chair, in a silence broken only by the tiny hiss of her pencil on rough paper and the tap-tap of the branches against the glass.

I spun Caitlin's hair between my fingers. It made a gold disc in the light as it turned. And it seemed to me then that I heard that hiss and tap, hiss and tap. It seemed to me too that I could sense something on the cool air: a perfume, a pure, slightly astringent scent. The dappled light fell over the chair, as it had fallen over another chair in another secret place years before, another place where she had been – just for a while – happy and safe. And for a moment, as I looked, she was there for me, her hair shining, in my crumpled shirt three sizes too big for her. She frowned with concentration as she worked, the ball of her thumb glossy from the pencil, the tip of her tongue showing pink between her teeth. And it was no longer years ago: it was here, and now, and always, as it would always be. Caitlin looked up at me then, across the room, across time itself, and smiled at me. I closed my eyes. And she was still there, smiling at me, at me alone.

The front door creaked.

I opened my eyes. I waited, but there was no other sound. I closed the portfolio, set it aside. I got up slowly from the bed, watching the rectangle of the open door. I could see a segment of the far wall in the main room, a corner of the bookcase, one of the wicker chairs.

My hearing and my vision grew preternaturally sharp. There was no movement. No flicker of shadow. No sound now except the muttering of the woods. I gathered myself and quickly stepped through the doorway. I had time to see that the front door stood open but then there was a violent blur of action and I staggered as the black dog cannoned into my legs, capering and barking in delight at our reunion. I bent down and spoke to him and stroked him, calming him, calming myself. He quivered in his excitement and extended a length of pink penis and gazed at me lovingly, swishing his tail in great sweeps over the floorboards. I rubbed his rough chest and he lifted his head in pleasure, and then his brown eyes widened and his ears came up, and I realised that he was no longer looking at me.

'It'd be a very good idea,' Barney Carrick said from behind me, 'if you don't do anything sudden.'

I stood up slowly, my back to him.

He said, 'Turn around.'

Carrick had grown the stubble of a beard and this made him look older than I expected. He was tanned and there were lines at the corners of his mouth and his eyes were very pale, unsettlingly pale. He wore a blue knitted ski-cap and a plaid shirt and khaki slacks. The weapon he held had grubby tape around the butt and he gripped it loosely in his right hand, muzzle down. I could not quite adjust to seeing such a thing here, in this room.

He walked past me, keeping his eyes on me, and glanced quickly out of the door. He clicked his fingers at the dog. It flattened its ears but trotted outside at once. He pushed the door shut and latched it with his free hand and came back to stand in front of me. He was a tall, powerfully built man, but he moved like a leopard, lightly and easily. He tossed his woollen cap into the corner and his dark hair fell free. He flicked aside the folds of my jacket, and looked me over with his light eyes. I could see no expression in them. He stood back a pace.

'Are you frightened, Michael?' he asked softly.

'Yes. I'm very frightened.'

'Good. It's important you know what it's like to be frightened. And you've got good reason to feel that way. Coming here. You of all people.'

'I know.'

His voice dropped. 'There's nothing for you in this place. This was our place. You've no business here.'

'I needed to see for myself.'

'And now you've seen. Did you find what you were looking for?'

'I found what I needed to find.'

Carrick cocked his head.

'You loved her,' I said. 'And she loved you. That's why I had to come. To learn that.'

'That's very fine. Very fine.' I could see a muscle tensing in his jaw. 'But it doesn't change things. I'm to blame, all the same. Just like you.'

'We have to draw a line under this, Barney. For everyone's sake.'

'Oh, aye,' he gave me a thin smile. 'For everyone's sake.'

He rolled his neck muscles and set the pistol down on the coffee table, where it lay like a power drill, ugly and functional. He was not, I knew, removing the threat of the weapon. He was demonstrating to me that he did not need it. He sat down in one of the cane chairs and crossed his legs. He jerked his chin at me and I sat too, on the edge of the opposite chair.

He said, 'How did you find this place?'

'Angie didn't tell me, if that's what you were thinking.'

'Oh, I wasn't. Our Angie thinks I can do no wrong.' He paused. 'I can, though.'

'Barney, all I care about is how this thing could have happened. When we both felt about her the way we did.'

He looked at me thoughtfully. 'You know, I used to think about how it would be, meeting you. I never was the jealous kind, I don't mean that. But I used to wake up in the night and look at her and think – God forbid she should open her eyes now, and see what's she's done, see what a mistake she's made. I lived in dread of it.'

I was silent.

'But now that I meet you,' he went on, 'I feel different. I can't believe how you could have been such a fool. How you could've just thrown her away like you did. Did you really have so many to choose from you could afford to do that?' He sat motionless in the dappled light. 'No-one so much as looked at me before. Not really *looked*. But Caitlin? She seemed to care about every bit of me. Sit there, she would, and draw me. Hour on hour.'

'It's the way your body fills its space in the world.'

He looked startled, as if a ghost had spoken. 'Yes.' The lines of his face moved and set. 'Yes. That's what she said.'

'It wasn't me who threw her away, Barney,' I said. 'Whatever mistakes I made, I didn't do that. If I have to face up to what I did wrong, then so do you.'

'Is that right? Well, you're the smart medical man. What do you think happened to make me do it?' He leaned forward half an inch. 'Let me guess. A momentary fit of madness? Iraq come rushing back? Post traumatic fucking stress?'

'If that's the way it was, it would make some kind of sense.'

'He's only an ignorant squaddie, when all's said and done. And look at his record.'

'Barney, I'm just trying to understand. You had a fight. Was it about the baby?'

'I didn't know about any baby!' His voice cracked like a whip and I could see his muscles tense. 'I didn't know she was pregnant until Angie told me.'

I kept very still for three heartbeats, four, five.

I said, 'We have that much in common, then.'

'The trouble with your scenario, Michael,' he said very slowly, 'is that I didn't kill Caitlin. I'd have died for her. But you won't believe that, will you? No matter what I say, it'll make no difference.'

'I found her dying. You'd just been in the house with her. My neighbour heard you screaming at one another. What should I think?'

'We argued. That's true enough. We went at it hammer and tongs for maybe five or ten minutes. Till we heard your car pull up, that is.'

'*My* car?'

'And then we heard you come walking down the back path. We both heard you.' He held my gaze steadily. 'She started screaming then. She told me to get out. And so I got out. Just in time. Just as you were turning the key in the back door lock.'

'Barney, that doesn't make any sense. I didn't even have the car. And I didn't come in the back door.'

'That's right, Michael,' he said, and smiled indulgently at me, as if I were a slow child who had finally got on the right track towards solving a riddle. 'It was in all the papers. You came in the front door, went upstairs, found her lying there. Tried to save her.'

'That's all true. I did everything I knew how to do.'

'Oh, I believe it, Michael. Which accounts for why you're still alive. Because if I thought you'd done for her, you wouldn't be breathing now.' Carrick put his hands together in his lap. 'But there was a time when I didn't think that way at all. There was a time when I thought about you just the way you're thinking about me now. After all, she was OK when I left. Then you walk in, and suddenly she's dead. What should I think?'

I opened my mouth to argue. But at that moment the image flipped in my mind, and I saw that his conclusion was exactly as reasonable as my own. It was like looking at an inkblot test: the marks on the card remain the same, but without warning the mind seizes on some wildly different interpretation. A dove becomes a demon, or an angel an ape.

He seemed to see this happening in my head.

'Don't worry, Michael. Our Angie says you couldn't do such a thing. Our Angie says that even if you had, you wouldn't run away from it. If she tells me, I believe her. That's part of my deal with Angie.' He smiled. 'Maybe she told you the same about me, once or twice. Only you didn't believe her. You still don't, do you?'

'Wait.' I passed my tongue over my lips. I struggled to hold the new pattern in my mind. 'You said there was a car?'

'That's right.'

'My neighbour talked about a car pulling up. He thought it was mine, just like you did.'

He watched me, his eyes narrowed. At that moment, from outside, we both heard the dog bark once, and then again, more urgently. I glanced around at the sound and when I looked back Carrick was on his feet and had slipped the gun into his waistband.

'Oh, you really *are* a smart bastard,' he said.

'No-one knew I was coming here.'

'Is that right.'

He backed away from me towards the kitchen door, never taking his eyes off me. The dog was baying furiously now. I could hear it running back and forth outside the front door. Then abruptly it yelped and screamed and a huge din broke out, a megaphone blared, a stampede of booted feet, hoarse voices bellowing.

I stood and tried to shout a denial to him over the noise, and perhaps he heard me, and perhaps not. Something splintered in the kitchen and he spun towards the sound and I heard the front door crash in and two men with their right arms extended burst yelling into the room and one of them hit me very hard across the side of the head and I stumbled down onto my knees and before I could get up again a massive explosion deafened me.

It was weird, surreal, to watch it in silence. Carrick seemed to be jerked backwards by a snapping wire, his body crashing against the bookcase and bringing down shelves and CD player and shining CDs and books in a cascade around him. Before he had even come to rest a fan of blood had sprayed three feet up the wall.

The room was crowded with armed men in blue flak jackets. There were probably only four or five of them but they were bulky men and they jammed the space, and as my hearing cleared their shouting jammed my head. I could smell adrenalin and cordite and sweat. I got to my feet and somebody thrust me back down, and this made me so furious that I stood up again.

A man bawled, 'Armed police!' into my face. And again: 'Armed police! Stay back!' and grabbed at me as I got to my feet. He was young and his eyes were very wide and he was panting. Perhaps I was still dazed but it seemed absurd to be shouted at by this excited boy at a time like this. I shook off his clutch, and shoved my way past him and on through the wall of blue backs. As if unsure what to do next, he bawled his warnings all over again, 'Armed police! Stay down!'

Carrick was motionless, on his back, and the fountain of blood rose vertically from his groin and fell back down over him and over the scattered books and splintered furniture. His eyes were open and they followed me. I knelt over him. His knitted cap lay where he had thrown it in the corner and I snatched it up and crammed it into the hole in his groin and got my hands around it and pushed down hard. For a moment I could feel the artery pulsing and twitching under my grip like a small fire hose. There was a lot of noise behind me. I shut my mind to it and tightened my grip. He looked down to see what I was doing.

'That's my ticket out, right? Femoral artery?' He might have been asking me the time.

I shifted my hands and took a firmer hold. 'Probably.'

He nodded and lay back.

There was some staccato talk behind me but the din had fallen away. I could hear the men crashing through the other rooms. Glass broke, a door banged, an occasional shout rang out. Heavy footsteps came up beside me and a man crouched down on his hams near my right shoulder. I knew even before I looked that it was Barrett.

'You followed me,' I said.

'Sorry if that interfered with your private agenda in any way.'

Barrett looked Carrick up and down, as if he were a specimen, an animal brought down during a shoot. Barrett was smiling slightly, pleased with himself.

I said, 'Get an air ambulance in here right now.'

'Not much chance of that, I shouldn't think,' Barrett sucked his teeth as if in regret. 'All these trees.'

The wool of the ski-cap was sodden under my hands. 'He'll die in a couple of minutes if I let go of this leg,' I told him. 'You've got to get some help in here right now. Do you understand?'

'A couple of minutes?' Barrett mused. 'Is that all it would take?' He rested his big hand on my shoulder and put his lips so close to my ear that I could smell his breath. 'Tell me, Dr Severin. How much did you love your wife?'

I shifted my grip and blood sprayed up over Barrett before I could strangle the artery again. He jerked back, his eyes like stones.

'Get the ambulance,' I told him.

He got to his feet. He pulled out a handkerchief and dabbed at his coat front, then strode quickly away.

'Half of fucking Al Qaida were popping at me one time,' Carrick said. His voice was dreamy. 'And some bobby who's never shot a rabbit has to get lucky.'

'Shut up. This is hard enough without having to listen to your memoirs.'

He gave a grunt, which might have been laughter, and shifted his shoulders a little. I glanced at him. He was pale and sweating. I hoped the artery would not rupture entirely. If it did it could retract up into his body out of my reach and nothing would save him. I struggled desperately to think of something I could use as a clamp. The muscles in my forearms were beginning to burn with the strain of holding on.

I called over my shoulder, 'I'm going to need some help here.'

The room fell quiet. Someone shuffled uncertainly.

'Listen to me, Michael,' Carrick said.

'Be quiet. I'm thinking.'

He licked his lips. 'Caitlin wasn't going away with me.'

I looked up at him. 'This doesn't matter now, Barney.'

'Now is just when it does matter.' He grimaced, shifted his back a little.

'Keep still, for Chrissake.'

'She'd left me, Michael. She'd come home. That was what we fought about.'

A policemen clumped up in his heavy boots and knelt beside me, pulling free the Velcro tabs on his flak jacket. I saw he was the young man who had bellowed at me just a few moments earlier, but now he seemed meek enough. He handed me a cloth, a tea-towel with a recipe printed on it. The recipe was for cottage pie.

'This any use?'

'Find me a belt or a strap. Anything to tie this on.'

He unclipped his own belt and pulled it out of its loops and handed it to me. 'Is he going to die?' His voice was a little high and he didn't look so tough with his body armour flapping loose. I guessed he was the one who had fired.

'Get your thumbs in there, where mine are. Push down hard. And keep pushing, unless you want him on your conscience.'

I slid the belt under Carrick's leg, twisted it and pulled it tight. The young policeman crushed his thumbs into the sodden cloth so hard that Carrick winced.

'I'll fucking haunt you, lad,' Carrick said. He rolled his head to look at me. 'You called her, didn't you, Michael? From some place overseas.'

'Yes.' I notched the belt.

'After that she came down here and she took her things and she left me. I followed her back to London, but I couldn't make her listen.'

I got the belt strapped tight and I freed one hand and flexed it, trying to get the circulation moving again. My fingers were sticky with Carrick's blood. I could not look at him. 'Caitlin was coming back?'

'She *had* come back. Her bags were there at the top of the stairs when I left the house.' His hand came up and gripped my wrist, a red claw. 'I let her go, see, Michael? I've never done a thing like that before, but I loved her that much. Do you think I could've harmed a hair of her head? Somebody else did that, Michael. Not you. Not me. Somebody else who came in the back way, somebody who was there between my leaving and your arriving.'

I sat back, the belt cinched tight at last. I looked down at his white and glistening face. I thought he might say more, but as I watched his eyes grew vague. I slapped his face a couple of times. My hands left red smears over his skin.

'Barney?'

'Is he dead?' The policeman's voice spiked up.

'Not until I say so.'

I felt Carrick's pulse. He was not dead, but he was no longer here. I knew where he had gone. He was back in Caitlin's eyrie, seeing her stand before him as he pleaded with her, seeing her tall and fair and broken with grief, her homecoming bags dumped at her feet.

'Chopper's coming in,' someone called.

Up on the ridge blue police beacons were flickering between dim trees. The helicopter rose from the ground and circled overhead for a second, standing motionless on a rod of light while its rotors socked the air, and then clattered away rapidly to the northwest. Radios squawked and car engines started in the middle distance. A burly policeman, still in his body armour, was standing near the broken front door of the cottage, dabbing with a handkerchief at a dogbite in his cheek. I lifted the lid from the water butt outside the back door. I broke the wafer of ice which covered the dark water and scooped out some and washed my face and hands as well as I could. The water was shockingly cold but I was glad of it.

Barrett moved up beside me. I pushed more water into my face, cupping it with both hands.

'For what it's worth,' I said, 'I didn't know where this place was until an hour ago. Not exactly where it was.'

'You just stumbled across it, like?'

'I know you think I've been holding out, but all I ever had was a hunch.'

He stood there in the chill afternoon, staring at me, his neck muscles bulging. Some of Carrick's blood stained his collar.

'I don't like you, Doctor Severin,' he said finally. 'I never have done, since the first moment I saw you. People like you think there's one rule for you and one for everyone else. And you know what pisses me right off? There usually is.'

I pushed the freezing water over my face again and again, saying nothing.

Barrett breathed hard for a while, snorting like a bull through his nose. 'Is he going to die?'

'I doubt it. He's not the type.'

'Pity. Would've saved the taxpayer a lot of money.'

I flicked icy water out of my hair. 'Before Caitlin was killed he heard someone come into the house. Someone came in as he was leaving, and before I got there. He thought it was me coming home.'

'That's what he told you, is it?'

'They both heard it, Caitlin and him. They heard a car pull up in the mews and then someone came in the back door.'

'Oh, your wife heard it too? Well, that's convenient. All young Barney needs now is a medium to get Mrs Severin to confirm his story and he's home and dry.'

'I believe him. Henry Kendrick said he saw a car pull up then, too. A dark red car.'

'This is bullshit. Cars pull up there and drive off again every five minutes.' He stepped close to me. 'You listen to me. I'm past giving much of a flying fuck what you think about anything. But just for the record, there isn't a killer in existence who doesn't deny he did it. They all do. They'll say anything at all. Anything. They got nothing to lose, see? There was no red fucking car. There was nobody come in the back way. There was just Barney Carrick and your wife.'

'I think he was telling the truth.'

'Barney Carrick's as guilty as sin. If I were you, I wouldn't forget that. For your wife's sake I wouldn't.'

He strode away between the trees.

CHAPTER TWENTY-EIGHT

When I got home I went upstairs and showered off the mud and the last traces of Barney Carrick's blood and the taint of fear and sweat.

I changed and went downstairs again, and poured myself a scotch. The images in my mind blinked through, one after another, like clips of film running in a loop. But gradually they slowed, blurred, flickered out. The last to go showed me a woman with a leather jacket, standing in a dim clearing, as fearful as a deer. She looked like a French Resistance heroine and she wore a beret, and that was why I couldn't tell whether her hair was blonde or black.

I fetched the bottle and put it on the dining table beside me and poured myself another and drank steadily, waiting for peace, or some facsimile of it. The scotch was rich and dark and the lamps gleamed on the polished wood.

Summer had already broken and the wet wind leaned on the windows and the lights of London were running down the glass. It was close to one in the morning, a blustery September night. It was only two days before Stella and I would leave for Venezuela. Miles Davis murmured on the stereo and candles reflected on silver and glass down the length of the polished dining room table. I was feeling mellow and I looked around the circle of faces, one after the other. At Anthony, with his silver hair and rumpled dark suit, presiding like a benign senator. At Caitlin, shining in grey silk. At Stella, growing strident opposite me. And even at Gordon, smiling nervously beside her, his spectacles flashing. They filled the room with their warmth.

Caitlin caught my eye across the table and smiled before turning back to her conversation. She had cropped her long hair a few months before. I had always loved her hair, and was nervous when she said she planned to cut it. But now that it was gone I found the change brought back the gamine look I remembered from years ago. I was filled quite suddenly with an aching tenderness for her, a need to hold her and protect her. I had not experienced this feeling with quite such intensity for some time. That realisation alarmed me a little, and for a second I regretted that I was going away so soon. The bright room seemed to shimmer. I could see the shadowed hollows under Caitlin's collarbones. I traced with my eyes the line of her jaw and the long curve of her neck. She had a swan's neck, a dancer's neck. I wondered how soon I could get rid of everyone.

Caitlin did not look across at me again. She and Anthony were talking earnestly. Usually Caitlin flirted with Anthony, and he would respond with lumbering old world gallantry. It was like watching a filly gambolling with a carthorse, a game they both enjoyed and which neither took seriously. But I had not often heard them holding so grave a discussion. A single sentence of Anthony's drifted across to me, and it seemed fitting that this should be the one thing I overheard.

'Quite early on, my dear,' Anthony was saying, 'I came to feel that the only truly important commitments are the ones we make to one another.'

I had not understood why at the time, but Caitlin looked troubled when he said this. Stella, who by this stage was not troubled by much at all, let her head sink onto the table and began gently to snore.

Later, when the house was quiet, I stretched out on the bed with my scotch tilted in my right hand and Beamish the bear tucked under my left arm. Caitlin moved back into the room from the shower and began to towel her shorn hair. I could not read her eyes. Concern. Affection. But something more. I knew I had had too much to drink, and perhaps that was the reason I could not decode her expression, and perhaps it was not. She gazed at me for so long that I began to feel uncomfortable.

She said, 'If Médecins Sans Frontières could just see you now. Intrepid surgeon and bald bear.'

I twisted Beamish's head so that he glared at her, his one eye fiery in the light. I held my glass up for the bear to drink from it. 'Do you think scotch will make his eye red?' I asked her.

'It's making yours red, all right. I'm glad you're not operating on me tomorrow.'

Caitlin walked a few paces to the window and stood with her back to me. I watched the way she held herself, the curve of her hip, the roll of muscle over her thigh. I waited but she did not say more. I sat up on the bed and propped Beamish beside me on Caitlin's pillow.

'You look gorgeous tonight,' I told her.

'*Gorgeous?*' She grimaced, then turned and for some moments stood watching me thoughtfully.

'Do you want to talk?' I said.

She noticed the towel hanging limp in her hand and tossed it over the laundry basket. She pulled up the cane chair from the dressing table and sat in it naked, close to the window. The window was open half-an-inch and the air stirred the curtain and a black-and-cream moth slid into the room and circled a couple of times around the light. Following its jerky flight made me dizzy and I was glad when it settled on the wall beneath the framed photograph of Lady Lavinia. Even in her antique black dress Caitlin's grandmother looked remarkably like Caitlin herself, with the same large eyes and oval face, her expression hovering somewhere on the edge of a smile.

'Not tonight,' Caitlin said, 'we shouldn't talk tonight.'

'We haven't talked properly since Italy. Maybe that's my fault.'

But she repeated, 'We shouldn't talk tonight.'

I wished Caitlin would not speak in code. She made me feel clumsy and stupid when she did that. The moth left the wall and swung in a figure-of-eight around the room and I silently cursed its giddy flight.

'Cate, do you want me to quit MSF?'

She stared at me.

'I'm not indispensable. They'll find someone else. I could spend a bit more time at home. We could sort this out.'

'I don't need to be *sorted out*, Michael,' she said. 'I'm not some clockwork toy that needs to be wound regularly.'

But then she stepped forward quickly and put her arms around me and pulled my head hard against her belly.

Some hours must have passed. I became aware only slowly that I was awake. I had the impression that I had lain here for an hour or more, dull spirited from alcohol and from some half-acknowledged doubt, floating between sleep and wakefulness. Certainly it was well on towards dawn, I could tell that from the breathing of the city outside, a subdued hiss, like distantly escaping steam.

Caitlin stirred beside me.

I stretched out a hand and touched her warm shoulder. 'You shouldn't be awake.'

She curled in tightly to me. 'Neither should you.'

I kissed the top of her head. Her hair was warm.

'I don't want you to stop,' she said. 'That isn't what this is about.'

I closed my eyes in the darkness. I knew that part of me had been angling for her to say this, to grant me a renewed licence. I cradled her quietly for a while. I felt I owed her an explanation, though I was sure she already understood better than I did.

'Sometimes,' I said, 'at a restaurant or at a party – or here, now, when we're warm and safe – I find myself asking if I should be taking time out like this.'

'Time out?'

'If only I was there – wherever - maybe I could help. As if every minute I spend living in comfort means that someone I could have helped goes unhelped, someone I might have rescued goes unrescued.'

She propped herself up on her elbows. She put her hand flat on my chest and felt for the key on its chain around my neck and folded her fingers around it into a fist and tugged it a little. 'It can't all be your responsibility. Can it?'

'I'm not saying it's rational.'

'Shall I tell you how I feel?' She put her cheek down against the muscle of my shoulder. 'Even though that isn't rational either?'

'Tell me.'

'My knight came galloping along, just like in the fairy tales, and he rescued me from the tower where I was locked up, and he rescued me from the ogre, and he pulled me up onto his white charger.' She turned her face a little against my skin and I knew she was looking up at me in the darkness. 'And then he carried me off to his own castle. And he made me mistress of it. And he gave me everything I asked for. And we lived happily ever after.'

She began to cry softly.

I left the house at nine. December London was as chill as glass under the flinty light, and the day dazzled me, but it was good to be out in the moving air. I walked for a while, threading through the morning commuters and last-minute shoppers. There were Christmas decorations strung from the lampposts, glittering explosions of red and gold tinsel – stars and comets which twirled and flashed and twinkled. They made my head spin and I could not look at them.

A red bus pulled up in front of me. It said Parliament Square on the front, and I climbed on, mostly because I knew where Parliament Square was, and the familiarity of the destination was comforting. I got to a seat and slumped against the window. I might have drifted away for a couple of minutes, for I was next aware of the smooth glass rocking against my face and the intricate spires soaring above me.

I got off the bus and at a stand outside the tube station I bought a bacon roll and a Styrofoam mug of milky tea and heaped sugar into it. I found a bench overlooking the river and sat and took the lid off the tea, so that it steamed extravagantly in the cold. I wasn't hungry but I ate the roll anyway, chewing steadily. At length I began to feel stronger. I sat there under the bare trees, with the red buses rumbling around the square behind me. I liked the sound. I liked to feel the river sliding seawards almost at my feet, and the dank smell of the water. I walked to the parapet and stared out over the steel grey Thames.

Brittle sunlight was filtering through the bare trees. I saw in my mind the rundown cottage of yesterday and the woodland light falling across the bed and the simple domestic things in the house, the coffee cups and the books and the handful of CDs featuring music I had never troubled to like. I saw the portfolio and I pictured Caitlin as she drew, hour after hour, the images of a man who sat still long enough to be drawn. I saw her handwriting on the yellow stickers on the fridge, reminders to buy food and wine for a man who would stay long enough to share them.

And I thought of Stella. She would be gone by now. I pictured her striding away across an airport concourse, her shoulder bag bouncing on her hip. I wondered who would take over her flat. It was impossible to imagine anyone else living there. I wondered where she had found a buyer for a beaten-up twelve-year-old VW Golf, hand-painted in two not-quite-matching tones of maroon. I had a vivid image of her on the thronged street outside Caracas airport, primary colours, blaring taxis, the taste of diesel and chilli in the hot air: she would be arguing with some driver, hands on hips, sunglasses pushed up into her red hair, her scuffed bags in the dust at her feet. Later, she would check into one of the cheap local hotels she favoured. I could see her testing the thin mattress, then opening the shutters and letting the aromatic tropical evening flow over her. She would shower and stroll down the noisy street to some pavement café, and drink a Polar while palm trees tossed their dark plumes against a lavender sky. Some ragged child would beg a coin from her. She would be generous. She could afford to be. She was free and clear. For all the absences in her life – perhaps because of them – she was free and clear. She was the only one of us who was.

I took the ticket Stella had given me from my jacket pocket, and looked at it for a while, and tore it very carefully into small pieces so that the fragments spun away on the wind.

An hour later the cab dropped me at the end of Anthony's street. I walked slowly up the hill, not anxious to get there, past the complacent suburban houses I remembered so well. Everything in order here. Worthy respectable lives lived out in a steady round of work, golf, the polishing of cars, the raising of children, pensions, holidays in undemanding places where the food was acceptable and the sun not too fierce.

Anthony's house stood out just that little bit, as it had always done for me. Just a little shabby, the garden just a little overgrown. Even from the outside it had that indefinable air of bohemianism about it. Dark furniture glimpsed through the bay windows gave it the look of an old curiosity shop. The old white Rover was standing in the drive. I ran my hand over the lovingly polished bodywork as I walked up to the front door. Though the day was still bright I saw a light on in Anthony's study and a curl of smoke lifting from the chimney and I was reassured. I had been afraid that he might be out, prowling the antique shops and the sales, but the place looked just as it always had, just as I remembered it from my childhood, a place of refuge in time of crisis. That was as it should be.

I got out my key and opened the front door. In the dark hallway I took off my coat and hung it over the banister rail and paused for a moment to listen to the familiar sounds of the house, the knocking of the clocks, the crackle of the fire in the study. And something I had not heard for a long time, music, wonderful soaring music: Callas singing La Bohème.

Anthony was standing in the centre of the room near the stereo. He was wearing his best dark pinstripe and a claret bow tie, almost as if he had dressed for some formal event but at the last moment changed his mind about going. He looked up as I opened the door and delight lit his face. He reached over and lowered the volume.

'Michael, my dear boy. I wasn't sure you'd come back. Not so soon.' He gave a twisted little smile. 'Perhaps not ever again.'

'You know I had to come back, Anthony.'

'I heard what happened. With this Carrick chap. Will he…' he hesitated, 'will he live?'

'Yes.'

'Thank God.' He let out a long breath.

'I thought you might rather see him dead.'

'Not any more. There's been enough pain and grief. Sometimes it seems to me that there is nothing but pain and grief in all this dark world.' He sat in his familiar chair next to the fire and looked up at me. 'But he is behind bars at last. One feels that rather brings things to a head.'

'Closure, they call it.'

Anthony puckered his mouth in distaste. 'Such an ugly word. And not even accurate.' He sighed. 'Standards are slipping everywhere, old chap, I'm afraid. Sometimes it's such a burden to maintain them.'

I noticed that there was a fine rosewood box on the hearthrug at his feet, the sort of box in which a man, growing old, might keep his personal treasures – a cap-badge from school, a ring from a loved one, a faded snapshot of a lost son. A crystal tumbler stood on the side table at his elbow with a bottle of cognac next to it. I had rarely known him drink alone during the day. From where I stood the firelight danced through the warm spirit. As my eyes grew accustomed to the low light, I saw that the rosewood box was not the only treasure on display. They were set out all around the fireplace, things I had not seen for years: antique clocks with tall numerals and cases the colour of port wine, a fluted silver coffee pot, some exquisite Meissen tableware, a cabinet of azure butterflies pinned in a spiral pattern, leatherbound first editions, a musical box with a ballerina pirouetting silently. As I watched, the ballerina came to a stop, her clockwork run down to stillness. Behind her stood the portrait of my father.

'All my pretty things.' Anthony selected a decanter and poured me a whisky and gave it to me. 'You look exhausted, my boy. Sit down.'

I took the glass. The music sobbed to a close and I reached across and turned it off.

Anthony said, 'Stella dropped in to say goodbye to me on the way to the airport. Which was very sweet of her, I thought. I always found her rather a brash young woman, I must confess, but seeing the sterling way she behaved in the last few weeks, well, I don't know. I was sorry to see her go.'

'It was the right thing.'

'Very likely. But her departure rather shatters what remains of our little circle, doesn't it?'

I took a step forward and lowered myself into the huge brown armchair opposite him. Between us the fire snapped and spat. Anthony gazed at me with his boxer dog eyes. I felt an unbearable sadness for him, sitting there in his jaunty damson bow-tie, his spirit bruised and bewildered. I reached across and put my hand over his pudgy fist where it lay on the arm of the chair. He looked down at my hand covering his. He closed his eyes for a moment. He moved his hand, patted mine, picked up his glass.

'I had never struck a human being in my life before, do you know that?' His voice was almost conversational. 'I had no idea of the damage it might do. You must know I didn't intend...what happened. Obviously. Who would? I struck her, and she fell. That grotesque marble bust she kept at the top of the stairs also fell.' He looked up at me. 'And it...' he groped for the word '...it broke her. Like a porcelain vase. Like a lovely thing, crushed.'

I did not speak.

'I liked to take care of her, when you were away,' he went on. 'I didn't like to think of her so lonely. I know all about loneliness, you see. And so I would call in at odd times.' He sipped his brandy and passed his hand over his face. 'Very often she would not be at home. More and more often over the past few months.'

'Anthony, why didn't you speak to me about what she was doing? Why?'

'About her grubby relationship with this Carrick fellow? But my dear boy, I never suspected anything at all.' He was aghast at the thought. 'I would never have dreamed that lovely Caitlin could betray our trust. I still can't believe it. And if I had not left Amsterdam just that one day early, I might never have found out. But I did leave. I couldn't face sitting next to poor Harry Judah at the closing lunch, listening to his little jokes. Oh, he meant well. He meant to show me he understood, I believe. But it was just so hurtful. So very hurtful. And so I flew back to London early.'

'And went to see Caitlin.'

'Straight from the airport. I had been out of touch for a whole week. I knew she would be so worried about you, after the earthquake. Of course we all knew you'd get involved in that business.'

'You used the courtesy car. That big red Volvo you picked me up in. Henry Kendrick mistook it for mine.'

'I parked in the mews at the back. And Carrick was there, Michael. In your house. This man. This stranger. He didn't see me, but I saw him for a second through the upstairs window. In your home.' Anthony breathed hard, controlled himself. 'I couldn't just walk away. I told myself I would handle the situation somehow, behave in a civilised manner.'

I felt immensely weary. 'Yes, I see.'

'I have always done so before, as you know.' He gazed helplessly at me. 'All through my life, I've always behaved in a civilised manner.'

'That's right, Anthony. Everything you've done has always been very civilised.'

'I let myself in the back door. I believe they must have heard me, because by the time I got upstairs he had gone. And Caitlin was screaming. I can't describe to you what it was like. Like a trapped animal. I couldn't bear this mindless *screaming*. She was quite hysterical. I had never seen such a thing. Screaming out how she'd betrayed you. Betrayed all of us. Betrayed herself. It was insupportable.'

His hands were shaking. He drank some more brandy and spilled a little on the lapel of his jacket and pawed at it ineffectually, embarrassed at his clumsiness.

'And afterwards?' I said. 'Did you think it would all just go away?'

'Afterwards, I didn't expect them to accuse anyone in particular.' His voice was calm now. 'I thought it might just be one of those closed police files. Person or persons unknown. It was naïve of me, but I even thought you might never have to know about Caitlin's…

lapse. I prayed you would be spared that. Perhaps you'd never have to know what I had done. I allowed myself to believe that.'

'That would have made it all right? That I didn't know?'

'All right?' he stared at me in confusion, 'how could anything have made it *all right?* Michael, you can't imagine I cared about myself! Do you suppose I could ever forget the suffering I had caused? I shall burn for it, of course. I burn for it already. Every moment. But how would it help for you to know? How is it helping you now?'

My head was hammering, little spikes of pain driving into my skull. I forced myself to drink some brandy.

Anthony stared into his glass. 'I didn't plan anything. I thought if I could simply pretend it had all been a dreadful nightmare, then that's what it would be, do you see? Just a nightmare. I didn't come back to this house after it had happened. I checked into some hotel. I realised that people would be trying to reach me, so I contacted Stella and told her I was stuck at Schiphol, pretended to be devastated at the news. I think that was the hardest part, pretending. But once that step had been taken....And then I picked you up at the police station the next day, and told you I had come straight from the airport. By then I half believed it myself. Until the last moment I thought that perhaps I would wake up and everything would be all right.'

He paused, looking back on this lost world of hope.

'But of course it wasn't all right. It could never be. She was so beautiful. To live with knowing I have destroyed such loveliness. It's not endurable.' He flourished his plum-coloured silk handkerchief and rubbed it between his palms and tucked it away again, taking care that it bloomed like an orchid against his breast.

'I can't let them charge Barney Carrick with this,' I said. 'I can't do that, Anthony. Not even for you.'

He looked shocked. 'But of course you can't, my boy.' He reached inside his jacket and took out a cream envelope and showed it to me. It was neatly addressed to Detective Inspector Maureen Dickenson. 'As you see, I find I can't do that either.'

I didn't like to see his face. I looked away. The firelight flickered over the polished rosewood box on the hearthrug, and on its bright brass fittings. The catches were unfastened. I could see the plate screwed into the lid and now I could read the inscription. 'Wheelers of London, Firearms of Quality.' Anthony got to his feet, tugged down the lapels of his jacket. He reached across and propped the cream envelope against the porcelain ballerina, still and silent on her musical box, and then looked at me, waiting for me to rise.

'I think it's time you left,' he said. 'Don't you?'

I stood up slowly and faced him. 'Do you think I'm going to let you do this?'

'Your father was a fine man, you know,' he said, as if somehow this followed from what I had said. He picked up the framed portrait and moved it so that the light fell on it, flashing on the glass. My father grinned out at us, raffish, handsome, forever young. Anthony replaced the portrait on the table and stood gazing at it. 'You must try to forgive us both, Michael. We tried so very hard to keep you from harm. But we are all such weak creatures. How can we change the world? We are not even masters of ourselves.'

We hovered there for a second, inches apart. I saw his eyes grow bright in the firelight. Without knowing I had moved I found that I was hugging his portly penguin body against me, and I could feel the small buzz of his cheek against my neck, and smell the tang of his old-fashioned cologne.

'Anthony, you can't ask me to just…'

'My dear old chap,' he said. He patted my back reassuringly and then pushed me gently away from him. 'If you love me at all.'

I was never sure whether I heard it or not. I had reached the bottom of the street, moving blindly past the mock-Tudor houses with their neat gardens. A red bus pulled up at the pebble-dashed bus stop and a woman with a push chair got off. People were drifting in and out of the off-licence over the road. A handyman was mending a fence a few yards further on. I stumbled a little, and the woman with the push chair caught my arm and steadied me and her well-meaning grip seemed to suck the strength out of me and my senses reeled and I thought, in the red rush of it, that there came a sharp small crack from somewhere behind me. But it might have been no more than the tap of the handyman's hammer against a nail. And when I came fully to myself again and looked past the woman's kind and worried face I could see only a flock of pigeons wheeling in the white winter sky, startled by some small alarm.

CHAPTER TWENTY-NINE

Two or three weeks slipped by. A lot happened, I suppose. An inquest, another funeral. Interviews with the police. I believe I did all that was asked of me. Yet it all seemed to glide over me, as if it were happening to someone else, a character in a film.

But at last the world fell quiet around me. For two or three days at a stretch the phone failed to ring, and that gave me the space to gather myself and, finally, to act. It didn't take long, once the machinery was put in motion. Somehow, I found myself in the middle of January, and the house was sold.

I stood in Caitlin's eyrie that last morning - a cold, ice-bright morning - listening to the removals men carrying out the last of our belongings from the downstairs rooms. They knew who I was, these men, and what had happened here, and they didn't laugh or say much or whistle while they worked. Throughout the morning they had treated me with a gentle deference which I appreciated, even if I no longer needed it. The work didn't take them long. There wasn't much for them to take. The saleroom people had cleared the place out pretty thoroughly. Some of the rest I had boxed and sent to Margot Dacre, and some had gone to other friends. All the rest was going to the York Road Community Centre. I didn't know what they'd do with half of it, but I had no doubt that this was its proper destination.

I waited until I was sure the men were finished. I'd felt no sentiment about the valuable items, but I did not want to see them carrying out the stuff of our everyday life, plates and mugs and knives and forks and paperback books and cheap sticks of furniture and pots for the houseplants and DVDs we had bought and never watched and the can opener and the soap dish and fridge magnets and tea-towels.

It fell silent down below, and I heard the front door click shut. The men would be waiting in their van, wheels up on the kerb, blocking the traffic, impatient to be gone but too considerate to hurry me. I stepped over the hollow boards to the window. This was her view, Caitlin's view, from her private place. Canted rooftops, the litter of pigeons' nests in a neighbour's gutter, and a great vista of pale sky. Day after day while I was away living, fully living, in some vibrant place. And I knew now what she had seen ahead for herself. Scenes in an ordered and decorous life, strung together like a necklace of promises, one fading into another, ultimately meaningless, none of them ever quite realised. She had told me once what she feared: a life without milestones.

I walked out of the room and went straight down the stairs without pausing, down the spiral staircase where I had last seen her, past the door of our bedroom, down the second set of stairs and into the hallway and along it without breaking step. I unhooked my jacket from beside the front door and shrugged it on and opened the door and stepped into the street and locked the door behind me.

The driver was a bald man with a bull neck and an earring. He said, 'Not much of a New Year for you, eh?'

There were three of them in the cab, and he was the boss, and I knew he had felt it incumbent on him to say something, but now felt awkward about it. The other two men stared fixedly out of the opposite window.

'Life goes on,' I said, to make them feel better.

I took the clipboard from him and signed where the driver pointed and found some money and gave it to him. He thanked me, and glanced past me and up at the house. I handed the clipboard back and found him looking at me. I could see it in his eyes, the kind of awed sympathy I had seen in the faces of others, wishing me good luck, but not expecting I was going to get it. He started the engine.

'You go careful, mate,' he said. He put the van in gear, bounced it off the kerb and drove out into the traffic.

The rumble of the truck filled the street for a moment and I did not at first hear the mobile buzzing.

'It's me,' Angie said.

It took me a moment to find my voice. I said, 'I've left messages. A lot of them.'

'Don't make this difficult.'

'I didn't even know you were still in London.'

'We're leaving. Today.' She paused. 'Look, can we meet? Just quickly. It's Uncle Stanley. He won't hear of us going without seeing you.'

'Where?'

'You choose.'

'Tower Bridge.' I said, picking the landmark at random. 'In the middle of Tower Bridge.'

'OK. Can you make it, like, now?'

'If that's what you want.'

'It is. I don't want to hang around.'

There was a silence.

'It's not that I'm ungrateful,' she said.

'I'll be there,' I told her. 'Besides, there's something I need to give you.'

I had the taxi drop me in a lay-by on the City side and saw them standing on the footpath in the very centre of the bridge. Uncle Stanley's ginger coat flapped in the wind. She stood a little beyond him, leaning on the parapet, staring downstream. I knew she was refusing to look, to watch for me. I paid the driver and shouldered my backpack and walked the last couple of hundred yards under the blue iron stanchions.

'Young Doctor Seven.' Uncle Stanley came forward to meet me. He had his pipe in his mouth, and the January wind whipping down the river tore away the smoke. He held out his bony hand and fixed his blue eyes on my face. 'I know my manners, even if she don't. And it's not polite to leave wi'out saying cheerio. Now I've said it.'

He released my hand and walked past me and did not stop until he was some distance away. There he leaned on the railings with his back to us, looking up at the bulk of the Tower and the shining buildings of the City beyond.

'Hello, Angie,' I said.

She stood looking at me, her face locked. Strands of her hair were coming loose in the wind. Her eyes were very black.

'He's right about one thing,' she said. 'I shouldn't leave without thanking you. For Barney. You saved him.'

'It's my job. I'm in the rescuing business.' I dumped the backpack on the paving stones between us and tugged it open. 'I brought something for you.'

She looked down and saw the two leather portfolios. 'I can't take those, Michael.'

'They don't belong to me, or you. They belong to Barney. Give them to him.'

She stood there staring at the folders for a long time. 'Caitlin's lovely drawings.' She wrapped her arms sadly around herself.

'Angie, why is it this way between us? There's no need for it now.'

I moved forward to touch her, but she pulled back at once. 'Don't.'

'Why won't you answer my calls? This thing is over now. We could talk, at least.'

'And it would stop there, would it?'

'So what if it didn't? There's no-one in our way.'

'And after that what am I supposed to do? Sit in my little flat in Leeds, waiting for my white knight to come galloping up the M1 whenever he's back from abroad? I don't think so.'

Her hair was lashing free now, and it made her look wild and dangerous. I thought: white knight. Caitlin's words.

'It doesn't have to be like that,' I said. 'I've learned some things.'

'What difference is it going to make in the end?' She turned to stare out over the river. 'It's like Uncle Stanley says. We don't have a blank sheet to write our story on. How could it ever work between us, you being who you are, me being who I am?'

'We could try,' I said.

She swung to face me. 'Michael, I've got a life of my own to live, and not just when you're between assignments. I've got people to look after.' She bent down and hefted the pack up onto her shoulder. 'You're not the only one in the rescuing business.'

I thought she would walk away then, but something seemed to hold her back. 'What will you do now?' she said.

'Nothing for a while. I'll go back to it in the end, I suppose. It's all I know how to do. Saving the world.'

She nodded, as if this was no more than she had expected. 'Can you take a bit of advice?'

'Try me.'

'You get in your posh car, Michael, and you drive for a week. South. Towards the sunshine. Go and find somewhere pretty by the water and you sit yourself down with a bottle of wine. Go and find your Ithaca. And give the world a chance to save you.'

'Maybe I'll do just that.'

'You won't,' she said. 'You can't.'

She lifted her hand and very gently touched the tip of her finger to the centre of my chest where the key hung under my clothes. I felt suddenly dizzy and closed my eyes for an instant and the images sprang alive then, a string of images, brilliant and clear, flashing up in my mind. Caitlin standing in the chill water, laughing with her mouth but pleading with her eyes and her body. Caitlin standing in the dawn meadow with her shoes slung over her shoulder from one finger, smiling at me. Caitlin guiding my hand down to her belly, letting the key swing in the darkness.

I looked directly into Angie's eyes. 'I'd locked the back door of the house. The night of the fire.' I was startled by the clarity of my voice. 'And I'd taken the key with me. I wasn't allowed to do that, to take the key. But I thought that if my father came down and found the door locked, he'd assume I was in my room, like I was supposed to be. He wouldn't know I was walking around the streets, cursing him for leaving me behind. Again.'

'You were a child, Michael. Just a child.' She stood with the wind whipping her hair, waiting for me to go on.

'When I got back I could see the flames through the glass. I knew they'd be trapped but I couldn't get in to warn them. I panicked. I didn't even have the sense to call a neighbour. I lost the key in the dark. I checked every pocket fifty times. I crawled about on the ground, feeling for it. I found it a week later about two feet away in the grass, but I couldn't find it then, not when I needed it. And so I couldn't wake them. I beat on that door until the police arrived. Somebody else called them, not me. I beat so hard on that door I broke three fingers. I put my fists through the glass and needed forty stitches in my hands. I screamed so hard it was a week before I got my voice back. But I couldn't find the key. I couldn't find the way to save them.'

She didn't move for a moment. Then she carefully put the pack down, and stepped forward and put her arms around my neck and held me and kissed me hard, and as we stood there locked together she suddenly thrust her hand into my shirt and ripped it open. She gripped the key and wrenched savagely at it so that the chain snapped, and then with a backward flick she tossed it high out over the balustrade. I watched it turn and flash in the thin sun until far, far below it struck the unquiet water with a tiny splash.

A slate grey gull swooped down to investigate, but, finding nothing, planed off again over the river. When I looked up, Angie was striding away across the bridge, her arm in the old man's, the pack on her shoulder. I saw Uncle Stanley shake his head mournfully, but Angie did not look back.

EPILOGUE

Nick brought the boat in through the rocky entrance in a smooth glide and throttled back, so that the clatter of the old diesel dropped to a steady thump.

The aquamarine water was so clear at this season that the boulders on the harbour floor wavered in the shadow of the wooden hull, like a child's building bricks. A plume of silver fishes turned below the boat and fled like smoke. Above us, blue and white houses climbed the rocky hillside. It was nearly six in the evening and I could smell cooking from the tavernas along the quay, herbs and hot oil and roasting meat.

I felt fit and relaxed and drugged by sun and exercise. There were other boats moving in the harbour – more boats than yesterday – and the third of the village's four taxis had been brought out of winter hibernation. The cab owner, a fat man called George, was already polishing the car on the dockside in expectation of new business. George also owned the taverna opposite, and the laundrette and the motorbike hire shop and the tourist office, so visitors meant a lot to him. But it was still only April and trippers had not yet started to arrive in significant numbers, and I would have the place largely to myself for a while yet.

Nick slid the boat up to the quay close to where George was working and stepped lightly ashore. I handed him up the baskets, one of them with the tendril of an octopus questing out into the sunlight. I felt a bit sorry for the octopus, but I could already imagine how it would taste in a couple of hours and this dulled my compassion.

Nick flicked the butt of his cigarette out into the water. He called, 'Hey, George - Mike almost catch fish today.'

'Sure?' George slapped down his leather on the car's bonnet and waddled up to the quayside. 'What kind fish?'

I said, 'It was a swordfish, I think.'

'Is pretty good,' George reached down to take my hand and help me out of the boat. 'Most times you almost catch only sardine.'

They roared with laughter and went through the backslapping routine and shouted the joke in Greek up and down the street not more than six or eight times, so that I would be sure never to hear the end of it.

I helped Nick tie up the blue boat and walked across the street to George's taverna and greeted a couple of the old men playing backgammon there. I helped myself to a Hellas beer from the fridge and took up my usual place at a table near the back under the awning. I liked to watch the activity of the little port from here. The Thursday evening ferry from Lefkas had just come in on the far side of the harbour. I could see the passengers getting off, some islanders returning from the market, but also a small knot of foreigners with their bags dumped on the cobbles and the local women gathering around them, offering rooms. They would be the more adventurous backpackers, maybe birdwatchers or people come to see the wildflowers, or one or two who kept apartments on the island.

The Lefkas ferry was a converted fishing caique which was run by a local family, when they felt like it. I supposed that one day someone would dynamite the old harbour entrance to let the bigger craft in and open up the trade. I hoped it would not be soon.

I stretched back in my chair and drank my beer. Nick and a brother and a cousin or two would be along later, when they had cleaned up and appeased their families. Others would join us – the local policeman, the Belgian owner of the classy bar which did not open until May, a few fishermen, perhaps a couple of the more inquisitive tourists. Then the place would begin to come alive and the evening would develop into that nightly Greek ritual of conviviality which anywhere else would be called a party. Meanwhile it was good to watch the sun sink into the sea and to dream about my swordfish out there somewhere, cruising uncaught in a comet of phosphorescence.

George finished polishing his car and carried some of Nick's catch through between the tables, and I heard him clattering around in the kitchen behind me. After a while he came out and set a carafe of the tarry island red on the table in front of me and put a thick glass next to it. He was wearing his apron, which meant he was officially open for business. Nobody got served before George put on his apron. I was allowed to help myself to a beer only because I rented the narrow white house next door, which of course he also owned.

'So, Mike!' George cried, in the voice he used to command the attention of the entire place. 'What fish you almost want to eat? The one you almost catch?' He slapped himself and slapped me and guffawed some more and poured the wine.

'Hello, Michael,' Angie said.

The taverna fell instantly silent. George saw my face and vanished. He returned before I could draw breath with a second glass and filled it and moved a chair into place for her, beaming, and then vanished again. I could feel him lurking in the shadows of the kitchen behind me.

She was wearing a white linen blouse and she had already caught the sun. Her dark hair was gathered to one side and shone like liquid over her shoulder.

'So you found Ithaca. I never thought you would.' She smiled at me and sat down. 'It was the devil's own job to find *you*.'

'How did you?'

'I kept asking. Some woman at St Ruth's took pity in the end. Meredith somebody? I'm not supposed to tell you that. But she only had a *poste restante* for you in Lefkas town. Even when I got that far it took me two days just to get a boat out here.' She drank some red wine, made a face, put her head on one side and drank again. 'Not so bad, is it? When you get used to it.'

'No. And I have. Got used to it.'

'Well, you look fine on it, Michael.' She put the glass down. 'It must agree with you.'

I was intensely aware of the quiet in the taverna. I could hear the backgammon pieces click from time to time, but nobody spoke. It was like trying to hold a conversation on stage in a crowded theatre.

'Don't worry,' she said, 'I haven't come to steal away your peace. In fact I've come to deliver a message. A sad message, in a way.'

'Oh?'

'Uncle Stanley. He died a week ago. Ten days now, I suppose.'

'I'm sorry.'

'They said it was his heart in the end, but he just wore out, I think. He was only in hospital for a couple of days. And he was ready to go. He was eighty-eight. Would you credit that?'

'I thought he was a fine old man. I liked him.'

'Well, he liked you too, apparently.' She lifted her bag onto the table and took out a fat white envelope. 'He made me promise to give you this.' She mimicked Uncle Stanley's accent and his mock-stern expression, '"Directly they put me under t'sod, lass." And he wouldn't have me post it. Deliver it by hand, he said. Right away. It had to be delivered right away. So here it is.'

The envelope was addressed, in a spidery hand, to Dr Michael Seven. I turned it over a couple of times. I wasn't sure whether I should open it here and now, in front of her. It felt bulky. I said, 'It must feel strange to you, losing him.'

'Yes. It makes me feel sad. And grateful that I knew him.' She took another sip of wine. 'And free.' She put her glass down and looked steadily at me. There was a stillness about her I had not seen before. 'Open it, Michael.'

I slit the heavy envelope and slid out the wad of notepaper. There were perhaps a dozen sheets. I shuffled through them quickly.

She said, 'They're blank, aren't they?'

I held the white pages up for her to see. She smiled and poured us some more wine. She put her elbows on the table and rested her chin on her clasped hands. Behind us on the evening water a boat chugged towards the harbour mouth. We listened to it until it was well clear of the port entrance, the putter of its engine fading away into the magenta sea.

- THE END -

IF YOU ENJOYED *THE END OF WINTER,* HERE IS A TASTER OF **T. D. GRIGGS'** NOVEL *REDEMPTION BLUES*

CHAPTER ONE

Before dawn, on the second anniversary of his wife's death, Sam Cobb left the farm and climbed towards daybreak.

Above and around him the rim of the black hills stood against the stars. His breath plumed from him in the bitter air. He moved mostly by instinct and memory: he had climbed this path many times before in the cold hours before the light, and he knew it well. First the crunch of frosted turf in the lower paddocks, crisp as spun glass. Then a wedge of sky marked a gap in the hawthorn hedge and the start of the track, muddy ruts frozen into lava, knocking like wood under his boots.

At length he felt for the field's top gate and found its timber, furred with frost. He opened it and stepped through, heard a beast shuffle and stamp nearby. Cobb could just make out the bulk of the animal's shoulder, then another beside it, and another, black humps against the starwash. He felt with his boots for the low turf ridge which marked the wall of the ancient churchyard, trod over it and took up his dawn station, seated with his back to the trunk of the oak which stood here.

He liked to think that the oak might have been growing here, a sapling unnoticed against the wall of the graveyard, when the lost village was populated by the living as well as the dead. That was in 1665. Twelve generations ago; not so very long. Recognisable people, speaking a language he would understand, making jokes he would laugh at, loving and cheating and working and sinning, crimes like the crimes he dealt with every day. Believing, all these vanished people, that it would go on forever, that, God willing, there would be a tomorrow. And then discovering, as Cobb himself had discovered, that God was not willing. That in fact He cared so little one way or the other that He allowed them all, of whatever virtue or beauty, to be swept away by a force whose nature they could not even imagine, for no reason that made any sense, following no discernible scheme of justice or mercy.

Cobb could see it now, the first fan of dove grey and pink far away over London. The rising air made the oak above him creak like a ship at sea and he felt the great trunk stir, a living thing, against his spine. To the south he could make out a scatter of diamond lights which must be Oxford: if he stayed here an hour longer he would see the needle spires piercing the roll of mist along the Thames. Somewhere below and far behind him he was aware of that ancient river, black water slipping eastward in dim channels, cold as death.

He heard Baskerville blundering in the gorse near him, panting and broken-winded. The old dog was searching for him in the dark, stopping at intervals to snuff the air, nearer, nearer, blundering and snuffing again. Then the rough warm head was in his lap, and Cobb put his own head down and dug his chin into the warm pelt and felt the dog shudder with delight and slap at his face with his tongue. Cobb rubbed the mongrel's ears and spoke to him, and the dog lay down on the frosted grass and thumped the crisp turf with his tail.

Cobb's spirit took joy in the warm presence of the dog and in the salmon wash of light that spread from the east. He took comfort too in the company of the dead beneath his feet. Against such casual extinction his own loss seemed at least part of a shared grief. He stretched back against the oak and it shifted against his spine once more. The net of its roots beneath him cradled the bones of the dead. Clea, for all the vigour she had brought into his life over twelve years, was as completely at rest as these long-dead villagers. Their peace was her peace and in their company he was in hers. He felt less alone.

The dog stirred at his feet and lifted his anvil head: he knew it was time for food. Cobb's stomach murmured in agreement and he stood up and stretched in the thin light. Cobb was not bitter. He had been bitter once, but not any more. It was less of a life now. He accepted that, and accepting it he was very nearly content.

CHAPTER TWO

Silver could not see beyond the blast of the lights but he could feel it there, the many mouthed beast he had to feed. He closed his eyes, his head thrown back, trying to shut it out. But the glare burned red into his brain just the same. The last shrill chord of his treble run hung there, ringing through the vast stadium, and the audience clung to it, invisibly, silently begging him to go on. At the last moment he did so, his left hand flicking up the frets, his head back, his eyes half closed, the patterns in his mind translated with perfect precision to the patterns of his fingertips, tapping, changing, dancing on the fretboard. And then back down - a barré at the eighth, a long glissade, the guitar howling in pain, and at the exact moment the crash of drums and bass smashing the cage of the music, releasing him from the song.

Silver bounded out of the light, the bellowing of the crowd breaking over him like a following surf. The band came after him, waving, as he had not done, at the audience. They blew like horses as they ran, their sweat flying in the lights. Silver stopped and let the musicians stampede past, laughing and cursing at one another, squinting in the darkness after the glare of the lights. He saw the familiar bulk of Tommy Hudson in the wings, clapping the musicians on the back, mouthing ritual congratulations over the din, though they were all too hyped and too deafened to hear.

Silver backed into the shadow behind the scaffolding which framed the stage, his heart bouncing like a triphammer from the adrenalin and sweat cooling on him in the winter night. From here he looked out on to the dazzling cone of centre stage, the abandoned instruments glittering in chrome and mother-of-pearl. He noticed for the first time that a fine rain was falling over the unprotected crowds in the stadium, curtains of drizzle drifting like golden smoke through the laser beams. The huge audience didn't care about the rain. They whooped and whistled and drummed the damp turf with their heels, baying for more. Up in the covered stands they stood and cheered, stamping on the boards and clattering their folding seats. Litter started to drop on the stage - flowers, programmes, hats - falling in the lights like singed moths.

Silver watched the crowd. He remembered the beginning, twenty-five years and more ago, when impatient audiences hurled bottles and chairs, and didn't always wait for him to get off stage first. It had been different back then, in rundown halls in Liverpool and Manchester and North London, crumbling theatres, off-duty cinemas, the back rooms of rough pubs. Back then there were no cordons of smart security guards keeping him safe, with their cellphones and their mace sprays and their crisp uniforms. Just Tommy Hudson's broad brawler's shoulders. Silver had a vision of one wild night at the Hackney Empire, long before the place was renovated, when a punchy drunk had hurled a bottle which burst clean through the bass drum. Silver remembered Hudson slipping the steel bracelet of his watch over his fist and sliding from the stage like a polar bear from an ice floe. The smack of knuckle on bone had silenced the whole screaming theatre for a full minute. Silver didn't know why he should remember this incident particularly. It was only one of many, and far from the worst. But there was something in the fierce protective roll of Hudson's massive shoulders that night, something that summed up the big man's faith and his devotion.

Out in the black gulf of the stadium the crowd was chanting, a hungry, pitiless chant. Silver could not make out the French words but he knew what they wanted. They wanted more. More of him. And then more. And more. They were lighting candles now. In a few seconds the small yellow flames were flickering all over the dark acres, a swarm of bright pinpoints, swaying to the chant, more urgent now, more urgent. Silver could not look away from those undulating lights.

"Look at the bastards," Hudson hissed the words into Silver's ear. "You know what you are, Mattie? You're the fucking Sun King." A man with headphones came running up and Hudson said "Piss off," without turning. "Give them what they want, Mattie. You know they only want one."

Silver pushed past him quickly, snatched the shining Gibson from the stagehand and bounded on to the stage. The audience erupted. But Silver stood motionless in the lights, waiting until the torrent of noise withered away. When the silence was complete, he held it for another twenty seconds, his right hand poised above the strings. Then he struck the first ringing chord and the audience bellowed their approval in a great clap of sound that drowned the first couplet.

You people climbing on that Narrow Way,
Can climb from cradle up to Judgement Day
You want to win, but first you gotta lose
That's what they call
That's what they call
Redemption Blues

Silver sent the aching chords across the stadium. The sound system picked up the buzz of his fingertips against the binding of the bass strings. Then the last line, hurled high in Silver's diamond-hard voice, and he was finished, flinging his arms wide, the guitar in one fist flashing like an unbuckled breastplate, his black hair swinging. And then he was running, racing the damburst of the crowd's frenzied adulation, hurling himself out of the dazzle of lights and into the wings.

Suddenly spent, Silver hung against Hudson's rough coat until his breathing steadied and the din engulfed them once more. The stage structure rocked as the crowd surged against it. Hudson felt it move and in an instant took charge, standing Silver upright, tossing the guitar to an aide, slinging a jacket across Silver's back.

"OK, my son. We're gone."

He gripped Silver's upper arm, steering him quickly away. Shouted orders, a hard, straight-armed, shoulder-barging rush down crowded corridors of grey cement and staircases smelling of piss and thronged with shouting people, then out into the sweet cold night behind the stand, where a stretch limousine stood with its back doors open.

Silver straightened, pulled his arm free. "You go ahead, Tommy. I'll meet you later."

Hudson glanced up at him. "Don't be a prick. Get in."

But Silver swung the jacket around his shoulders like a hussar's tunic, cocked his head mockingly at Hudson's tone.

"Get in, for Chrissake." Hudson growled. "We've got a meeting, remember?"

But Silver was already backing out of Hudson's range and into the darkness, smiling.

CHAPTER THREE

He moved among the chaos of trucks and generators and trailers behind the stadium, breathing the stink of diesel and fried food. The drizzle was heavier now, glistening on the sides of the vehicles and gathering in pools on the tarmac. The shouting men and cranes and arc lights made him think of a depot behind the front line of some forgotten war. Staring up at a reversing truck, he stumbled on cabling and fell against a toiling man who swore at him in French. The man was wearing a tour tee-shirt with Silver's face on it but gave no sign of recognition.

He found himself coming down. The anonymity helped. It was a while since he had kicked over the traces and it felt good - irresponsible, unprofessional, and good. Unprofessional because he would miss one of Tommy's late-night business gatherings in some exclusive Paris restaurant. There was a time, and not long ago, when Silver had enjoyed this sort of thing. He would listen to Tommy talking big money with the dealmakers while he sat back, pulsing with that after-show energy that was better than sex.

He caught the smell of onions on the night air and found a hamburger stand and bought a paper thimble of coffee as thick as tar and leaned against a trailer in the shadows to drink it. The cold rain slanted through the lights. Something, perhaps the foreignness of the accents around him, flung him back thirty years to Dr Gottschalk's tiny basement studio at the Conservatorium in Kensington, a place of yellowing sheet music, and hot water pipes, and the smell of stale cigars. He saw himself again, a truculent boy of sixteen, hunched over his guitar, staring rudely out of the window at the garbage cans in the light well.

"You are a very bad classical student, young Mr Matthew Silver," Dr Gottschalk told him in his clockwork English. Then the old man folded his sere fingers over the neck of his own instrument. "But you haff something very big to say. Get out from my sight and say it."

The memory depressed him. Something to say. But what story was so important that this vast weight of manpower and equipment and transport and technology was needed to tell it? There had been a time when Silver had said whatever he had to say with an old acoustic guitar and no more gear than would fit into the pockets of a donkey jacket. He finished his coffee and screwed up the paper cup and tossed it away among the big wheels. He was not a romantic. He did not believe in the good old days. They had been hard days, hard and squalid, and he had no faith in the improving power of poverty. But he also knew he had lost touch in some way, somewhere between there and here. At some point his own voice had been drowned out by the grinding of this great machine designed to project it.

Twenty thousand in the crowd tonight, many of them unborn when Dr Gottschalk had confronted him with his destiny all those years ago. What could *Redemption Blues* mean to these young French people?

The song had come to him as he huddled in a bus shelter on the outskirts of Hull on a bleak November evening a hundred years ago. Their Dormobile had finally packed up on the ring road and Tommy was off scaring up new transport, though how he would do it without money was beyond Silver's power to imagine. Exhausted and near defeat, Silver was not even sure that the big man would ever return, and he could not have blamed him if he had not. From the grim council estate across the road came the jagged sound of a kitchen shouting match, people yelling above the chatter of a television show. Lauren, feverish and ill, slept curled in a sleeping bag on the spit-stained concrete of the shelter. A solitary bus prowled past, a patchwork of yellow light. It did not trouble to stop, and Silver remembered the desolate whine of its gears as it pulled away. He did not know why it depressed him so. They had no destination in any case, and no money to take them there.

At his feet Lauren moaned softly in her sleep. He knelt down and stroked her hair, murmuring to her, to himself. She nuzzled against his hand. Then unbidden, the refrain was in his mind. He let it play, finding its form, until it was clear enough for him to hum it aloud. When the girl was sleeping again, he moved quietly away and found the cardboard lid of a takeaway container in the gutter and scribbled on it in fitful blue biro, scribbled and scribbled, until the cold locked his fingers, and then scribbled more with the biro pushed through the barrel of his fist. It took him perhaps twenty minutes to get the verses down. No longer than that. When he had finished he looked up to find Lauren watching him, the sleeping bag pulled tight around her. She looked like death under the yellow streetlight, sick and shivering. But she smiled at him, a smile of such confidence and courage that he felt his heart lift, and he knew it would be all right. It had been her song from that moment.

Silver dragged out his mobile and punched the keys. Busy. He swore, tried again. Her mobile, then the landline. And again. And again. Hunched in the wet night while this toiling army of strangers deconstructed the world around him, he dialled and redialled endlessly. His knuckles shone white where he gripped the phone.

Printed in Great Britain
by Amazon.co.uk, Ltd.,
Marston Gate.